Personal Geography

Personal Geography
A Novel

Geoff Rips

Welcome Rain Publishers
NEW YORK

for Dan

Personal Geography

Copyright © 2022 by Geoff Rips

All rights reserved, including the right of reproduction in whole or in part or in any form, electronic or mechanical, without written permission from the publisher.

Designed by Laura Smyth

10 9 8 7 6 5 4 3 2 1

Library of Congress Cataloging in Publication Data is available from the publisher. Direct any inquiries to Welcome Rain Publishers, LLC.

Printed in the USA

Paperback ISBN: 978-1-56649-410-6
Hardcover ISBN: 978-1-56649-411-3

We passed from one strange tongue to another,
but God our Lord always enabled each new people
to understand us and we them. You would have thought,
from the questions and answers in signs,
that they spoke our language and we theirs.

—Álvar Núñez Cabeza de Vaca

I

The Beginning

THERE ONCE WAS A WORLD.

There once was a world where nothing had to be explained, where nothing went unspoken. The grasses and birds spoke to each other. The trees spoke to the wind, the fish to the water, the water to the land.

There once was a world of hunger and stark, bare survival. Digging a hole in a sand dune to escape the hurricane. Buried there. Walking 200 miles for pecans. Children dying on the way. Eating berries. Eating toadstools. Turning your insides out and seeing god.

Where brothers were bound together at the heart. Where the enemy was anyone not touched by the glow of home fires at night.

There once was a world lived in the open. At the mercy of all elements—drought, wind, flood, wolf.

And it was in constant conversation.

Peter Proust overheard that conversation. In the dark of moonless nights, with the first light of dawn, lying in a creek under the noon sun, he overheard.

He stood naked on a hillside facing the sunset. He took a knife and cut lines in the flesh of his belly. Droplets of blood hugged those lines or dribbled down through his dark, curly hair.

To purge the hunger eating him up inside. The constant, gnawing self. The persistence of self-preservation. The self-consciousness that kept him from entering the general conversation—grasses to birds, water to land.

He stood on the hillside. The noise was deafening. He wanted to become part of it. To roar with the general roar.

There once was a world. He heard it still. He covered his ears and heard it. He opened his mouth so that world could use him as its instrument, a great clamor moving through him. But nothing came out.

There once was a world.

Shipwrecked

SHIPWRECKED. Giacomo Berg had washed up on a green couch in a prim yellow living room. A Bible on the table. A crucifix mounted on the wall by the front door and on the TV.

Shipwrecked. He'd been hurtling through the night on Greyhound, past Texaco stations like incandescent bulbs in the darkness, under the brief ribbons of blue highway lamps at four-leaf clovers, over rusted bridges over creeks and rivers giving off a yellow-red corroded glow, past the cafes, truck stops, Shoney's Big Boy balancing a burger somewhere in Tennessee, blocks of red brick buildings in Memphis before getting spit out of the downtown corporate wall and across the great gray Mississippi, a dog track behind the Sirloin Stockade, tenant shacks in Arkansas lit up by purple television lights, waking and sleeping, waking to see the capitol in Little Rock, smaller than a credit union, shooting the gap through miles of forest in the gray dawn light. To be disgorged by a broken-down Greyhound in early afternoon in Hope, Arkansas. The fellow next to him offered to take him along to his daughter's house in Texarkana for the night. Giacomo Berg had no other options. In less than an hour, the two of them were ferried to these alien shores by kind strangers offering rides. Giacomo was tired but eager to begin his hunt.

Beginning here, on a green couch in a yellow living room overflowing with knickknacks and carefully penned, framed verses from the New Testament on the walls. Under a slowly turning ceiling fan. In Texas. He lay back, bringing one leg up on the couch, keeping the other foot on the ground, as seemed almost appropriate. Time was slowing down.

He heard shuffling in the other rooms. Muted conversations. He also heard crickets outside the window by the couch. And a high-pitched din that seemed a little wild but became soothing in its regularity. A swampy edge of the world.

The swinging kitchen door opened into the living room. "Mr. Berg, in a few minutes will you join us for supper?"

He raised himself on his elbows, then flopped back on the couch again. Two nearly sleepless nights on a Greyhound only to be coughed up into this room, onto this couch, staring at the framed words, "Jesus is all."

Mary Lou Vlcek was standing in front of him. "Anything I can get you, Mr. Berg?" She held a pot of tea and a cup and motioned to give it to him. He sat up, took it, and settled back against the pillows of the couch. "I'm fixing dinner," she said. "You'll stay, of course."

Of course, meaning he had no place else to be. Meaning he wasn't even sure where he was.

"Jesus!" is right, he thought.

He'd seen the sign for Texarkana from the smudged Greyhound window just before the bus broke down near Hope. Coming off the interstate ramp. Then catching a ride to Texas. The dark creeks and wooded ravines radiating from the highway. Gray moss hanging from the trees. Deadwood flopped across creek beds. Green willows slowly leaning into their eventual demise, roots half-exposed, screening the paths of streams so the horizon at those points was no more than fifty yards from the highway, with darkness sucking behind it.

Translucence

B.C. BOYD HAD NEVER mentioned swampiness when talking about her Texas. She'd never mentioned wild chirping sounds. Or feeling hemmed in by dark ravines and heavy air. She never mentioned that everything felt too close.

Was it two days ago that he was sitting in his office on Union Square, trying to figure his next move? Half a country away?

The old office door with translucent glass had opened slowly. The shadow from behind the glass walked in. B.C. Boyd. He knew it was her. He'd heard her boots clunking their way from the elevator to his office door.

B.C. stepped in. Her eyes darted to all the corners of the room. She took a seat facing him across his old wooden desk.

"I was in the neighborhood," she said.

Never as he remembered her. Except her legs. They scared him. Starting out in the deep wells of her cowboy boots, they emerged like birdlegs and were bony at the knees. But by the time they reached her hips they were two Greek columns holding up the pediment that was her waist. And everything above it swayed. Now, as she sat across from him, her legs crossed, her calves seemed to twist around each other like vines. He could figure out a lot of things, but he couldn't figure out her legs. Few things scared Giacomo Berg the way B.C. Boyd scared him. He liked that. Did she know she scared him? She wanted to scare him.

He was hanging it up. The building was being sold. The job he'd fallen into fifteen years ago, tracking cheating lovers and workers comp fakes, following scheming husbands down endless streets, hanging out in coffee shops, talking to bartenders, waitresses, nurses, doormen, was now spent day after day at his computer, substituting binary computations for conversation, tracking bank records, money transfers, identity thefts, credit-card records, hacked conversations. Bloodless. Had he told B.C. this was the end?

She stood up—dark hair, dark eyes, almost translucent skin, Roman nose, those legs. Her eyes darted around the office, taking it in. Fewer books. Posters off the walls. But the air hadn't changed. The same air trapped in that office for two decades. "Damn, Jack," she said. "There's even less here here than there was before. You're disappearing right before my face.

"I was just stopping by to see if you were going anywhere interesting?" she continued. "I've got to get away—at least for a few days. You know the Millennium will be here in a few months. This could be our last chance to get out of town." She ended that sentence with a nervous laugh. "As long as a town exists to get out of," she added.

B.C. felt hemmed in by world events. By the family living across the airshaft from her back-of-the-building apartment on West 98th, treating their landing off the fire escape like a private patio, the father sitting on a big pillow in warm weather in his boxers and wife-beater, the kid with binoculars looking into everybody's windows—the little creep, the mother handing food out the window to keep the two guys happy. She felt hemmed in by long elevator rides and crowded subway cars and the uncertainty of queues at crowded bus stops. She felt hemmed in by the glances of strangers on the street and by the people who looked straight through her as if she weren't there. She missed the wide-open spaces of Texas, the sun taking a good hour to set on the horizon, the quiet evenings punctuated by screech owls, cicadas, or crickets.

She felt hemmed in by the silence at the other end of most of her communications about the political refugees she worked with. A big gulping silence.

She'd decided to quit her work. She couldn't exactly call it a job. She got paid for it by a board of directors she rarely saw. She just made lists: the killed, the disappeared, people seeking political asylum, people looking for their uncles and aunts and sons and daughters who had dropped off the face of the earth. Sometimes she organized a letter-writing campaign for a medical student with three children held in detention in El Salvador or Venezuela. Or for a journalist who'd gone to a remote Mexican village in Guerrero and was never heard from again. Sometimes she put together a protest by exiles, mothers of missing college students, maybe a state assemblyman, and sympathizing American celebrities in front of an embassy. She called the press. She got one or two cameras and a reporter from the *Daily News*. Was anyone ever freed by these actions? Did anyone ever move up on the President's negotiating list? She never knew. She considered it a small victory when the mutilated bodies of missing journalists didn't end up on the front page of a Mexican newspaper. Maybe they were still alive.

Damn, she had to get out. Bonita Carriker Boyd. What the hell has happened to you?

Sometimes she felt like all she had left of her former self were her boots.

Two more months. Then a break in Italy? Or back to Texas? Or maybe even back to singing for a band. Could she find any bands to sing for? Were her old musician buddies wanting to try it again? She was almost ready to pull her guitar out of the closet to see if she still had the urge. Tonight maybe. Should she say anything yet to Giacomo Berg? Would he care?

He enjoyed watching her enter his office. Slowly sliding through the half-opened door. Glancing at him sideways. Her nervous smile. Her eyes evading his. Her agitation amused him and the way her legs twisted around each other as she slid into the chair in front of his desk and began the defoliation of his office. No plant was safe, even if plastic. She reached across his desk and pulled the potted fern toward her. He watched it go. Adieu. She pulled the fronds off the fern as she talked. He'd seen her at a party work the big leathery leaf of a rubber plant, a couple of centimeters along the edge at a time, back and forth as she talked, one hand on the stalk, the other pinching the leaf edge with her long red fingernails. And by the time she walked away, the woody rubber plant stalk was bare. It was enough to scare any man.

What brought her there so often? Why sometimes at Union Square did she leave the subway, climb the 14th St. steps, sit on the bench in Union Square, deciding her next move? What brought her to the elevator doors, to the bronze hand above them, to the drab brown elevator cubicle, to the eighth floor button on the panel that did not light like all the others when it was pressed, to an instant's panic each time the elevator stopped at the eighth floor and the doors hesitated before opening and then hesitated again, stranding her in the elevator outside the eighth floor hallway, until the doors suddenly slid open? Why did she laugh to herself every time she read the sign on the office door, "Giacomo Berg—Private Investigations," why at this door did she see herself standing outside her fourth grade classroom on her first day of school in Lockhart or, later, outside the hospital room in which her father lay after his first heart attack? Was it the sight and feel of translucent glass?

What sent her past Pilar Moreno, who nodded while reading at her desk? What caused her to look in through the inner door, to smile as if in apology, to take the chair in front of him, waiting for him to look her way?

Why did she always see his hands first? They always seemed to be in his way. He never quite knew what to do with them. Both arms were crossed in front of his chest, but each hand held something—a pen, a scrap of paper with a scribbled note. Or one hand was holding the place in a book on his lap while he raised the other one in greeting. Or both hands gripped the edges of his desk as if to keep it from flying away. Why did she come here? Was it his black hair curling out above his collar? Was it the way he looked at everything as if it were at some great distance? Was it her one-year marriage at eighteen that brought her here? Her married year spent in the trailer park in Austin reading all the works of Melville with the tiny fan blowing all day and night? Was it the years working as a waitress and then a bar singer while putting herself through college and graduate school? Was it the distance between those years and life as she now found it? Was it the distance between Lockhart, Texas, and New York City? Was that the same distance between her loneliness and his? She had to get out.

Pilar Moreno opened the door to the office and looked in. Her long dark hair brushed the inside door knob. "I'm out of here, boss," she said. "Will you be here tomorrow?"

A loaded question, he thought. She knew they were shutting down. "Should be," he said. "Tomorrow." His loaded answer.

She waved her child psychology book at the room and closed the door behind her. Her hair brushed the door's translucent glass.

Pilar's footsteps across the tile floor of the outer office. The door to the hallway closed.

What brought B.C. here? "I have to pick up new glasses on Delancey tomorrow. If I get a chance, I'll stop by. I really want to know if you're going somewhere. I have to get out. If you're not going anywhere, then I am. And maybe I'll invite you."

Now looking at her. "That's a deal," he said. "Maybe I'll be able to make you a real offer by tomorrow. You can see nothing's going on here."

What was it? B.C. went to the door, rubbed her hand across the translucent glass. She leaned back in. "How about a few days at the Cape?" she asked.

"We'll see," he said.

"Maybe I'll send you a postcard," she said, closing the door more forcefully than usual, but not hard enough for the way she felt.

He'd first met her in a bar in the Village, called the Lone Star. She'd just come in from the rain. Dark hair. Dark, darting eyes. Dark raincoat. Almost translucent skin, aquiline nose.

Those legs. Those brown-and-turquoise cowboy boots. She walked right up, ordered a drink at the bar, and began pulling a napkin apart while she waited.

"Don't like paper products?" Giacomo asked.

She blushed and put her hands behind her. "Just a nervous habit," she said.

He introduced himself and held out his right hand. His left hand held on to her shoulder as if keeping her steady. Or was he steadying himself? He couldn't hear a word she said because just at that moment an electric train took off on the track that ran above the bar, whistling and blowing smoke. So he just held on.

They Look Away

NOW MARY LOU VLCEK was in front of him again with two dimpled, green glasses of iced tea on a tray she held out to him. "Mr. Berg, I'm sorry supper is taking so long," she said. "We didn't really expect visitors."

He hadn't expected to be one.

She set one of the glasses on the coffee table in front of him and sat down with the other one on a foot stool across from the couch. "New York," she said. "I don't know that I've ever met anybody who actually lived in New York. Isn't it dangerous?"

He shrugged. This could be dangerous.

A lacquered plaque on the wall behind her bore the title "Family Prayer" with a verse in script too small for him to read at that distance. Below the plaque was a framed photograph of Mary Lou, maybe ten years earlier, wearing a light blue dress, her blond hair in a beehive, two blond boys wearing red blazers and blue ties standing on either side of her—one boy about fifteen, the other seven or eight—and in front of her a brown-haired girl of nine or ten wearing a blue organdy dress with a white-lace collar. The picture may have been hand-tinted. Mary Lou's lips were unnaturally red. The children's lips were pink. All the eyes were blue. While Mary Lou and the boys were looking directly into the camera, the girl held a Bible and looked off slightly to the right.

She was watching him. "That's my family," she said. "You can see by the picture of me it was a few years ago. You'll probably meet the rest of my crew at dinner. We always try to eat together. Do you have a family, Mr. Berg?"

"Please call me Jack," he said.

"All right, Jack. And call me Mary Lou, won't you? Well?"

He was staring at the photo of a young woman on a wooden fence, surrounded by wildflowers. Maybe 19 or 20. Maybe taken in the 1940s.

"That was my mother," Mary Lou said. "She looked like a movie star. Don't you think, Jack? In fact, don't you think all young people look like movie stars? Some days I catch myself looking at that picture and just thinking of all she went through after it was taken. One brother was killed while he was fishing. Went out and never came back. Her little brother died in Korea. She helped her mother run a little soda and candy store. Look at her smile. She was beautiful and she was innocent. She didn't know what life was like. I guess that's what makes all kids look like movie stars. They don't know what life is like yet. She was smart. She kept up with the news, but she didn't know. I know she laughed a lot. You could tell people wanted to be around her. You can tell it from that picture. She was so alive then. It's funny how alive you can be in an old photograph. Even ten years after you're gone.

"Do you know how she died, Jack? Of course you don't. She was hanging out the laundry like she did every day. Must have been a heart attack. With her dying breath, she clothes-pinned the shoulders of the dress she had on to the laundry line so we wouldn't find her in a position she would rather us not. It took us a while to realize she was gone.

"After she died, I found things she'd kept from when she was young. Invitations to parties. A few hair ribbons. Not much. But just enough to know that she would daydream. A school notebook with thick cardboard covers with "PRIVATE" written on the cover. And inside were drawings. They were drawings of flowers. Drawings of birds. Sketches of people facing the other way. You always saw their backs, and they were looking out into a field or across a pond. Maybe she didn't want to draw faces. They were always looking away. She didn't have an easy marriage—even after he left. Four kids. But she was always good to us. When I think of her, though, I always think of her leaning against the sink in the kitchen looking out the window, looking out at birds or flowers, always looking away."

Berg was staring at her hands, holding the glass in front of her knees.

"I'm so sorry, Mr. Berg, Jack. Why am I telling this to a complete stranger? A complete stranger from New York?" She smiled, and her eyes disappeared behind her cheekbones.

A screen door slammed behind her.

She shot up. "Oh, the dinner," she said. "It won't be long." And she ran back into the kitchen.

Disasters of War

"YESTERDAY MORNING THE ARMY came into our town of San Juan Cotzál. I stayed with many others in the church while they were here. I do not think these walls or my collar will protect us much longer. After they left, I went through the village and made this list: eleven men dead (one a schoolteacher), four women dead, two little boys dead and one little girl, five hands missing, three eyes, one tongue, four rapes, eighteen people taken on the bus to Guatemala City to the doctors, and nine boys, three men, and one woman disappeared. It is my belief that they will make the boys into the soldiers who will attack the next village of Joyabaj. That is what they do. This is what I report. I alone of all the literate people have lived to tell what happened."

B.C. Boyd recorded the facts. Eighteen dead (one schoolteacher). At least eighteen wounded. Rape. Thirteen disappeared. She took off her glasses and closed her eyes. The end of the Maya. The girl who used to come by the office to translate letters. Broad Mayan face. Upper class. Art history student—not Mayan but Olmec. Pretty girl.

B.C. looked at her glasses. Her eyes hurt. The optician on 8th Street told her one thing. The optician on Delancey had told her another. She decided to try another optician on Delancey Street. She had seen gray, almost translucent frames in his window. If he agreed with one of the other two, she would buy the glasses and those frames.

She thumbed through the files on her desk. "The Children of the Disappeared in Argentina." "The Private Armies of Paraguay." "Land Confiscation in Guatemala." She picked up the Guatemala file, walked to the window, and watched an argument between two old women, each pointing to an empty space on a bench on the Broadway median. She decided to go to Delancey Street and then see if Giacomo Berg was ready to go somewhere.

Why? Because she liked his thick ethnic presence, his substantial nose, his peasant hands, the light that sometimes emanated from his eyes and was sometimes aimed directly at her, she thought. But great deserts of silence lay between them.

Besides, at the moment she had no better options. Maybe he wasn't worth all the thought she put into this. She resented the fact that here she was thinking about him again. Time to move on.

She closed the file on Guatemala and turned to look outside. Below a waiter and his family were waiting for a taxi. The waiter's family stood stiffly on the corner. He had his right arm raised. He was wearing a blue waiter's jacket. He was also wearing black pants, white shirt, black bow tie. He was definitely a waiter. He held his right hand in the air looking toward the line of traffic stopped in front of him. A woman wearing a brown coat and a black head scarf stood beside him. She held a child bundled in white. She looked straight ahead. A little girl stood beside her. She wore a green coat and a green hood. A green scarf hung out at her knees. It's too warm to be dressed like that, B.C. thought. A boy stood next to the girl. His hands were in the pockets of his red jacket. He shifted weight from one foot to the other. He was standing by the light pole. They all stood so erect. The traffic light on the pole was red. Then it was green. Then yellow. Red. When the light beside the boy turned green, the waiter waved his right hand in small arcs above his head. When the light turned yellow, he brought his arm down and rubbed his hands together. When the light turned red, he lifted his hand again.

The night before, B.C. had heard this story on the subway going back to her apartment. A woman sitting to B.C.'s left, either from India or Pakistan—she couldn't tell which, wearing a head scarf, told it to an older woman, also from India or Pakistan, sitting beside her. A man sitting in a window saw a young man on the street pushing at a derelict. The derelict held a carton of rotten vegetables from which he'd been eating. The young man knocked the derelict down into the street and sent his box of vegetables rolling through the intersection. The man in the window was now standing, people on the ground later said. Then he saw the derelict get up from the street, gather the vegetables into the box, and start walking toward the young man, who was still standing there. The derelict took a tomato and threw it at the young man, who ran over to a pile of debris and grabbed a brick. The man saw this from his window and decided to stop the young man from further violence. By the time he reached the street, the man saw the young man waving the brick standing not more than ten feet from the derelict, who was waving a two-by-four over his head. There was a great deal of shouting, the young man saying things like "bastard," "cocksucker," "fuck," the old man yelling and screaming things no one could understand. There was a small crowd of people standing across the intersection. The man from the window stepped in front of the derelict and faced the young man, telling him, "Leave the old man alone." Just as he said "alone," the derelict swung the board he had grabbed and hit the man from the window on the side of the head, crushing his skull and killing him just like that. The police were called. Some people held the old man down. The young man told the cops that the derelict had chased his children, had knocked his wife's grocery bags from her hands, and had kept everyone in their building awake, including his baby, by standing in the entranceway ringing all the doorbells all night long. He said he was trying to teach the derelict a lesson. So the police took the derelict away. An ambulance came for the body. Later the young man learned that the old man had been placed in a veterans' hospital. He found out from a social worker there that the old man thought he lived with the young man's family in their building. No one knew anything about the dead man from the window. "Such a shame," the woman next to B.C. said, ending her story. She looked down at her hands and shook her head.

The light turned green. The waiter waved his hand above his head. A taxi stopped. The waiter opened the door. The woman and children got in. The waiter stood beside the taxi. It pulled away. He turned around and walked swiftly up the street. He turned left on W. 82nd and disappeared.

It was time to go downtown. She found the glasses she wanted on Delancey. Black that came to slight points at the corners. They would tell people she was serious, but not entirely.

She decided to stop at his office. Was she wasting her time? What else could she be doing? Anything else. She took the elevator to his floor. There was a note taped to the door to his office. "OUT OF TOWN. CLOSED UNTIL FURTHER NOTICE."

God dammit! God dammit! She beat her right fist into her left palm. Giacomo Berg, that's it. Good riddance.

Instead of taking the elevator, she walked slowly down the stairs. She needed a drink. A deep sadness blossomed inside her. Not because he'd disappeared without telling her but because she cared that he did.

By the time she got to the lobby and then the street, it was getting dark. She stopped dead still. Things kept moving past her. Kids on scooters. Bike messengers with always urgent business. The masses dodging trash cans and other barriers as they rushed to disappear into dark subway entrances. Everyone had somewhere to go.

At Home

A FIRE AT THE EDGE of the road. How had it started? He scratched the skin under his beard. He slowly picked his way downhill through rocks and scrub brush to the flames. He squatted a few feet from the fire, watching it almost die then grab a dried-up shoot of Johnson grass and pull itself forward. The black patch, outlined in red with a yellow spark here and there, was slowly expanding, moving away from the edge of the road. The red line approached his boot soles. He stood, unbuttoned his overalls, and pissed on the red line, where it was picking its way through the grass. There was a slight hiss, and threads of smoke rose along the edge of the black half-moon. Farther on, he walked along a line where flames jumped up not more than an inch or so from the ground. If he walked slowly enough, would the flames melt through his rubber soles before they were snuffed out by his weight? He tried to discern the heat brushing the bottom of his foot before being trampled. Behind him now was a long, thin line of ash. In front, only about ten feet left of the smoldering ribbon. He decided to let nature take care of the rest. He squatted, scratching his chest under his overalls, watching the black stain grow in tiny leaps, moving to a dry branch, one dead grass blade to the next, taking in a few, tiny, oval brown leaves, dried deer scat, mesquite bean shells, and goat turds. It stopped at one end before an expanse of ten feet or more of dry, hard land without a twig, a weed, or a snakeskin to feed on. At the other end, the fire line was confronted by a patch of green weeds, a live oak tree, an outcropping of limestone. Little by little, the sparks burned out, puffs of smoke rose from the ground, the black patch stopped growing.

He stood up, buttoned his overalls, and slowly climbed back up the hill. A gray rock lizard went with him, crossing his path several times as he climbed over rocks, slipped on gravel and loose caliche, and eventually reached a shack near the summit of the hill.

He picked up a bucket of water on the porch and poured a small amount into a blue tin bowl. He dipped his left hand, then his right into the bowl, then rubbed them together and dried them on his overalls. He poured what remained in the bowl over his head, letting it run over his face, trying to keep his eyes open, closing his mouth and holding his nostrils closed.

A cloud of dust rose from the road below. He stood on a rock to examine the road. Not a car. A jackrabbit? The wind? He returned to the porch, sat down, and scratched his beard. He went inside the one-room shack and inspected a pouch full of prickly pears he'd picked the day before. He tried to bite into the fruit. Still hard and bitter. He took a handful and laid them on the porch in the sun.

He took off his overalls, picked up a towel from the porch, placed it on the ground, and sat on it in full lotus, facing the sun. He leaned forward and put his right forefinger down his throat. He gagged but nothing came up. Empty. Purged. Starving. Bony. He reassumed the position: straight backbone, open palms, thumbs touching forefingers, backs of hands on knees, eyes open, staring at the sun.

The skin on his back was red. Acne. Welts up and down his spine and on his chest under the curly black hair. The bone of his pelvis stood out like a saddle. No fat on his buttocks. The bone showed there, too. Ribs and shoulder blades prominent. The thin bones of his feet. Every line of sinew and bone was defined, except those under the thick black beard, extending to the middle of his chest, and under his black hair, falling to the middle of his back.

He stared straight ahead. A lizard darted in front of him, stopped beside his right knee, looked at the shade under the knee, then scooted away. A breeze started in the cedar trees on the hill. Mesquite beans rattled. He would sit like this until sunset, until the sky was as dark as the blackened stubble by the road, until something in nature moved him. Peter Proust at home.

How They Lived. What They Ate. What They Believed.

WAS IT JUST TWO EVENINGS before that B.C. had walked out of his office, rubbing the door's translucent glass as she left, saying she'd return the next day? Was it just two evenings before when, knowing he would be closing his business that week, he wanted to jump up from his desk and go with her, as he'd never done before?

Two days earlier, after she'd left, he put the items on top of his desk into a box. His books were already packed in boxes against the front wall. He took down the framed poster of the Jasper Johns painting of the United States. He took down his framed diplomas, his framed Garry Winogrand photos of people at the Central Park Zoo, carefully cut from a book, the framed tickets his uncle had given him from the last game at Ebbets Field. He turned off the lights. He walked out and locked the front door. The phone began to ring.

A boy about twelve swung the door open to the living room, poked his head through the opening, and announced, "Mr. Berg, my mama says to tell you supper is on the table."

Dinner was served at a long table with benches on either side and chairs on the ends. Mary Lou motioned for Berg to sit in one of the chairs. She sat in the other facing him. Her father and the kids settled onto the benches.

She looked him in the eyes as she commanded Little Henry to say grace and later as she served the greens. For a few minutes there was only the passing of food. The greens went to the left, the dinner rolls to the right. No one said a word. Just the clanking of serving forks and spoons against dishes. Each person took a swipe at the bowl of mashed potatoes. Each speared a piece of fried chicken from the platter in the center of the table. Each ate a chicken part and set the stripped bones back on the plate, wiped his mouth or her mouth, then drank from the green dimpled glasses of pre-sweetened iced tea. The ice clattered to their lips.

Mary Lou's brother, Bob Sidell, Jr., pulled his long legs out from under the table and stood up. "I wisht I could stay and talk tonight, Mr. Berg. I'd like to hear about New York. But I've got to go to a meetin'. There's a lot of folks dependin' on me for a ride if for nothing else. But tomorrow, if you need a ride somewhere, I'll be glad to take you as far as you want to go or, leastwise, until I get tired of taking you there." He bowed slightly at the waist and took off out the back door.

"Mr. Berg, I'm afraid we don't have many rooms here, but you are welcome to stay on the couch for the night," Mary Lou said. "That's as long as you don't mind waking up to find a cat walking on your face." She almost giggled.

Mary Lou's dad, Robert, motioned his fork toward the girl with braces across the table from him. "Margaret Ann, I'll bet the boys are starting to pester you now that you're getting to be a lady."

Margaret Ann turned to her mother and whined, "Mama."

"Daddy, don't you talk like that to her," Mary Lou said. "She's too young to think about those things, even if she is a pretty girl. Especially because she's so pretty." Robert looked down at his plate.

She picked up the basket of dinner rolls to pass to Giacomo. "We're a very religious family, Jack. Daddy doesn't understand it because he didn't raise me that way. But that's how we are. This world is falling apart, so the only thing there is to do is to believe in doing the right thing by each other and to wait for Jesus Christ Our Lord and Savior to come retrieve us. Sometimes I think the worse things get, the better off we are, because it means we are that much closer to the End Time."

"Amen," said Little Henry.

"Do you think about those things, Mr. Berg?"

He put down a chicken leg, cleared his throat and said, "Truthfully, I try to think about the future as little as possible. I have a hard enough time putting one foot in front of the other." He fiddled with his plate, turning it a little to the left and then back to the right.

"Pardon me for asking this, Mr. Berg," she said. "I hope you don't take offense, but are you Jewish, Mr. Berg? I think I've only known one person who's Jewish. Mrs. Michaelson downtown. She has a dress shop. She's very nice. There just aren't that many Jewish people around here."

"No offense taken. I haven't met many Southern Baptists myself," Berg said.

"Church of Christ, Mr. Berg. We're Church of Christ." She put her hands in her lap and smiled.

"Now it's my turn to be sorry," Berg said. "My father is Jewish. His family came from Lithuania. My mother is Italian. Hers came from Sicily. I'm 100 percent immigrant."

"That's so interesting, Mr. Berg—I mean Jack. Daddy, how far back does our family go?"

"Oh, hell," Robert said.

"Daddy," Mary Lou said, raising a forefinger.

"Sorry. But we're just a bunch of Appalachian hillbillies, one of whom married a Czech accordion player. They turned him into a hillbilly, too. For as far back as anyone can remember. Her mama, of course, was Church of Christ, and that added a wrinkle. Nothing special about us, though."

"We're all special in the eyes of the Lord, Daddy," Mary Lou said, coldly staring him down. "But Mr. Berg, does that mean you don't believe in a Hereafter? The Millennium's on our doorstep. Aren't you at least a little worried about what might happen on the Millennium?"

Giacomo Berg picked up his dinner knife and then laid it down. He did the same with his water glass without taking a sip. "To my way of thinking, it's just numbers. Somebody started counting about 2000 years ago, so 2000 had to come up sooner or later. I can't think about the Here-after because I have a hard enough time thinking about the here-today or tomorrow. We could all be vaporized by some giant space rock in a matter of seconds," he said. "So that's why I just try to think about where I might eat my next meal. I certainly wouldn't have predicted having a sumptuous meal like this."

"Oh, Mr. Berg, Jack. Thank you, but that's so sad. I can't believe you really think that. We have to believe in something bigger than ourselves. If you don't object, I'll have you in my prayers tonight," Mary Lou said.

Damn, if she didn't just wink at him. Now he was confused, but pleasantly surprised, to find himself inside the prayers of a Church of Christ true believer in Texarkana, Texas.

Mary Lou brought banana pudding from the refrigerator. She spooned it into bowls, standing a vanilla wafer on the top of each serving and passing around the bowls. When they finished, she and Margaret Ann began to wash the dishes. Robert went out the back door followed by Little Henry. Giacomo Berg returned to the couch.

This is the Story of...

WHEN THE PHONE RANG in his office, he'd hesitated. Who would use that number? He put the box he was carrying on the floor, unlocked the door, and lunged back in, picking up the receiver on Pilar's desk.

"Hello. Hello?"

"Jack. Is that you Jack?" a woman's voice at the other end. Not unfamiliar. "This is Sara, Jack. Sara Proust."

"Sara? Sara. Are you in town? Is everything all right?"

"Jack, it's not all right. We can't find Peter. We don't know where he is. The last we heard he was in that commune, Jack. In East Texas. But it's been months. Things sounded like they were falling apart. Have you talked to him?"

"I hate to say this, but it's been at least three or four years. Maybe more. I just lost track." He looked through the door to his office, out the window of his office, and toward the west, past the Hudson, toward the lights that could be the end of the sunset but were more likely the lights of Jersey City, the Meadowlands, Secaucus.

"We all have. He's not right, Jack. Can you help us? Can you go look for him? I'll pay for it. Can you, Jack?"

"Yes," he answered slowly. Then "Yes. Yes. Where do I begin?"

"I guess you have to start with that commune. I hate that place. I went there once to see him. They wouldn't let me talk to him for more than an hour; then I had to leave. I told him to leave, but he wouldn't."

"Okay. I'll go. But where?"

"You have to go to Texarkana, Texas. Then you go south near a town called Marshall. You got this, Jack? Then you ask somebody for the Refuge. That's the best I can tell you. Is that okay, Jack? When can you go?"

"Tomorrow. I'll go tomorrow."

"Thank you, Jack. Thank you. Tell me how to send you money. Call me when you find something."

"Of course. Don't worry. We'll find him." He took down her numbers. He hung up the phone. He left a note for Pilar and put a sign on the door. He carried his box of office mementos home. He called Greyhound. A bus was leaving for Dallas at midnight. It stopped in Texarkana. He took that bus.

B.C. Boyd lay on her bed and stared at the ceiling in the light of early evening. She watched the darkness grow across the white plaster, from the wall by the hallway toward her window. She wondered if she had a cigarette. Lying there, she thought her way through every drawer in the house, but came up empty. She had quit years before, twenty years before, but every once in a while....

She got up and walked to the kitchen. How could she be so stuck? She found an old opened bottle of pinot grigio in the refrigerator. Almost vinegar, but not quite. She took it to the couch and began to drink.

Where was B.C. Boyd, lead singer for Athena, Austin's all-woman band? Up on stage wearing black boots, black jeans, and a black cowboy shirt unsnapped as far down as she felt like, strumming an autoharp and singing Hank Williams? "Hear that lonesome whippoorwill?" Where was B.C. Boyd, working on her Virginia Woolf dissertation in the University town by day, slugging back vodka and singing all night, going to an all-night party at a farmhouse outside town, flying on brownies laced with LSD? Where was that woman, living in a communal house that was raided for drugs and harassed by police because the school radicals camped out there, the woman followed from campus to the Split Rail saloon by rumpled English professors, singing a sultry "Jumpin' Jack Flash" right in their faces? Where was the woman who drove all night to hear the wailing of Ornette Coleman in the bars of black Dallas only to be back defending her dissertation on Woolf's use of mirrors the next morning? Where was she? Where was the woman who jumped twenty feet bare-assed into the cold lake water of Hippie Hollow, who got her Ph.D., then drove straight to New York City to get a job as a waitress at the Frog Pond on the Lower East Side? Keeping track of disappeared people and lately tagging after an only mildly attractive misanthrope who has apparently given her the slip? Impossible.

When she woke up the next morning, the first thing she did was get down on her hands and knees and reach under her bed for her guitar case. She pulled it out, brushed and blew the dust off, and opened it up. There it was, almost glistening in the light filtering through her curtains. She pulled it out of the case. The phone rang.

He had been awake to see the signs for Bristol, Tennessee, then Knox-ville. It was still dark when the bus driver announced, "Folks, on your right is Oak Ridge, Tennessee, the home of atomic science." The bus driver was on his microphone. "The pine trees you see at the edge of the highway are part of the Atomic Energy Reservation. You should all come back some time and visit the American Museum of Science and Energy they've got set up there. It's truly amazing." He thought he could see a glow among the trees. He fell back to sleep.

The bus descended the off-ramp into downtown Nashville. Red brick buildings. He looked for any signs that this was indeed Nashville—guitar stores, beehive hair. He really didn't know what to look for. They stopped for an hour. He ate a warmed-up burger in the bus station café. Sweet iced tea. He could imagine smooth-faced Willie Nelson, weird young Roy Orbison, emaciated Hank Williams showing up here with a guitar case and nothing more. He looked around the bus station. Only sad people waiting to leave. Or waiting to wait some more. Another coffee, then they announced his bus to Dallas.

A line formed in front of the bus. He followed it back on board. He helped a white-haired white woman hoist her bag onto the overhead lug-gage rack. She wore pleated khaki pants, black alligator-looking boots, and a button-down pin-striped shirt. Nashville. They all took their seats. The bus driver got on. He was laughing and holding up four fingers to show another bus driver, who was laughing behind the glass of the bus driver's dispatch room. Jack leaned against the window.

It was almost a lifetime ago that Peter had taken him to visit a com-mune in Massachusetts, near Vermont, crossing the Connecticut River a dozen times to get there. They followed a dirt road for miles. They stopped at a creek that crossed the dirt road. They listened to the three or four inches of water running across the gravel of the road. They sat long enough for horse-flies to find them. They walked in the yellow light that filtered through the leaves. Dead leaves crackled. Branches broke. Peter took a shit in the woods. Said he wanted to memorialize their being there in that way. They returned to the car and drove up a slowly curving path that brought them to a clear-ing. The trees fell away on either side, and they saw a field marked off by giant sunflowers, a frame house painted purple, a large building like a barracks made of new wood, junked cars, a rock-and-roll band playing in the middle of the field beside a trailer parked there with huge black wires running to the band, and men and women and children, dogs and goats, dancing in the field. Peter wagged his head from side to side. Berg told Peter, "I don't believe this shit," and they both started laughing.

While Jack took in the spectacle, Peter found the friend he'd come to see. The friend explained that CBS News had been there filming all morning. The commune's rock band had been asked to play. The leadership had declared it a holiday. The friend took them to the dormitory being built. He asked them to carry wood planks up to the second floor for later construction. They were taken to the big hall of the purple house, where they ate lunch with the communards. Giacomo remembered someone reading announcements, babies crying. After lunch, while Peter went with his friend to talk to Paulie Polidor, the commune founder, Jack and two other visitors followed a man and a woman to a swimming hole at the river. They undressed and walked into the cold water. Scores of naked people were standing in the water, splashing each other. The TV cameras were there but said they were only filming above the shoulders.

Later he found Peter in the middle of a commune football game. Peter played like a wild man. Once Peter knocked Jack down with an elbow to the rib cage while blocking for a runner. He landed several inches from the mud overflowing a pigsty. He looked up into the snout of a sow. They went to the bathhouse to shower. There was a door for men and a door for women. Peter didn't like that. While they were showering, a hand pulled aside a curtain, and a wet woman asked, "Is there any soap on your side?" Peter smiled and said, "I'll wash your back if you wash mine."

As they walked to the car to leave, a woman holding a little boy hugged Peter. A woman with braids squeezed his hand. Peter's friend handed them a bag of apples. They drove back through the woods. They crossed the creek. They crossed the Connecticut River several times.

They got high. They stopped at a diner for coffee. Two highway cops sat down beside them. They stiffened. Then one of the cops said to them, "This is the night that cracks the camel's back." What did that mean? They laughed. The cops laughed. They drank their coffee and split a slice of apple pie. The highway cops left. Jack found Orion before getting in the car. They opened all the windows, turned the radio up as loud as it would go, and drove full speed down the highway.

They were approaching Memphis. Memphis—until now just a marker. The assassination of Martin Luther King, the home of BB King, Graceland, slave markets, the great river. A great ball of ideas. But now here it was in the flesh. Men and women walking the sidewalks in front of blocks of red brick neighborhoods. He felt like an ignoramus. A woman across the aisle held an open book face down against her stomach and stared straight ahead. They pulled into the bus terminal with the morning sun illuminating the building's chrome outlines.

A two-hour delay in the Memphis bus station while they changed drivers. He ordered a cup of coffee. He didn't want to use up the meager charge in his cell phone, so he called B.C. from a pay phone near the counter. As he drank, the brown veins of the cup were revealed.

"B.C., this is Jack."

"Where are you? I got your note taped to your door—if that was a note for me."

"I'm sorry I had to leave that way. Something came up. I'm in Memphis."

"Memphis? Memphis, Tennessee? Why are you in Memphis? Is everybody nuts? My brother called me last night to tell me that first a psychic, then a local team of scientists have predicted that his town in Ohio would probably be struck by debris from a disintegrating space capsule. He's taking his family to Florida until the capsule falls. Space officials have shown up in town to deny all allegations. Insurance companies are selling special policies covering the loss of home by falling object. He told me not to sit on the roof, Jack. On the roof, the way I like to do with the rest of the building in the summer. He told me not to go outside more than necessary during the time of 'likely fall.' That's what he called it—'likely fall.' He told me to keep track of the capsule's course, to keep the radio on night and day, and to have a plan for escape. Escape, Jack. From New York City? He's flipped. And now you're calling me from Memphis."

Giacomo Berg listened without answering. He watched a cockroach carry its egg sack across the gray tile of the wall around the telephone. It hesitated before crossing a strip of aluminum. It turned left, then right, then proceeded across the aluminum strip to the darker tile that continued to the ceiling.

"Are you there, Jack? Are you hearing what I'm saying?"

"No telling what can fall on you, B.C. I got a call. I had to go."

"Sure. Sure," she interrupted. "They always get excited out there about aliens. Ohio, Iowa, Indiana. Martians landing. Bright lights in the cornfields. They could sure use an ocean or some other large body of water. They need another source of possibility. Something strange. Otherwise, it's just corn and more corn. Otherwise, what's there to hope for? It must have finally gotten to my brother. He never used to follow those flying saucer stories much. He used to be too smart for that."

She stopped talking. He listened to her breathing. He heard New York City behind her. Out the window. The dull gray run of traffic. Hip-hop from somewhere and then it disappeared.

"Do you remember," he started slowly, "I told you about my friend Peter, the one always on a spiritual quest? Years ago I used to think that he had it all together, that he was thinking about the big questions while I was worried about my next job. Well, apparently he's still wandering in the desert. His sister called me not long after you left my office. She says he's lost. They can't find him. She says he's been acting strange and distant for the last four or five years—like he's already left this world or wants to. So they want me to find him. I can't say No."

"But why are you in Memphis?"

"I'm on my way to East Texas. Your Texas. The last place they knew to look was that commune called The Refuge. He lived there off and on for years. So that's where I'm going to start." He waited for a reply. He didn't know what else to say.

Then B.C. said, "East Texas isn't my Texas. It's swampy and racist and full of alligators. You better watch out over there."

"I don't know exactly what I'm doing," Jack said, "but I've got to start. I'm waiting to board a bus. When I get somewhere, I'll let you know."

"If you end up somewhere else in Texas, let me know. I might join you, if that won't put you out. You could end up in my Texas. But be careful, Jack. Some redneck may want to use you for target practice."

"I'll call," he said and was about to hang up, when she said, "Wait, Jack, wait. I have something else I want to say. I was thinking about this all last night. And now that I'm about to say it, it sounds way stupid. But Jack, I've been thinking about this for hours. I've been thinking about the space capsule and how everyone in the world feels helpless and terrified it will fall on them. And there are people thinking the Millennium will be the end of everything.

"And I've been thinking about this woman I saw standing on the curb while I was riding the bus from Delancey. A dark-skinned woman with dyed red curly hair and a tight short dress on. She was overweight. She was looking down the street so expectantly. Like she was waiting for something great or something terrible. And as I passed her, I saw that she had little red lips painted on her big brown lips. It was beautiful, Jack, in a sad way. And I couldn't help thinking that the world is amazing and it is horrifying all at once. Not one or the other or one then the other, but both together. All at once. What's wrong with me, Jack? Sometimes I want to dance and at the same time I want to scream. I don't know. I started crying right there on the bus. And I'm crying now, Jack. Isn't that stupid? I should go. Call me." She hung up the phone.

Water

ALL HE COULD THINK ABOUT WAS WATER.

The hard scrabble hills. Granite, flint, sandstone. Gray, brown, red. Dry as the moon. A brown rock lizard at his doorstep. Rock lizard on rock.

Even the water he kept in buckets and barrels seemed dry. It didn't have the deep coolness of water, even at night. It didn't flow across his skin. It simply made the dust cake.

He heard it long before he saw it. A trickling coolness beneath his feet. Unlike anything in the open air. The smell of water.

Now he lowered himself inch by inch. Peter Proust was wedged between two rock walls. His back was flat against one. The rubber soles of his boots worked the granite slab less than two feet from his face. Slowly, slowly he was going down. His knees were up against his chest. The muscles in his thighs and lower legs were taut, intent on maintaining the pressure that kept his back against the wall while grabbing and releasing the wall in front with his feet and hands, descending three or four inches at a time.

He'd found this place while walking the circles he'd charted, moving out and away from his cabin. This was how he was learning the world around him, in circular forays, widening the gyre each time, gaining incremental understanding, so the circle that took him to the bottom of the hill was replaced the next day by a circle along the edges of the two hills just beyond his.

Then up those hills in later days. And so his world grew.

The day before this he'd come across this opening in the red rock at the top of a hill two hills from his own. A crack in the moonscape. A sound like life cleaving the bone dryness.

Shielding his eyes from the sunlight, he'd looked deep into this crevice. Down below, no more than several body lengths below, he saw green moss growing on the red rock and a fountain of clear water trickling from no apparent source or break in the stone.

He determined that he had to drink that water, coming, as it seemed, out of nothing. A creational force more than a physical presence, that water and the sound of it hung in Peter's mind. He had to get down to it. He had to drink it, let it run over him.

He retraced his circle down one hill and over another until he'd returned home. That night he didn't eat or drink. He tested his strength by using the rafters to pull himself up to the ceiling of the cabin. Then he slept stretched out on the floor. When the sun came up the next morning, he ran round and round the cabin singing the Navajo "Heyaho, Heyaho!"

To descend into the opening he tied a blanket around his middle so that would protect him as he braced against the rock at his back. Slowly he descended, palms and soles flat against the rock face, as if he were some ancient rock bug skittering slowly into oblivion.

And he went down. Working his way by inches, he disappeared beneath the earth's surface. Almost instantly it was cool and wet. The heat of the sun was above him. He could hear the water trickling below. About twelve feet down, he rested. He was by then far removed from the world above.

The opening had not grown narrower or wider. But the muscles in his legs had begun to tighten. He continued down the flue. Painfully, hesitantly, he reached the spring in the rock. The cold water trickled against his right hand. He went farther down. He worked to position himself so that, by leaning forward, he could put his mouth against the water's source. He locked his knees, braced his legs, closed his eyes and, bending forward, brought his mouth to the water running from the cool rock. His tongue on stone. Purest water. Earth, air, fire forgotten.

He blocked out all thought. Connected to the source of water.

Then he opened his eyes, raised his back against the wall behind him. Pushing down with his feet, his palms, his hips, slowly he ascended to the blue opening above him, brought forth, up out of the rock, out of the earth, like the water.

Peter Proust once more walked the surface of the earth, water percolating in every cell.

Crossing Over

THE MISSISSIPPI. Tall, steely buildings and a white stone civic center stood massed at the water's edge. Through a break in that wall, the bus had emerged onto what seemed like a hair-thin bridge across the great gray river.

It all seemed freighted with meaning to Giacomo Berg. He just couldn't quite figure out what it was trying to say to him. The East spitting him forth across this plain of water and into the swamps on the other side. The green fields half-covered with water, the viridian trees, 3-Dollar motels, truck stops, dog track, flat, swampy land. This meant something—going west, but he was too tired to try to understand it.

Along a dirt road running parallel to the highway and not twenty yards away, he saw shack after shack after shack, a black woman or man or child in front of some, most closed up but some showing a plume of smoke from the chimneys. Houses on stilts. Water in ditches.

How do you live a life?

When they'd stopped in Little Rock, Giacomo got out and walked an eight-block circuit around the bus station. The squat capitals of the South. Limestone and sandstone office buildings with hints of green mold growing between the blocks, in the cracks, filling in the fossil imprint of shells in the limestone. An old hospital: red brick surrounded by patches of gravel and dirt, roots from huge live oaks, their long branches nearly scraping the ground. Around a corner, then he could see the cluster of glassy office buildings and condos that spring up in all these cities.

Maybe three blocks' worth. Here's the money, it says. Then back to the blue plastic wall panes and chrome strip-molding of the bus station.

To return to his window seat, Berg had to climb over a large man who had apparently just boarded and was already asleep. The man wore a blue windbreaker with a logo for "ABC Sports" and gray work pants. He turned away from Berg and continued sleeping, facing the aisle. As he turned, Berg's seat rose.

They ascended the on-ramp to the highway and quickly left the city. Three men sat on a bridge west of Little Rock fishing in the river. Their lines dropped thirty feet to the water. A boat moved under the bridge as he crossed over.

At that moment, B.C. Boyd was probably walking down a sidewalk on the Upper West Side carrying her briefcase with the names of the lost and the martyred. A thousand miles away he was riding a bus toward her Texas, an inexorable ride away from her. Add to that Peter Proust. Somewhere. Can desire move in more than one direction? The three rays of his thoughts: a point, a direction, a memory.

Just before the bus stopped in Arkadelphia, the body next to Giacomo roused. A gray-whiskered face turned to Giacomo Berg and offered to get coffee and doughnuts for both of them if Giacomo would watch their bags. As soon as the bus stopped, he was gone. He returned breathing heavily, "Can't do this much more."

The bus left Arkadelphia, the man breathing loudly through his nose as he ate. Then, staring straight ahead, he said, "Yes, sir, I've lived a lousy, complicated life." Giacomo barely nodded, hoping not to encourage him.

"What you see here is the mere package of a man. Look inside," he opened his jacket, symbolically Berg guessed. "It's nothing, nada, zero sum and total. No wife. No fortune. My children barely remember me one visit to the next. Yessiree. You are sitting next to one genuine American. Which way are you headed?"

"East Texas, out in the country somewhere north of Houston, near a town called Marshall."

"Going that way myself, though not that far. Just to Texarkana to see my daughter and grandkids. I hope she remembers I'm coming. Every time I go there I'm afraid she don't remember me. She can be kind of cold, you know. She lives on the Texas side. A miserable little town, Texarkana. Just miserable." He took another doughnut out of the bag and chewed it thoughtfully.

Arkansas was more rugged than Giacomo thought it would be. Irrigation sprinkler heads turned slowly in fields that were green in the center but brown along the fence lines. Other fields were just plain brown. Stubbly crops. Dry dirt, beige with a little purple running through it. At least through the tinted bus window. Near the cutoff for Hope he saw a coyote running through the dust. They passed a brush fire spreading from the shoulder of the road. The bus stopped under the five oaks of Five Oaks Café, where the driver announced the bus had broken down.

Giacomo followed the large man through a screen door and to a table in the Five Oaks Café. Near the door, three middle-aged men with pink faces and white straw Stetsons drank coffee and stared out the window at the road that curved by the oaks. Not a word said among them. At the counter, which ran the length of the café, five African American men and two African American women listened to a seemingly unending monologue coming from the fry cook standing behind the counter facing away from her audience, flipping eggs.

"Call me Bob," the large man said, reaching his hand across the table to shake Giacomo's hand. "I don't believe I caught yours."

"Jack, call me Jack."

"You see, Jack, this here's Hope. Everybody knows Hope now from the President. Lots of old families. Old houses. Spanish moss hanging from old trees. I lived here a couple of years myself. But there's no money, unless you tell people you're related to the President, so they'll pay you ten dollars for a tour of his boyhood home."

A man wearing a Caterpillar cap brought their eggs to the table. Bob buttered a biscuit while studying Giacomo Berg, who pretended not to notice as he ate. "So, Jack, what's it like up in New York? I could tell you were from New York just by looking at you. I was there once, but that was over 20 years ago. I suspect it's changed considerable."

"You could tell by my nose?" Jack asked. "Or do you think all Yankees come from New York?"

"Well, Jack, I couldn't help but notice that you said 'dunkey' for donkey and 'dungarees' for jeans and any number of words you folks get wrong."

"Okay," Jack nodded. "You win."

The bus driver walked in from the back of the café and announced that it would be at least three hours until the next bus from Little Rock could pick them up.

"Shit," Bob said, "It don't take that long to walk to Texarkana. C'mon, Jack, let's you and me go catch us a ride out on the highway. I've got a son who'll drive you anywhere you want to go from there."

They paid the bill and walked to the side of the road. He was content to be led. Not having to think much helped conserve his strength. A whirl-wind of gnats followed them up the road.

They walked along State Highway 67. The trees were heavy with Spanish moss. Every ten or twelve paces, Bob spit in the dust and shook his head. A few cars passed without slowing down. The fields along the road were dry. Tailwinds from the cars raised clouds of dust. But where the road crossed a creek, trees stood in a foot of water. Pine trees, hanging moss, browning fields, parched clay—did it all cohere? They got a short ride in the back of a pickup truck to a cutoff that disappeared into a stand of trees.

From the edge of the highway, Giacomo saw a small African American woman hoeing in a field. Beyond her, someone, who from that distance could have been Peter Proust, was also hoeing. Giacomo climbed the fence and approached the woman. "Good morning," he called, though it was well beyond morning. The woman turned around. She was old, had white hair underneath her bonnet, and her hands looked like wire gripping the hoe.

"About how far to Texarkana?" he asked, studying the man at the other end of the field.

Dark beard, long dark hair like Peter. The way he stood more than anything. "Don't know for sure. Never been there."

"What are you growing here?"

"Trying to grow soybeans. What they need is water. Not doing much good by them this year."

"Who you got working with you?"

"Just a fellow."

"Mind if I ask you his name? I'm looking for someone who looks like him."

She looked toward the bearded man, who was moving away from them as he hoed. "Yep, I do mind. We got work to do."

A car stopped, and Bob called to Giacomo from the road. Giacomo looked at the bearded man. Probably a little too heavy, a little too tall. Besides, it didn't make sense to find him this way, so easily, off a side road, hoeing a field in all these United States.

He ran back to the fence, climbed over, and followed Bob into the back seat of a white '84 Buick. A young black man was driving the car. The young maybe Hispanic woman beside him didn't turn around. A baby girl stared at Giacomo over the back of the front seat. By the time they reached Texarkana, she was asleep on Bob's lap.

Intimacy and Distance

AS HE LAY ON THE COUCH in the living room in the stillness after everyone had gone to bed, Giacomo listened to the crickets outside the window. He also heard a strange, high-pitched rattle that grew louder then softer then louder again as if on cue. Almost eerie, almost soothing. There was definitely something swampy about this part of the world. He heard shuffling by the kitchen door, the door open, and the shuffling coming toward him. He turned on the couch to see Mary Lou standing over him.

"I hope I didn't wake you," she said, sitting down in an easy chair a few feet from his knees. "I thought I heard you turning over and over. It's just that I don't often meet someone from your part of the world. Do you mind if I turn on a little light? I don't like it much talking to someone I can't see."

She turned on a lamp. Light seemed to emanate from her skin.

"What interests me, Mr. Berg, is that you seem so quiet-like. Not at all what I expected or have even seen in the few New Yorkers I've come across."

What was she after? He raised himself on his elbows. He'd taken off his shirt. He pulled the blanket up toward his shoulders. "I don't know what to say," he said.

She moved her hands to cover her knees. "I'm just interested, that's all. The Good Lord sets strangers before us for a purpose, and I'm trying to get it right for His Sake and for my own."

Was he being seduced by homily? Was it working? Was this the polyester conclusion to the antebellum South? Were these vestiges of Southern gentility passed on from one generation of women to the next, mansions giving way to town-houses then to apartments and tract housing? All the while, not thinking about the others still laboring in the fields.

Her hands clasped at her knees. The lamplight picked up the curves of her hips inside her nightgown, inside her robe. She looked him right in the eyes and through them, as if she were looking at a picture on the wall behind his head or out a window with a view of mountains way beyond Texarkana, one thousand miles to the west.

"So what's it like in New York? Is it as bad as they all say it is?" She leaned forward. "It's just that I've always thought that all you people up there were so pushy and had such hedonistic ways. I'm sorry if that sounds rude, but that's what I thought. But, Mr. Berg…"

"Jack."

"But, Jack, you don't seem that way entirely. It's just a first impression, of course, and I hardly know you, but I'm usually right about these things."

What should he say? Should he plead innocence in order to do the devil's work? Such a swamp here among these slow, pure syllables. "It could be that we are more devious than you imagine," he said. "Maybe we've learned how to hide our sinful ways. Beware of Yankees, especially those not bearing gifts."

He almost felt like using her name when he spoke to her, the way she stared deep into his eyes, leaned so close in. He could have begun his last sentence with "Mary Lou." But for Giacomo Berg addressing someone by her first name represented a commitment, a kind of intimacy he wasn't ready for. It crossed too many boundaries. He had to keep his guard up.

As he spoke, she stared at his lips, then looked into his eyes. She laughed. "You don't seem so dangerous. Besides, we're not so simple-minded either."

She sat there by his knees looking into his face. "Tell me, did Daddy make you walk down the street and talk to you about one side being Texas and the other being Arkansas?"

He sat up against the back of the couch, making sure the blanket was still in place. "That was interesting," he said. "We'd caught a ride after our bus had broken down. Then Bob had the car drop us off at the end of a road that, he said, ran down the middle of town. We walked by a few salvage yards and garages with cars up on blocks as we headed toward a row of light-colored buildings that he said was downtown Texarkana. He told me that the road was right on the Texas and Arkansas border. He said that if you committed a crime on one side of the street and crossed the street, you'd need a court order to extradite you back to the side where you committed the crime. I couldn't buy that. He said one side was wet, where they sold liquor, and the other side was dry. Maybe I'd buy that. Then he had me walk on the line down the center of the street, saying half of me was in Arkansas and the other half was in Texas."

"He was pulling your leg, Jack. He was close, but it's not nearly that crazy," Mary Lou said. "He's been saying those things since I was a little girl." She sat there and smiled vacantly, as if thinking about something in the past or about something else that could happen in the future.

He didn't tell her about the fact that Bob had kept muttering, "Miserable, miserable little town." He didn't tell her what Bob had said as they'd arrived at her gravel driveway, ducking under the clothesline of white and yellow underwear, dodging the whiny, gray, non-descript dog.

Before they approached the front door, Bob had grabbed Berg's elbow and said, "Now before we go in, there's something you've got to know. They don't always take to me too much. My daughter's a very religious type of person. She got it from her mother, that's for sure. And her kids are like that. And her husband before he ran away. And my son, Bob Sidell, Jr., who lives in the house, is also a little bit that way. I don't know exactly what to make of it myself, but that's just the way it is. So watch what you might be wanting to say."

Then they walked up to the front screen door and Bob knocked. Mary Lou had met them with her extraordinarily prominent cheekbones and graying blond hair. "Hello, Daddy," she'd said, and looked Giacomo up and down without opening the door. "And who's your friend?"

"His name's Jack. He's from New York. We were on the bus together when it broke down, so I brought him here. I thought maybe Bob Junior would take him down toward Marshall."

She opened the screen door and shook his hand. Her eyes sank behind her cheekbones as she smiled, saying, "That's nice, but Bob Junior may have other plans, Daddy. He may be too busy. I hope my father hasn't led you on. Won't you come in?"

She swung the door open.

Bob looked at his feet and motioned for Giacomo to follow his daughter. He stayed behind, tightening his grip on the back of a porch chair until his hands turned white. Giacomo followed her through the kitchen and into a living room. As they walked, he suddenly understood how a moving body could affect the curvature of space.

He didn't dare say any of that. Instead, he said, "Since I've never been to Texas, I wasn't sure what to expect." She listened, biting her tongue, the tip protruding slightly from her teeth. There was something about her unrelenting chasteness that excited him. She gave off a kind of physical strength without muscle, a combination of softness and determination. He followed the soft white skin of her arms and the line of her jaw, tight and controlled. He was no match for whatever she wanted. He figured she knew that.

She was leaning in toward Giacomo Berg as he still lay on the couch. "I want to ask you something, Mr. Berg, Jack, because I'm sure you have a different perspective than anyone else in Texarkana I could ask. I believe in the Rapture, Mr. Berg, and the Second Coming. I have little doubt about those things. Doubt can eat away at the soul. We know that.

"But I don't necessarily believe in these things the way some people do. Take the year 2000. People are running around saying that in a few months, exactly at the Millennium, the world is going to come to an end, Jesus will walk among us, and those of us who are ready will be escorted into Heaven while the rest of the people will have to figure out how to cling to Purgatory so they don't drop forever into Hell. I believe that most of that is true, but it doesn't have to happen in our time—in a calendar year that people put up in their kitchen and write doctors' appointments on.

"We have to understand that we are dealing with a bigger picture than that. We can't just expect these monumental changes to occur in our time. They have to come in His Time. And we can't really understand all that's meant by His Time, can we Mr. Berg? It's just too big for us to wrap our arms around?

"What do you think, Mr. Berg—Jack? I've got to stop chattering on, but I want to know what you really think."

"You're not going to like what I have to say," Jack said, raised up on his right elbow.

"Everything I do, everything I believe, is based on doubt. I couldn't do my job if I didn't start out by doubting anything and everything people tell me. Even what you might call the hard facts. I don't believe in any of that. I believe that what we do on Earth is fully responsible for what happens on Earth. No tricks. No mirrors. It's all physics and chemistry. All disconnecting and reconnecting molecules. And to the extent that we can affect anything by our tiny actions, then we're responsible for any earthly outcomes. Like global warming. But I do plan to have a bottle of Irish whiskey by my side on the night we hit 2000."

He waited for her to say something. She just sat there, seeming to gather herself up inside. She glowed.

She stood. "I hope you visit us again, Mr. Berg," she said. She patted the arm of the couch, turned the lamp off and shuffled back into the darkness. "I hope you can sleep with all the racket outside tonight," she said. "I bet you don't hear that in New York."

"Now that you mention it, what is that sound?"

They both listened. High-pitched chirping started up a few feet from the window. "Oh, that," she said. "That's our tree frog. It's got a little wildness in it—the sound, I mean. But I think it's beautiful. Tree frogs don't like disturbances. It means we're going to have a peaceful year in this house. I'm glad of that. Goodnight, Jack."

Silence inside the house. He waited for sleep to sneak up on him. He listened to the noises outside. Crickets, a car door slamming, the tree frog, leaves scraping the window screen.

Modern Life

ON THE SIDEWALK across the street two little girls stood with their hands on their hips. The one with long, dark hair began to dance, starting with a little hop on her left foot. The other girl followed, one step behind.

This on her desk in the morning: *La Voz del Pueblo, Prensa Libre, La Libertad, Gloria del Pueblo, Paz Tierra y Esperanza, Diario de la Independencia, La Revolución Agrícola.*

"*El Salvador.* Sanchez Muñoz, editor, *Prensa Libre*, 41, killed while drinking coffee. Pablo Quetzal, independent journalist, pulled from car in downtown San Salvador. María Pettí, journalist, companion of Quetzal, clubbed from behind. Body of Quetzal found four days later, country road, eyes gouged out. Sonia de la Cruz, social worker, 28, kidnapped, beaten, left for dead in suburbs, recuperating in unspecified location. Four Maryknoll Brothers found dead in jungle, sunk neck-deep in mud. 'At first we thought it was just the heads,' said the campesino who found them." *La Voz del Pueblo.* San Salvador.

And now the unending migrations. Not something she'd dealt with before. Individuals, martyrs—those she helped get papers. She'd find them housing, resources, safe transit. For those who are eligible, she'd find them lawyers to secure visas or political asylum. But now she's called to meetings to deal with mass migrations. Thousands and tens of thousands of people fleeing war, poverty, and hunger produced by roving gangs of thugs, small-town despots, mushrooming armies of 16-year-olds, drug networks, the IMF and international markets. Her list from the last meeting: Afghanis, Palestinians, Chechens, Albanians, Croatians, Eritreans, Sudanese, Salvadorans. People from Uzbekistan, Serbia, Somalia, Pakistan, Myanmar. Streams of people becoming rivers of desperate people. Is this the New World Order? Millions displaced, roaming the globe? Running from the dangerously unlivable to create new hotspots of overcrowding, hunger, sickness, and inevitable violence? Call their new country "Chaos." Give them each an ID and passport with that as their home.

She had to let this go. By the time she was awake before dawn this morning, she couldn't put it out of her mind. Third cup of coffee.

Not a way to start the morning. What could she set against this? Giacomo Berg? Not a chance. Not enough there, yet, if ever. The call from a Memphis bus station. Was she the rock in the middle of his waters? Did he think he must be dutiful to something, so he chose her? Steady B.C., the rock, the anchor.

Arnulfo the same way. Her heart jumped. She grabbed the report from her desk and quickly read through it again. Arnulfo? Arnulfo? No mention of Arnulfo. Not that his name not appearing on a report meant anything. He could be dead and rotting in the ocean somewhere, eaten by fish, or buried not neck-deep—that beautiful mustache—but entirely in the mud at the edge of a swamp. Seven months since any kind of sign. Since the letter he sent her from California through someone named Maceo, who knew him in their student days. It read: "They know who I am and they don't know who I am. The best of situations. I dream of your thighs leading to their inevitable conclusion, your ass like holding two live pigeons each with a pounding heart, your kiss damper than the jungle, your back, your shoulders. When I hold certain fruits, I feel your breasts." Jesus Christ, Arnulfo, give it up. If she thought he were alive and well, she'd just laugh at this. But now.... "Your eyes are in the jungle. But also and always there are other eyes. They watch me. They know me. And I know you...forever. Arnulfo." Seven months. And when must that have been written? No response when she wrote to the address for Maceo. No answers from their mutual friend in San Salvador, the lawyer who handled only matters of taxes, wills, and insurance, but on the side produced money and papers to smuggle out those in danger. "Even hidden behind actuarial forms and the estates of rich widows, I was discovered by the world," he once wrote her when writing to say he had no news. And he no longer wrote.

Two years ago, Arnulfo had simply arrived, had been given her name, had appeared at her office door on an October day just after she had noticed for the first time that fall that the leaves were no longer green on the trees in the median. He stood there, elegant mustache, khaki shirt, brown pants, brown boots, windbreaker, beaten attaché case in his left hand.

"Where's your scarf, your beret?" she'd wanted to ask.

A heavy-set man wearing dark glasses stood just behind him, wearing a sport coat of one plaid with pants of another, worn green shoes, a mouth of incredible sadness. They came to her sent by the lawyer in San Salvador, seeking asylum for the heavy, somber man. He had been marked for death. He wrote columns for his newspaper denouncing the conspiracy of rich coffee merchants, the bankers, and the Unification Church. They had warned him in different ways: messages were passed under his door; women came up to him on street corners and each touched her right index finger to the right side of her nose; twice his house was bombed, the second time killing his daughter's parrot in its cage hanging in the patio. He kept writing. They threatened his family. A reporter working with him was dragged from a bus and held with a knife at his neck for four hours. He wrote another column. Then they said it would be before Monday. Then by Sunday night. Then, exactly, on Friday at noon. The lawyer gave Arnulfo and the man false passports. They crossed through Guatemala and into Mexico, where they took a flight to New York. Arnulfo went because he spoke English and because he wanted to see the world and because he thought he might die fairly soon.

She took them home. She made dinner. While making soup, she called an immigration lawyer in Los Angeles, who agreed to handle the appeals for political refugee status. While seasoning the salad, she contacted a church organization that would house and feed the writer and send him on to Los Angeles to wait for his appeal. Then she served the wine. The writer saluted her work. Arnulfo saluted her resourcefulness. She saluted their bravery. They drank more wine.

The writer spoke several times about his wife and children. Arnulfo asked about the Empire State Building, the Statue of Liberty, whether the drug addicts he saw on the street were recruited to addiction to solve the unemployment situation or whether it was more subtle than that, whether it would be possible to hear some jazz, whether the centers of power in North America lie hidden from plain sight or whether they drive by every day in limousines to rub people's faces in it. The writer complained of exhaustion and fell asleep on the couch soon after the meal.

She and Arnulfo took another bottle of wine into her bedroom. She asked about his life of action. He asked about her life in the capital of commerce.

She said, "You're still a student."

"Always," he said, touching her shoulder.

"And what are you studying now?"

"Your eyes. Your neck. Your breasts."

"Okay, Latin lover."

"Okay," he said. The Yankee word. Modern life. They went to bed.

He tried to tell her how he may not live very long, the dangers of the revolution, but she stopped him. "You don't need to say another word, *mi estudiante.*"

Sometimes it became too much for her—the killing, the disappearances, the not knowing.

She had to do something besides be a witness. If only she'd gone to law school or medical school. She'd have a skill. Maybe she could get a job with Oxfam and distribute rice shipments in Africa. Or maybe she should leave it all behind. She'd done her stint. She knew people who did this kind of thing their whole lives. Either they carried an inner glow, a burning bush that did not burn out, or they were bitter and used up and self-righteous. That could be her. She had to get out. Just a few months ago, she'd come to the realization that most of what she did was not about people. It was about absences—holes in humanity where real flesh and blood had been. The woman in Argentina, 25, medical technician, two children, engineer husband, dark hair, dark eyes, staring out of her photograph, white laboratory jacket, the slightest hesitancy in one eyebrow, a tiny bend in the bridge of the nose, upper lip slightly arched—indicating uncertainty? Fear? Impatience? Graduation photographs, employment photographs, missing-person photographs. It was too much. On the street below, a man in an oversized overcoat was spitting on the windshields of cars stopped at the light, then holding up a squeegee with an offer to clean up what he'd done. Three women sat on a bench in the median staring straight ahead at the empty bench across from them. At some time, Arnulfo, at some time, Giacomo Berg, at some time the world will come to an end.

Running. Jumping. Standing still.

THEY DROVE SAYING NOTHING.

Red clay and red sand. Fields of dry grass. Then a dip in the road, a creek, bushes, willows, sumac, pine trees farther on. Then dry fields, grass burned out along the edge of 59.

"A scissortail," Bob Junior pointing to the darting bird trailing the forked branch of a tail. They stopped where a sign pointed for a roadside park. A cement table and bench and an aluminum trash container. Giacomo opened the paper bag Mary Lou had given him on the way out of the house—along with a pat on the shoulder and the admonition to come visit again. A ham sandwich for each of them, a half-gallon of iced tea.

Bob Junior pissed behind the trash container. From the sticky green leaves beyond the barbed wire, a scream of cicadas.

When they reached Marshall, Bob Junior said, "I think I'll drive a little more. Don't get out that often myself these days."

The road signs: Carthage, Palestine, San Augustine, Moscow. So many towns misplaced. At Tenaha they cut west to Nacogdoches. They passed a gas station at Attoyac Bayou with three dogs lying in the driveway and a sign on the pumps: "NO GAS. NO WATER. AND WE BARELY GOT AIR."

A few miles later Bob Junior said, "It's funny how you can have a swamp and you can have parched fields laying right up against one another. It's funny and it's a shame. You just don't know what to think."

When they crossed the Angelino River, Giacomo saw a green field to the east in which Brahma bulls were grazing. Snow-white egrets walked among the bulls or rode their backs.

They entered a state forest. On either side of the road for many miles there was either thick, green forest or thick, dead wood standing in water, covered with vines.

He let himself be carried along. He was determined not to be carried forever, to act when it was time for action. But, for now, he let himself be carried along.

When they reached the Neches River, Bob Junior said, "Well, I've brought you this far. Might as well take you all the way into the Thicket. I'll go as far as China if you want me to."

They came to Doucette. They slowed down and pulled off the road next to a stand of ash trees, where they stopped. Staring straight ahead, Bob Junior said, "She thinks our Daddy killed a man some time back. She's got no evidence, except her feeling. I thought I should explain." He left the motor running, got out of the car to piss in the trees, got back into the car, and returned them to the road. "That tea goes right through you."

They came to Village Mills, the left turn for China, the right turn for Honey Island, the town of Thicket, where they stopped in front of a white building set back from the intersection.

The building sat in the middle of a gravel and caliche lot, worn down and rutted by the entrance of trucks and cars, several of which never exited again but sat on blocks with wheels missing or the hood propped up and a door flung open or the doors missing entirely. A row of gas pumps stood in front of the building. They were red and partly rusted cylinders from the '50s with the tops rounded off and a circular sign mounted on each and blank except for the figure "9/10." At the end of the row of pumps was a smaller cylinder for dispensing air and skinny hoses running from that.

Giacomo Berg spotted a tall, big-bellied man standing behind the screen door of the white frame building. The man was barely discernible from the shadow that he stood in. He wore the Barg's soft drink sign in the middle of the screen door like a belt buckle for his khaki pants. As Giacomo approached the screen door, he heard the rustle of dogs behind the man. Then he heard a bark.

He asked the screen door for directions to the Refuge. There was a growl from between the man's legs. The man said, "The Refuge. Oh it must be about four miles that way to where you turn off on Blackmoor Road, then a few more miles through the woods there until you get right near the Trinity." A bark from between his legs. "Don't know exactly though." Another bark. "I only been there once and that was to buy some truck to sell in the store here—tomatoes and lettuce and what all. Just that one time. Another fellow brings it to me now." Steady barking from between his legs.

Giacomo backed away from the door while nodding his head and returned to the car. They began the drive into the woods. Giacomo relayed the instructions to Bob Junior, who said, "Just point the way and I'll go to it. I got to start heading back, but I want to see this through."

They came to the sign for Blackmoor Road and turned. The road began as pavement, but soon the pavement began breaking up. Deep holes appeared and patches of gravel and mud. The pavement ended altogether, and the car dropped to gravel and caliche. The tires threw the popping gravel against the bushes on either side of the road. The gravel ended, and they were on dirt rutted with mud and water. The large gray car plowed through the countryside, raising a plume of dust behind it.

Several times they came to a place which, by means of various indications, Giacomo took to be the Refuge. At some spots it was simply a clearing by the side of the road—a place someone had used to turn around and return to the main road to take off as fast as he could and which others, following this example, had since used as the farthest point they cared to wander before realizing they were lost. Or it was the place the children of Thicket and Votaw and Honey Island pulled off the road in the night to be alone until the owls, the coyotes, and other night noises spooked them so much they withdrew their hands from the deep recesses of the flesh and headed for home. At other places, there were actually gravel roads leading from the dirt road, entering a gate with a silver mailbox attached. But in those cases, the name on the mailbox was Duchamp or Poteet or Bouchard. In another place there were antlers tied to a tree branch hanging over the road. Finally there was nothing but trees and dips and turns in the road and barbed wire on both sides and more trees.

About every thirty seconds Bob Junior looked quickly at Giacomo Berg.

Giacomo Berg looked straight ahead, determined to be carried along. He watched both sides of the roadbed for any aberration.

Suddenly they were startled by a blue heron that started out of a bog by the side of the road, pumping its blue-gray wings as it followed the road ahead of them, gradually rising to the height of the treetops. They were almost under it when it veered to the right and disappeared. At that very spot, on the right, a dirt road appeared and a plain wooden sign, "The Refuge." The car stopped. Giacomo Berg got out, grabbed his bag, and waved as Bob Junior turned the gray car around and headed back into the diminishing light of late afternoon.

How to survive like a lizard

PETER PROUST RAN OUT of the shack screaming. That light. What were they doing now? He was sitting on the floor of the shack with his right hand in the bowl of water where the mountain laurel beans were soaking. It was completely dark. He'd thought he heard the scraping of the earth's turning against the air, producing breezes. He did hear the sloshing of the lake he could see from the second hill to the west. He may have been sitting for a hundred years. Then that light.

He felt it first on his hand in the water. Not warmth as with sunlight, but more like a steady gaze, like feeling someone's eyes on his hand. Were his eyes open or closed when he first felt it? Turning to look at his hand in the bowl of water required an effort he decided was worth making. That light on his hand among the laurel beans in the bowl of water.

What were they doing now? Were they putting up streetlights on the dusty road at the bottom of the hill? Streetlights for jackrabbits? For coyotes? Or for developers to sneak among the hills at night secretly designing model communities? He stood up and screamed in a convulsion that shook his entire being. He was naked. He breathed heavily as he pulled on his overalls, then sat on a wooden crate while tying his bootlaces. He managed to control his breathing, making sure the deep inhalations were matched by forced exhalations, that the rhythm was at once strong and regular. He felt a certain wiry strength enter his arms and legs and a lightness enter his brain. He stood up and screamed again, then charged out the door. That light!

It was in front of him—huge, round, yellow, just over the crest of his hill, hanging over the road below. So huge. How dared they? So huge. He stopped. Or was it the moon? He looked.

He concentrated. It was the moon.

What did this mean? He scratched his chest under the overalls. How could he have made this mistake? He ground his boot heels into the dust. He stared at the moon. The moon. He laughed loudly. Not good enough. He screamed, shaking his entire body. From far away he was answered by a howl. He laughed again, holding his sides. He picked up a large rock and threw it at the moon. He went back inside, laughing and scratching his chest.

He picked up the bowl of soaking mountain laurel beans and bit one of the beans. It was still hard as a pebble. He figured it would make him sick. But would he see things? The grapey smell of the mountain laurel blossom promised something.

He picked up another pot, in which green mesquite beans were soaking. He put a mesquite bean into his mouth and bit down. It gave way slightly, a kind of pulpy softness like wet wood. He poured the beans and water into an iron pot and took the pot outside to the halved steel drum that he used for cooking. He lit twigs, paper, and dry brush and let it burn down inside the drum. Then he placed the pot of mesquite beans just above the fire on three metal rods he had managed to push through holes in the side of the drum. He picked up two dry cactus leaves and one green, tender pad from a box on the porch. The dry leaves he threw in the fire. Then he eased the tender pad onto one edge of the smoldering mound inside the steel drum. He watched the prickly pear pad simmer, then the soft thorns on it catch fire. They burned off, and the green skin began to peel back. He turned the leaf over. The edges of the leaf were black. The liquid in the pad was sizzling. As it began to curl up, he fished it from the fire and put it on a red cloth to cool. He stirred the mesquite beans. He picked up the cactus pad, pulled it apart, and ate. The blackened parts were like paper. The rest was pulpy but tasted something like seaweed or artichoke. A delicacy. The water in the pot never boiled, but the beans gradually softened. Peter Proust drained the pot, then mashed the beans with an iron spoon. He was intent on this. He pressed the spoon against the beans along the side of the pot. He was methodical, pressing every bean. They did not give way easily. Finally he was satisfied. He ate the paste he had made. He could still taste the dust and gravel they grew in. Occasionally, though, a bite tasted like piñon nuts. He chewed thoughtfully, rubbed his stomach, and looked at the sky. The moon was directly overhead.

After eating, he put more brush in the fire in the steel drum and blew the smoldering ash until a flame or two appeared. He found a blanket in the shack, spread it on the ground not far from the drum, and lay down to look at the stars. At one point he got up, walked into the brush, and retched dryly a few times before vomiting. He thought he had been sleeping. He was not certain. He returned to the fire in the steel drum, adding a few sticks. He wanted to keep the fire going as long as possible. Matches were the most difficult article to find. Except for matches, he could live up here alone forever.

There were two left in the tin box on the shelf. It meant a walk into Mountain Home before too long.

He went into the shack, found the journal he kept in the crate nailed to the wall. The crate also contained a copy of William Blake's *America: A Prophecy* (illustrated), Ken Kesey's *Sometimes a Great Notion*, a candle in a tin candleholder, and, tacked above the candle, a picture of his sister and her son. He began to write in the section he had marked "Recipes":

HOW TO SURVIVE LIKE A LIZARD

Gather dry leaves and branches together. Using a branch, sweep clean a space in the dirt. Lie down in that space. Cover yourself with the leaves and branches. Wait for the wind to spread a thin sheet of dust over you. Be so still the bugs will walk up to your mouth. When the sun is low, lie on a rock. When the sun is high, find the shade. Let the dust work its way into your skin until your skin is the color of the dust. Exercise your tongue. Stretch it as far as it will go. If a dragonfly passes by, beckon it with your tongue. If it descends, then you will eat. If it does not, then practice by beckoning in the same way to women.

He closed the journal, returned it to the crate, and went back outside. He looked around for the moon, but it was gone. He lay down on the blanket. He looked at the stars. He missed Sara. He missed her son, Seth. He missed the quiet woods behind his home. His clueless parents—they were good people. He missed sleeping by the fireplace in their brick home. But that was another lifetime. Another world. Even if he wanted to, he couldn't find his way back there. He was out in the universe. Alone. The fire crackled. Far away a truck geared down on a highway.

How They Broke Bread

GIACOMO BERG WALKED DOWN a dirt road into the trees. The earth was soft, rich, black. Ferns growing under the trees. Everything a deep green. In several places, the road came within twenty feet of the swamp. Reeds stood three and four feet high out of the water. Between swamp and road, willows wept, cottonwoods quaked in their formal, soft wood; flowers dotted the earth. He saw brown birds riding the tops of cattails. A rustling in the treetops to his right.

It was early evening, and the gray-brown light seemed to emanate from the tree bark and the soil. He came to a wooden gate across the road, on either side of which were the shells of two flatbed trucks, whose hoods were painted with the words, "The Refuge." Dogs began to bark.

Giacomo Berg was not fond of barking dogs. Two bearded men carrying poles appeared. They asked his name. They asked his purpose. He told them he was looking for Peter Proust. They did not respond. He told them he had heard a great deal about the Refuge. They stared into his eyes. He told them he had been traveling for three days and would like to spend the night. The taller man nodded to the shorter, who swung open the gate. Giacomo passed through the opening between the two trucks. The men did not hold the dogs back, and they rushed up and surrounded him, barking at his knees. The hot breath of nondescript black and brown dogs barking at his knees. The short man closed the gate again. The men called off the dogs, who trotted away, and they led Giacomo to a hut by the side of the road.

There, under a sign proclaiming, "NO ALCOHOL. NO LEATHER," they told him to take off his belt. They asked for his wallet. Then his shoes. They removed the contents of the wallet and placed the wallet, belt, and shoes in a box. They handed Giacomo the money and cards from his wallet and asked him to write his name on the side of the box. They asked his shoe size. Nine. They opened a knapsack marked "9," pulled out a pair of sneakers, and threw them on the ground by Giacomo's feet. He put them on. They asked if the small backpack he'd been carrying had any leather. He said it didn't, but they kept it anyway.

The men left the hut and motioned for Giacomo to follow them and the two dogs deeper into the woods. He walked five feet behind them, afraid to lose them in the semi-darkness. He heard their tramping, the high-pitched drone of cicadas that rose and fell in the treetops, and an occasional bullfrog belching in the swamps. At one point he realized he was following his guides by sound rather than by sight. The darkness had become a swamp.

Every once in a while, he saw lights through the trees. He thought he heard voices. Then only darkness and cicadas. Finally the two men stopped at a gate and waited for him to join them. They pushed the gate open, walked him across a cattle guard, led him under what appeared to be a long grape arbor, then stepped into a large, well-lit clearing with five long wooden buildings forming a semi-circle across from them. At one end of the row of buildings a line of doorless and hoodless flatbed and pickup trucks rested on blocks. At the other end, a few horses stood in a large corral, motionless except for the flicking of their tails. In front of one of the buildings, three women holding buckets stood in line while a fourth pumped water from a well.

"You'll be staying over there," the taller man said, pointing to a small building on the right. "The rules are: One. No one stays for more than two nights and three days. Two. Everyone who stays does his share of work. Three. Everyone gets one audience with Joseph or one of the Counselors. Four. You may speak to any brother or sister on any subject, but you may in no way touch a brother or sister physically unless he or she touches you first nor call him brother nor her sister unless you are so called. Five. No leather may be used or worn in the Refuge, and no furry or feathered animal may be eaten or in any other way exploited, as we are all fellow creatures made of the same earth and sun. You may join us in the middle building now for supper. Your leather belongings will be returned to you when you leave. Are we agreed?"

Giacomo nodded and said, "I'll be glad to leave as soon as I can find out something about Peter Proust."

"Joseph will see you when it's time. The middle building."

Giacomo followed the men into the building. They were in a large room filled with rows of picnic tables where long-haired men and women sat, talking and gesticulating over bowls of steaming food. Other women moved among the tables carrying platters of food and empty trays. It was a scene from some archaic hippie dream. How had this survived for so long or was it simply lost in time?

Giacomo threaded his way across the room toward a table marked for visitors. Uneasy without his belt, he pulled up the waist of his pants several times during his trip across the room. A gray-haired man and woman sat at the visitors' table and smiled uncomfortably as Giacomo sat down.

Two women with hair tied up in braids attended the visitors' table. One of the women appeared to be nearly nine months pregnant. She had white hair.

The gray-haired man began to cut into the cheese, but the pregnant woman's hand grabbed his wrist, as she said, "Wait, first the blessing." The man folded his hands on his lap and stared at the edge of the table.

Across the room a man with a full red beard and red ponytail stood. "May the food be blessed for we have made it. As Joseph says, 'The karma of the hands goes straight to the stomach.'"

A bald man at a table behind Giacomo stood. "Bless this food that we guarded from the rolly-pollies and covered when it froze smack dab in the middle of May."

As he sat down, a woman across from him stood. "Bless this cheese that the dairy crew made for us. You outdid yourselves, boys, this time." Light clapping from all the tables.

Another woman stood. She rubbed her stomach. "Bless this supper that I feel will be the last one we eat before a new baby brother or baby sister comes to join us. That will make seven." More clapping. Then no one was standing.

Then a man with a long black beard shouted. "We need a blessing from the little brothers and sisters before we eat." He went to one end of the hall and picked up a little boy with blond hair and stood him on a table. The boy said, "Bless this food and bless our home. The earth's our bed. The sky's our dome." Everyone in the hall said, "Amen." Then only the clatter of knives and forks, plates and glasses was heard. The older man again began to slice the cheese.

The woman beside him said to Giacomo, "We've come here because our son Edward lives here with his lifemate Sarita. They have five children. He's sitting over there." She pointed to a row of tables.

The other woman serving them stood at the far end of the table and leaned slightly toward them as she said, "If you have any questions, ask me. My name is Hannachild, and I've been here since Joseph first found this place and went back for the flat-bed truck, the one you probably saw mounted by the gate with 'THE YEAR ZERO' painted on the windshield. I probably know anything you'd want to know about the Refuge." She fingered a gold ring.

"Oh, no," the older woman said. "We don't have any questions. We come here every year to see our son and his children. We really think you folks have an awfully nice place."

"Nice," nodded the man beside her. "Real nice. And clean, too."

The woman's ponderous breasts nearly rubbed the table as she leaned now toward Giacomo Berg. She wore a wife-beater shirt, like the older immigrant men in New York wore every day of their lives. "And you?"

"Me? I'm trying to find a friend named Peter Proust. He used to live here. You must have known him."

She stood up straight and wiped her forehead with the back of her hand. "Seems like I vaguely remember that name. Of course, he had a different name here. Joseph gives you a name. Like their son Edward. He's Micah here."

"That's right. Micah," the woman nodded.

"The other woman serving this table—she's Satyavanda. I happen to know that her former name was Tinka Rubinstein, but that was before the Year One, so it's like it never happened. What did you say the name was?"

"Peter Proust. From Massachusetts. He had a black beard, long black hair, pockmarks all over his back, and a way of rubbing his hairy chest while he daydreamed that made him look like the soul most at peace with the world."

The woman and man were watching Giacomo Berg. The woman smiled at him sympathetically. Hannachild started to leave the table. "Sounds like a lot of people. Some people join us and others go away." She walked away.

The man and woman stared at the bowl of okra. Giacomo sliced the cheese. The only sounds in the hall were those that accompany the acts of eating. Throughout the meal, women moved among the tables carrying platters of food or trays of dirty dishes. As soon as a plate was emptied, it was removed. As soon as Giacomo crossed his fork over his knife to indicate he had finished, Satyavanda appeared at his left shoulder to take his plate.

"Great service," Giacomo said to the couple. They smiled.

When Satyavanda returned to take the plates of the couple, he asked her, "Say, do you know anything about someone named Peter Proust?" She smiled, wiped the table where the plates had been, and walked away.

Hannachild reappeared to announce that Joseph himself would be speaking that evening. Giacomo asked, "Well, thought any more about Peter Proust?"

"Yes, I've thought about it and I asked the women in the kitchen, and, familiar as it seems, no one knows that name."

"So when can I speak to this Joseph about it?"

"Joseph will see you when it is the proper time. Joseph says, 'Truth only comes at the time that it comes.'"

She put two fingers to her lips and pointed to a table at one end of the hall where a tall, gray-bearded man was standing, waving his left hand above his head showing the two-fingered peace sign. This sign was answered all around the hall by hands raised in the same sign and shushing sounds.

A thin man with the hairline of a friar in front and slate-gray hair hanging halfway down his back stood, raised his left hand in the peace sign, and began: "Brothers and sisters, Refugees of Earth, the subject of the rap tonight is 'Space and Place.' Now, if you remember what they told you in public so-called school, one of the things they mentioned when they discussed where life came from was this far-out theory that life here on the planet Earth may have been started by a chunk of some other planet flying out of the great cosmic order and landing here, planting itself, as it were, in the soil of this lifeless rock. Now if they taught you in anything like the way they taught me, the teachers said something like, 'Some people think this, but science shows they're wrong. And here are some more dumb theories.' Then they'd talk about Martians and starships and leave the story of the seeding of the earth lost somewhere in outer space."

He picked up a clump of black dirt from which a green seedling was sprouting and held it above his head. "Now look at this. You all know what it is. You see it at least twice a year. You walk along the rows of earth and from way up in space—compared to the worms or the roots or bugs, that is—you drop these seeds. And the miracle is that the seeds do their thing. They get straight with the dirt that's as alien to them as one planet is to another. The seeds send out their roots and pretty soon, in a week or two weeks, you've got a whole new culture growing. Now to my way of thinking, that's a miracle. But it's also science. And there's nobody who can say it isn't. So, if a seed can do it, why can't an amoeba or a worm or a man or woman, for that matter? Why can't a whole civilization in its seed form land somewhere after flying through space and take root and grow into what it is today or will be tomorrow? That's what I think about when I think about science." He put the dirt back on the table.

"I'll tell you something else. That's the way we started, all of us coming here, flying off through the outer space of decadent everyday shopping-mall and TV-dinner culture. First a few of us landed here in the flatbed truck. More people arrived. And they're still coming all the time—more seeds flying off from their pods and landing here to build a new civilization.

"But here's the second point. If you fly off and land somewhere else, you've got a mission. You've got a mission to survive and you've got a mission to grow. Every seed knows that. There's a reason you flew off and landed where you did. And that reason is so you could grow and propagate. That's why the babies are so important. We may be the only people left on earth who recognize that kind of mission. We know that we're just refugees here, and our duty is to make a refuge for ourselves and to watch it grow and to become a whole new universe.

"I'm sure you know that some folks are saying the end of this year will be the Millennium when the earth is destroyed and true believers will rise up to heaven. Well, I'm not worried. You want to know why I'm not worried?"

"Yeah," a man shouts from the rear.

"I'm not worried because, for one thing, I think the people saying this are a little short-sighted and self-serving. Somehow it will work out that they'll be the only ones saved. In the great scheme of things, that just doesn't make sense. But I'm also not worried because if they are right, and the world as we know it does end, then we are positioned exactly right to start the new Millennium. We will inherit the earth and spread the seeds of our teachings across the universe. So, why worry? Either way, we are blessed.

"Maybe one day someone will arrive from that original planet that we flew off from, and we'll recognize them, the same way you recognize your old-life parents when they come here on a visit. We'll feel close to them, but at the same time we'll realize that this refuge is a home and a civilization unto itself. It will start sending off seeds of its own to take root somewhere else in outer space.

"That's why each of us has a job to do. That you landed here may be regarded by some as an accident, but you yourself know it's part of a larger plan and reason that we are only now beginning to understand. It's the same thing as when people say it's an accident whether you're born a boy or a girl, a brother or a sister. But I say it's not an accident. It's part of a bigger plan. And that's why the women here have their work filling their wombs and delivering babies and raising the kids and getting right with all the parts of home life. And the men have their place, working on the trucks or building irrigation ditches or working in the fields. We all land where we land and the way we land for a special reason. Our job is to take root where we land and to grow and fulfill our roles in life. That's the reason some of us have to go into the city to work in the mills or down to Houston to build houses for suburbs. It's in order to fulfill a greater purpose—to help the whole Refuge grow and to grow within yourself for the purpose you were destined to fulfill. Don't take who you are lightly, brothers and sisters. We are each put here to build a refuge for the greater purposes in life. They say there is a time and a place for everything. Well, you are already in your place. All you have to do is live and grow and the time for true understanding will come to you. Now we want to play a new number we just wrote today for the Refuge Band. We call it 'Get Right with Planet Earth.'"

He raised his left hand again in the peace sign and was answered by a room of raised hands. A band assembled behind him. The people in the great hall were clapping and whistling. Some were pounding on tables. Two long-haired men tuned electric guitars. A drummer hit a cymbal and the music began. The gray-haired man held a microphone, into which he sang, "We were brought here on a flying cloud...."

A voice near Giacomo's left ear whispered, "When you leave the Great Hall, linger around the pump that's on your right. I knew your friend Oman."

He turned to see a woman with yellow hair, carrying a baby in a sling on her back, walking to the kitchen door. She looked back at him as she pushed on the door.

Now people were dancing between the tables. Men alone and women alone and women and men together. A dozen children had formed a circle and skipped around and around. The older woman at his table was clapping in time to the music, moving her hands so left was above right, then right above left, then left above right. Her husband leaned back and stared at the floor under the table.

A woman with blazing red hair grabbed Giacomo's hand and pulled him after her. At a certain spot she began to dance, waving her arms and twirling, looking at the ceiling. He watched her a moment, then started to move his legs, bending them slightly at the knees, trying to pick up the beat, desperate to slide out of this spot. The woman twirled and twirled. He stopped moving his legs. He returned to his seat at the table. The woman was still twirling.

One song moved into the next. The older woman stopped clapping. Then she started up again. Her husband was asleep, his chin in his hands on the table.

The music stopped. More clapping and whistling from the crowd. The gray-haired band leader said, "Just one more number. It's time for the little brothers and sisters to sleep. All those scheduled for the mushroom feast should gather early on the eastern hill tomorrow night. Captains, they should be excused from work a little early. Now one more song."

The music finally stopped. Hannachild appeared at his side and walked him to the door. She pointed to a small house across the clearing and said, "That's where you stay. Someone will be by in the morning to assign you to your chore."

A large light on a telephone pole lit up the clearing. A small generator whirred at the base of the pole. Giacomo looked for a pump on his right. People and dogs but no pump. A shed on the right. He walked around the shed. No pump there. He searched among the half-rebuilt trucks set on blocks. He looked between two long, low buildings. He circled behind the Great Hall. He found a pigpen with a huge sow asleep on its side. Strange. He nearly stumbled into a plot of vegetables. The light picked out small pumpkins and squash among the vines. He was on the other side of the Great Hall now. And there he saw the woman with yellow hair and the sling with the baby. The woman was leaning on a pump.

As he walked up, she was already apologizing. "I was afraid of that. I never get it straight. It's a curse to be ambidextrous."

He tried to be charming. "Oh, I thought maybe I was wrong. Maybe in the South everything reverses. Or maybe in the country. I'm a city boy. Or maybe in the Refuge."

She Looked for a Message

A short brown man was standing at her door. He wore an academic's brown tweed jacket and carried a brown suitcase with orange tape wrapped around the handle and at strategic corners, holding it together. He said the name, Flores Chacón, the friend of Arnulfo, and handed her a letter.

So, you thought of Arnulfo in the morning and by evening something of him appeared.

She had to be careful what she thought about.

She led him into her small office, picking up papers from chairs as she went. An hour earlier she had watched the sun set over New Jersey, and she had not been able to leave. A morning spent staring at newspapers. She had come across a story in *Le Monde* reporting that among six killed while attending the meeting of the teachers' union in Huehuetenango was Irina Quiché. She found the letter in her files that Irina Quiché had once written to her:

> Last week a commissioner from the Education Bureau came into my classroom and asked me who my best male students were. How proud I was to have Victor Solís, César Xaratango, and Edmundo Casón come up to the front of the room and shake the commissioner's hand. I thought that maybe at last for one of these poor boys some good luck was coming in and they would be recognized for their abilities and given the chance to make something of themselves. But instead the commissioner looked at the boys and said, "You have been chosen for the officer training school." And then he took them away with him. Since that time, no one, not even their families, has heard a thing about those unlucky boys. From now on I just smile for the government officials and tell them, "No, these poor indios—they're all as dumb as pigs."

While reading correspondence from various human rights outposts, B.C. Boyd had spent the afternoon following a knot of old men who had begun by standing across the street where the sun hit the sidewalk in front of a candy store. Then they'd followed the sun to the median, standing there shaking their fists as the cars passed by them on either side. Then they were on the sidewalk underneath her window as the last sun sliced across their hats. Now they were gone: it was night, and B.C. Boyd still could not get up until the knock on the door, leading to the short brown man.

He sat across from her with his arms on the arms of the chair, his feet braced as if to be ready to rise at the slightest sign, as she read: "I am sending you Israel Soría. I remember your kindness from the time of Arnulfo. This man was in the refugee camp in California that no one knows about. The way they are treated there is second only to the death that waits for them in El Salvador, Guatemala, and the other places they are managing to get out of with only their lives. (Thanks to your help, I was a fortunate one who did not have to endure their humiliation.) Now they are deporting people back to where they came from. No one knows about it, but it's true.

"Already fifty people have been put on airplanes and sent back to the airport in San Salvador, where they will step down from the ramp and disappear. Without a doubt, Israel Soría, a school teacher by profession, would be one of those who disappears."

She looked from the letter to the silent man in the brown suit. He removed his sunglasses and leaned forward to look her in the eyes.

"Two weeks ago Israel Soría came to me after having escaped the camp with five others while the garbage was being removed. The night before, the union leader in the bed next to his killed himself because they told him he would be sent back. He cut his wrists and wrapped them up in plastic bags and lay on top of them under the sheets so they could not see he was bleeding until the blood ran out of the bags and spread over the sheets. Israel Soría told me that through it all the union leader did not make a sound."

She looked out the window. She tried to absorb as little as was necessary of what she read. Even as this man sat in front of her, it all seemed so distant and so sad. Every move she made—to smooth her hair, to touch the envelope in her lap—was followed attentively by this Israel Soría.

"We arranged for his bus travel to New York. We have arranged for an airplane ticket to take him from Montreal to Paris. We ask you to find him a place to stay for the night in New York City and to find him the bus ticket that will take him to Montreal. He carries the papers necessary to see him across the border. This is too much to ask and this is all we ask. Flores Chacón."

She quickly read through the letter again. No mention of Arnulfo. Why didn't he mention Arnulfo? Why should he? Those things were not so important.

She looked up at the man and nodded her head. His right arm fell to the side of the chair. He sat back. He crossed his right foot over his left. He looked out the window.

She slid out the sheet with the list of church centers, refugee groups, human rights offices to call for assistance. She stared at the phone numbers without seeing them and slid the sheet back in her desk. She straightened a few papers, walked to the door, motioned for the man to follow, turned out the light, and closed the door behind them.

They walked to her apartment. B.C. tried to think as little as possible. Israel Soría stayed about one pace behind her and about ten feet to her right, walking as if he carried a weight that was not entirely confined to his brown suitcase. B.C. slowed down, and he remained a step behind. Was this for her sake or his own? Seeing them, she thought, you could either think he was with her or he was not.

In her apartment, the man removed his sunglasses and almost immediately pulled a chair to the window, sat down with his suitcase between his knees, and watched the street below. She scrambled eggs. She had trouble understanding his almost guttural Spanish, so they ate without speaking. She fixed a bed for him on the couch. She went into her bedroom to read. She left him sitting by the window.

The next morning she opened the door to find him still by the window, this time with his sunglasses on. The sheets on the couch seemed untouched. She served him coffee. She took him to the bus terminal, where she bought a ticket for Montreal and handed it to him. She led him to the proper gate. At the door to the boarding platform, he held up his passport and handed the ticket to the driver, who separated the layers of the tissue-like paper and handed one portion back. The man stuffed this in the pocket of his brown suit jacket, nodded to B.C., who nodded back, and went through the door to board the bus.

B.C. walked away from the boarding platform. She left the terminal and walked through blocks of produce stands and stalled traffic. She walked through streets of lofts half-occupied by small industry. Paper and cardboard littered the sidewalks and streets. At a corner, a blue glove fell off the dangling left hand of an old woman waiting in front of her for the light to change.

B.C. picked it up and discovered it was a blue sock rolled up into a ball. She tapped the woman on the shoulder and handed her the sock, saying, "Excuse me, you dropped your glove." The woman pulled on the sock and nodded. Then she crossed the street.

Trucks blocked the sidewalks. Their drivers sat on loading docks eating lunch, not saying a word. A wolf-whistle took a long time to catch up to her. Then projects: tall, lifeless, gray-brick projects. Kids hitting trash cans with sawed-off broom handles. Racks of meat rolled out of butcher sheds. For about a block by the crumbling highway she walked behind a black transvestite wearing a blond wig, who waved at all the cars. B.C. watched the smooth rocking of the hips inside the tight black skirt. A truck slowed down, and the transvestite pointed a long index finger to her mouth, "Over here, honey, over here."

B.C. sat down at the counter of a diner and ordered coffee. "Anything you say, sweets," the large woman behind the counter replied. The man beside B.C. ordered, "The usual, Lucille," and the woman called to the cook behind her, "Brisket roll, make it wet."

The woman working the tables called to the man sitting at the counter, "Say, Al, did you hear Lucille's old man got out of the bone bin, and the doc said he don't have anything left for her."

"That ain't what he said," Lucille yelled back. "He said no more bending and lifting, but that don't mean the woman can't get on top. Or ain't you never heard of that?"

"Oh, sure. But in your case that'll kill him sure. Where's my little Bud?"

"Hold your wagons. Anything else you want, sweets?"

B.C. shook her head, slid two dollar bills halfway across the counter and left. She walked across landfill, garbage mixed with sand. A helicopter circled overhead, veered in front of her, no more than fifteen feet off the ground, then stopped there, hovering as two men wearing aviator glasses looked out at her from their bubble and smiled. The helicopter settled on a red circle painted on an asphalt square beside the landfill. What would Giacomo have thought? That they had come for him, had found him walking on landfill after having put an illegal Salvadorean on a bus to Montreal? The two men now stood hunched over under the turning blades and waved at her with their arms parallel to the ground.

It was time to do something else. Time for a change. She was ready.

She reached the tip of the island and leaned out over the water, her waist against the railing. She tasted the salt in the wind. Brooklyn, Staten Island, New Jersey, buildings, ships, birds. The water was brown and choppy. Nothing about it could have been said to dance.

Swamp

THEY WERE WALKING by a creek. In the moonlight, the creek looked like mercury. It didn't seem to run. On either side the woods were black. Her name was Thrush. Her hair seemed nearly white as were her hands when she threw them up while talking as was her face when the moonlight penetrated the branches. The rest of her was dark. The baby on her back was dark. Giacomo Berg was also dark, walking between her and the trees.

They stopped by a small tree that had fallen over into the creek. She sat down on the trunk near the short roots that had been pulled out of the soil. Branches grew straight up all along the length of the trunk, even where it entered the water.

"I think a fox lives under here," she said pointing to a darker spot under the dark clot of roots and dried dirt. "That's the kind of hole it is, anyway. These willows barely get their toes under the ground. You can lean on them and they fall right over." She swung the sling around from her back. It gave out a muffled whimper. She unbuttoned her shirt and nursed the baby, holding its head like an overripe fruit and rocking back and forth very slightly. "This one's a black willow. Not many around here. It's mostly sycamore and hawthorn and locust. No one will tell you about Oman, will they?"

"We're talking about the same person?" Giacomo asked.

She nodded. "They won't talk about him because for everybody here he's as good as dead. Joseph says, 'When you come to the Refuge you are born, and when you leave the Refuge you die.' That's what he says, and it almost seems like it's true. You leave the Refuge and it's like you leave the world. I tried it once." She looked at the creek while stroking the baby's head. "Name of this creek is Little Tight Eye, but Joseph says to call it the River Jordan."

Above them, branches moved and there was a deep hoo-hooing. Giacomo spun around. She laughed. "Great horned," she said. "And over there, almost exactly across the creek from here, I spotted the nest of a great blue heron. Almost impossible to see tonight, but it's up there. I saw the mama standing on it once, looking down into the water."

"Okay," Giacomo said. The latent wildness was beginning to get to him. He felt it itching to creep up his pants or drop down on him from the trees. "Okay. So everyone here except you has written Peter, or Oman, off. Is that it? No one remembers you once you're gone?"

"Oh, more than me remember him. They just won't talk about it, that's all. But I'm just about fed up myself." She took the baby from the sling and held it in her lap. She buttoned her shirt. She balanced the baby on her legs while she twirled her hair around one hand and secured it on top of her head with a comb. "1 don't know if I can leave. This creek, these trees, brothers and sisters. I've got nowhere else to go. But I don't know if I can stay much longer either."

He was becoming more and more uneasy. Did snakes slide around at night? How could he tell what time it was or whether the whole night was rushing by? He was not used to this.

Here in the swamps, every question took you farther in. The water got deeper and the ferns blocked your view. Where were the snakes? He was waiting for the snakes. What he wouldn't give for a bench in Washington Square or a booth in a diner or a seat at a bar. She was taking her own sweet time. "So?" he asked.

"So Oman had questions. Simple questions really. Nobody thinks of them until the first person does. Then it's like everybody had these questions in their mind."

"Like what?" Giacomo snapped a twig in two.

"Well, Oman liked to bake bread. But Joseph says that's women's work. It was no big thing, really. Oman stood up at one of the general meetings that Joseph calls sometimes, and he asked if he could spend some time baking bread with the women on kitchen shift instead of working full-time in the truck farm. That was right after he first got here. I'd been here almost a year by that time, so I knew that Joseph would answer that we each have a purpose and a duty to fulfill the greater purpose of the Refuge. And if a brother wanted to do a sister's work, he should make every effort to come back in the next life as a woman. Oman stood there and shook his head, but he accepted it. I remember he just sat down and kept shaking his head and rubbing the hair on his chest under his shirt."

It was Peter Proust they were talking about. That was Peter all over. He was on the right track. "What else? Tell me everything you know about him."

"Well, he can stare right through you. He has those blue eyes, you know, and almost womanly eyelashes, and when he looks at you, you think he can't just be looking at me. I'm just not all that interesting. That's what it makes you think. But I shouldn't say any more right now. Someone might be around here and hear us."

"Come on. I've come all the way out here to find him. The least you could do is say a little more."

"Okay, real fast. He just never got along, that's all. He'd always be having these meetings with Joseph. Like once he wanted to study with the midwives, but Joseph wouldn't let him. Joseph wouldn't even talk to him about it. He just had the counselors keep turning Oman away. That time Oman went on one of his fasts. Two days on one of the eastern hills. No one knew where he was, but I found him out there in full lotus, sitting on a rock. I asked him what he was doing. But he didn't answer me. I told him I'd talk to the midwives myself to see if something could be worked out. But it was like he didn't hear me. He stayed there for another day-and-a-half, staring straight off to the east. When he finally came back, I made a squash bread for him from the bits and pieces I'd saved up."

"So you like him."

"I miss Oman. If he weren't so stubborn."

The baby on her lap opened her eyes and whimpered. She was building up to a full cry. "See. Now we've got to go. They'll find us for sure, and they'll know what I'm out talking to you about. Let's go back." She got up, holding the baby in front of her, and started to walk back into the woods.

Giacomo did not get up. "Who cares?" he called after her.

"You'll see," she called back to him and disappeared into the trees.

Where did she go? He jumped up and followed the sound of her into the trees. She was waiting for him about ten feet in. He looked back toward the creek. It was still a silvery presence. She started walking through the darkness, and he followed no more than two steps behind.

Names

PETER PROUST HAD A DREAM. He was walking through a field of grain. It grew above his knees. In the dream he was given the power to name the grain. He called it Sunlight-Rising-Up. He then took it upon himself to name everything around him. It was as if all memory had been erased, all inherited knowledge had vanished.

He came to a stream. He called it From-Here-To-There. The tree beside it he called A-Moment-To-Think. The wind he called Going-Forward. The rocks he called Noticing-Them. The clouds he called Better-Than-Ideas. He came to his cabin. He named it What-Divides-Knowing-From-Not-Knowing. Then he went inside.

He woke up. He walked outside. The sun was rising. It lit a wall of his cabin. He decided to name his cabin. He called it "Strong Enough to Hold Back Sunlight."

Then he retrieved his journal from inside in order to write a story. He wrote, "One day Coyote and Possum were arguing. 'At night,' said Possum, 'the animals who can see well own the earth. We gather at the river, divide the earth among us and roam and eat at will. You think you are so strong, Coyote, but we just let you think so. We let the weaker ones hunt our leftovers by day.'

"'That can't be so, possum,' said Coyote. 'I do whatever I please.'

"'You are completely fooled,' said Possum. 'If you could see what I see at night, then you would understand.'

"'Let me borrow your eyes, then,' said Coyote. And before Possum could cover his face, Coyote had plucked out his eyes, leaving Possum to climb blindly up into a tree.

"That night Coyote sneaked down to the river. He found no one there. Angered, he returned to Possum's tree. 'There is no one by the river,' he said. 'You have lied, Possum.'

"'No,' said Possum. 'Give me my eyes and I will show you where we gather.'

"Coyote gave back the eyes but then grabbed Possum's tail. 'I just wanted you to be able to see who is more powerful,' he said. 'I wanted you to see who will be eating you tonight.'

"And with that, Coyote ate Possum."
Then under "Recipes" Peter added the following:

Mock Possum Pontchartrain
Ingredients:
1 large butternut squash 1 large onion—finely chopped
1 green onion 4 good-sized carrots
1 baked yam.
Some cabbage or kale or cauliflower.
1 turnip or rutabaga.
Dill, parsley, sage oil.
Halve squash—one possum should serve 4. Scoop out seeds and set aside. Scoop out as much squash as you can. Sauté onions. Mix scooped-out squash, onion, mashed yam, chopped cabbage and spices and stuff into both sides of squash. Fit squash back together and tie, nail or staple together. Cut out four plugs—two on each side of the squash. Fit the carrots into these holes. These are the legs. Cut a plug in the large end of the squash and stick in bulb end of green onion. This is the tail. Cut another plug in the small end of the squash and attach root end of the turnip. Rub all over with oil. Cook in 350–400-degree oven until squash is tender. Possum should look like this when done.

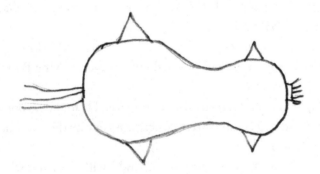

Folkways

IN THE MIDDLE OF THE NIGHT he heard scraping all around the cabin. Like snow shovels clearing sidewalks. But there was no snow. There were no sidewalks.

He was awakened by a big hand on his shoulder. "Good morning," a red-bearded face said. "You've been assigned to the fish transport system. There's breakfast in the main hall if you hurry. I'll find you there and take you to your work group."

Giacomo Berg looked out the window. The only light came from the light pole in the middle of the yard, the generator chugging beside it. He got dressed in the dark. He stumbled around outside the cabin looking for an outhouse and finally found one. He walked to the main hall with his eyes half open.

The main hall was filled with the din of hundreds of knives and forks clattering against plates, scores of earnest discussions, and screaming children. Women walked back and forth, carrying platters among the tables. Bright lights scraped every angle in the room free of shadows. No place to rest his eyes. A tape recording of banjos and mandolins was issuing from speakers hung in the corners of the hall.

He looked around for Thrush but didn't see her. He found his way to the visitors' table. The gray-haired couple was eating dark brown pancakes covered with syrup. The woman looked up at Giacomo and smiled. The man did not look up from his pancakes. In apology, the woman said, "Harold always has to keep his eyes on what he eats."

The woman named Satyavanda appeared, holding a brown-haired child.

"Good morning. Did you sleep well? Would you like our whole-wheat flapjacks with apples or pecans?"

"Apples," answered Giacomo Berg, "and coffee."

"I'm sorry, we don't drink coffee here. It depletes Vitamin B, throws off your gastric juices, and, as Joseph says, 'makes everybody so goddamn irritable.'" She walked away.

Giacomo looked at the table and muttered, "Yeah, well you've just made me irritable." The gray-haired man looked up from his pancakes and almost smiled. They exchanged a knowing glance. "Goddamn health nuts," the man said, and looked back down at his pancakes.

Satyavanda returned with the pancakes and a cup of herbal tea. She sat down on the bench beside the older woman and began to nurse her child. "If any of you need something," she said, "just say so. Usually we have more visitors than this, so there's plenty of food to spread around."

The gray-haired man glanced sideways at her from his pancakes. The red beard appeared next to Giacomo. "When you're finished, I'll take you to your station. You'll get some exercise today."

"So when do I get to speak to Joseph? I've got to get going."

"So does Joseph. He'll call for you when the time is right."

Giacomo ate slowly. He tried to feel out his metabolism, searching for some caffeine-like kick from the herbal tea. It didn't come.

The bluegrass music stopped. A short man with a long, gray beard stood on the platform and called: "Announcements. Those taking part in the sunset ritual will be excused from their work details one hour early. If you plan to take part, let your crew chief know before you start work this morning. Now some brothers and sisters have been seen searching for mushrooms in the cow patties at Old Man Schroeder's place. Leave that to the psilocybin crew. They're specially trained. The tallest corn stalk measured yesterday was three feet, four-and-one-half inches. That's a good six inches taller than last year at this date." Applause. "Joseph's class on love tripping will be delayed for two weeks because of a new gig the band signed up for in Chicago and the Midwest. The city crew should leave now in order to get back for the sunset. They tell me they are nearly two houses ahead of the other subcontractor down in Neches View Estates." More applause. "This is the twenty-third day of the fifteenth year since the year Zero. The news from the rest of the world is as you would expect. Fourteen percent unemployment in this country among the unskilled and poor and unhip. A terrorist bomb in Milan kills three.

"With the Christian Millennium just half a year away, some people are getting ready to be beamed up into heaven. Others say it's the end of the world. Joseph says it's just the beginning. And we are that beginning. The Republicans and the Democrats are fighting each other for tax loopholes. And marijuana is still illegal. The space capsule is still wobbling around in space. Joseph says maybe we'll get some sense of it at the sunset ritual tonight. In sports—those wanting to play softball again this spring must meet on Saturday to clear away a field. You know the old field went for lettuce this year, so you may have to do some chopping. The weather today will be sunny and a cool 83 degrees. Go figure. The sun will set at 7:38. The moon will rise at 7:56. The sun will be coming up as soon as I get through with these announcements. Tonight squash bread and sweet potato soup for those not out on the hill. Remember: What you put into your work comes back out in your love. Have a good day, everybody. Move the way the Spirit moves."

Red beard reappeared. "Okay. It's time for some work now. Come on, and I'll show you what you'll be doing."

Giacomo stood up and nodded to the gray-haired man and woman. She said, "Have a nice day."

He followed the red beard through the tables. Just before they reached the door, Thrush passed in front of them. She turned her head toward Giacomo for a split-second and then looked straight ahead. She held her right hand by her right breast and moved her fingers up and down in a half-wave. Some kind of signal.

The baby on her back looked back at him with her head nearly upside down. Red beard led him out the door. He stopped Giacomo by the light pole.

The generator was silent. He pointed to the left: "I'm going to keep this simple. Over there is the River Jordan. The fishing group is already over there trying to catch us some fish." Then he pointed to the right to a space between two two-story wooden buildings. "Now over there is the cornfield. You can't really see it from here, but it's back there a ways. Now your job is to take the fish they pull out of the river and transport them to the planting crew that's over in the corn. You see, not only did the Indians give us corn, but they taught us that the best fertilizer is fish, especially the fish bone. You remember back in school when they taught you that in some ancient weird corn worship Squanto the Indian planted fish next to his corn. Well, that was no weird ritual. That was agricultural science. Got it straight?"

They stood there staring in the direction of the cornfield. Apparently red beard was giving Giacomo the chance to absorb the import of all he had seen and heard. What kind of folkway did they have planned for him now? Giacomo took the opportunity to look around in the daylight. Three two-story buildings stood to the left of the one-story visitors' house. Those were probably dormitories. Following the arc of buildings to the left, he found a building as tall as those beside it but appearing to have only one story. A star was painted over the doorway. A building of similar design but smaller proportions came next with a painting of a thundercloud over the door. A water pump stood ten feet in front of that doorway. A mottled dog sat by the pump, lazily lapping water from a puddle at its feet. Then the long, low main hall behind him. Then a squat brown shed surrounded by pickup trucks, flatbeds, and rutted ground. A field of truck and auto parts spread out behind the shed. At the end of the semi-circle of buildings, set somewhat apart, was a round, wooden, red building. It was no more than ten feet in diameter with maybe eight sides, which were no more than five feet in height. A pitched green roof rose another three feet to a point. No door was visible from where Giacomo stood.

Then there was the path he came in on. The light pole and the generator.

Farther off, beyond the circle, he saw for the first time a barn and a silo. A fenced plot of flowers lay between the barn and the visitors' house, completing the circle.

Giacomo figured he was allowed one question about all this. "The round building?" he motioned with his head.

"That's the pantheon. Has a hole right in the middle of the roof. You can sit in there in the middle of the night, and it'll be completely dark. Then the moon will pop up right over that hole and it'll be brighter than day. What I really like, though, is that you can sit in there and hear everything in the Refuge going on around you and everything in the Thicket going on around that—all the birds and crickets and bullfrogs. Or you can tune it all out and just hear your own pulse or tune that out again and hear nothing at all. Joseph calls it 'the original silence before the world.' It can be heavy."

Giacomo nodded. A life of homilies. He wanted to get this over with. "Okay. What do I have to do?"

The red beard started walking on a path that began between the silo and the plot of flowers. Giacomo followed. The path led through a large stand of tall trees. If they were going to the river, it seemed to be taking longer than it had the night before. Maybe they were going to a different part of the river. Several times he realized that what he had written off as the silence of the woods was actually a tumultuous rising and falling of the screech of cicadas.

As they walked, he became increasingly aware of ferns. Some were taller than he was, while others rose no more than an inch from the spongy ground. He had to keep pushing fronds more than a foot long away from his face. Tiny barbs on fronds around his ankles caught on his pants legs. He heard red beard ahead of him, but he could no longer see him, obscured as he was by the undergrowth. They couldn't have passed this way the night before. Nothing had brushed his face. He was beginning to get the creeps.

Bends in the path began to look familiar. The sumac growing between two rocks—they'd passed that once already. The blackened hollow of a tree stump—there couldn't have been two looking exactly the same next to the footpath. Was this what happened to Peter Proust—they wanted him to lose his way? He tried to take careful note of everything he passed. Three rocks that looked like a double chin. An open space of dry grass twenty feet across bordered on one side by green sumac. He balanced a stick in the fork of a tree. He pulled fronds off a fern and arranged them on a rock. Next to the rock he pushed a twig into the dirt so that it stood erect, two feet high and out of place. He was careful to make the markers inconspicuous so the red beard ahead of him would not notice them. Should he have used his red bandana? Too conspicuous? He took out his pocket knife and cut a corner out of the bandana as he walked. He punched a hole in this corner and slipped it over a dead branch a little lower than eye level.

Red beard called, "Are you coming? We're almost there. We took the scenic route."

Almost where? The ferns rose up. Red beard was standing in front of him now, waiting for him to catch up. Red beard was smiling. Giacomo was ready for anything. He gritted his teeth and walked toward red beard, who stepped aside to reveal a bush of pink hibiscus, then the stream, then three men fishing and a fourth standing behind them holding a bucket.

"Okay. Here we are—the River Jordan. Abdo here will show you what to do."

The man holding the bucket stepped toward Giacomo. As red beard started back for the path, Giacomo called after him, "Hey, when do I see this Joseph?"

Red beard waved without turning around: "All in good time. Don't work too hard." He laughed and disappeared behind the pink hibiscus.

Abdo motioned for Giacomo to come toward him. He handed Giacomo a bucket and pointed in the direction of three men standing about one hundred feet down river. Giacomo walked up to the fishermen, one of whom turned and handed him a stringer of fish. Giacomo stood there, staring at the fish, lethargically flapping against one another on the stringer. He gathered that he was to separate them from the stringer and put them in the bucket. No one said a word. He worked the metal end of the stringer through the gills of each fish, while those below on the line slapped helplessly against his pants leg. Finally they were off. Some flipped around in the bucket. Others just lay there, working their gills open and shut. From the little he knew, he guessed they were perch or sunfish with yellow bellies. He washed his bloodied hands in the stream, rubbed some clay from the bank between his palms, then washed them again. He let a little water run into the bucket and handed the stringer back to one of the fishermen, who said, "Hey, man, you'll be sorry. They'll flip right out of there."

Giacomo didn't respond. The water in the bucket was roiling.

"Well, what are you waiting for?" the fisherman with the stringer asked. "Go take those to Abdo, and he'll show you what to do."

Giacomo walked back over to Abdo, who nodded, picked up two buckets and motioned for him to follow. Abdo led him back into the ferns, but this time on a path not marked by pink hibiscus. They crossed a clearing where a single live oak stood surrounded by dead grass. They entered a part of the woods in which the ferns were denser than before and the ground was wet and spongy. The tapping of small ball-peen hammers surrounded them. Some of it was measured, steady knocking. Some was a rapid staccato that sounded almost like a drill. Now it was more like a typewriter, or a typing pool, high in the trees. Ferns along the path grew several feet above his head.

As he passed a stand of irises, there was a splash in the bucket, and a perch leaped out into the flowers. Giacomo kept walking. Anyone else? He looked into the bucket. The water was deep red and barely stirred.

He no longer heard Abdo foraging ahead of him. The woods ended abruptly at a fence, and there was Abdo, leaning against it. They slid under the fence wire and were now among rows of corn, most between two and three feet high. On every row, men and boys were bent among the corn stalks, pulling weeds and burying fish. Abdo emptied his two buckets into a trough from which a teenage boy began grabbing fish and throwing them into a rucksack. Giacomo poured his fish and bloody water into the trough. A few tails lifted and dropped.

A heavy, gray-bearded man, maybe sixty, walked up to the fish trough and began loading a rucksack with fish.

Giacomo caught his eye. "How long you been here?"

"Oh, a little over four years now. Four years last June. They got you doing fish transport, huh?" He laughed, continuing to load fish.

"Yeah. You like it here?"

"There's no like or don't like about it. It's my family. It's all my money. It's where I'll die." He put down the sack and leaned across the trough. His nose nearly touched Giacomo Berg's nose. "I don't know where you're coming from, mister, but I came from a ranch-style house in a suburb of Charlottesville, Virginia, with a sprinkler system in the lawn, a smooth, white cement driveway, and a wife and two teenage daughters who left me a note when I came home on Thursday, May the twelfth, 1984, that said they were gone and never coming back, don't come after them. They were gone just like that. That's where I come from. I closed the front door of the house, didn't lock it, got in the car and started driving. I went north, then I went west, then I went south. Eleven years. Then I woke up one day in Port Arthur, Texas, with about eleven dollars and fifty-seven cents left on me. A fella told me you could live out here in the woods for almost nothing. He said there were cabins in the Thicket that no one's touched for years. So I came out here. Couldn't find a cabin. Couldn't find solid ground to park on. Then I ran out of gas. I pushed my car onto the road leading to the Refuge, and I've been here ever since. Any other questions?"

He hoisted the strap of the sack onto his shoulder and began to walk away. Giacomo called after him: "Yeah, one. Did you ever know anyone by the name of Oman?"

The man stopped and turned around. "Oh, I don't know. Doesn't ring a bell."

"Doesn't everybody here know everybody else?"

"Sorry. You've used up your quota. That's an entirely new question." He turned again and walked away.

Giacomo walked up to Abdo and handed him the bucket. "Don't think I'll be needing this anymore," he said. "I'm ready to see Joseph." And he walked back into the woods.

This time she was waiting for him. He pushed aside fronds brushing his neck, and there she was—Thrush recumbent on a moldy log.

"What took you so long?" she asked. For the first time, she almost smiled.

"Slime," he said. "You walk back and forth through here enough times and your skin starts to turn green. It's so goddamn sultry."

A cloud of sound descended from the treetops. "The cicadas are heating up," she said, looking up, tossing her hair like a model on a shampoo commercial. Wave after wave of the high-pitched scratching passed over them.

He sat down on the other end of the log. "And another thing—you can't breathe with these ferns grabbing at your throat. So what's going on here?"

"What do you mean?" A spiral of gnats passed between them, circling out into the stillness. "How well do you know Oman anyway?"

"Fair question." He got up and began to pace in circles around the log. "I used to know him. I used to know him well. We lost touch once he came here."

"You seem so different is what I mean."

"At some point you've got to let go. There was a time when I believed in all this, but not anymore. You ever been to New York? Try smiling at people on the subway platform." He watched her eyes for some sign of recognition. She showed none.

"Bitter old man." She leaned back farther on the log and pulled her ankle-length dress up to her thighs. "You like my legs?"

He was confused—didn't know which way to go in this swamp. "Where's your kid?" he asked.

She smiled and hiked the dress up another inch. "What's the matter? You don't like my legs?" She laughed, lowering her dress again. "You looked like a catfish when the mud dried up. Just another city slicker out of his element. Oman and I used to come out here when we could and get it on in a little clearing over there," she jerked her head to the right. "It's something not allowed, you know."

"I gathered that."

"See, Joseph says once you're attached, it's for life. You make a pact, and Joseph gives the blessing; then you drop acid and move into a room in the family barracks. They give you a week off without duties. It was fine. I came here with an old boyfriend. Right away I got pregnant, so that set me straight with Joseph. They gave me a job at the lying-in center to help other sisters deliver before it was my time. It was when I came out of the lying-in center and started back to working in the food center that I met Oman. Right away it was those eyes. They're so blue, and I just kept falling into them. You know, every meal in the Big Hall I just kept feeling his eyes following me all over, and I'd turn around and there'd they be, those two blue holes above the dandelion greens, through the soybeans, behind the pecan pie. One morning I was walking in the clearing over there, carrying my first baby, Paco, trying to burp him, when Oman showed up in front of me. He didn't say anything. He just took the baby and started swinging him up and down until Paco spit up all over his shirt and beard. Oman just laughed and started walking with the baby over to the Jordan. I followed them, of course, and he handed me Paco and took off his shirt, then his pants, and waded into the water to wash himself off. When he came out, we put the baby on his pile of clothes and made love under a willow tree." She was sitting up on the log, looking Giacomo in the eyes.

"My old man at the time, Segan, took it to Joseph and the Council, who said I was the woman of Segan and the baby, and Oman was my brother. Our crime, therefore, was incest and could not be allowed."

"So Oman was banished to the lower circles of Hell?"

"No. He was advised to listen to the spirit in the Pantheon every night for a month."

"What did he hear?"

"He heard my name. He told me that. And before the sun came up he'd meet me in that clearing or over by the Jordan or beyond the second cornfield, and we'd get it on. That wasn't what did it, though."

"Did what?"

"Drove him out of here. It was his questions. Not that he wouldn't have had them anyway, but I think the Pantheon speeded up the process. Sometimes Joseph doesn't know what's in his own best interest. It was after that month in the Pantheon that Oman started asking a lot of questions. At one of the meetings he stood up and asked Joseph why certain work was assigned to women and certain work was assigned to men just like it was in the straight world. Joseph gave his 'man-force and woman-force' rap. I remember Oman just stood there pulling at his whiskers and barely shaking his head. He set his jaw, and all his weight was shifted onto one hip, so you knew his mind wasn't changed."

Now she was leaning forward on the log, her nose not six inches from Giacomo Berg's. Her deliberate speech was speeding up. She touched his leg with her right hand and covered his mouth with her left. "Shh," she whispered. "I think 1 hear something."

They didn't move. He didn't hear anything. Not even the hammering. The cicadas, of course, but that was a constant. How did he get so bugged out in the middle of nowhere?

She slowly stood and motioned for Giacomo to follow. She picked her way among the sumac, ferns, and dead wood. He followed, his every step sounding to him like a bull moose crashing through the underbrush. He lost her. He stepped into a clearing. A hand waved from a stand of tall grass. He found her lying in the grass, her right arm behind her head. He stood over her. Thrush horizontal again.

"This is where we used to come. Oman found it. And no one ever found us here. Sit down. It's safe."

He sat uneasily beside her. The grass got in his face. "Come on. Lie down. Otherwise they'll see you."

He stretched out beside her. She put her head against his shoulder. "I almost went with him. That is, I might have gone if he would have told me he was going."

Giacomo tried to regain the momentum. "Okay. So Peter looks for an authority, finds an authority, then questions that authority, hoping to be convinced, hoping that the authority would legitimize the faith he's placed in it. And it doesn't work."

"Of course it doesn't work. He's so stubborn. I told him, Oman, let's take the baby and get out of here. We can make it by ourselves. But he wouldn't leave, he said, because there was no place else to go. He came here because of the chance for perfection the Refuge offered, and it had to be made to work. He said there wasn't any other way. He finally convinced me."

"But he still split anyway?"

"That's what I don't get myself. Except that he started getting weird on me, the way he was doing with everybody else. He'd go for days without saying anything to anybody. I'd find him sitting out in the woods at night and I'd do everything I could think of to make him say something to me. I slapped him in the face. I lay down on the ground and got off right in front of him. But he wouldn't say anything. He just watched. And his eyes started getting darker and more deep-set. Big, dark circles started growing under them. You couldn't tell what he was thinking, but you knew it wasn't good. Then a few days later he'd say something to you as if nothing had happened. And you couldn't get him to shut up. He'd start ranting and raving at meetings or when we were lying here in the grass, and it wouldn't be good for anybody."

She took Giacomo's left hand, squeezed it, and placed it with her own on her stomach. This threw his left shoulder into a slightly awkward angle. It was hard for him to concentrate.

"Once it was about the work crew he was on. They started sending him out to work in the Elysian Fields housing development outside of Beaumont to bring in money for the Refuge. It was partly because he was a carpenter by experience and partly because he was making a little trouble, so they wanted to get him out of here. I remember at his first meeting after starting to work in the Fields, Oman stood up and said he didn't think it was the clear way for some people to be working for money, putting up unnatural and prefab housing for a real estate concern to sell to poor little bookkeepers and hardware store managers with three kids to mortgage their lives away in order to live in these crummy little boxes in relative unhappiness and spiritual starvation.

"Now Joseph was sitting back listening to the meeting. So he stepped up to the podium and said we all have to work for the good of the whole, and the whole would not survive to show another way without the workers in the Fields and that it served as a good reminder of what is and what we're trying to show that isn't and that we all do the work of the Spirit in one way or another.

"But Oman wasn't satisfied, and every meeting after that he would stand up and say so. He wasn't alone in this, but he was the most stubborn about it. I wasn't quite decided myself at that time, although I did see he had some points. I just wasn't sure Joseph didn't have some bigger plan floating in his head that we were just not ready to comprehend.

"One day Oman takes off. He just disappears. That was the first of his major disappearances. He was gone over a year. He never said goodbye to me. I didn't know anything about him until one day he just came walking back in. He said he'd sent me postcards, but they must have been confiscated. He said he'd been living in western Massachusetts for a while, working on cars. He said he'd met a woman there and lived with her. But then she'd just upped and ran off.

"By the time he came back, it didn't really matter to me anyway. I had almost forgotten most of him, and what I hadn't forgotten made me feel kind of sick. He was complaining all that much more about how this was an imperfect world. I told him, 'Oman, what else did you expect? We're just trying to get by.' But he expected more. That was his big problem. Joseph told him that a number of times."

Giacomo's left hand and forearm started to go to sleep. He tried to drag it off her stomach, but she resisted, squeezing it tighter and pulling it down along the top of her right thigh. At least at this angle he could feel the blood returning to his hand.

"Oman took to wandering off into the woods and no one sees him for hours. He started doing things like not drinking the water here anymore. He'd go out to the little stream behind the second cornfield and get his water there because he said he'd figured out that water was coming from due west and not from northwest like the water that ran through the center of the Refuge and could look awfully dirty before it drained into the bedrock where our well water came from. He started criticizing the Refuge Band for going off on tours of Europe and South America while the sisters worked in the kitchen and the brothers built houses for straight contractors. 'They may think they're spreading the Spirit,' Oman would say, 'but the only way to spread the Spirit is to live the Spirit, and Joseph and the Band were living off the backs of their brothers and sisters.'

"It got to where he didn't trust a soul. We'd get out here in the grass, and he'd spend the whole time looking all around for somebody spying on us. He'd be lying here and then jump up stark naked and run into the woods and leave me. I'd wait and wait for him to come back, and then finally I'd have to get up and go back to the kitchen. Or we'd be walking here, and he'd say I was leading him into a trap. He'd say I was leading him into the field so they could catch him with his pants down and disprove everything he said.

"He said Joseph had my mind controlled like all the rest. That was about it for us. I mean I couldn't be around him anymore. That's when I went to see my old man again. That's when I got my baby. But Oman opened my eyes to some things. I'd like to leave here now myself. I'm getting ready to leave. If I could only figure out where to go or what to do with the kids and all. I have to give Oman credit for some of that. But he had just gone too far to deal with anymore."

Giacomo had been watching the sky through all this. He couldn't tell whether it was cloudy or whether he was looking at a blue-gray haze. Ends of branches and green leaves were at the periphery of his vision.

Thrush rose on one elbow and put a hand on his chest. "Shh. I think I hear someone." His left hand was now under her.

Not the hammering. It had stopped. The cicadas were a constant. No. He heard thrashing in the woods. It was nearby. "What's everybody afraid of?" he whispered. She pressed her hand against his mouth.

"Hey fella. New guy." The voice of Abdo.

"You'd better go," she whispered. "Meet me tonight in the Pantheon when it's completely dark." She started to push him away, then pulled him back to whisper in his ear, "When you go, I might go with you." She kissed his ear then pushed him away again.

Giacomo stumbled off toward the trees. He found a rock and sat, waiting for the thrashing Abdo to reach him. Abdo emerged from a stand of ferns.

"What's the matter with you? If you're not going to work, I'd say it's time for you to leave."

"That's fine," Giacomo said, "once I talk to Joseph."

Abdo spun around. "Look, man. Joseph calls for you if and when he's ready."

Giacomo tried to decide whether these hippies had violent tendencies. He measured Abdo's wide shoulders, his limp, the length of his beard, his eyes. "I think I'll stick with my plan."

Abdo stalked away. "You'll see. Be cool or be gone. You'll see."

Giacomo waited for Abdo to disappear. Then he returned to the clearing to look for Thrush. He found their imprint in her place. Not a great surprise. He walked through the woods, trying to find his way back to the settlement proper.

Then B.C. He thought of her long, thin fingers stripping the fronds from the fern by his desk, one frond at a time. In the middle of this forest of ferns he thought of B.C. He couldn't exactly summon up her face. Her mouth at times. The gap between her teeth. Her shoulders in a white shirt. Her long legs. Her voice above all. Over the telephone—calling him from his daily reverie, denouncing torture somewhere, fascism, tyranny, modes of production that exploit the producers, telling him that two kids mugged an old woman in her building not for the money or for the sport or for what she represented but because they were already living in the next world where there were no reasons and that people better do something about it or that next world would be where we will all be living soon enough.

He came to a cornfield. He saw the settlement beyond that. Why did he hear her voice? Why did her name pop into his head right now? Was it the way she looked at him when she thought he wasn't looking? Just B.C. Interesting that she should appear here, while he was wandering around in some palmetto bog looking for a lost friend among throwbacks to an age long gone. He wanted her there. Because he was in her Texas?

Nothing could be that simple. It was something to think about. He walked into the clearing ringed by buildings. B.C. Strange.

The Sleep of Reason Produces Monsters

B.C. WATCHED THE Italian family in the building behind her, maybe twenty feet away. They had built an arbor on their landing of the fire escape. A green, translucent panel served as the roof, providing semi-tropical light. A yellow fiberglass wall was braced at one end of the landing. Plastic vines and grapes were glued to the awning and the wall. A patch of blue-green Astroturf had been laid across the iron slats of the fire escape. A narrow picnic table, a bench, and three plastic chairs were arranged on the Astroturf, and there the family sat eating watermelon. The man's fat white legs tested the plaid tension of his Bermuda shorts. His black shoes and socks were planted firmly on the Astroturf. His castle. He kept his eyes on the watermelon slice in his hands. The boy was soft and white in his striped t-shirt and pajama bottoms and bounced as he ate. He usually spent days like these sitting in the green shade in his underwear or pajama bottoms, beating the cardboard rolls from paper towels rhythmically against the railing of the fire escape. The woman sliced watermelon. She rolled the sleeves of her purple housedress up to her shoulders. Bags of flesh waved from her arms as she sliced. The white of her undergarments stuck out in spots through the frayed purple dress. She wore black flip-flops. She had the most trouble in the family climbing out the kitchen window to sit on the landing. Every once in a while she got up, walked around the table, and leaned over the railing, looking down into the air shaft as if at water or looking up at the sliver of light between buildings, shading her eyes, as if looking at a blinding sun in a blue sky marked by occasional clouds or migrating birds.

B.C. sipped coffee. She turned on the radio. The all-news station. This morning she'd awakened, sat up in bed, and said out loud, "Oh my god. The satellite! What's with the satellite?" She'd nearly forgotten. She hadn't heard from her brother. Where was he? Had it come down? She listened:

"The tracking station in Melbourne has reported a significant wobble. So far this wobble had not been detected or confirmed by scientists working on Midway Island or in Hawaii or in California. It was first reported by scientists working in the Azores and then on Madagascar. In the Seychelles, scientists were divided concerning the possible wobble, which, if present, would indicate that the empty spacecraft was finally succumbing to the final, fatal gravitational pull. Experts remain at a loss, however, to explain why there has been no significant descent in the orbit of the satellite in the last 36 hours, an occurrence that defies all the known laws of physics. Meanwhile, new sites are being predicted for the likely fall of the satellite. The Chamber of Commerce of Harrison, Nevada, has already dubbed its town, 'Crash Town, U.S.A.' Bleachers have been erected on the edge of town facing a small ravine, which a local psychic has said will be the site of the final fall. A campsite is filled to capacity with RVs waiting for the spectacle. A daredevil motorcycle team has been hired to jump the ravine in varied configurations to entertain the crowd until the satellite arrives. In contrast, we have the reaction of the mayor of Racine, Wisconsin, mentioned by Russian scientists as a possible crash site. When asked to comment, the Racine mayor, W. Arthur Snell, said, 'Oh, I've heard those reports. All of a sudden you news folks will believe anything those Russians have to say. I recommend Racine to anyone as a nice place to land, but I'd just as soon the space capsule stayed away.' Stay tuned for further developments in the final flight of Dogstar II. In sports, the Yankees traded...."

B.C. turned off the radio. What if it hit Florida in the spot her brother has gone to take refuge? Or Texas? She knew Giacomo wasn't thinking about it. For him, it was not a constant threat, like radiation. It was a variable. Giacomo got a kick out of variables. It was the constants he was afraid of.

She should go to work. She figured it must be at least noon if the Italian family was already eating watermelon. The old man was spitting seeds over his left shoulder onto the garbage cans eight floors below. She heard the light pings of the seeds on the aluminum lids. She stared into her coffee cup, then looked back out at the fire escape. The man was following the woman inside through the window. The boy was still sitting on the astroturf, his legs through the railing. He was getting older.

The buzzer for the door. Now what? She asked who it was through the intercom. "Western Union. I have a telegram."

She hesitated. They still do that? She took a deep breath. "Come on up. To the right when you get off the elevator."

She put on a robe and stood by the door, biting her lip. Giacomo? Her brother? A massacre in Guatemala? Was this really Western Union? In Guatemala people had to wave from the sidewalk before being let in. They had to show their faces so you knew it was not a death squad or the police. Who was this? A knock on the door. She opened it to find a teenage boy with a few hairs for a mustache wearing a Western Union shirt but no hat and dark gray pants.

He held an envelope in front of him, saying, "We don't usually deliver anymore, ma'am, but since our office is only three blocks away I thought I'd run it over. I do that a lot in this area. People appreciate it being like the old days. A phone call's just too impersonal."

She nodded and took the envelope. His hand remained outstretched, waiting for a tip. She'd forgotten about the tip. She had him wait while she found her wallet, handed him some change, and closed the door.

Tearing open the envelope, she tore the message in half. The first time she skimmed the message too fast for it to register. What did this mean? "Air to Paris one hour. Gracias. Israel."

Then she saw Montreal. Of course. She remembered the day before. Was she that far gone? She was still shaking from the idea of a telegram. She tried to laugh at herself; then she cried. She turned on the water for a shower, took the shower, got dressed, and left for work.

She waited with the crowd on the subway platform. Each time a train approached, the crowd pushed toward the tracks. At the same time, an undercurrent of scurrying sneakers, sharp glances, and quick hands wove in and out of the crowd. B.C. hugged a concrete support in order not to be consumed by any of these tides. A train arrived, and the crowd surged forward. She was now inside a car, and a group of twelve-year-old boys was dancing in the center of the car to the sounds only they could hear through their earbuds. The boys began moving up and down the car, their eyes on the necks of the passengers, their heads no more than two feet away from those necks. A boy pulled the gold necklace off the neck of a woman across from B.C. and stuffed it into his pocket. The passengers did not move. They stared straight ahead or into their newspapers or books. B.C. glanced at the boy in the middle of the car, apparently directing his accomplices. A switchblade poked up out of the right pocket of his basketball shorts. Another kid, under five feet tall in blue shorts and sneakers, was looking at the woman sitting next to B.C. Then at B.C. His little hand grazed her left breast. The boy laughed a high-pitched laugh. The train pulled into a station. The doors opened, and, as quickly as they'd appeared, the boys were gone.

B.C. exhaled the breath she hadn't known she was holding. Her hands shook. She still didn't look around. At her stop, she walked slowly up the steps to her office, did not read the mail, sat staring out the window, stood up, looked absently through the files, turned off the lights, walked out, locked the door behind her, and began to walk aimlessly in the direction of a meeting about amnesty she'd agreed to attend. It wasn't for another five hours. Those meetings in a church basement. Linoleum and fluorescent lights. Everyone was a good soul. Everyone was tired and gray. She wouldn't be able to stand it.

A young woman approached her holding leaflets and a coffee can. Money for water wells in West Africa. "I can't," B.C. mumbled. "I give all day. I have nothing else to give. Ask a banker." She skirted around the outstretched coffee can.

At the corner, while waiting for the light to change, she jumped when a little boy and girl ran up to the curb and stopped. Now she was terrified of children.

She stepped into a bar on the corner. She ordered a gin and tonic and drank it slowly. She pulled apart the mint leaves that were perched on top of the drink. She decided to leave the city for a while. She decided to join Giacomo wherever he was as soon as she heard from him. He'd have to let her. Where else could she go? Lockhart? Maybe she could persuade him to go with her there? She'd show him the courthouse and the crape-myrtle trees. She'd show him the house where she grew up, whether he wanted to see it or not. She had to get away.

Where was he now? Surely in Texas. But where? When she thought of Texas, she thought of crape-myrtle blooming on every corner, in front of every house in Lockhart. The blossoms on the tree by her window were white, dazzling sometimes when she woke up in her bedroom with the pitched roof and dormer windows and found the sunlight streaming through the blossoms.

She got on her bicycle and rode through the gravel streets of Lockhart pulling a sprig of blossoms from every crape-myrtle she passed. No two were alike—the colors ranging from deep purple, almost lavender, to maroon to red to pink to white. She carried them in her bicycle basket to the county courthouse in the town square, and on the polished granite monument for veterans of World War I she arranged the blossoms in an artistic manner. She sat in the grass by the monument, and everyone smiled who walked by.

She took a deep breath, stood up, and walked toward the last daylight and out of the bar. She walked back toward her office and the subway. Two little girls sat in a laundromat window, staring at the window of a washing machine. A woman was mopping the floors in back. Get me out of here.

B.C. came to the subway entrance and descended. A kid wearing black chinos, a black jacket, and white shoes was walking up and down the platform singing loudly, "If you were the only girl in the world, and I were the only boy...." He tested his tremolo in the echo chamber of the station. B.C. hid behind a column. The train came, and she got on.

She was trying not to think. She concentrated on the vibrations of the subway car.

Arnulfo came to mind, so she immediately began reading the ads on the subway in order to push the name away. Then Giacomo Berg. Texas. She stared at the black combat boots on the woman wrapped around a subway pole a couple of feet away. A man entered the car wearing a red, plastic, slotted bowl over a black cap on his head. It looked like a red helmet with a black bill. He walked down the middle of the car, waving a can back and forth to clear a path. As he passed, the woman on B.C.'s right pointed to the cap and said to the woman on her right, "That's the kind of salad spinner I was mentioning the other day." The other woman said, "Uh-huh. Uh-huh." The man opened the door at the end of their car and proceeded to the next.

B.C. was facing a woman of about her own age. The woman had very large legs, fat ankles, fat hands, wide shoulders. She wore a brown cloth coat. She had beautiful brown eyes. The woman looked at B.C., smiled, and pulled a tan pamphlet out of her black purse and started reading. B.C. read the back of the pamphlet:

You are a very unique individual.
We have a very unique program for you.
Just answer the following questions:
    Name?
    Address?
    Social Security Number?

The woman licked her thumb, getting ready to turn the page. B.C. looked for the black combat boots, but they were gone. The next stop was hers.

She left the woman reading the pamphlet. She walked up the steps to the sidewalk. The full moon was still just above the rooftops. Not over Texas for a while.

As B.C. approached the steps to her building, a little girl ran from a doorway on her left and stopped in front of her. "Say, Miss," she asked. "When's Lent?" B.C. shrugged. The little girl skipped back to her doorway.

B.C. nodded to her super, who was sitting on the front steps with a folded red bandana on top of his bald head. He did that when he got hot. She walked up the stairs in her building. She entered her apartment. The room was lit by moonlight. She sat on the bed still made on the couch. She had to call Giacomo Berg.

She took out her phone and held it on her lap. She looked at the guitar case leaning in the corner. There are songs in all this somewhere. But she didn't want to write them or sing them just then. Certainly not folk songs with a guitar and autoharp. Did she have an inner Janis Joplin or Tina Turner? Could she sing angry? She'd never thought about that before. She lay down, putting the phone beside her. She fell asleep.

To the Mountaintop

GIACOMO BEAT ON THE DOOR of the building marked with a star.

A thin, black-bearded man in a wheelchair, whose head and limbs were in constant, erratic motion, opened the door. "Yesss?" he said, whistling the "s."

"My name is Berg. I'm looking for a friend of mine—Peter Proust or Oman or whatever you want to call him. I've been waiting for a day now to talk to Joseph about him. Can I come in?"

The man shook his head back and forth, smiling. "Berg is a funny name. Like 'iceberg?' Is your last name lettuce?" He paused as if waiting for a laugh. "My name is Adam. Joseph is busy now preparing for the European tour, Berg. You wait." He held up his right hand. It waved in Giacomo's face.

The modulation of his speech was so erratic that Giacomo could barely understand what he was saying. But, of course, he did understand. He surveyed the doorway and Adam in constant motion in his chair. He surveyed his own will. He couldn't push Adam aside or slip by him with his own dignity intact. Giacomo nodded and backed away from the door. He sat down by the building in the shade. The door closed. A mustard-colored dog lay down next to Giacomo Berg.

He watched the work crews come in from all parts of the Refuge and enter the main hall for lunch. He watched some of those crews leave again. He wasn't hungry.

He searched for Thrush among the women in the yard, but didn't see her. He was fairly sure of that, even though everyone looked alike. Everyone in overalls: men, women, children, next the dogs. So goddamn many tan, healthy blonds. Not like the commune they'd visited in Massachusetts years before, peopled by a bunch of Italian and Jewish kids fed up with cities and college. They, at least, had still carried the pallor of generations of urban squalor. Not here. So much aggressive good health made Giacomo long for the ugliness and sickness-unto-death that inhabited the faces of New York.

The mustard-colored dog licked his foot and broke his reverie. Giacomo noticed four men working on the trucks on blocks in front of the garage. He walked up behind a bald, short man leaning over an engine. The man leaned way over, pushed something, shouting, "Now!" and a man in the cab turned the ignition. The only noise was a tiny click. The bald man said, "Shit!," fiddled some more, and shouted, "Now!" The key was turned. The same click. "Shit!" This happened four or five times, creating its own cadence, before the bald man lifted his head abruptly and spun around to face Giacomo Berg.

"What can we do you for, brother?"

"Did any of you fellas ever know someone called Oman? He used to like to fool around with trucks."

The bald man said, "Nope," turned around and leaned back over the engine. The man in the cab threw up his hands. A man leaning over the other side of the engine shook his head. "Nope," from a man standing on the front bumper of another truck, "but I just came here four months ago myself."

"What you want to know for?" asked a man with a blond beard, speckled with grease, who pulled himself out from under a truck behind Giacomo.

"I'm an old friend of his, and I've lost track of him. Last I heard he was living here."

"Well, hell yes, I know Oman. Crazier than horseshit, but that brother sure did know a truck." He looked around at his coworkers, who kept their heads bent over their engines.

"Now I can only speak for myself, but see that green truck over there? Oman nearly got that runnin'. In fact, he did get it runnin' for a few hundred yards. Then it just died, right where it's standin' now. That's the closest we ever got to putting one of these old wrecks back on the road. Oman was the genius behind that, so I got to put in a word for him."

"It must be kind of frustrating," Giacomo said, leaning on a fender, trying to be folksy.

"Well, yes and no. You might think it's kind of funny, but we don't get a whole lot of support here with the mechanicals. You know all these brothers and sisters—a lot of them don't like the idea of trucks or cars or any kind of machine being out here at all. Like they aren't natural or something. Well, you know hippies. I can kind of see their point, but I don't agree with it. I don't think Joseph does either. He says our first duty is to survive, and in this world you got to have a certain minimum of machines or you won't survive. That farming part of it won't survive without some machines, at least. Joseph says, 'It's all a matter of how you go about what you're about.'

I think that's true. I mean it's not like we got a fleet of Diamond Reos all spouting diesel and churning up the soy fields. So, a lot of brothers and sisters don't like us, and we ain't real popular when we go to grinding engines and blowing smoke."

He was about to say more, but Giacomo cut him off. "So what happened to Oman? Do you know where he went? When did he work around here?"

The blond man looked around at the others hunched over engines and said, "I guess I've said enough already. I just told you what I know. The rest I don't know. I just know that fella Oman sure did know a truck." He slid back under the truck.

Giacomo stood over the man's feet for a minute, then walked back to his vigil by the mustard-colored dog, still sitting in the shade of the building with a star. Just after he sat down, the door to the building opened, and two women and five men, three carrying guitar cases, filed out and headed toward the main hall. Adam appeared and, rolling his head in a circle, said, "Okay."

As Giacomo entered, Adam forced a wink and patted Giacomo tentatively on the back. Joseph sat in full lotus across the room and motioned for Giacomo to sit on the floor in front of him. A short table with a teapot and cups was on Joseph's right. An old hookah with seven separate tubes running from it was on Joseph's left. Giacomo sat down uneasily on the floor. He crossed his legs in front of him, then straightened them out, brought his knees near his chin, crossed his legs again, coming as close to lotus as that would bring him. Joseph waited for him to sit still.

Giacomo tried to assert himself: "I am here looking for…"

Joseph interrupted him by raising the first and middle fingers of his right hand in the peace sign. "I know what you think you are here for. But first, let's discuss who you are. You are a private investigator from New York City. You are looking for someone you claim lived here, someone named Peter Proust. The first night you are here you meet one of our sisters at the Jordan and try to cross-examine her. The next day you lie down with her in a field and try to cross-examine her that way. You do not perform your work assignment that is essential for the survival of the Refuge and that is a requirement for staying here for any length of time. We cannot tolerate freeloaders and work-force cheats."

"Look, I'm sorry you feel that way, but I'm only here to look for a friend whose family can't find him because he has simply disappeared, and this is the last place from which he communicated with anyone that we know of. Is that so difficult to understand or so uncool or anti-hip to deal with?"

Joseph raised his right hand again. "Please, Mr. Berg. You are someone who thinks of yourself as having once been a hippie. I'm sure you once dropped acid, shared a house with five or six people and a bed with two or three. You would not touch meat, were committed to enlightenment through hallucinogenic substances, picked up all hitchhikers and thought the power of love and the forbearance from all but bare necessities would one day conquer the world. We've all been on the same trip, brother. You just got off the boat too soon."

The voice was getting to him. He could never argue with authority figures who spoke in round, golden tones. He felt some sort of humiliation and slight nausea at his own weakness in the face of such measured sonority. But he kept on: "I'm not asking for guidance here. I'm just looking for somebody, that's all. Are you going to give me the information I need or should I go somewhere else?"

"Hey man, cool out. You're taking my time, which is my people's time. You're eating our food; you're sleeping in our bed. You hear me out. Now, fifteen years ago we came out here to the middle of the Thicket to start all over again after we were driven out of Virginia. We're the future of the universe. You understand? In the same way, we've got to start the universe all over again or there's no hope for anybody. The world—the way your folks are running it now—is one fucked-up place. So we're out here making a go of it not just for ourselves but for you, too, brother, and for everybody else. We're out here having babies and raising them right and eating off the land without using anything unnatural and without partaking of meat. Are you aware that an acre of wheat has ten times more protein in it than an acre of cows? If you feed an acre of corn to the number of pigs it will sustain, those pigs will produce one-twenty-fourth the number of nutrients a human being needs as would the corn itself outright. We're out to show the world how to feed itself and how to raise its children and how to take care of the land so it will take care of you. We're doing all that here, and we've taken on the business of enlightenment, too. The enlightenment of the universe is our religion, and marijuana is our incense, and organic mescaline and psilocybin are our wafer and wine. All this costs a price. A heavy price, man. I was in jail for two years just to prove that these drugs are religious sacraments. They came in here one day and chained me up and led me off in handcuffs because I was the ringleader of this racket, as they called it, and I stayed in prison for nearly two years, where I did some teaching to the brothers there. Meanwhile, the brothers and sisters here went right on with the sacraments and sowing that karma among the neighbors hereabouts, so by the time I got out we were all straight with everybody. No one said another word about what we do because we're good neighbors and good farmers and we're straight with everybody."

"I appreciate that, but what about Peter Proust, the one you renamed Oman?"

"Things reveal themselves in their own true time. I'm just trying to come on to you like one brother to another. You have to open up to me so we can relate like two men on a higher plane. I just wanted to point out to you that it's not easy trying to save the world. You have to understand that. There have to be certain rules. You have to segregate yourself and all your people from the rest of society or you'll be poisoned by what's poisoning the rest of the world."

"And if the world goes, you don't think you'll go with it?" Berg asked. "You don't think some cloud of poisonous gases that accidentally get turned loose one day over Beaumont won't float into the Thicket and envelope your secluded heads?"

"You'd better listen more carefully to me, brother. This is how it goes down: It was decided long ago, when the first truck pulled in here, that all life beyond this Refuge was no longer life at all. Instead it is to be considered like what comes before birth and follows after death. You come into the Refuge and you are born. You must be taught how to walk, how to talk, and how to think just like with any baby. We give you a name, and we hold you to our bosom and nurse you until you can get along on your own as a member of the community of brothers and sisters. This must be your whole world. You must renounce everything that went before. The first thing you do when you commit yourself to us is give us the clothes off your back and your bank account and your car and your stereo and your baseball glove. And we give you a family and food and a place to sleep and a fully guaranteed future with a pension of constant care. Not a bad trade. So when you ask me about Peter Proust, I say there is no Peter Proust. But there once was a brother named Oman, who lived in this world for over ten years, except for the two he took off, and then he died to us in his early adolescence as quickly as he was born."

Giacomo had been lulled into a near-stupor by the warm air inside the small building, by the pervasive smell of marijuana, and by Joseph's monotone. But the mention of Peter Proust, then Oman, awakened him. "Okay. Where is he? We're finally getting some place."

"I've told you he is dead to us now. Where some other reincarnation of him has gone I have no idea nor have I thought a single instant on the subject. I will tell you that Oman had a difficult time getting straight with himself and, therefore, getting straight with his brothers and sisters. He used to come here often, much more than most others, to tell me what he thought was wrong with the Refuge and our life here. I had to remind him of his own karma. I remember telling him, 'Oman, you must get clear with yourself before you can become clear about others.'

"But I don't think it ever got through to him. He was so full of problems brought here from another life. Once I recommended that he visit the family from his former life to straighten out some of the residual bad vibrations that were crowding him here. He did, but he returned seeming more troubled than before. Many times I would tell him to go sit with himself all night in the pantheon. He would follow my advice, but then he'd return the next day with more questions than ever. He became so angry with everything and everyone here that he began to disrupt a small part of the fabric of our life. Finally I had to take Oman aside to tell him that for the good of his people he should leave in order to get straight with himself so that he could return some day and get straight with everybody else. He left for two years. And two years later he came back for a gathering of the tribe. But he was still angry. It was clear. Finally, we asked him to leave for good. This doesn't often become necessary with the brothers and sisters here. We have a policy whereby anger is not allowed to fester but is confronted forthrightly out in the open. If a brother or a sister is angry with another, the two confront each other either in front of all of us at a meeting or alone, either physically or verbally—whichever they agree upon—they have it out then and there. But Oman was angry with himself and he dealt with it by confronting me. But I was not his problem."

Giacomo realized that Joseph was trying to stare into his eyes. It was the same look Joseph had probably used as a teenager to try to pick up girls. Giacomo stared back. "So when was this? When did you kick him out? Do you know where he went?"

"I've told you all there is to say. You are free to leave the Refuge now or you may stay another night. If you stay, you will be required to attend the sunset vigil. In addition, you may not question anyone about this Oman and you may not meet again with Thrush. I'm sure you will convey to the family of Oman that there is no need to bother us again in this matter. Go in peace."

He raised his right hand in the peace sign. The door behind Giacomo opened, and the doorman wheeled in and pointed the way out, smiling all the while. Giacomo returned to the mustard-colored dog lying in the shade.

He didn't join the dog but instead wandered around the compound trying to fit things together. At least he knew Peter was here. And Peter couldn't stomach this bullshit. That was reassuring. But where did he go from here? What kind of head start did Peter have on him and in what direction?

A sign saying "Refuge Press" hung from the side of a building. Giacomo opened a door under the sign to find a blond, pink-skinned man sitting behind a desk displaying brightly colored books with such titles as *The Gospel According to Joseph*, *Straightening the Straight* and *What I Say*.

"Mind if I look through your books?" he asked the man, who shook his head side to side in reply.

Pages and pages of longhairs. Beatific smiles. Sagacious beards. People in full lotus crowned with rays of the sun. He scanned the photos for Peter. Among all the longhaired, black-bearded men, he looked for the angle of the tilt of the head, the penetrating eyes. Once or twice he was almost sure he'd found Peter. He tried to will it, but it was never unmistakable. He borrowed a magnifying glass, put it over one face, then another. Some could be Peter, but he couldn't be convinced.

He handed the books back to the man. "Have you got anything else?"

"You're into pictures, ain't ya? Well, maybe you'd like to groove on the latest. It's the five-color picture for the cover of our next book, *Stoned Counsel*. You can actually see the sun's penumbra hit the auras of the tripping brothers and sisters in this photograph. Take a looksee."

He handed Giacomo a folded book jacket on which the colors had been intensified beyond natural color. Giacomo began at the lower left corner of what would be the book's back cover. He scanned slowly to the right, picking out the few dark beards and hair scattered among the sea of faces. He moved to the upper right and across again to the upper left. Something caught his eye. He moved back to the right. There. Near the edge of the crowd. The nose. The tilt of the head. He thought he could even see the deep-set eyes. He could almost hear the laugh from the open mouth. There. Peter. Not even looking exactly as Giacomo remembered. Nor like the photo in his bedroom taken of the softball team: Peter with his Red Sox cap on backwards, throwing an imaginary ball. But it was Peter. That was unmistakable. He was here. It was probably not that long ago. No one could deny it. Giacomo put the photo in front of the blond man. He pointed to Peter. "This one. Do you know this one?"

The man looked through the magnifying glass and said, "I can't really make it out. They all look alike, if you know what I mean."

"I don't know. Try a little harder."

"Nope. I've used all the brain cells I own."

"When was this picture taken?"

"Oh, can't be too sure. I'm in there, see?" He pointed to a blond ponytail on the left. "So it had to be in the last three years."

"Yeah, but when was it taken exactly? When did you take pictures for this book?"

"Oh, all along. We go through and see what we've got to fit with certain raps we want to print. Got a photo file just like any place else."

"Look. Make a guess. Last year? Last week?"

"Couldn't be last week because we wouldn't have gotten it together as a cover fast enough. Takes at least two months to put something like this together."

"Okay, over two months ago. What else? Who took the photo? Maybe that person would know."

"Don't know. Could be one of a number of people. We don't sign our photos just like the other brothers and sisters don't sign the corn. Someone comes in here and checks out a camera. There's a darkroom out back. That's all. We all do it all."

"Look, I'm trying to find this guy," Berg said, summoning his New

York attitude. "I've got to know when this was taken to get some idea of when he was here."

"Hey, man, back off! What are you doing? Are you a cop or something? Let me take another look." He picked up the photo again and studied it carefully, holding it no more than four inches from his eyes.

"Don't know him. But the trees still have leaves. So that makes it either before November or after February around here. They've got sweaters and ponchos on, so it's still kind of chilly.

"Joseph has that kind of heavy baldness that set in last year, so you've got your year now. I'd guess it was March of this year and no later than March 15 at that, judging by the fact that the leaves are still fresh green and not brownish or that gray-green color they get when it starts getting real hot. You can learn a lot from your colors. Something to keep in mind, detective."

"I'll make a note of it," Giacomo said. "Anyway, thanks. You'll make a good cop yet."

Giacomo walked back outside. He was not that far behind. Maybe five or six months at the most. But where did he go from here?

He found himself in a stream of people walking toward a hill. Lemmings? Giacomo approached the gray-haired couple standing off to one side. The woman, her lips pursed, was sucking hard on a joint of marijuana. Her husband was turned away from her, facing the east, where the sky was beginning to purple over.

She handed the joint to Giacomo and smiled. "This is the second time. The first time I tried it, it didn't work either."

She turned toward the groups slightly higher on the hill in order to lead his attention there. Giacomo could hear Joseph's voice among those emanating from the top of the hill.

"Our son is up there," the woman said, nodding her head. "He's taking mescaline tonight." Her husband continued staring east.

Giacomo returned the joint to her and walked to the edge of the crowd on the hilltop.

Joseph was speaking: "With the moon we partake of the psychedelic wisdom of the planet, the dark underside of knowledge that comes out when the sun goes down." Joseph held his hands out in front of him, motioning for the gathering to sit. They sat in formation, a triangle with Joseph at the head. He turned to face the setting sun in the west. All were full-lotus, some naked, some wearing robes, some wearing work clothes.

Giacomo sat down behind them in his nearest approach to full lotus. Three stone columns formed a triangle in front of Joseph. The sun set between two of the columns. The horizon grew dark. A low "om" rose from the gathering and mingled with the emerging sound of cicadas and crickets.

Without a word, the gathering stood, turned, and sat down in full lotus, facing Giacomo.

He tried to appear nonchalant, cool, stoned as he got up and sidled off to join the gray-haired couple sitting on a rock and staring at the rising moon.

Another "om." More full-throated. Gradually bodies began to peel away from the group to wander around the hillside, to stretch out on the ground, to weave through the underbrush and dance. Giacomo looked for Thrush but couldn't find her. Shapes moved about the hillside, exchanging burning joints. A man sang bird calls—first the barn owl, then a hawk, then a potpourri, like a mockingbird.

The gray-haired woman slid off the rock onto the ground and leaned against the rock, smiling absently at the moon. Her husband faced west. Giacomo got up and walked among the bodies. He tried to make out faces, but had no luck. A large man, like a wall, appeared in front of Giacomo and handed him a joint. As Giacomo drew on the joint, the man said, "You shouldn't be around tonight."

"What do you mean?"

"Full moon and mescaline. People could get freaked. You ask too many questions. They're sure you came here to spy. Or you came here to sleep with our sisters. You came here asking about the dead. People get freaked real easily."

"I thought everyone was out here for enlightenment."

"Man, let's just call it bad vibes. You've been spreading them, so you better get out. The highest trip a man can make is for the survival of the whole. There are a few brothers here willing to make that trip if you give them an excuse. Savvy?"

The wall walked away. Giacomo decided it was time to meet Thrush in the pantheon. He picked his way down the hill in the moonlight. Bodies moved up and down the hill on either side of him. He worried about snakes.

Snakes and bodies. He retraced his path to the compound, found the pantheon, and opened the door, quietly calling for Thrush. There was no answer.

He sat down in the dark, looking at the silver moonlight hitting the hole in the roof, where it was projected to the top of the wall across from him. How long should he wait?

Everything about this place was giving him the creeps. The light at the top prevented his eyes from adjusting to the darkness. Something moved against his thigh. A mouth covered his mouth before he could scream.

Light in Dark

THAT IS, if he were going to scream. But Giacomo Berg wasn't driven to screaming. Instead, he inhaled quickly with a short choking sound. And instead of air, he found a tongue filling his mouth. It was slowly removed, lips lingering for a moment about his lips. Finally, he could breathe. The weight against his thigh disappeared. There were shuffling sounds to his left, followed by the whining of a baby. Then silence.

He waited for his eyes to adjust to the darkness. They did not adjust. The only light was a cylinder that shot from the hole in the roof to the wall across from him fairly high up. The shaft dimmed and brightened. Looking up through the hole, he couldn't see stars, but he thought he could discern passing clouds.

Not another sound from the room's other inhabitants. He did hear the cicadas in the trees.

He heard the wind rustling the treetops. He heard an owl. He thought he heard chanting. What the red beard told him was true—you heard everything else; then you heard yourself.

He decided not to say a word. He decided not to say her name, not to reach out a hand to find her in the darkness. He decided just to breathe for a while without thinking and then, perhaps, to think more clearly. Being Here Now was insidious. Too late—he was already thinking. He breathed deeply. He concentrated on the name Peter Proust. He thought of Peter spending days in this room, probably weeks, in full lotus breathing deeply through his nose, forefingers and thumbs forming circles resting on his knees.

It was dark. It was perfectly still. She didn't make a sound. Giacomo took off his sneakers. Why was she so quiet?

He considered his libido. He measured it: it was almost absent. Flat-lined. He looked for it. Was it the spirit of survivalism that deadened his lust? Was it fear? He wasn't very fearful here. Was it the proliferation of babies? The constant smiling? The caring looks and encouraging pats and squeezes all around, even when they don't mean it? Especially, when they don't mean it? Did he require intrigue for lust? How could he lust when everyone was a brother or sister? He knew it was mystery that drove him wild. He was glad to admit that. In the Refuge, he was a relic from some infernal machine powered by imbalance and inequity. He felt more secure chained libidinously to the uncertain order outside the Refuge than the faux serenity within.

The room was getting to him. He was thinking too much. She was sitting there somewhere in the dark, holding a baby no doubt. Could these people sit this way for hours? Could she see him? Was she watching him? Were they joined by others? She wouldn't have allowed that. She would have been compromised. But what if it was a set-up? No. He trusted her that much. They were cut off from the world. They were together in this darkness. He could sense the warmth of a human presence. But she wouldn't be finding any warmth in him. He wanted out. Utopian communities gave him the willies.

Why didn't she say something? He was no longer floating in the darkness listening to rustling leaves. He was waiting for a signal. He wanted to get out of there and be on his way. But, again, where should he go? There had to be a clue. He saw how Peter would have liked it there. For a split second, he'd almost felt cut free from the world himself. But only for a split second. He was sitting in a dark room with a woman and her baby, and he was no further along in his search for Peter Proust than he was when he stepped out of Bob Junior's car. Now some hippie vigilantes want to do him in. Fuck. He had to move this thing along.

"So here we are," he said to the darkness.

"Yes," she said. "We have to talk softly, so they won't hear us."

"I talked to Joseph and I witnessed the moonrise trip, and all I can find out is that Peter couldn't get straight with anybody, as Joseph put it. Now what's that supposed to mean?"

He was getting louder. She grabbed his arm. Then slowly she let it go.

"We went through that before. He couldn't get along with Joseph in particular, so that made him weird for everyone." She paused. "I think the baby here and I want to leave with you."

Giacomo stared at the shaft of light hitting the wall in front of hm. It had been moving down the wall and now seemed to be at just about eye level as he sat on the floor. The room itself was much lighter. But he didn't turn in the direction of her voice. He decided not to respond yet, if at all, to her proposal.

"How many people do you think leave here in a given month?" he asked.

"Not that many leave. Maybe one or two. Some months no one leaves. I can think of maybe three people who left for good that I knew pretty well. My old man walked off once after they found me with Oman. But he came back after a while and changed his name, and they sent him off to live on the second Refuge they started down in Mexico. It's hard, you know, after you give this place everything you've got, and then you have to go back out with nothing and face your parents and everybody else and show them that you failed. But I'm ready to go now, all the same."

"More."

"What do you mean?"

"Just keep talking. Maybe we'll hit something. There must have been more to it than that. Peter's pretty stubborn. He'd stay with it if he could."

"It's like I said before. He was getting paranoid. He wouldn't drink the water, and he'd only eat raw food, whatever he could sneak out of the kitchen or I could get for him. Lots of times he'd go without food altogether for long stretches. The last time he disappeared before he left altogether was for over two weeks."

"You don't know where he went?"

"No idea. By then he wasn't talking to anybody. He'd given up on all of us, and I just couldn't stand the sight of him for it. So I wouldn't know where he'd been. Why don't you answer when I say we're getting out of here with you?"

"One thing at a time. And you didn't hear anything from him after he left?"

"That's what I brought to show you if you let us leave with you. I'm taking a big chance here, you know."

"Let me see it. Then we'll discuss your plans."

"I don't think so," she said in a soft voice. Her hands rubbed up and down his left thigh.

The moonlight made a right angle where the wall hit the floor. "First things first," she said.

Nothing ever came easily. Did she really have something? He was getting edgy. They probably didn't have much time before people started returning from the hill. They'd be walking all around this building, maybe coming inside to zone out. He had to have some clue before he left, and he had to leave right away. Just some direction. B.C., get him out of here!

B.C.? She'd been with him all day, hadn't she? He couldn't shake her and didn't particularly want to. She was out there. She was civilization. She kept him from completely foundering here. If only B.C. were in this darkness with him, he could sort things out.

He turned and faced Thrush. "You can leave with me if you want. I'm not stopping you. But I've got things to do. You don't need to feel me up to walk out of here with me, but once we're out, you and the baby are on your own. We'll find a bus station and probably get on two different buses and that'll be it. It's been nice knowing you, and maybe our paths will cross again, but right now I'm in a hurry. Okay? Now show me what you got from Peter."

Her face was well-lit by now. "Nice knowing you? I don't get a better brush-off than that?" She turned and reached for the baby sleeping on the ground beside her. When she picked him up, he started crying.

Suddenly, there was yelling outside the pantheon, then voices at the door: "What's a kid doing in there? Come on out!" The door opened and two men entered.

"Hey, who's in here? Don't you know there's no kids allowed in here? We have to keep it mellow."

A third man pushed his way through the first two, looked at Giacomo and Thrush, and said, "You know what Joseph told you about fraternizing with a sister. I think you'd better leave."

Thrush stood. "I'm going with him, and so's the baby."

"I don't think so. You know the rules. You have to check out with Joseph first. Come on."

They began to lead her out the door. She stopped them, pulled Giacomo's boots and wallet out of her knapsack, and said, "Tell him hello for me." They led her out.

"Hey, what about that information?" Giacomo called after her.

She shrugged her shoulders while walking between two of the men.

Now what? Should he wait around for a day or two to see if he could get to her? The man standing in the doorway made that option seem unlikely. Should he go to the nearest town and wait? Who knew what direction she'd take when she left or where she'd stop, if she left at all? Fuck.

He picked up his wallet, pulled on his left boot, then his right. He had some difficulty with the right. The inner sole had apparently come loose and was bunched up in the toe. He took off the boot and reached in to straighten the sole. But the sole was in place. Instead, he found a crumpled postcard in the toe. He smiled, put the card in his shirt pocket, and pulled the boot back on. Good job.

"Come on, man. Other people want to use the pantheon," the man guarding the doorway said.

Giacomo got up, walked out the door, looked around the compound, found the path to the front gate, and headed that way, followed by two men. He reached the front gate, where he was stopped by a couple of dogs. "I see you already got your leather. How'd you manage that?" a man in the gate-house asked him, handing him his knapsack.

"Friends in high places," he replied.

They opened the gate. Giacomo walked out and stood under the light post marking the Refuge so he could read the card she'd given him:

"With the dinosaurs. Learning to walk backwards. Waiting to be born. Oman."

Great. Peter had turned cryptic on him. He tried to make out the postmark. "Flour...ff, TX 78.8." Better. Something to go on. Giacomo turned to the three men leaning on the closed gate watching him. "It's been real," he waved and walked into the Thicket.

The Fourth Element is Fire

HE HAD VISIONS. Some came while he was sleeping. A coyote was running. It was running over the hills, weaving through the dry brush like a wind. It came to a creek and lapped at the water caught in a limestone cavity. It looked up; water dripped from its tongue. It was running again like the shadows of the clouds racing over the ground. He was running with it. It did not turn to look at him. It kept its nose to the wind. He felt the burning yellow fire in the eyes of the coyote in his own eyes. He drooled beside still water. He stayed low to the ground. He skimmed the top of gravel. Where the coyote stopped, he stopped. When the coyote moved on, he ran. In the visions, the coyote came to a cliff, paused, sniffed the wind, and then sprang forward. He came to the cliff, felt the wind in his hair, and jumped. He always woke up from these dreams just as his back foot left the pressure of the ground, just as the dust raised by his leap was kicked into the air, just as he began to fly.

Several times he had awakened from these dreams to find a coyote sniffing at the edges of the shack or lapping water from his bucket. He felt it more than heard it. Naked, he went outside and held out his palms to the coyote. The coyote did not shy and did not come forward. It stared at him with its yellow eyes, turned and slowly walked away.

Sometimes he saw the coyote running in the middle of the day. He was sitting on his blanket, naked, in full lotus, his eyes closed, when the coyote ran by. He rose and ran in pursuit. They came to the creek and drank. They ran through the underbrush. They came to the cliff.

They jumped. Then he returned to his body on the blanket.

Today he had dug a hole about twelve inches in diameter and two feet deep. He had pounded it smooth with a large rock he used for pounding mesquite beans. He lined the hole with a sheet of plastic he'd found by the highway. He poured mesquite beans into the hole. He poured enough water to cover the beans. He took the large, smooth stone and began pounding the beans, breaking open the hulls, which he picked from the hole, leaving the beans to soak. Later, he returned and pounded a while longer, picking the remaining twigs and hulls from the hole and leaving the beans to continue their soaking. He threw a handful of dirt into the hole. He had noticed that dirt added a salty taste and more texture to the beans.

He sat on the blanket and considered the next move. He had two matches remaining. He considered walking in to Mountain Home. He should have left earlier for that. He decided instead to walk to the creek for water and to check the persimmons there to see if they were ripe.

He carried the bucket and two plastic gallon containers tied on a rope over his shoulder. He walked down to the road and along the road over three hills to a bridge, where the creek ran under the road. He climbed down to the creek, put the containers down, and lay on his stomach by the edge of the creek. It was no more than six inches deep and three feet wide. The clear water moved slowly over cream-colored pebbles and was barely audible. Water walkers skittered on its surface.

He watched the water intently for signs of life. He would only drink water in which fish lived. If he were desperate, he would drink rainwater, wincing at the metallic taste of fallout.

This creek had provided him with decent water so far, but it could turn at any moment. Some pollutant, some uranium isotope, could get into its system and that would be the end. He watched the water. Finally, he spotted two tiny, black one-inch streaks darting in the water. He knew they were fish by studying their motion, since they moved too fast for him to actually see them.

Satisfied, he filled the bucket and the plastic containers with water. He inspected each for fish. Finding none, he put the containers aside, took off his clothes, and lay down on his back in the creek so that the water almost covered him. Then he turned over, pressing his lips to the pebbles, letting the water wash over him. He got up, shook himself dry, and walked among the trees and bushes by the water looking for persimmons. Some were nearly ripe. He picked one, peeled back the skin, and bit into it. Its tartness made his body pucker. He shook his head from side to side, spit out the seed, and continued eating. He picked eight or ten more persimmons, put them in the burlap bag he'd brought for that purpose, tied the bag to the bucket, got dressed, hoisted the rope over his shoulder, and began the walk back over the three hills and up to the shack. Food and water for another two days. Only matches could be a problem.

In the shack, he pulled a pink prickly pear from a jar he kept in the coolest corner. He cut open the pear, licked its wet interior, and squeezed a few drops of pear juice into a jar. He drank the juice, cut the pear in quarters, then scraped out the inside of each with his teeth, savoring the sweet pulp.

He reached for his journal. He counted the blank pages remaining in the notebook and closed his eyes, as if calculating. Besides matches, paper for the notebook was something he had to buy. He should learn to make paper somehow. And pencils. He'd forgotten pencils. He hadn't weaned himself from anything. He was disgusted with his dependence on manufactured products. Soon he would give up this writing vanity. Should he throw the notebook away right now? Not yet. He had more to write. He found the first blank page and carefully printed:

"I will not say what I did today. I do not do things in order to write them down. I keep this notebook to try to get clear. Not to record. Not even to record dreams. A question: do dreams have life when they are not remembered? I think so. That is the ideal life. Beyond consciousness and into complete presence. If I went to the stream today, do I remember how it felt? Is that memory the same as that feeling? I don't think so. Then why remember? Then why be conscious of existence? To be conscious of existence is to exist no longer. The rock lizard moves in direct relation to the sun, yet it does not study cosmology. To be like the rock lizard, then like the rock, then like its shadow."

He returned the notebook to the crate and went outside to check the mesquite beans. They were soft. He tasted a bean. Almost tasteless. He threw in more dirt, pounded the mixture with a stone, then carefully scooped it into a jar to be cooked later when a match could serve more than one function.

He watched the sun. It would be setting soon. He had to run. He had been intent on running lately. He ran. At first, he picked his way among stones, jumped ravines, dodged the brambles of dry chaparral. Then he lost all sense of the ground. Faster. He was running faster now, barely touching the loose earth. He didn't notice changes in grade, stones, brambles. He felt the wind against his chest, in his hair. He ran straight for the setting sun. Faster over the hills. He felt himself being chiseled by his speed into an arrow, a streak, a will.

He stopped. He was at the bottom of a hill, standing by a mountain cedar slightly taller than he was. He exhaled what seemed to be the breath taken when he had begun his run. Sweat poured off his body. He turned around and walked back toward the shack. It was three or four hills away.

Once inside, he dug through the little bag hanging on a nail containing the dried psilocybin he collected after rains. He took one mushroom and rubbed it between his thumb and forefinger until it formed a powder. He licked the powder off his hand.

He used one of his two matches and built a fire in the steel drum, put the mesquite bean mixture in a pot on the fire, then walked about twenty feet away and vomited in the chaparral. He wiped his mouth and returned to the fire, grinning. The mesquite mush bubbled. The sun went down. He ate the beans. They were gritty. He walked into the chaparral and vomited again.

Purging was necessary. He believed almost everything worth eating contained its own purgative, so that we are only briefly inhabited by other elements of the world, which, in their turn, do not get trapped inside of us. So that we are full but not gluttonous. So that we remain the essential vacuums that we are.

He returned to the fire and ate more beans. He removed the pot from the fire and replaced it with an empty pot, into which he dropped a few holly leaves taken from a sack on the porch. The leaves turned yellow and curled in the heat. He poured water into the pot, and let it heat up. This water he drank from a cup he dipped into the pot. He sat by the fire still burning in the steel drum and sipped this tea. The moon hung heavy. There was a breeze. He thought his jaw might be growing slightly. It felt a little off. He slowly moved his jaw around, trying to feel for any changes. No. He took off his clothes and sat full lotus on the blanket, occasionally sipping the tea. The breeze sometimes felt like a gale. It blew so hard he couldn't keep his eyes open. At other times, the moonlight burned his skin. He looked straight out into the darkness. If he sat still long enough, would he petrify?

How He Re-entered the World

GIACOMO BERG had started out on what he thought was a road, but pretty soon it was no longer a road. Had he missed a turn in the darkness or had it simply stopped? He had noticed the earth getting spongier, and his last step had been into almost two feet of water. Fucking swamp. It had all been easy up to that point: the postcard with almost a zip code, maybe even the date. He couldn't read it by moonlight, but surely later with a light somewhere he would be able to make it out. It had to have been since last March anyway. If he'd only had time to ask her when she'd received it. But it couldn't all be resolved right away. That would put people like him out of business. Then he remembered: he was already out of business.

He had been bounding along in the moonlight—nothing to it—when he plunged into water up to his knees. He backed out of the swamp and looked around. It was hard to distinguish much of anything. The moonlight was less helpful among these trees. And when clouds moved across the moon, the white outline of everything suddenly went dark. No sign of what could be a road or a path. In fact, he couldn't distinguish a sign of any kind. No clues. No signals to follow. He tried to retrace his path a short distance. But with each step, the earth gave a little, producing a tiny sucking sound. Uncertain ground. He turned around and headed in the direction he thought would be roughly south, judging by the moon. He felt for the water density in the earth. From step six to step seven, he thought he could tell a significant change for the better. The ground wasn't giving, so he walked more slowly, feeling for the relative pressures on his soles. In this way, he thought he could skirt the swamp and eventually reach a road.

He was concentrating so hard on the ground that it took him a while to realize he was surrounded by walls of sound: rustling in the treetops, bellowing bullfrogs, night birds calling, every creature probably warning of his timid approach. No matter how cautiously he shifted his weight into the next step forward, the ground gave way. He ran into logs. He again stepped into water up to his knees. He pulled himself out and tried another approach, veering to the right, but he ended up in water again. He backed out, went left, walking very deliberately. He figured snakes had to be slithering all around his feet and waiting under every log. It was becoming noticeably darker. Was the moon already setting? He'd lost it. Was it going to rain? He stopped several times to sit on fallen trees. But swarming mosquitoes and the idea of snakes pushed him on. Once he thought he saw a light through the trees. Then he lost it. Then he heard singing. Had he been going in circles? He kept walking, and the singing subsided.

Finally, he came to a break in the trees. The ground was harder. It seemed to be a field. He decided to wait for the moonlight to reveal what lay in front of him. He waited for a break in the clouds, which now seemed to cover the sky almost entirely. Eventually, the moonlight revealed a field of silver forms, monuments he thought, standing four feet tall and ten feet apart, looking like stalagmites. Safe enough, he guessed. He walked up to one of the columns and felt it, finding it to be wood. He sat down on the ground with his back to a column and tried to sleep.

He thought about the Refuge. Cynicism was its own reward. Peter didn't have that kind of protection. Giacomo almost fell asleep but remained teetering on the edge of wakefulness by the wind in the tree-tops, by all kinds of animal calls foreign to him, by the idea of snakes, the occasional flapping of wings overhead, the thought of B.C. lulled to sleep in civilized New York by sirens, people arguing on the street, rear-end collisions, more predictable danger.

He got up and looked around. It was getting lighter. There must have been a fire here. He looked for a road but only found huge tire tracks that zig-zagged among the stumps. He followed a track that seemed heavily used. He couldn't see any real evidence of fire. Branches were stacked as far as he could see. Nothing seemed charred. Instead, the stumps and larger branches were white and dry, desiccated like bone, cut clean across or cut part way, then ripped asunder. This might go on for miles. He followed the tire tracks on a winding course over several hills. A buzzard flew up from a stump in front of him to join others circling overhead. Slowly they spiraled away over the trees behind him.

At the top of a rise, Giacomo came to a large cleared area, devoid of stumps, with piles of ashes at regular intervals on either side of the tire tracks. Still no sign of civilization, unless, of course, this was civilization. He kept walking. The tire track eventually became more substantial, more like ruts, something approaching a road. He took heart. The road climbed another rise, and Giacomo followed. From the top, he saw a large hole gouged out of the earth. The space satellite? Had it fallen here? No. The explosion would have carried for miles.

On closer inspection, he saw the earth had been dug out in sheets to form terraces down to the bottom of the hole. Huge earthmovers and bulldozers stood silently on every terrace level, many with their raised jaws poised over the backs of dump trucks. Beyond the hole was an aluminum shed, and beyond the shed was a real road, leading back into the trees, and back in the trees he saw smoke rising in a single thread, as if from a chimney. But he didn't see a living soul.

Nevertheless, there was a shed and there was a road and farther on there must have been someone burning a fire. He walked down the hill, around the hole, and up to the shed. The heavy machinery in the hole was marked "Anahuac Contracting," as was the shed. Giacomo tried the door. It was, of course, locked. He could see two desks inside, chairs, a file cabinet. On one desk was a pair of work gloves and a lamp. No telephone that he could see. Was it Sunday? He couldn't quite make the calculations required, but it seemed too soon for Sunday. And his phone had been dead for several days. He could use something to drink, but that didn't seem to be available in the shed either. There were probably keys to the trucks and earth movers in the office. He could drive right out of there. For some reason, he didn't feel desperate enough to break into the shed. The road there probably led fairly soon to a bigger road and then to a town or, at least, to a house. Better to spend a few more hours walking than to get nabbed for stealing the Anahuac dump truck and end up in a backwoods jailhouse without a Jewish Yankee prayer. He did check the ignition of a truck parked by the shed. No key, but there was a bottle of Southern Comfort on the seat. He downed the four swallows that were left and threw the bottle away. Not much help for his thirst, but he was finally alert and eager to get this ordeal over with. He began to follow the road.

The trees closed in again. The road wound. He grew agitated. Where did this road end? He sat down on a stump by the edge of the road. He tried to ignore his hunger, thinking he was bound to reach a main road soon. Surrounded by trees. He was heartened by the fact that there was so much uninhabited land. Heartened in the abstract. Two thousand people on a city block and no one out here for miles. He could use a block full of people right now. Maybe it would all even out. Maybe we wouldn't multiply ourselves into oblivion. Not that he had any desire to multiply. He was thinking about everyone else. Was hunger bringing on delirium? No sleep.

Nobody lived out here because nobody could live here except a bunch of crazed hippies who will end up selling off their trees to survive. Christ. The Southern Comfort had given him a headache. He got up and walked on.

Finally, there was a clearing ahead. He walked faster and saw an aluminum shed. He walked slower, fearing the worst. He arrived at the clearing, confirming his fears. He was back where he'd started. The road was a circle.

He picked up a rock and threw it through the shed's window. He reached inside, opened the window, climbed in and looked around. He looked through the desk drawers for keys. No keys. He found a small, white refrigerator beside the file cabinet. Inside a half-eaten bologna sandwich, an apple, two beers, and a Coca-Cola. He ate the sandwich and apple and drank the beers. He stretched out on the floor, figuring if they found him, they could arrest him and take him to a town. It made no difference to him. He tried to think of a lawyer in Texas he could call, but found the effort too much for him right then. They must have an ACLU in Texas. Maybe. The kind of thing they do? Maybe. Of course. He fell asleep.

He woke up to find that no one had come, he had not been arrested, he was still in the middle of nowhere, and the afternoon light seemed to be fading. Shit! He jumped up, found he needed a key to unlock the door from the inside, and went to the window to climb out. When he was halfway out, he remembered the Coca-Cola in the refrigerator, climbed back in, drank it, and scrambled out the window. He walked to the top of the rise on the other side of the big hole to try to get his bearings. Trees one way and wasteland the other. The thread of smoke was still rising from the trees not far away. He decided to head for the smoke, even if it meant falling into the hands of some hick lunatic. He'd take that chance. New York had prepared him better for handling lunatics than for handling swamps and trees. In order to reach the smoke, he had to walk right into the trees. The paths and clearings didn't seem to lead anywhere. He'd certainly make it before it got too dark.

He walked back down the hill, past the shed and into the trees. Plowing through brambles and bushes, he was determined not to veer from what he believed was the direction of the smoke, though he'd lost sight of it. He did think he saw a light ahead. He'd see it through the trees, lose it, then see it again. That was his beacon.

The Thicket was growing darker. It was well into evening. But the light was getting brighter. He saw it for ten steps, lost it for another ten, then picked it up again. Walking faster now, he pushed the undergrowth aside, desperate to make it before it was completely dark. Now the light was constant and clear, probably no more than two hundred yards away. Crashing through a wall of brush, he was suddenly on all fours under water. He stood up quickly in the chest-deep water, fell down again, pulled himself up, and screamed, "Goddamn it!" A flashlight clicked on, shining right in his eyes.

"Shouldn't take His name in vain like that," a raspy voice said.

Giacomo was able to make out a couple of yelping dogs running along the opposite bank and a dark rifle in the crook of the arm of the figure carrying the flashlight.

"Fell into the bayou," the voice said. "Better pull yourself out of there or you'll stink till you die."

The butt of the rifle appeared in front of Giacomo's eyes. He grabbed it and was pulled onto dry ground. The dogs inspected him while he sat on the ground. Circling, they sniffed his hair and face.

"Them's leopards," the man standing over him said. "Ugliest damn dogs there is, but smarter than a snake. They're telling me now that you ain't dangerous, just a damn fool."

Giacomo nodded to show his gratitude for this assessment. He got up and followed the man, who with a wave of his rifle had signaled the dogs to run ahead. They came to a small, frame house covered with tar paper with an old pickup truck parked right in front of the door. Giacomo couldn't discern more than that in the dark.

"You're gonna have to take them clothes off if you expect to come in my house," the man told Giacomo. "Leave them in the back of the truck to get some air. We may not be fancy, but at least we don't smell like a possum's ass."

Giacomo got undressed and followed the man into the gap between the truck and the front door, then through the door into a room with a table and benches, two rocking chairs, and a wood-burning stove with the dogs taking their places on the floor around it.

The man came out of a back room with a blanket, which he handed to Berg. "No women around to see you, but I ain't too keen on having your what-for staring me in the face while I eat. You hungry?"

Giacomo nodded.

"Okay. You got your choice—mush or grub?" The old man laughed. "That gets 'em every time. Actually, I got continual stew. Right now it's pretty mean. I can spot some pig's ears, a little possum, greens, and lots of chili pepper mixed up in there. It's your only choice."

Giacomo nodded again.

The old man put a pot on the stove, stirred the fire around inside, then walked over and stood directly in front of Giacomo Berg and extended his hand. "My name's Jacques Fourier, spelled like the French because my people were Cajun but pronounced around here like the number. 'Jack Four' is what most people call me. Yours?"

"Berg. Giacomo Berg."

"Okay, Jock. We got the same name. What else? Where you from? You're some kind of Yankee. What the hell are you doin' in the bayou in the middle of the night?"

"New York. I was sent out here to look for somebody."

"In the bayou? Ain't nobody dumped in the bayou, that I know of anyway, since some ol' boys threw another ol' boy in there who was poachin' in on their poachin' territory. And that was over twenty years ago. I ain't heard nary a scream since then. Of course, if you'd stayed in there any longer, you'd have been poached pretty good yourself. That's why you stink so bad. Course it's always stunk somewhat in that a bayou don't run like a river runs. But since these lumber outfits pushed into these parts and the miners after them, the water's been dumped so full of chemicals that it puts out an odor worse than a sulphur pit. Now that I think of it—and since you've been sitting here inside for a spell—why don't you go around back and find the pump and bucket and pour some water over you a couple of times. We'll both find it more agreeable for eating. And rinse off those clothes while you're at it."

Giacomo followed the instructions. The dogs followed Giacomo. He emptied a few buckets full of water over his head. He did feel somewhat better. He rinsed the clothes in the bucket and hung them back on the truck. He kept thinking that it was a good thing he wasn't black. He went back in to find Jack Four eating from a bowl at the table, motioning for Giacomo to eat from another bowl. Giacomo ate. Jack Four wiped his mouth and put his bowl on the floor a few inches from the dogs' snouts. Without raising their heads, the dogs worked their tongues around the edge of the bowl.

"So, you're a Yankee. You a Jewboy, too?" The old man put a stare on him.

A sweat broke out on Giacomo's brow and in his crotch. Here it comes. "Half," he said and continued eating. He didn't look up. He refused to let his face turn red. It pissed him off—this physical response. It had to be millennia of ancestors sweating inside him. He was not about to step and fetch. Still, here he was, naked, in a shack in the middle of a swamp with some crazed old redneck, who was surrounded by hunting dogs and carried a shotgun and called him "Jewboy." Great. He kept eating.

The old man had not removed his eyes from Giacomo. "Couldn't help but notice you had the ring reamed from your lower finger," he continued. "It don't matter to me, you understand. It's just that I'm always curious about a person's originations. I like to know what I pull out of the bayou. So where do you people keep all that gold you've stored away for centuries?"

The thing to do would be to get out of there as soon as possible, even in the dark. He would say as little about himself as he could get away with. So he got down to business. "How do I get to a town? I've been walking for two days out here and haven't hit a good road yet."

"What's your hurry?" The old man looked him straight in the eyes, then broke up laughing. "You know I'm just fucking with you. Where you coming from—the Refuge?"

Giacomo nodded. The old man was enjoying his haplessness. What could Giacomo do about it? Grab the shotgun? No. Get his clothes and walk back into the dark? Not a good move.

"I get some of them comin' through here every once in a while," Jack Four went on. "But they don't look like you. Not bad folks. Just a little too righteous, that's all. Some of them come by here when they're out selling pigs or eggs. I don't mind talking to them, but they're so goddamn sure of themselves. They think the whole world's gonna turn out like them. Motherfuckin' idiots. It starts to get all over a person. What's the matter—you didn't like it over there?"

"They asked me to leave, and I wanted to leave. So it worked out, except that it was the middle of the night, and I couldn't find a road. Yesterday I started to follow your smoke."

"Well, I ain't the only sonofabitch living out in this swamp. You just gotta know where to look, that's all. There's the Refuge, there's the strip mine, there's the lumber companies, a few oil jacks pumping away, and then they's hundreds of folks snookered up all over this Thicket, and they've been that way for a hundred years. I've only been here thirty myself. Some of them old bastards regard me as an interloper. Now I ain't that. Just took me the first thirty-five years of my life to figure my way out here."

Giacomo twirled the spoon inside the empty bowl in front of him. His twinge of fear had rapidly devolved into boredom. Rather than being a hostage, he felt more like a guest at a dull dinner party. He realized it was his turn to ask questions.

"So where were you before this?" he asked.

"Oh, here and there. I heard about this place while I was roughnecking over near Lufkin. I was always unsettled up to then. Didn't know why, but I was unsettled. Also, I was sure the world was going to end back then, and I'd be caught dead in my tracks on somebody else's land. The Russkies were advertising they had the bomb, and we were advertising we had a bigger bomb. I just knew that sooner or later they were going to have it out. And when they did, they were going to do it in the cities. So my first rule was to get out of town. Then my second rule was that I wanted to be in my own house on my own place with the rest of nature packing in around me when the bomb dropped. I figured that, if anything survived, it would be something living out in the swamps. Swamp life has a thicker skin, so to speak. Besides, who would waste part of an atom bomb on a swamp? Wouldn't get more than four or five people per ten square miles. Hell, a firing squad could take care of them. So, while I was working over in Lufkin, a fellow told me about this here Thicket and about how there were houses standing around empty just waiting to be inhabited and land so bad that it was yours if you wanted it."

"So you've been here thirty years? I see you survived the Bomb?"

"Bomb? What bomb? Don't fuck with me, Jewboy. I know what goes on in the world. There ain't been no bomb yet, but don't you worry about that. They'll still kill us off in due time. Of course, now they've got it more

so-phis-ticated than I had them figured for with computers and what-not."
He peered into Giacomo's eyes to see if he was going to follow the argument
Jack Four was heading into.

Giacomo nodded to show he was.

"Here's how I got it pictured. For 50 years, the Russkies emphasized
all this nuclear buildup just to get us to do the same thing. We didn't even
know if they were doing it for real. We just had to take them at their Communist word. That's the way they were going to get us, even when they said
they weren't no Communists any longer. They added five megatons, so we
added six. They added 500 surface-to-air; we added 600. I've studied on it,
see. Sooner or later it all has to go. Blow up right in our faces. Some missile
silo in Kansas or some nuclear reactor they got buried under a sidewalk in
Chicago. Or an earthquake cracks open some uranium bins like little bird
eggs, and that will be all she wrote. Yep. Even your New York City probably
has a couple of reactors locked up behind steel doors just waiting to bust at
the seams. Those Russkies knew what they were about. They put all their
missiles out in Siberia, where there was nothing but prisoners and ice and
bad news. And if they blew one or two, who cared beyond a few caribou?
Hell, one popped off a few years ago, and all it did was burn off some trees
and dig a hole to pour more snow into. You follow me?"

Giacomo nodded again.

"Hell, no, you don't. You probably think I'm crazy as a turkey buzzard.
But I tell you this. I bet half of what they got is no more than cardboard or
something the Russkie Walt Disney put together. All those comrades and
commissars were just sitting over there laughing into their vodka. And I
know you're going to say that the wall came down and Russia is free. I hope
you don't believe that for one second. You know the KGB? They ran the
Communist Party and now they run their so-called democracy. It's all the
same people pulling all the same shit. They were calling our bluff, and we
were just licking it up all the way to the cemetery. But there won't even be a
cemetery left. Oh, maybe they'll find some fingernails dug into a door or a
footprint melted into the pavement or little bits of bone scattered in a field.

"And here's the real bitch. The damnedest thing is we've both done
spent our way to the poorhouse anyways. We spent so much money on our
missiles and reactors, and they spent so much trying to scare us and everyone else, so neither of us will have anything left to defend anyway. China

has all our money, and it's putting together its nuclear bombs, and it's got hundreds of millions of Chinamen just waiting to invade. You tell me who outsmarted who?"

Giacomo nodded. "I think we pretty much agree."

"What are you talking about? I ain't gonna kill you or turn you out if you think I'm a mad sonofabitch, so long as you mind your manners. Now I might kill you because you're a damn Jewboy and don't eat pork." Jack Four hung his head down toward his knees and couldn't stop laughing.

"C'mon, man," Berg said. "Lay off. There are maniacs running this world. And we don't know how to stop them."

"I knew you had an honest face, even though it was covered with swamp shit when I pulled you out. Now see if you're smart enough to follow this: I'd go tell some general or some Wall Street tycoon what I've figured out, but I know they don't care. They're in on it, too. That's the damnedest part. It's their line of work to be part of the system that fucks the world. If you're supporting a wife and kids by selling cigarettes, you just go right on selling, even when the black hand of tobacco is wrapped around your lungs. That's what I call the 'human weakness' about this thing. The human weakness is that you can always count on the human being to look after his own little world of self-interest before he thinks about any other thing. So those generals and Wall Street wizards just go on turning out missile heads and nuclear reactors until one day some tiny charge says, 'Wait a goddamned minute—I ain't ready to jump,' and throws off every law of electricity known to man, so that a string of cells heats up inside some reactor, and the whole country explodes, quiet-like, on the inside, sucked in at the heart, and we're gone."

He tried to read Giacomo's reaction. "You goddamned poker-faced Yankee. If you're so goddamned smart, how come you still live up there in one of the first places to go, where everybody's going to die climbing all over each other?"

Giacomo had an answer for this. "I don't see you running from the reactor they built south of Houston."

"Yeah. I guess I'm just too old. I should be running, but I'm just too old, that's all. This is what I know, and this is where I'll make my stand, and this is where I'll die, one way or the other. It's good to know ahead of time where you're going to die. Makes you feel more restful.

"Besides, I figure if you ain't safe from nuclear in the Thicket, then there's no place left to hide. They got us so scared, we're putting those suicide makers everywhere."

"So what do you think about all these people talking about the world disappearing at the Millennium?" Berg asked.

"More fucking lies. There's a reason we're all going to die, and it's not gonna come from the ticking of a clock. Unless that inspires some trigger-happy fucker to decide to celebrate the year 2000 by starting the unstoppable. There could be that," he said. "I read, you know. I'm not just some stupid Cajun guzzling moonshine and barking at the moon."

He pulled aside a curtain to reveal a small bookshelf. Berg spotted titles that included *Atlas Shrugged, Fountainhead, Be Here Now, The Martian Chronicles*, and *Stranger in a Strange Land*.

"I ain't no dummy, New York Jewboy," he said, waving a stack of magazines at Berg. "These here are thirty years of *The Bulletin of Atomic Scientists*. I subscribe and pick it up at the post office every month. I've even got my own Doomsday clock." He pulled the curtain farther aside to unveil an old school clock without its glass face. "The Bulletin always sugar-coats its predictions. They say we've got seven minutes left until Doomsday. By my calculations, it's no more than two-and-a-half."

Giacomo suddenly felt complete exhaustion take over his limbs. He had difficulty keeping his eyes open, even in the face of Doomsday. He strained to watch the embers in the stove, hoping they would interest him enough to keep his eyes open.

The old man stared at him. "If you don't like all the preaching, you're getting it anyway. I figure you owe it to me for a place to sleep and the food. Pull two chairs together, and you should be all right. Tomorrow I'll take you into Liberty, where you can catch the bus to Houston, and that'll get you almost anywhere."

Giacomo pulled up a chair for his feet. He watched Jack Four blow out the lantern. The dogs were curled up by the stove. He watched the last embers die. The old man was walking around outside. Too tired to think or hear or smell or feel anything more, Giacomo fell asleep.

The next morning Jack Four led him to the pickup truck without saying a word. Giacomo got his clothes from the back of the truck, got dressed, and seated himself beside Jack Four in the cab of the truck. The old man was short and wiry, much shorter than Giacomo had thought the night before. He was wearing a black-and-red-striped welder's cap. The dogs stood in the bed of the truck. Thus arrayed, they drove through the woods.

After a few minutes, Jack Four said, "You know I can still smell you. Good thing I've only got you for another ten minutes. Then you'll be Greyhound's problem."

They came to an intersection with a county road. A sign read, "Liberty." When they pulled up to a gas station with a Greyhound sign, Jack Four signaled to Giacomo with his head.

Giacomo obeyed, getting out. He thanked Jack Four and reached through the window to shake the old man's hand. Jack Four didn't take his hands from the steering wheel, but did say, "When you get on that bus, do everybody a favor and sit all by yourself." He tipped the bill of his welding cap and drove off.

Giacomo bought a ticket for the bus to Houston and waited in the shade by the gas pumps. Back in civilized society. It was hot and dusty in Liberty. He needed a shower and a shave. He needed more money. He had to call B.C. He couldn't figure out what day it was. B.C.—how long had he been gone? Was he hot on the trail or just wasting time? He felt pretty far from everything.

After a while, the dust announced the chrome bus for Houston. It stopped in front of the gas pumps, idling like a huge refrigerator.

The station attendant appeared, calling, "Big dog to Houston. All aboard!" as if addressing a crowd and not just Giacomo Berg.

The driver stepped off the bus and handed the attendant a package from down below.

Giacomo boarded the bus, the door closed behind him, and the bus pulled out of Liberty.

Geological Optimism

THERE WAS ICELAND TO CONSIDER. She could go there. It was growing. The only land mass that could claim a few more feet each day. Or was it inches? Was it inches per year? Anyway, there was some future in that. There was a little more land every day. You could make promises to future generations. You could say, "We have what's ours, and when you are of age, what new land exists by then will be yours." Unless the oceans rise at a faster rate. There's that. But miles of hot springs and geysers. She'd read that Reykjavik was heated by the hot water underground. What an idea. The Romans did that in Bath, didn't they? She could use a bath.

B.C. went into the bathroom and turned on the water, making it a little warmer than usual. She kept testing the water temperature with her finger, and when the tub began to fill, with her toe. She turned the knobs to approximate an ideal the pores in her flesh were imagining. As the tub filled, she got undressed. When it reached the right depth, the right temperature, she stepped in and lay down. For an instant her legs were buoyed up, then they lowered to the porcelain bottom.

Where was she? Iceland? Yes, Iceland. Every day lava seeped from holes, ran over what ran before, came to the edge of that, met the water, and in a rush of steam began to cool, arrested, hardening, adding another step or half step out into the ocean. She could imagine rivulets of lava running for days over cooling rock, water bubbling in pockets, steam rising. She could see orange ribbons at night against black earth, black water, black sky, those in the distance seeming to run through the sky. She could imagine Iceland slowly advancing on the rest of the world, which was shrinking, cracking, and breaking off.

She'd just read that the earth's temperature had risen over one degree in the past ten years. She thought it had to be more than that, just from her own experience. At least in the past twenty years it must have risen at least five degrees. Five degrees hotter in the summer for sure and at least four in the winter. Just in the last four or five years, the plants on her windowsill had dried up faster, it had been hotter on the summer streets, and on the winter weather map the snow didn't go as far south as it once did. Except for the blizzard two years ago that stopped New York in its tracks and froze the grapefruit crops in Florida and Texas.

It snowed three times in Lockhart that she could remember. The first time, there was no school. No one could drive. They all walked to the courthouse square—the old people, mothers and fathers with their kids. No one had ever seen snow like that. They just stood on the street around the square and looked at the snow respectfully. She remembered the courthouse clock's minute hand had supported a small pallet of snow until it reached the half hour, when the snow cascaded down the building. Why did she remember that? She had tried to build a snowman but didn't know how. The second time was on Abraham Lincoln's birthday. She was in fourth grade. She remembered exactly. It had snowed the night before. When she woke up, everything was white. But the streets were black like mud, and everyone went to school. She had walked the deepest parts of the snow on the way to school. She could see grass wherever she left a footprint. She knew the snow wouldn't last long. The teacher wouldn't let them go outside for recess. The whole class whined and begged. Some even cried. They could see patches of grass opening up in the snow. The teacher told them that Abraham Lincoln's birthday was not a holiday the way George Washington or Jefferson Davis was. When they were finally let out in the afternoon, the snow had, for the most part, vanished. She ran to the small patches that remained in the grass, a few mounds under trees and out of the sun. She walked through as many as she could find going home. Once home, she scooped up a handful of snow and put it in a plastic bag and put this in the freezer of the Frigidaire. In the summer, when she got it out, it was a lump of ice, and she herself couldn't believe it was ever snow. The last time was more like an ice storm. She was a freshman in high school. The boys piled up walls of ice and snow and threw iceballs at each other. Everyone had to walk to school because cars were sliding all over the road. She was sure there were a few wrecks that day, especially among the farm kids, who had to come a long way and drove like they wanted to die all the time anyway with their special rural hardship driver's licenses they got when they were twelve. But she didn't remember any wrecks. She did remember the tobacco juice frozen in the ice outside the schoolhouse door. She couldn't wait to graduate and get out of town. By the time school was over that afternoon, the ice had melted.

But Iceland. You never thought of it as being cold. Not like the tundra and glaciers of Greenland anyway. Funny how those names should be changed—Iceland and Greenland. To Steamland for Iceland and Iceland for Greenland or something like that. Who named them? First impressions nearly always fail.

The bath water was getting cool. She turned a knob and added hot water. The heat spread through the water in currents she made by waving her arms. She shifted so her weight was held by her spine along the porcelain. Her legs floated up slightly. Did they wave like seaweed? She would like to imagine they did. If the temperature of the earth rose between two and three degrees, was that enough to melt the polar ice caps? Half the Arctic could be sloughed off in ten years. The seas would rise. That would take care of Lower Manhattan. Below the tenth floor at least. The lady in back would get her view of the ocean. That would take care of the Eastern Seaboard. Miami, New Orleans, the South Texas coast, and Houston for sure. It might even reach from the Gulf of California up into southern Arizona, the way it used to be an ocean eons ago. In forty years, nothing would be left of California west of the foothills of the Sierras. Western Europe, Southeast Asia, Leningrad, Istanbul, Guatemala, and Nicaragua would be a series of islands, some wrapped around green mountains. Iceland? Would it be gone? There was every reason to believe it would. But she wasn't sure. She thought it might float, almost like a lily pad on the ocean's surface. The lava would continue to build, to force its way out into the air. The mountains would remain. And the Gulf Stream. Does that mean something that the Gulf Stream finds Iceland in the middle of the cold seas? That's probably why people have lived there. There are so many things B.C. wished she'd studied. There was something about centrifugal force pulling the added water to the equator and redistributing it from there. Maybe she'd be able to stand on the edge of the lava fields and watch the icebergs float south to break up in the Bermuda Triangle, to run aground on Vero Beach, to overtake and drown St. Kitt.

The water was cool again. The bar of soap floated through the channel between her knees. The trouble, of course, was the missile tracking station. That would have to be destroyed. No good reason for it with the Soviets gone. There was always China. But would it come at them from the east or the west? No good reason for the U.S. to care enough to station troops or missiles. Iceland. Destroy the tracking station and you remove Iceland from the atomic world. It might even be a haven from radiation, if nuclear war still came and were limited. Minneapolis for Novgorod. Seattle for Shanghai. The clouds might hang on for months. The radiation would filter down. But underground would be heated. And the heat could provide power. Food could be grown hydroponically. Iceland might be far enough away that two-thirds would survive without contracting cancer, without damage to the chromosomes. In a limited war, at any rate, if there were such a thing. The tracking station had to be destroyed.

At least with Iceland there was hope. The picture she kept returning to was the one of little green spongy plants, tiny yellow and purple flowers, in the holes and crevices of black lava fields. She must have seen it in *National Geographic* in a doctor's office. The roots of tiny plants worked through the lava, breaking it up. Later this would be pasture, fertile farmland. The sea would be miles away. The seabirds would appear before a storm. She might have a child or two. She'd better hurry. They would live in a stone cottage heated from underground. New York would not exist. Lockhart would not exist. All she would know of the world would be Iceland.

She got out of the tub and grabbed a towel. She stood there dripping, watching the soap float across the waves of dirty water. If Giacomo didn't call that night, tomorrow she'd be packing for Iceland or some other place. Any place else. She fished the soap out of the water and slowly began drying her legs, her back.

The telephone rang. Perfect timing, Giacomo Berg. She wrapped the towel around her and went to the phone.

"B.C.?"

"Yes?"

"It's Giacomo."

"I know. I wondered if I'd ever hear from you again." She didn't want to act like this, but she'd already written him off for not calling that night. And now he called.

"I'm sorry. You don't know what it's been like. You didn't tell me Texas could be such a labyrinth." He tried to insert a kind of laugh at his end of the line.

"You didn't ask," she said, bidding Iceland goodbye for the moment. "So where are you? What do you need? Are you coming back or going somewhere else?"

"Money. I need money. I'm just about broke. Can you wire some to me? Have you got any? Nobody seems to trust me when I try to use plastic out in the sticks. If the Prousts want me to keep on the trail, they'll have to foot the bill from here. I hate to ask them, but that's the way it is. In the meantime, if you could send me some cash, I'll be your slave for life."

"You already are," she said, brightening slightly. "You just don't know it yet."

He ignored that. "I've got the thinnest thread to follow right now, so maybe they'll want to call the whole thing off. If they do, I'll have to decide whether or not I'll just keep going on my own. I want to see this through. Anyway, I'm in Houston. I'll give you the hotel information so you can send money. Is that okay?"

"I'll tell you when I see you."

"That could be a while."

"No more than half a day, if you can wait that long. I'm bringing the money to you."

"Why would you want to do that?"

"I've just got to get out of here, that's all. I thought maybe we could go to Lockhart for a day. I could show you around. I really do have to get out of here."

He wasn't sure what to say. It would just complicate things if he had to look for Peter and think about B.C. at the same time. But he would like to see her. He saw her now picking apart the plant on his desk. He made one weak attempt: "What will you do if I spend three days on the telephone and in various police stations going through files?"

"I'll sit in the sun. I'll read a book. Things I can't seem to do here anymore."

He gave in easily. "Okay," he said. "When do you arrive?"

She told him she'd call him back with the flight and time. She'd bring enough money to make a vacation of it. She didn't tell him that. She told him she'd be happy to follow him around wherever he needed to go. But if they worked Lockhart in, she would be very pleased, she said.

Despite his weariness, despite his growing anxiety about finding Peter, despite himself, Giacomo Berg was pleased as well or excited or maybe even aroused. He tried to picture her face and smile exactly but didn't succeed. He said, "Goodbye."

B.C. returned to the bathroom to dry her hair. Before she put on a robe, she began to pack what she called her "sundries"—eyebrow pencil, hand lotion, diaphragm. There was a frantic purpose to every moment. She was getting out. Iceland. Lockhart. It didn't matter where. Giacomo Berg? Not sure about that port in this storm. But what the hell?

She was about to leave the bathroom with her small bag in hand when she saw the soapy water still standing in the bathtub. She opened the drain. She stood there, naked, watching the whirlpool of gray water swallow itself.

"Hot damn," she said to herself. "Hot damn." She danced naked in a circle for five seconds.

II

Trouble in Paradise

"THE MASS OF MEN lead lives of quiet desperation" read the carefully lettered, framed document on the wall of Stephen Seltzer's office. And on top of the careful lettering, "BUT NOT ME" was stamped in red ink.

Stephen Seltzer was disturbed. Life had been running right on schedule for so long, and then his neighbor's child got sick. Tommy Perkins, the boy who mowed the grass. Here he was, Stephen Seltzer, law degree at 24, wife at 26, daughter at 28, son at 30, second home at 31, a partner at 32, second daughter at 35, still uncompromising at 46.

Then Tommy Perkins became seriously ill. In one day, as if the life had just been kicked out of him. He saw Tommy, white and waxy, lying on the Perkins's living room couch, his hand on a box of chocolates, as if he were too tired to lift a candy from its paper wrapper—the boy who cut the grass and then went to the Lions Club field to play a doubleheader under the lights. They'd taken him for tests, of course. They hadn't been told what it was, Stephen, that is, and his wife, Cara Fenster, a potter. They didn't know the Perkins family all that well. Just Tommy. The boy who mowed their grass. But you could tell it was a blood disease or cancer or something to be backed away from. Stephen could tell, somehow.

It bothered him. Not just because it was Tommy Perkins, poor kid. There was always a Tommy Perkins in every school. When he was a kid, Stephen Seltzer knew one or two of them, just barely. A girl who rode in his sister's carpool in elementary school. Leukemia—before the days when any kid survived it. The little girl's twin sister got in the car the fall after her sister died and moved away from the door, as if to make more room for her sister following after. There were always one or two kids with weak hearts. One passed out after running two laps of the 300-yard track in junior high. He was dead by that afternoon. It was announced on the school's intercom. A girl in tenth grade sat down at home one evening after pep squad and died.

Kids who knew these kids huddled in the hallways by the lockers, trying to figure it out. Stephen had it figured out, even then. It was a scrape, a brush, it was a reminder, it was the passage nearby of that presence called death that would come by again and again, sometimes closer, sometimes

farther away, whittling away at that buffer of other people his age until a
final swoop would catch him right between the eyes. He'd had it figured
out for a number of years.

But this Tommy Perkins thing was something else. It was something else because Stephen Seltzer had heard rumors that there was another
Tommy Perkins two blocks away, and two old ladies living next door to each
other down the street had both come down with a case of "the nerves" all
at once, and a woman who buys his wife's pots was losing her sense of taste.

And three days before, his older daughter Tessie had come home with
some sort of rash on her hands, saying kids all over school, who didn't even
know each other or come close to each other in the lunchroom, were coming down with this rash.

Something was wrong here, he kept saying to himself. But something
had better not be wrong, he also kept saying. Stephen Seltzer was a man
who believed in seizing destiny by the balls. But he was also a man who,
deep down, knew that destiny was a woman, weaving the fabric of his life,
to which he might be able to add a little embroidery at best. It was that East
Coast liberal arts education that had done him in. How could he continue
to survive in the world of Houston go-getters, pock-marked as he was by so
much doubt?

But here they were: Stephen Seltzer and Cara Fenster, Tess Fenster-Seltzer, Josh Fenster-Seltzer, and Lucia Fenster-Seltzer—all called Seltzer at school and when discussed at the law firm, as for insurance coverage,
for example, securely domiciled in a four-bedroom home, in a Houston
suburb of four-bedroom homes, forested lawns, parks built around sluggish
bayous, pine trees, weeping willows and cottonwoods breaking the flat tra-
jectories, schools of red brick with special programs for the gifted in science
and in the dramatic arts. Here they were with a shop in the second-best
shopping center in affluent West Houston committed to selling Cara's pots,
a thriving legal practice in the midst of a recession, owing principally to Stephen's foresight, making himself an expert in bankruptcy law. Here they
were: well-situated and, Stephen believed, relatively uncompromised. Until
now, he might have said "bullet-proof." He wasn't exactly storming the Pen-
tagon, but then that had never been his game plan. He'd simply gone along,
carried by the tides of the times. But now he was spending his money where
it counted, backing the reform slate in Houston city politics, sending money

to anyone running against the old order in the state capital, contributing to full-page ads opposing new U.S. aggression in Central America, sending money only to humanitarian efforts in Israel. Not how his college friends would do it, Stephen would angrily find himself mumbling while writing out a check for a campaign contribution. But now that they were entering middle age, this was the way it was going to get done. Stephen Seltzer hated himself whenever he realized he was still justifying his actions to his college cronies.

Like B.C. Boyd. Why had she called?

They'd been lovers one year in college, not even a full year really, thrown together by mutual friends and events. A process of elimination when you really thought about it. A few parties, drank some beer, smoked some grass, got to know each other in that way. Then the Earth Day Save-Mother-Earth March in Washington. They'd chartered an old Bluebird school bus to drive them down and back. The driver, a nice guy, fiftyish, had kept his headlights on all the way down as a sign of solidarity with the President. Symbols, after all, provided the most meaningful plane of existence. Someone discovered the bus driver's subversion at a turnpike service area, and the driver was engaged in dialectical debate from that point on into Washington, D.C. It was this same driver, Stephen remembered, who braved barricades and tear gas to pick up his charges two days later to ferry them home, headlights still burning. Integrity, Stephen thought upon remembering. A kind of integrity foreign to us then.

Anyway, they'd arrived in Washington and immediately boarded chartered city buses to take them to the Arlington Cemetery for a candlelight parade for all those who had died worldwide at the hands of toxic chemicals and nuclear power. Probably not many, if any, at Arlington Cemetery, but it was a symbol, understood at the time. As the bus pulled away from Capitol Hill, a voice with a familiar timbre came over the bus's p.a. "All right cowboys and cowgirls," it said, "I'm an ol' cowhand from Sweetwater, Texas, and while we're riding, you've got your choice of Merle Haggard or Conway Twitty. What'll it be?" Twitty carried the day, and Stephen remembered exchanging a knowing smile with B.C. across the aisle, his Texas compatriot.

That night they'd assembled after the march at a church, God knows where, in Washington. Someone gave them a slip of paper saying a woman not far away at the address shown had room for seven people. They'd grabbed their sleeping bags and backpacks and headed off, found the apartment, were shown to two large rooms and a bathroom. There were cats everywhere, he remembered. Somehow he and B.C. had ended up in sleeping bags on the floor next to each other. Somehow, by morning, they'd ended up in the same sleeping bag.

It was not the most sanguine relationship. He was careful about his political involvement, not wanting to ruin his chances for law school, not wanting a felony on his record, wary of joining political organizations that might be fronts for something else. She gave him hell at every turn.

They'd lived in her dormitory room for a while, in a suite with the son of the head of the World Council of Churches, who would drop acid, then play a cello sonata that began with Bach and ended with the cellist leaping around the room, cello held above his head. She'd pull out her autoharp and jump around the room with him. There was also a student radical leader, several years their senior, who shared the suite. He'd just returned from two years of therapy for a broken neck suffered while competing for the college wrestling team. B.C. and Fazio, the wheelchair radical, had immediately hit it off. He'd always suspected some love interest there that B.C. had never quite figured out how to exploit, given her predilection for letting such affairs happen to her. She always went with Fazio when he had to confront school authorities about some issue. Invariably Fazio would do a wheelie in his wheelchair while bartering with school officials, who were conscious, Stephen realized only later, that the school was aware of its continuing liability for his injury and thereby scared of what further responsibilities his balancing act portended. Stephen would sometimes tag along, helping lift Fazio up the long steps of a school administration building, for instance, demonstrating as much because they cajoled him into it as because it was something he believed. Not that he supported the corporate culture that was screwing the world or even, at the time, believed in electoral politics. It's just that he knew he would someday return to that system of belief, and it was to his future that Stephen wanted to remain reasonably true.

But not B.C. There won't be any future, she would say more often than not. Or, on one of her more optimistic days, she might allow as how there would be a future only if the current order of existence were changed radically. Their relationship wasn't meant to last—he'd known that from the start. It had just happened, and then, over a summer that he'd spent back home in Houston while she'd stayed in Connecticut, it had ceased to happen. They'd both pretty much had it figured that way. It had been as much a solution to the college housing problem as anything else. And a large part of his sexual and social education. Hers, too, he imagined. Part of the college experience, he liked to think. The next year or two he spent aiming for law school, while she seemed to drift through the liberal arts. She went to Austin for graduate school while he went to law school, but they never saw each other. Maybe once or twice, thirty seconds' worth of conversation, but that was all.

He hadn't heard from her for two or three years. She used to call or write when she made her yearly pilgrimage to Lockhart. But since her father died and her mother had moved to Sun City, she no longer came that way. A few years ago she'd called from the airport while changing planes to go to Arizona. But that was about it.

Until now. He couldn't exactly understand what she was telling him. She'd be in Houston for a few days with a detective and would like to stop by. A detective? Was she in some kind of trouble? Or was this her latest flirtation with adventure? Next thing you know, she'd end up marrying a cop. Wouldn't that be a rich turn of events?

But he couldn't worry about it now. If she called again, she called. He had to think about Tommy Perkins now and about Tessie's rash. There was some poison ivy growing in the trees on the back of his lot. He thought he'd killed it off, but maybe it'd come back. He'd have to check. Tess said she hadn't been back there, but maybe she'd forgotten. She couldn't have given it to all the kids in school. Unless there's some poison ivy growing around the school. Had they checked that? He wasn't sure what the reaction to poison ivy looked like. But somehow this wasn't exactly what he would have guessed. It was more like bad acne. Anyway, it had him bugged. He couldn't concentrate on the Smithson brief. It had him bugged; that was all.

And then B.C. Boyd.

There was a time for a few weeks when it had seemed like they never got out of bed. John and Yoko, their friends called them, visiting while he and B.C. lay entwined beneath the sheets. They always seemed to be in bed. That must have meant something. It wasn't that way with Cara. Even at first. He wasn't sure what that meant. Probably nothing more than the remission of adolescent hormones.

What could B.C. be doing now? His secretary buzzed to say more Smithson files had arrived. Back to work.

Songs from Home

Airports made him agitated. Airports and teeming freeways out to airports and miles of airport parking lots and circular lobbies with a phony French cafe serving plastic-wrapped croissants on one side mirrored by an identical phony French cafe on the other, so you didn't know where you were. It was impossible to pace amid so much mindless replication. Anxiety was riding Giacomo Berg as if he were a mule.

Another half hour. He went into the shop marked "Sundries" on one side of the lobby or the other and bought a can of shaving cream and a disposable razor. He also found a *New York Times* and produced a credit card to take care of his end of the transaction. The young strawberry-blond cashier, wearing a sun visor marked "Houston Astros," rang it up, and upon returning his credit card, told Giacomo Berg, "You could use a shave." Then she laughed that coquettish laugh he associated with ingratiating clerks and high school cheerleaders. It agitated him all that much more.

Feeling tormented by youth, Giacomo Berg took his full week's beard, speckled with a little gray, into the terminal men's room. It was not easy, and it left the razor nicked and twisted, but after three or four passes, inch by inch, he was able to clear the stubble from his face. While his forehead had begun to brown, his cheeks still bore that pale luminescence of New York City half-light. His eyes still peered from their gray-brown vaults. No one could call him a redneck, the way so many of these ol' boys seemed to parade the streets of Houston like fighting cocks in heat, the fair skin of their necks actually turned permanently beet red and slightly jowly from years of days in the sun and years of nights at the bar.

He'd noticed this about most of the white people he'd been encountering: the seamlessness of their faces in youth did not serve them well in later years. It had nowhere to go but get fatter and start to slough off their cheekbones, sagging and wagging, dying on the vine. They were either red-faced if they drank or waxen white if they feared God. It paid to be ethnic in the long run. All those imperfections added up to history and character when you turned the cusp of middle age. At least he liked to think so. He considered it a modest revenge.

He looked in the mirror again. He seemed to have lost more hair on top. Had this trip been that rough? Was his scalp beginning to shine? He could take losing a few hairs, but not true baldness announcing itself. He lathered his hands and washed his face, scrubbing his hairline to dim that oily luster.

He was ready for B.C. And for a change of clothes. Glad he didn't have to submit his cellular makeup to a security x-ray, he waited in the terminal lobby. He positioned himself in a chair from which he had a clear view of the entrance to the corridor connecting the lobby to B.C.'s gate. Then he settled into the *Times*.

Right in the middle of the editorial page, the arrival of B.C.'s plane was announced. He hurried to the sports pages, reduced for the consumption of the outlying regions to a couple of columns and the box scores of New York teams. Nothing to sink his teeth into. Instead, how to maintain the condition of the outfield at Yankee stadium as revealed by a retiring groundskeeper, the short careers of ice hockey referees. What did he care? He raced back through the front section of the paper looking for any mention of the wayward satellite and its projected time of fall. Each time he turned a page, he looked over the top of the paper at the corridor from which B.C. would soon emerge. No sign. A woman dragging a child dragging a teddy bear. Three young business executive studs, walking hurriedly, talking seriously, each carrying a briefcase, wearing a dark suit and black cowboy boots. After a glance at the business pages, he looked up again to find an older man with a big beer belly hanging over a belt buckle shaped like Texas with a diamond reflecting light from just about the location of Houston. And this big-bellied man was wearing an oversized cowboy hat and laughing so loudly that the sound of it vaulted through the general din and past Giacomo Berg and around a curve toward one of the French cafes. In one hand he held a small brown travel bag. And the other patted the upper back of B.C. Boyd, leading her into the lobby proper.

She laughed at something the big man said, then stopped to look around. It was one of those places where the ceiling was so high that everyone looked diminutive and the same. She couldn't stand those rooms, particularly in places where you're supposed to recognize someone at a great distance. The big man kept talking, saying something about empty office space, something about its being as big as Philadelphia, something like that.

Where was Giacomo Berg? Just like him not to be standing at the entrance to the lobby where she could see him.

Quickly to the left and to the right. She couldn't get her bearings. Then straight ahead she saw him, folding his paper, getting up from a chair and coming toward her. Was he wearing the same clothes he'd worn the last time she'd seen him in New York? For a split-second, she wished she hadn't come. And then he was standing in front of her.

She smiled. The big man stopped talking. "This is the friend I told you about," she said to the big man. He extended his hand to Giacomo.

"Bobby Mayfield, my friend. Used trucks, cars, and tars. Mighty sharp gal you're meeting here. Now you two stay out of trouble, and if you ever get to Rosenberg, look me up—'Bobby Mayfield's.' Everybody knows me." He handed the brown bag he was carrying to B.C. and walked away.

"Tars?" Giacomo asked.

"You know," she said, "They go on the wheels of cars. I brought some money and got your clothes. The super helped me pick out your wardrobe. He said I could rob you blind for all he cared."

Giacomo Berg nodded and started walking to the baggage claim area. B.C. walked beside him. Texas. Somehow she felt a little safer, on a little firmer footing here. They waited for her bags. For at least ten minutes a lone blue suitcase rode the carousel while several hundred people stood staring intently at the rubber fringe through which the luggage would emerge. Each time the blue suitcase passed, they gave a collective shrug and started their watch again.

"How was the flight?" he offered.

"Okay."

"And Bobby Mayfield?"

"Just a good ol' boy. Nice enough."

To a small cheer, the baggage began to emerge from an antechamber. B.C. stared at the mouth of the carousel.

"There they are," pointing to her two gray bags and his brown.

They extracted the bags from the river of luggage and themselves from the multitude converging on that river. Then on to the rental car parking lot, into the white rental car, and out onto the expressway. After driving a few miles, Giacomo Berg pointed to the skyline. "Houston," he said, then said no more.

Funny, she'd stayed there a few times with her parents as a kid, B.C. thought as Giacomo pulled into the parking lot of the Gulf Hotel, south of downtown Houston. The old green-roofed Shamrock Hilton used to be just around the corner. Her uncle had once taken them swimming there in the Olympic pool, around which all the swells gathered sipping cocktails after a few sets on the Shamrock's tennis courts. Her uncle had called it "the good life," making sure to point out the women in furs in the middle of a Houston summer scurrying through the hotel's lobby to the limousines parked out front. The Gulf had a pool, of course, but it was only kidney-shaped with a concrete bridge crossing over it at the midpoint. No one sipping cocktails there. No limousines stationed in the front drive. A four-floor orange, green, and white-paneled main building with the more expensive bungalows stationed around the pool.

And across the street, the cancer hospital. Beyond it, the Houston Medical Center complex. He would get a room across from the cancer hospital, B.C. thought.

He led her to a room on the second floor. "I got a suite," he said. "A few bucks more than a single room." He swung the door open and nodded for her to enter. She did.

Inside were two rooms. One, a living area with a kidney-shaped table and white naugahyde couch and easy chairs. The details of the room: the trim, the lamps, the desk, and chair were turquoise. The drapes, still closed, were orange. She pulled them aside to reveal a view of the kidney-shaped pool surrounded by palm trees beside which a man and a woman in wheelchairs sat talking while a maid emptied ash trays set on poolside tables. B.C. looked into the next room: one king bed, a "Magic-Fingers" machine attached to it, a table, and three chairs. The bathroom door closed behind her and she heard the shower begin to run. Here they were.

She opened one of her bags in the living room, looked through it, and closed it again. She looked through the phone book on the table between the two beds. "Seltzer, Stephen and Cara Fenster." How cute. How much extra did they have to pay for that? She copied the number, which she already had somewhere in her purse, on a pad beside the phone. This was a strange obsession, she thought. If he'd lived in New York, she would never look him up.

She picked up the receiver, but just as she began to dial, she thought she heard the doorknob turning in the bathroom. She put the receiver back down and walked into the living room. Why a failure of nerve? Not that he would care one way or the other. Later, she decided.

He had not yet emerged from the bathroom. She picked up a promotional magazine from the coffee table and started looking through the restaurant ads. He came out of the bathroom, and she called, "How about Vietnamese?" assuming he'd know what she meant.

He did. "Fine," he said.

"They've got a lot of it here," she said.

"Fine," he called from the other room.

This was great. Stuck in Houston by the cancer hospital with a brooding, speechless semblance of a detective. Just great. She went into the next room. "It's early," she said, "so maybe we could take a drive around. See what Houston looks like. Does the Astrodome still exist? What else? What do you want to see? A little drive out to NASA?"

He shivered.

"No NASA," she continued, "but it all must have changed so much since I was here last for any length of time, maybe ten years ago. C'mon. Let's drive around."

"Fine," he said.

And off they went.

"So are you ever going to tell me what happened?" She'd just driven him around town, had shown him everything from the ship channel to the mansions of River Oaks. Then they wandered into what the hotel magazine called Little Saigon, just west of downtown. They stopped at a place called "Truong's Blue Space—Floor Show Nightly." Inside, she was a little taken aback to find almost all men sitting around small candlelit tables, a jukebox playing disco music in the background, and a small stage lit by multi-colored klieg lights. Had they stumbled into a Vietnamese gay bar? she wondered for maybe ten seconds. When they sat down at a table, they were greeted by a waiter who appeared to be Central American, maybe Salvadoran, she thought, who handed Giacomo the menu, while saying the floor show would not start for another hour. The food was served. She watched Giacomo Berg take it all in.

"Not what I think of when I think of Houston," he finally said. "I kind of like it here."

"So," she tried again, "what did you find out?"

He sipped a little beer, put his glass down, and, still staring at the glass, said, "It's too depressing to talk about. Mind numbing. If I were Peter, I would disappear, too. He goes out there looking for sweetness and light, and what you run into are a bunch of Moonies, real end-of-the-line, be-here-now, true-believer, peyote-popping control freaks in long hair and beads. And they've been doing this for twenty years. Lost in space." He drank some more. "Then, as if that weren't weird enough, on the way there I ran into a family of Bible-thumping Christians in Texarkana. Nice folks, but unquestioning. And getting out of there, I was taken in or brought in or held hostage briefly by an old fart who had total faith that the world is about to end. He did have a kind of native intelligence. I'll give him that. But I'll tell you, B.C., there's no crisis of belief out here. I guess the word 'agnostic' doesn't apply to anyone in Texas."

"Oh, fuck you, Jack. You love it. It's not New York. That's a good thing."

She finished her Mai Tai and stared straight into his forehead. Not his eyes. He'd avert those. But she wanted to hold his attention for a second. "So what are you going to do? Any clues?"

"Not much. A few words on a postcard and some drug-assisted ratiocination from a few hippies. I've talked to his parents. They're wiring me a little money tomorrow to see if I can work out anything from the postcard. That's pretty much all I've got to go on."

What did she do to deserve so much conversation? He was almost charming. He must have been starved for company. They finished eating. Suddenly, the men all around them were clapping. A man stepped up on the stage. He said he was Truong. Then he said a few things in Vietnamese and pointed to a woman who climbed onto the stage and began singing in French with recorded instrumentation playing behind her. It was a slow, melancholy ballad, obviously filled with a great deal of pain.

"I guess they've listened to a lot of Edith Piaf," B.C. said. She watched the men around her. As the candlelight caught their faces, some seemed close to tears. The woman sang three songs, her voice sounding to B.C. almost as much like a reed instrument as a human instrument. This woman gave way to another, who introduced herself and began singing still another mournful ballad. This one was in Vietnamese. As the first singer made her way from the stage through the tables, men stopped her to shake her hand, some pressing bills into her palm. The second woman gave way to a third and fourth, each singing two or three doleful songs. The fifth singer was a white woman with a blond bouffant. Like the other women, she wore a long tunic slit up the side. Her ample build pushed the tunic to its limits. It was soon clear that she was the headliner of the show. Her appearance was greeted with loud applause. Her singing, to Giacomo's ear, sounded like that of her predecessors, but when he listened closely, he realized it was in English. A small entourage of men followed the woman off the stage and from the room.

After the white singer, B.C. turned to Giacomo to say, "I've got an old friend here I'd like to see tomorrow. Not a bad guy. I'd like to work that in somehow."

He nodded. "Do what you like."

"He's got a good law practice. Maybe I can get him to take us to lunch."

He nodded again. "Don't commit me to anything. I may have some work to do."

Not a categorical rejection, she thought. Get him away from home and he softened up a little. Better than she'd expected. Maybe there was hope for Giacomo Berg.

A sixth singer appeared on the stage. She was a good twenty years younger than the others, late teens at the oldest. Her black hair was tipped in gold, and instead of the long tunic worn by the other women, she wore black Spandex tights and a black sweatshirt. She was joined onstage by a young kid with a set of snare drums. He started the beat, then she started gyrating around the microphone, singing songs whose melody B.C. thought she recognized from the radio in her building's elevator. Top 40 hits sung in Vietnamese. A few older men got up and walked to the bar in the back. Younger men moved up to the tables in front to take their places. As she and Giacomo paid their bill and got up to leave, the singer launched into a Vietnamese rendition of "Girls Just Wanna Have Fun."

Back at the Gulf Hotel not much was said. B.C. went into the bedroom and closed the door in order to change. By the time she reopened the door, he was lying on the daybed in the front room, reading *The Discovery and Conquest of New Spain.*

"Is it my imagination, or are you holding books farther away from you every time I see you?" she asked, trying not to smile.

He watched her over the top of the book. He was trying to figure out what to say. He had hoped in her Texas they would not fall into the same ruts they'd traveled before. She sat down beside him, put her hand across his chest. "This is going to be awkward," she said.

"Let's get awkward then," he said, reaching for a bottle of rum and two cans of Coke they'd brought to their room.

And so they did.

The Deal Maker

NOW THIS. Josh came home with a bloody nose. They'd called Cara from her studio to pick him up. He was sitting at his desk during geography when his nose started running. He wiped it once then noticed red drops falling on the map showing the raw materials of India, obliterating Mumbai. First he went to the bathroom and sat with his head upside down for a few minutes, but it wouldn't stop. He went to the nurse's office, where she put a cold cloth under his upper lip.

That didn't help. Finally, they called Cara. By the time she got there, the bleeding had subsided. But Josh was looking pale, so she took him home. When they pulled into the driveway, the bleeding started again. The doctor wanted to do a blood count that afternoon. Stephen couldn't help but think of Tommy Perkins, his hand draped across the box of chocolates.

If only this weren't happening. If only his kids were not getting sick. He would give up his legal practice. He would do more pro bono work. He would become a poverty lawyer altogether with a storefront in the Fifth Ward. If only his kids don't come down with anything life-threatening, then let it hit him. He would make that sacrifice. He would spend more time with his kids, hoping that turned the tide. He wouldn't stay late at work. He would make any deal, sign any bargain, if it would keep this menace, whatever it was, away from his children.

Stephen Seltzer was forever coming up with deals he would make. They applied only to things he could not change. This had been going on ever since his first child was born. As his wife was in labor, he vowed never to raise his voice to Cara again, or to whatever children they produce, if this child would be born healthy. The birth was perfect, Tess unblemished, Cara ecstatic, and the vow broken not many weeks thereafter. But Stephen Seltzer continued crafting deals with the unknowable.

B.C. Boyd was due any minute for lunch. Not a good day for it. The Smithson brief and all. But maybe it would take his mind off Tommy Perkins and Josh's bloody nose. It had him worried. He would admit that to himself, but not to Cara. Not to the kids. Not yet. And Tess's rash. It seemed to come and go. Nothing seemed to bother Lucia, thank God, except the fact that she was not bequeathed at birth the absolute authority to run the house. Here he was at 46, and here it was, the nuclear family, and already there were little tears in an otherwise perfect picture, the one he would have painted twenty years ago if he'd been asked to conjure up the image of how he would like his life to be shaped, all things considered, twenty years hence.

His secretary buzzed to announce the arrival of B.C. Boyd. The door opened. She walked in, never as tall as he remembered her, looking younger than he thought he looked at 46.

He got up, extended his hand. She came around the desk, took his hand, and kissed him on the cheek.

"You're looking more prosperous every year," she said, sitting down in a leather chair across from Stephen's desk. "Do you have time for lunch?"

He smiled. "Sure. You're not looking so bad yourself. What brings you here?"

"New York," she laughed. "Had to get away. This friend of mine, Giacomo Berg, the detective, was down here, so I thought I'd join him. One excuse is as good as another. Thought maybe I could get back to Lockhart. Or at least breathe some fresh air."

"In Houston?" he said, thinking immediately of Josh, Tommy, and his own anxiety. "Not in Houston. But maybe in the Hill Country or on Padre or at some roadside stop somewhere.

"Why don't we go?" he said, his anxiety driving him, getting up, motioning to the door.

She followed his direction, surprised a little by its abruptness. Not what she expected from a Texan, even Stephen.

The elevator ride from his office was one of continuous descent.

"It used to take hours to make this trip," Stephen told her. "There were waiting lists for office space in here. Now whole floors are empty. It's a free fall almost every day for me. Good for business, my business, but a little wearing on the spirit."

Later, driving out of downtown in his Volvo, he picked up the theme again. "Prosperity needs a little camaraderie, you know. I like that confirmation of success that an elevator full of well-tailored lawyers reading the *Wall Street Journal* brings. You can't get a racquetball game in the building's athletic club without arranging one with a prospective partner in advance. It used to be that you couldn't get a court. Now you can't find anyone to play with. Times are bad, even, I say it again, if not for me."

"Pobrecito," B.C. said, as she used to when they had been together. "How's your family, Cara and the kids?"

"That, too," he said. "Tess has a skin rash. Josh's nose has been bleeding all day, and the kid who mows our lawn has come down with some kind of blood disease. It's not what you expect."

She couldn't believe he was starting out with so much gloom and doom. Usually he seemed bent on impressing her with both his material success and political engagement.

Something was not right.

"Of course, those are the little things. The everyday annoyances of family life. It's hard to appreciate how large they loom inside the nest if you've never been there, I guess. In the larger scheme of things, life couldn't be better. Cara's having one show after another and selling quite well. Even in this depression. The dealer said it's because she's got real recognizable talent and her work is not high priced. So people are buying it as one of many talismens that indicate that they will be included in the next cycle of prosperity and shrewd collectorship. Tess is a genius on the violin. Josh is going to a Quaker camp on an Indian reservation next summer, and Lucia is well on her way to grooming herself to be President. We've got a heated pool we built last year. You ought to come out tonight and go for a swim. I was going to ask you anyway. Bring your friend, too. The last private detective who worked for us was a character named Billy Thousands from Abilene, who wore a silver belt buckle with the number '1000' in gold on it. I suspect this New Yorker won't be quite like that."

"Not so much," she answered. That was more like it. She was afraid she'd caught Stephen off his feed. How she would get Giacomo Berg to join her for dinner in the 'burbs was quite another question. So maybe he wouldn't go. Who cared?

He pulled into the parking lot of an upscale Mexican food restaurant. Next door was a health food store advertising fresh caviar and truffles. And beyond that was a book store with a display of prisms in the window above another display featuring books by Krishnamurti and Jane Fonda, as well as a video on "How to Make Your First Million."

"Yuppie nirvana," Stephen said. "But I love it."

He opened the restaurant door for her to enter and held up two fingers to the bartender as they walked to a table. "Margaritas for two," Stephen said.

"Yes, sir, Mr. Seltzer," the bartender answered.

Stephen smiled, momentarily content. B.C. smiled, highly amused.

Giacomo Berg's Uncertainty Principle

"THIS WILL BE SO GOOD FOR YOU," B.C. said, as Giacomo Berg inserted their car into the river of late rush-hour traffic. "A good home-cooked meal in a suburban home. Kids playing on the big green lawn. Maybe a patio with a brick barbeque and floodlights. A heated swimming pool. Real life. What more could you want?"

"A Vietnamese bar. A big white woman singing Vietnamese love songs. A little weirdness to remind me of home."

"This will be weird enough. I promise you. If you get bored, spend your time watching Stephen try to justify his life and prove his political purity to me all evening. He goes through some hoops."

She was feeling pretty good about herself, Giacomo thought. Still an independent woman showing up at the house of an old boyfriend, dragging another man along to somehow attest to her New York independence.

Giacomo's eyes began to burn. He thought the air smelled unusually sweet, almost like parts of New Jersey. He didn't like it. They'd been tooling along at 30 miles an hour when suddenly the traffic on the freeway stopped.

"We'll never get there at this rate. You said it was 30 miles away?"

"Twenty-eight," she said. "I should be driving. You're a nervous wreck. They bought the house about twelve years ago when it was in an older, country-style development, called 'Glasgow Country Estates.' Then the city built up around them, leaving room, of course for all those beautiful industries that follow refineries and petrochemical plants around. Of course, we could take off for Lockhart from there."

He glanced at her.

She looked straight ahead, then laughed. "Just kidding. Don't get tense. Did Peter's family send anything besides the money?"

"Yeah. A postcard his sister Sara had gotten about three months ago from some place called Rockport. They'd forgotten about it since they thought he was still living at the Refuge when he'd written it."

"So what are you going to do?"

"I'll try this place Flour Bluff that I've decided the first postcard refers to. Maybe I'll try Rockport first to see if anything comes of that. The

Rockport card only says something about the fish jumping, so there aren't many clues there."

The traffic moved twenty feet, then stopped again. "You know, this missing person business is not for me. I'm more of a who's-been-sleeping-with-my-wife man, or a trading-corporate-secrets man. Or a who-really-owns-a-piece-of-property-my-client-is-trying-to-buy-from-a-front-organization-that-refuses-to-sell kind of guy. People you can watch and get a line on and touch. But a disappearance, an absence, a hole in the world that is sealed over as soon as it appears—I'm at a loss. And because it's Peter, it doesn't seal itself off for me. It's cold and it's lonely."

There was a break in the traffic ahead. The car in front of the car in front of them moved. Then the car in front of them moved. Then they moved, twenty, thirty miles an hour, forty-five. The brake lights went on ahead of them, and another full stop.

"If there's anything I can do to help," she said.

"Get us a helicopter," he said.

About one-half mile ahead, they saw flashing police lights. As they began to inch toward the lights, she watched Giacomo's fingers tighten, then relax, on the steering wheel. He put his little finger in his left ear. He turned on the radio, fooled around with a couple of stations, then turned it off again.

She held a bouquet of flowers they were taking to their hosts. As they rode, B.C. picked at the leaves, pulling them off, one by one. By the time the traffic moved, no leaves were left.

"Not the flowers," he said, glancing at her sideways. "Oh," she said, examining the bouquet. And she smiled.

As they got closer, she saw a large trailer turned over on its side, while the truck's cab stood upright. A line of police motorcycles and cars had cordoned off the two right lanes. The traffic siphoned into the two lanes on the left. As they approached the accident scene, she saw two paneled police trucks marked, "Hazardous Materials Disposal Unit." The overturned trailer was marked "Texas Toxics Disposal," and painted on the rear doors was the warning, "Danger—Hazardous Material." She looked at Giacomo Berg. He was sweating profusely. His fingers were white on the steering wheel.

Following B.C.'s directions, Giacomo crossed the bayou three times on two different roads before coming to a small island in the middle of the roadway. On the island was a brick wall, maybe four feet high and ten feet long, holding a metal plate announcing, "Glasgow Country Estates—The Misty Moors of Texas—Established 1964 on the Bayou."

"Here we are," she said. They drove on. Some twenty yards beyond the sign, there was another small island. A guardhouse stood there. The guardhouse was empty and seemed to have been so for a while. Painted on one window of the guardhouse was "Buffs '94."

B.C. pointed one way then another while looking at a hand-drawn map. He drove as he was told. The streets had names like Heather, Gorse, Lilac, Linden, Loch Loman, Loch MacIsaac, Ferguson Mews.

"I wonder where Loch Ness is," he said at one turn, though he found himself being somewhat impressed. It was not the characterless suburb he'd expected, with one neo-colonial perversity after another laid out on perfectly leveled, perfectly spaced lots extending ad infinitum. Instead, it was a community of what could have passed for country lanes, uncurbed, running through patches of pine forest that seemed to appear after every five or six houses, which themselves were set, for the most part, way back behind long green lawns and long red-clay driveways among more stands of pine. He could have mistaken it for some idyllic bedroom community in Connecticut or on Long Island, near the eastern end, were it not for the stifling absence of a breeze and the mosquitos that seemed drawn to the inside of the car as if by a magnet every time they stopped to debate the next turn. He looked for the kids that B.C. promised would be playing outside but didn't see any.

"Have you ever been to Glasgow?" he asked. "Nothing like this. This must have been built by someone four or five generations removed from the old sod. Smokestacks, gray sky, and dull brick buildings brought to you by the Industrial Revolution. All this linden and lilac crap would have coughed and died in one day in Glasgow."

She wasn't paying any attention. "It should be here," she said, pointing to a lane marked "Bobby Burns Rd." "Just a minute now," she said, reading the numbers on mailboxes they passed. "23145 Bobby Burns," she said, pointing to a silver mailbox just ahead. "That's it. Turn here." He turned and drove down a long clay driveway, wondering where the other twenty thousand-some-odd houses of Bobby Burns Rd. might be. He parked under a basketball hoop beside a long, low red-brick house. B.C. jumped out of the car and headed for the door. She was announced by a Yorkshire terrier, yipping from a front bay window.

Soon they were eating chateaubriand. Giacomo wondered if they ate like this all the time.

B.C. took this for another attempt by Stephen Seltzer to impress her. She didn't mind. At the same time, she'd been hoping Giacomo would say something interesting or outrageous, something New York and streetwise to break the monotonous mealtime patter, in which she had found herself asking Cara about her pottery and the two girls about school. Instead, Giacomo, the shithead, had said practically nothing. The meal had been interrupted several times by Cara or Stephen, who left the room by turns briefly to minister to the yelled requests of Josh, who was lying down on the couch in the den watching television, waiting for his nose to stop bleeding. Each time Cara or Stephen returned to the table, they exchanged worried, almost quizzical, looks.

Once they'd finished eating, Cara began to walk around the table pouring coffee, telling them at the same time that Tess had announced for the candidacy for library club president. "Tell them what that means, Tessie," Stephen said.

"Well," said Tess, "it means I have to read 23 books next year in the recommended order and hand out book report assignments to the other members of the club. And then at each meeting I have to call on three club members to present their reports. And then I have to lead the discussion of the reports. That's why I have to read all those books. And then at Christmas we have a big library party for all the kids in school, where we make exhibits of our favorite books and collect old books kids have at home to give to poor kids in Houston. And then at the end of the year I present the gavel to the next library club president they elect. And one of the things I like best."

"She hasn't won it yet, of course," Cara interrupted. "There are three other girls and a boy running, so that gives the boy an edge. But we're having the poster party over here tomorrow."

"And how's the violin?" B.C. asked. Tess winced and wiggled in her seat. "Fine," she said.

"Maybe she'll play something for us in a few minutes," Stephen said. "A little after-dinner music." Tess winced again, as did Giacomo Berg.

"At this point, she seems more interested in Gary Miller down the street than in Jascha Heifitz," her mother said, serving bowls of strawberries and whipped cream. Tess winced again.

"So you're a detective," Stephen Seltzer said to Giacomo Berg, abruptly turning the conversation away from his squirming daughter.

"Not a detective, really. A private investigator. And I'm about to try something else—maybe teaching at a community college."

"I don't think I've ever met one before," Cara said.

"A junior college teacher?"

"A private investigator. What do you investigate?"

"It's mostly jealous husbands and wives," he said. "Spouses wanting child custody after a divorce they are secretly planning. Or I track spousal kidnapping of kids lost in a custody fight. Or I work for people who don't think they're getting an even break from city government. They think their competitors are getting special favors. Then there are small-time business people who think their trade secrets are being snatched. I plug into a few databases for that. What else? A lot of real estate stuff lately. People hire me to find when an apartment or a coop in a building they want to live in will go on the market. Then they hire me to find out how to get a lock on that co-op or condo ahead of 40,000 other people. I've had a few, mostly friends, hire me so I could intimidate their landlords or building managers by letting them know I'm watching them. That never works. Most of what I do is a lot of watching and waiting. It's wading through phone directories and databases and talking to people, everybody there is to talk to. I do a lot of discrediting witnesses for defense lawyers. That's a big part of my business. A guy gets mugged. Three witnesses say a kid wearing a green jacket did it. I get hired to show the three were all dealing smack in the middle of Union Square and couldn't have seen the mugging even if they were able to see straight enough to be witnesses. That sort of thing. Not the kind of excitement I bet you were expecting."

"Not really. What brings you here?"

"I'm looking for a lost friend."

Cara went back to her dessert. B.C. watched Stephen. Her disappointment at Giacomo's performance showed. She sighed once and started to say something about her own work but then said nothing. Just then, anyway, her stop on the Central American underground railroad seemed much more intriguing to her than Giacomo Berg's machinations. Why hadn't she thought about it that way before?

Cara finished her strawberries and cream and looked at Giacomo again. "Forgive me for being such an inquisitor," she said, "but how did you get into the business in the first place?"

"I can't really remember," Berg said. "In retrospect, it seems to have had something to do with a proliferation of doubt. I did all the usual things: went to college, wrote for the college paper, protested Reagan imperialism and Iran-Contra. Did some graduate school. I read what you were expected to read: Wittgenstein, Derrida, Foucault. Finally, I woke up one morning and said to myself. Is this a life? Is this the real world? What am I doing? Kind of like the Talking Heads. So I left. I wandered around Europe, then I wandered around this country for a couple of years. I started writing for a couple of alternative newspapers and studying people like I. F. Stone and Norman Mailer and reading a bunch of journalists like A. J. Leibling and Mark Twain. Dreyer. I spent my years honing my skepticism and refining my doubt."

B.C. looked down at her dessert. Did he really say that?

"Western civilization is based on doubt," Giacomo was continuing. "That's where the power lies—in the ability of those who take power to play upon the doubts of those they rule and then to con these same underlings into suspending their doubt for a new reality. I realized that all authority is premised on the absence of doubt. And all authority is vulnerable to an attack of doubt. I also realized that I liked investigating, actively practicing doubt, but not writing about it, as I'd been doing in the little bit of journalism I turned out. So I went to work as an investigator for a company that specialized in corporate intrigue. Then I got a license and set up my own office in New York, did some free-lance copy editing to earn a living, and tried to get people to hire me so that I could infuse seemingly ironclad situations with a healthy dose of doubt and, thereby, maybe, initiate some understanding. Does that make any sense?"

"It does to me," Cara said. Stephen nodded. B.C. stared at her plate. He may believe some of this bullshit he was handing out, but she was convinced most of it was a show meant to impress Cara. Clearly, he was flirting with Cara. That's how he flirted.

"Of course, most of what I do is far removed from such grand purpose— neither earth shaking or earth moving," Giacomo continued. "It becomes like any other job, only so many times so much more depressing: people out to get even, people spying on each other, people wanting to know what no one has a right to know. Wives tailing husbands. Husbands tailing girlfriends. Competitors tailing each other and their girlfriends. When I think about it too hard, it gets to be pretty depressing. I wonder how I ended up here. I've almost quit a thousand times. But then I don't. Something comes along. You solve a very minor mystery. You help someone almost get even with a corporation. The juices start flowing. Generally, I try not to think about it too much. This time when I get back, I think I'm quitting for good. I need a better take on life."

He finished his glass of wine. Everyone was still looking at him. "What's wrong with your son?" Giacomo then asked.

B.C. couldn't believe his soliloquy. And she couldn't believe his interest in their son. He was, indeed, flirting.

"We don't get the results of the blood count until tomorrow," Stephen said, looking at his daughters. "Probably nothing, though it's got me a little bugged. Tess show him your arms. Go ahead, show them your rash."

"No," Cara said. "You don't have to." Tess kept her arms, covered in long sleeves, crossed on her lap.

Later, they were sitting in the living room. Stephen had lit a fire in the red-brick fireplace, though the evening was warm. The kids were in their rooms. Josh's nose was reported to have stopped bleeding for an hour, then started up again.

"There's something going on here," Stephen said. "Something."

"Stephen thinks we've been sprayed with Agent Orange or something," Cara said, filling four tiny glasses with Kahlua. "I think he may have been working too hard."

"She thinks I'm paranoid is what she thinks. But what would she know? She has her head half buried in clays and kilns and glazes all day long. She'll probably solidify before they cart her away."

B.C. glanced at one, then the other.

"We moved here, this direction," Stephen said, "because, not only did it have a home we wanted to buy surrounded by pine trees and the traffic into town wasn't as bad, but also because it seemed to be shielded from most of the petrochemical swamps farther to the north and the south. But somehow they've found us anyway. Now I can't drive to our golf club without feeling those little carcinogens working their way into my cells. It makes my protoplasm tighten up."

We're in Giacomo Berg's territory now, B.C. thought.

"So we move out here. Idyllic semi-urban life, complete with a pine forest and red clay drives. Blue jays and nuthatches. When we first moved here from our condo in town twelve years ago, we thought we were living in fucking Yosemite. They all think I'm paranoid. The air's pretty clear. The water looks clean. Tomatoes thrive in our garden. The squirrels aren't comatose. And my kid's nose won't stop bleeding. The schools are good. I'm in great shape. Go jogging every morning. And my daughter's entire class develops a mystery rash. Something's going on. It's either in the water or in the air. There's something out there."

"Does anybody else feel this way around here?" Giacomo asked. "Are you the village paranoiac or is everybody upset?"

"Who the hell knows? They're all Republicans out here. They'll believe anything that doesn't upset their notion of things."

"We were the only Democrats at our precinct meeting," Cara said, "except for that drama professor from the University of Houston. We divided it up. I was precinct chair. Stephen was delegate to the county convention, and the professor was alternate. You should hear the ideas the kids come home with. We don't drive a BMW or Mercedes, so we must be poor. We use a maid service instead of a regular housekeeper, so we must be some kind of hippies. Tess used to play on a girl's kickball team, and they got their uniforms from Neiman-Marcus for $125 each. Cute little shorts and shirt with matching socks and ribbons and a team logo stitched onto the shirt. And all for one night a week for eight weeks in the summer. You wouldn't believe what goes on out here."

"But we do our best," Stephen said. "You have to ignore the county commissioner out here and the township officeholders, but we get involved with statewide campaigns and send some money out of the state, wherever a liberal actor tells us to send it."

"We're big on medical aid to countries we've destroyed," Cara said. Was that a jab at Stephen or U.S. foreign policy? B.C. wondered.

"I've got some theories here," Stephen said, lowering his voice to show his seriousness. "I've been asking around, and I find these two old women a few blocks away, both coming down with Hodgkins on practically the same day. And a woman Cara knows who's lost her sense of taste. Then there are all these kids at school with the same ungodly form of heat rash. Now

Tommy Perkins, who can no longer mow our yard. And Josh, whose nose won't stop bleeding. There's something going on. I just don't know what to make of it, how to get a handle on it. But I've decided tomorrow I'm going to go check at the medical center to see if there's any unusual incidence of illness in Glasgow in general. Or if it's just our bad luck. For all we know we could be sitting on top of another Love Canal. We moved out here just to get away from that. But that could be what we're dealing with. They'll have a lawsuit on their hands."

"And what have you been doing, B.C.?" Cara asked, apparently determined to move the conversation from her husband's current obsession. "Still working with the refugees?"

B.C. had found a potted fern by the edge of the couch and was stealthily pulling thin fronds from it one at a time. When Cara turned to her, she quickly hid the fronds in her hand.

"Just a minute," Stephen said. "I'm not quite through. What do you think, B.C.? How about you, Giacomo? What would you do next?"

First to Cara, B.C. said, "Yes, more refugee work every day," smiling in a way she couldn't remember smiling since high school.

Then she turned to Stephen. "You've got to be careful, Stephen. You're asking a man who quakes at speed traps. I think you need more to go on. It could just be coincidence. You know, pre-adolescence with kids. A girl in my junior high came down with mono once, and I remember we all thought we had it. There were fainting spells up and down the hallways. Not that you may not be on to something. When the wind blows the smoke from some chemical fire over in New Jersey, I'm surprised the entire West Side of New York doesn't fall over dead. But I think you need more to go on. Have you smelled anything funny? How about the school? Have you checked the food in the cafeteria?"

"But the old ladies with Hodgkins?"

"I'd go for it," Giacomo said, looking into his hands all the while. "There's nothing that can't happen with organic chemicals. Nothing. A teaspoon of something or other in the water supply of New York could wipe out three million people in a day. You don't fool around with this stuff. Go for it. You're in the heart of the petro-kingdom. These guys don't give a shit about anyone."

He suddenly noticed the reddish brown stain on Cara's hands as she gathered the aperitif glasses. She seemed pretty dead-ahead, he thought. A belief in order and reason. He'd never known a potter who wasn't like that. Centering. Watching that wheel go around and around.

Water and clay steered into some sort of natural expression by the pressure of the thumbs. He always thought of potters as people whose feet were embedded in the earth, rooted, unmoving, even stolid. Cara moved pretty quickly for a potter. She was into the kitchen, then back out, and into the den, where Josh was calling for help. She called Stephen, who ran to the den. B.C. followed a few minutes later. She found Josh's head in his mother's lap and Stephen staring into a pool of blood on the den's tile floor. The pale boy looked up at B.C. and weakly smiled. "It's stopped bleeding," he said.

A few minutes later B.C. and Giacomo were going out the door. "But we never got to hear what you're doing?" Stephen said to B.C., "Not at lunch or tonight. I'm so obsessed with this thing."

B.C. shrugged, "Let me know about Josh," she said.

"How long will you be around?"

"I'm not sure," she said, looking not at anyone but at the car. "It's hard to say."

"What's with you?" B.C. asked Giacomo Berg as he turned the car around to drive out the long clay driveway. "Why all the sudden interest? Why'd you talk so much?"

"Let's drive around a little," he answered. "I want to see what this place is all about." They drove, not seeing much of anything. There were streetlights only at the corners, and those were far apart, given the Glasgow penchant for country living.

After a few minutes of driving, she tried again. "What is it? I've never heard all that stuff about your personal trip through modern Western Philosophy 101. Pretty soon I'd expected to hear you say Kierkegaard made you do it. Was that really you or some kind of persona you concocted to pass the time? You've never talked so much in your life."

"That's where you're wrong. That's how I work." They were stopped in front of a post office in the shopping area of the town. An insurance office next door sported a sign in its parking lot, saying, "You need liability insurance today." A billboard behind the insurance office parking lot featured a man in a white jacket with the words "Tired of Hurting? Glasgow Chiropractic Center."

"See that," Berg said, pointing to the sign. "That tells you something. It tells me, at least, that your friend Stephen may be on to something."

"What about that?" she said. "Why do you care so much? I'm the one who knows him, and I'm not sure I care all that much."

"It's not a matter of caring. It's a problem to solve. Here I was preparing to passively wait out a night with you in the suburbs and then, emerging from within the parameters of homogeneous affluence and chateaubriand, is a dark mystery: Why won't my kid's nose stop bleeding? Why does everyone at school have a rash all over their arms? Maybe there's a bad batch of kitty litter they're selling in the IGA here in downtown Glasgow. But at least it's got people worried. At least there's a little doubt thrust into the lives of this bankruptcy lawyer and potter. In spite of the house, the lawn, the cars, the kids, the perfectly scripted life, now they're grappling with uncertainty. Now they're part of what life's all about. What a revelation to them.

"The solid floor they thought they were standing on all these years has now become a flimsy lattice of spinning molecules. They're falling through space like everybody else? Don't you see? The world's become a whole lot scarier to them and a whole lot more exciting.

"Besides, how else was I supposed to get through the evening? So I open up. I tell them about me, and the bankruptcy lawyer starts to tell me about them, about his fears, about the dark side of life behind the endless lawns. It was better than talking about swimming pools and mixers back in college and listening to the girl scratch her way through a little Czerny or whatever they play on the violin. At least we learned a little something. That's better than sitting around the hot tub sipping Kahlua, isn't it?"

B.C. hadn't been in a hot tub in a long time. It didn't sound so bad to her. At any rate, she wasn't going to answer Giacomo Berg.

"Look," he said, turning to face her. "I listen. That's what I do. I look for a story. And in order to hear the story I want to hear, I usually have to tell my own story first. I open myself up. That's the rule. We exchange stories. We have to trust each other at some level to do that. By exchanging stories we build a relationship. And we need that relationship, that understanding, in order to move toward solving whatever problem we're dealing with. Now, I'll admit that sometimes the story I tell may not actually be the life I've lived. But it's at least a consistent fiction. It could be a life. It could be my life. It operates at least on a level of fictional truth, and people respond to that.

"What I said tonight happened to be true. It didn't have to be, but it was. After all, I realized you were there, and that kind of makes veracity imperative. I don't want you undermining my sincerity, you see."

"Okay," she said. "That's enough. Once you start talking I can't shut you up. Besides, you seem to enjoy the fact that they're in pain. That's pretty sick."

"I don't enjoy it, but I figure most people are dealing with puzzles they can't solve, so they bury them. Your friends, at least, are past full denial."

"You are so full of shit," she said. "Let's go back to town."

"All right. It's your call. I found our clue for the night." He pointed again to the chiropractic sign. "It's an indicator. Tell your friend Stephen tomorrow to call that chiropractic clinic. That sign could be a symbol for the entire town." They got back on the highway.

"You can't let these little guideposts go unnoticed," he said.

"I just think he may be having a midlife crisis," B.C. said. "He's about due. His whole life has been based on denial. Something has to give. Besides, what chiropractor isn't going to tell you that you're in pain?"

Giacomo waited a beat, then two. He let her finish thinking whatever she was thinking. "I can't have a midlife crisis," he said, "because I just can't believe this is midlife."

"There's the rub," she said. "Midlife crises aren't about midlife. They're about the growing fear that this isn't midlife at all. Midlife isn't a place: it's the beginning of the slalom to life's end. Once you're over the hump, it's a fast slide downhill. Old mortality occupies the big chair in your living room."

"I don't know," Giacomo said. "That may be too easy. At least Dante made his midlife crisis resonate, finding himself in that dark wood as he entered middle age. Entering middle age as he left the Middle Ages. That was a midlife crisis worth talking about."

"Well, Stephen's no Alighieri. So his crisis has to be about nose bleeds and rashes. It's all perfectly to scale. Dante at one end with his crisis of Western civilization. You and Stephen at the other, worrying about chemicals and radar guns. I'm sorry, Jack. That may just be the truth."

She was smiling fairly broadly. She'd enjoyed that interchange even if he could be an ass. One of the best conversations with another human being she'd had in several years. She leaned against the car door, playing it through again.

"Why don't you ever tell me your story?" she asked. "Don't you want to hear mine?"

"We're telling a story right now," he said, knowing that wasn't enough to say. "I just don't know where it's leading. The hardest stories to tell are the ones where you don't know how they'll end."

"I thought so," she said. "That's good." She fell asleep as he steered toward Houston.

Ancient Evenings

HE'D DECIDED TO USE a back road on his drive down the coastline to Rockport and Flour Bluff. He was sure it was something Peter would have done if he'd come this way.

B.C. was going to remain in Houston at the Gulf Hotel. She wanted to rest, lie around a swimming pool, and read. Do nothing. But he had to get going. Distance was important here and the perspective it allowed.

As they ate breakfast in the hotel coffee shop, she opened the front page of the *Houston Chronicle*. "My god," she said, "my god. A man walked into a maternity ward in Boise and shot three babies. What the fuck is going on?" She closed the paper, slid the front page section into the other sections, walked over to the trash can near the cashier, and threw it away. "I can't take any more of this. Is this ever going to stop? Babies now? Innocent babies?"

They ate in silence. He quickly drank three cups of coffee.

"Okay, I'm better now," B.C. said. "Not really, but I'm going to lie by the pool and read some shitty, engrossing novel. If I swim twenty laps, I should be ready to start again. But you have to call me several times a day. Don't leave me here alone with all this bad news."

He only nodded.

As they parted outside the motel coffee shop, a gardener was spraying the lawn with some kind of fungicide or insecticide. Giacomo beat a hasty exit. He was to call her as soon as he knew his next move. She, of course, said she wanted to go to Lockhart fairly soon. It wasn't in his plans, he'd told her, knowing they'd get there sooner or later.

He'd made copies of a photo of Peter that the Prousts had sent him. B.C. was to take copies to the Houston Police Department and the Department of Public Safety. The Prousts had contacted the Texas DPS first thing, but DPS still had no one to match the report they'd been given. Giacomo had tried to talk to DPS at length the day before on the telephone, but all he'd gotten were "Yups" and "Nopes." Was this the same as the Texas Rangers? The Department of Public Safety sounded a little too Orwellian for his money. Anyway, Peter's photo would be on their dot pattern soon.

And he was off, through rice fields and brush country. Low, flat, green farmland, cattle grazing, not twenty miles from the Gulf of Mexico. Places with names like Chocolate Bayou and Sugar Valley. Approaching a town called Bay City, and there was nothing like a bay anywhere in sight. What was there, he soon discovered, was a huge nuclear reactor rising out of the sandy loam. There didn't appear to be much activity around the reactor. Maybe that meant it was shut down. Not that you could be sure. He pressed on.

A little later, at a town called Blessing, the road turned and went straight to the Gulf. It crossed inlets and bays. There were water birds standing in marshes. It was getting hot. No breeze. The air smelled of rotting vegetation more than it did of salt. He drove on. In the town of Port Lavaca, he saw a number of fishing boats, shrimpers, and a Vietnamese grocery and restaurant. There were a couple of kids, maybe eighteen years old, in Army uniforms standing around a jeep parked at the grocery. Another long, flat stretch of land broken up by trailer parks, bait shops, small groceries, all-you-can-eat fish restaurants, miniature golf courses, and double-wide trailers turned into lounges, located seemingly haphazardly along the road. He crossed a long, narrow bridge over Copano Bay and entered the town of Rockport. A little fancier here. A development of condos offering time-shares with boats docked at the back door. A sign for Blue Wave Estates, with an arrow pointing to two- and three-story houses built on stilts behind a tastefully landscaped entrance, complete with gate and guardhouse, this one occupied.

Giacomo drove into what he figured was the middle of town. A dock advertised boats for fishing excursions, and beside the dock a small white building with a sign hawking both fresh fish and fish cleaning.

It seemed as good a place as any to start. He approached a teenage kid sitting on a crate scaling fish. "How you doing?" Giacomo asked, trying to slow down his speech without seeming to.

"Yep," the kid said.

"Catching anything around here?"

"Yep."

"What do they catch?"

"Mackerel mostly," he said, never looking up from his scaling.

"Mackerel?"

"Today, that is."

Enough foreplay. He pulled out a copy of the photo of Peter and held it up to the kid. "I'm looking for an old friend of mine that I was told has been hanging around here the past few months. Ever see him?"

"Can't really tell. Could have. Hundreds of people get on those boats."

"You don't know him or you do?"

"Can't tell. He don't strike me, though."

"Anybody else around here?"

"Nope."

"Anybody else near here who sees a lot of people come and go?"

"Over to the cafe. They're open all night and day. You know, when I'm scraping fish, I don't look up much."

Giacomo looked around for a cafe. He saw Port o'Call Cafe across the street and headed that way. It was like pulling teeth. Give him the loquacious East Coast every time. They may give you a long worthless storyline, but at least there are a few words to work with. Here everybody's Gary Cooper. These one-word answers drove him nuts.

He entered the Port o'Call and took a seat on a bar stool in front of the counter that formed a horseshoe in the middle of the cafe. Red booths lined two walls of the cafe, and a few tables occupied the space between booths and counter.

"Menu?" asked a waitress with a leathery face, whose distinguishing characteristics were not the sensory organs but the brown creases and wrinkles surrounding them. Her name tag said she was "June."

"Yep," Giacomo said. He surveyed the menu. It was an eggs-and-sausage place with shrimp and eggs an advertised specialty. He ordered shrimp and eggs.

"How hot you want it?" she asked, pointing to a sign on the wall: "One. We take your tongue. Two. We burn away your gut. Three. Just one big hole from here to there."

Giacomo held up one finger. "Baby hens and seabug. Make it sissy," she called through an open door to the back. Giacomo was glad to hear the universal language of greasy spoons.

He felt more at home.

When she brought the shrimp and eggs, he tried to start a conversation. "Lot of people come through here?" he asked, knowing it was a lame attempt.

"Honey, we get all kinds. Who you looking for?"

Giacomo gained an immediate appreciation for this woman's wizened skin. "A friend of mine," he said, pulling out a copy of the photograph. "He was supposed to have been here around three months ago."

"Three months? You might as well say three decades. How am I supposed to remember three months? Let me take a look. Yeah, he looks like just about everybody. With that beard and that long hair, he might have caught on with a shrimper. Lots of shrimpers looking like that. Or he might go out on one of the excursion boats. Tell you what. Your best bet is to come in here at three or four in the morning and talk to the shrimpers before they go out. Around five in the morning you can catch the excursion boat crews. Or you can catch them this afternoon around three or four when they come back. But they're more likely to be in a remembering mood in the mornings before they've had a chance to sit at the trough long enough to drive away the thirst they catch from that sun and that wind, if you know what I mean. Can't say I know that one specifically, though. Shrimpers might. Shrimpers are a funny people, so make sure you catch them on a good day. That's all I can tell you."

Giacomo Berg checked with the local police. They took a copy of Peter Proust's picture and threw it into a file folder. He asked where someone might latch onto a job around there, and they suggested he try Seadrift, where a lot of shrimpers dock their boats—the base for a lot of small shrimping operations. "But let me tell you," a wiry little cop with a nose like a parrot's beak told Giacomo, "they's shrimpers and then they's shrimpers. And if you don't know what I mean, you'll find out." The three uniformed men in the room chuckled, not looking up.

Giacomo decided he would spend the next few hours, while waiting for the excursion boats, in a drive up to Seadrift. It took almost an hour, the road straight as a carpenter's level though fields of maize and tall grass, broken only by more small settlements consisting of bait and convenience stores, lounges, and mobile home parks.

He made the turn for Seadrift and eventually came to a strip of double-wide mobile homes, each with a sign in front advertising "Full Body Shampoos." There was the Oriental Spa, then the Swedish Spa, then the Total Pleasure Spa, and the Girls Just Want to Have Fun Spa.

Then the Seadrift city limits. The docks themselves were at the mouth of what was called San Antonio Bay. First he tried a long wooden building advertising beer and bait. A long narrow pier ran from the building. A single shrimp boat was moored at the end of the pier.

Inside the building he found a couple of small, leather-faced men drinking beer, playing dominoes, and a big red-faced man behind a cash register, pulling on a stick of beef jerky with his teeth. "What can I do you for?" the man asked.

"I'm looking for somebody," said Giacomo Berg.

"Nobody here," the man said, causing the men at the domino table to laugh.

"Somebody who might have been here," said Giacomo, pulling out the photo.

"Don't know him," said the man, looking at the photo. "Don't exactly look like a shrimper. From that kind of beard, he looks like he might be more like a hippie. Ain't no hippies here."

"Think your friends may have seen him?"

"Look. I don't know where you're from, but they's several things shrimpers can't tolerate. That's hippies and gooks and Yankees." He leaned out over the cash register, staring right into Giacomo Berg's eyes.

Giacomo didn't flinch. Fat son of a bitch. But he couldn't keep himself from jumping when there was a sudden slap of dominoes at the domino table behind him. The fat man laughed at that.

"Look, Bud," he said, "they's a bunch of gooks at the other end of the waterfront. Maybe one of them will hire a hippie. If you don't find him there, try Indianola."

Giacomo walked out the door. Great bunch of guys.

He tried the other end of the waterfront. Inside a long tin shed he found a couple of Vietnamese women counting crates and three old men playing cards. Giacomo approached the women first. He showed them the picture of Peter. They shook their heads, said they'd never seen him, told Giacomo to try the white boats at the other end of the waterfront. The old men passed around the photo. One said, "He looks like a communist. We don't hire. The only white men we hire are the ones, once in a while, who go lose their boats over there and know what they are doing. But most of them don't come to us. He looks like a hippie. We don't hire hippies. We're 100 percent American over here."

Nice little hellhole. Giacomo studied the map. Still had a few hours to kill. Indianola was not far away. The redneck did say to try Indianola. He drove away.

What he found at Indianola were a few mobile homes up on blocks, a garage advertising used tires, and a frame building strung with multi-colored lights and gas pumps in front, calling itself "Dorantes and Son Grocery." A paunchy, older man was leaning over the counter by the cash register sipping a cup of coffee. He had blackened patches of skin covering his cheeks and creeping down onto his brown neck. Diabetes. Giacomo asked where he could find the shrimpers in the area.

"Oh," the man said, "they're down in Seadrift. Nothing here."

"They told me to try Indianola."

"Then," he laughed, "the joke's on you, my friend. Trying Indianola is like saying, try shit. Try nothing. Try nada. Try a big zero. Try the place that has been wiped from the face of the earth. Try your mother. Get what I'm telling you?"

Giacomo nodded, pulled a beer out of a cooler, paid for it, and started to drink. "Indianola," the man started up again. "This is the place that got blown away completely by a hurricane, not one but two times." He held up two fingers, the middle finger missing its final joint. "Here's your history lesson for the day. This was a nice town, pretty important a long time ago. Big ships used to come here. Then boom. In less than two days, houses, boats, people, horses, gone. They said the wind was so strong it swept the bay water over the houses. Only eight buildings were left. But they try it again. They build it up, not as grand as before, you understand, because of what they know happened, so they're a little afraid of that. But it was pretty nice all the same. And no sooner than they were able to get it started again, with the school and the stores and the bank and the post office and everything going again, where people started forgetting about a hurricane and started thinking instead about what they would wear on the Feast of the Assumption, then suddenly, boom, another hurricane comes eleven years later and levels the houses and the stores and the school and the churches all over again. That was it. It's not like they could tune into some weather channel to tell them what was coming. That's what you're looking at here. It happened a hundred years ago, but people can't get over it. People come to see the place where the hurricanes wiped out a whole town just like that Vesuvius volcano did. They come to read the marker down the road and to go to the state park where they used to have a town.

"Other people live around here now. But they don't say they live in Indianola. That would be like saying they were marked for disaster. But I like to fish myself. I had a cousin who bought this land more than fifty years ago. So I started this grocery a few years after that, and now my son is in it, too, except that he's also got that tire store and garage on the side because of all the people who break down out here. Now, we don't mind calling ourselves Indianola because you can make some money off that. Not much, but some. We've got the Indianola postcards in here and even a post office, so we've got the postmark, too. That's good for something. But when they tell you to go try Indianola, they're just telling you to give it up. Was it a shrimper who told you that?"

Giacomo nodded.

"Shrimpers. With house painters it's the paint fumes. You can figure that. And with roofers it's standing up there in the hot tar in the middle of the summer. Their brains probably get cooked up like *huevos revueltos*. You speak Spanish? But shrimpers. They've got the sun, too, but it's not that hot. And they've got the wind and the water. I don't know what it is. Probably just from what they call the elements. Too long out there with just a bunch of other shrimpers. They're just mean motherfuckers. That's all. I don't know why they are. But now that you got me on the subject, let me tell you that it might be because we are all living in a place that's been doomed for centuries. That's one of the theories I have."

Giacomo decided to take a seat at a table not far from the counter behind which Dorantes was pontificating. He flipped through an old *Field and Stream* lying on the table, not really looking at it but also not looking at Dorantes as he talked. A way to pass the time since there was nothing else in Indianola.

"This area here, see, is a peninsula stuck out here between Matagorda Bay and Espiritu Santo Bay and San Antonio Bay." He was holding a roadmap up with his finger pointing to a star designating Indianola. "And you know what happened here? This is where the first white people came to explore Texas, what we call Texas now, that is. Cabeza de Vaca—did you ever hear of him? He was right here, right here in this area. He got shipwrecked with a bunch of other Spanish people and then he wandered around living with the Indians with two or three others from his boat because the rest of them were killed. And they lived here six, seven, maybe ten years. Nobody knows for sure. They lost all track of time. They came down from around Galveston where they were shipwrecked and sooner or later after six or seven or more years they managed to walk back to Mexico. But they went the long way, up past Austin and then out west by El Paso and New Mexico and then back down to Mexico. They didn't know any better back then. They followed rivers mostly. I read all about it in some magazine.

"But what I want to say is that Cabeza de Vaca spent a big majority of his time right around here. And I read up on this. He lived near here with what they called the Karankawa Indians. And he didn't live with them by choice. He was a slave to them, except they kept him around and didn't kill him like they did most enemies because he knew something about medicine. He helped heal a few important leaders, so they figured they'd better keep him around.

"Anyway, the point I want to make is that the Spaniards claimed they were cannibals. Some accounts say they killed and ate their daughters because they don't intermarry and they didn't want their enemies to reproduce with Karankawa women. But I tell you, I did some studying on this over at the library in Victoria. And you know what I found? It was just more white racist propaganda. The Spaniards spread this around to justify their attacks on the Indians. Típico, as we say. If anybody was a cannibal, it was Cabeza de Vaca himself. He wrote that at first he had to eat body parts of his shipmates who washed onshore." He shook his head.

"I don't know. That's the kind of place this always was—with not enough food to go around and people scraping the ground to survive. The place was mean. In my opinion, that's the reason we had two hurricanes wipe out the city altogether years ago. And it doesn't surprise me that you used to see the Ku Klux Klan all around over here. My son can't understand it. He fought in Nam and he says so did those shrimpers, too, and so did the ones from Vietnam, all on the same side. And so did the Ku Klux Klan for that matter. He says he doesn't understand it. But I do. That's the way it is here on the peninsula. It's one mean son of a bitch. Yessir."

Dorantes had been leaning on the counter while talking to Giacomo Berg. He stood up, folded the road map, and put it in a drawer behind the counter. Then he walked around to the front of the counter to straighten a display of packaged cupcakes from which a few cellophane containers had fallen on the ground. "What did you want to talk to shrimpers for?"

"I'm looking for someone," Giacomo said, holding up the photo.

Dorantes looked at the photo and shook his head. "Don't remember seeing him. But not many people come through here, except for fishing season. Does he fish?"

"Probably," Giacomo said. He decided it was time to return to Rockport to meet the excursion boats coming in.

The drive back seemed to take forever, distinguished by no landmark of any kind. At one point, a great blue heron flapped up from a body of water on one side of the highway and flew across the road in front of him, no more than ten feet from the ground, to settle in a body of water on the other side of the highway. That was it. Nothing else to report.

By the time he reached the Rockport docks, a few excursion boats were tied to the moorings, rocking in the water. He moved from one to the other, poked his head into cabins and into holds. He found people who seemed to be in charge on three of the excursion boats. None recognized the photo of Peter Proust. A white-haired, red-faced man on *Molly's Dowry* told Giacomo that each boat has a crew of only two or three and they stay fairly permanent year round. He said he knew the crews of all the boats and hadn't seen anyone looking like the photo Giacomo was carrying. "The shrimpers are another story. Try them," he said. "But try 'em in the morning. I used to live up North myself. I'm giving you some good advice."

Giacomo Berg decided to take the advice. He stopped in at the Rockport Baptist Museum. It consisted of a few stuffed sea turtles and sharks, a sandhill crane, and, for some reason, a mountain lion missing patches of fur along its taxidermed back. There was a diorama of American Indian life on the coast. Two female mannequins sat by a campfire pounding maize. Two male mannequins stood, each holding a rough-hewn spear, staring off into the distance. A sign beneath the display read: "The Indians worshipped a happy God. They were a primitive people." The next few displays showed the bringing of Christ to the Texas Gulf Coast. Giacomo made a quick exit.

With maybe two or three hours of sunlight left, he decided to drive to a wildlife preserve he'd passed going and coming. Maybe he'd be able to think there, get into an investigative rhythm, a rhythm more like Peter's. At least if he had to be out in the sticks anyway, he should take the opportunity to see some wildlife while it was still living and breathing.

He followed the road through the wildlife preserve. At one point he stopped to climb a viewing tower overlooking a marsh in which, the sign said, whooping cranes and sand cranes were often found. No cranes. But two large brown pelicans were rowing through the air over the marsh, one twenty yards in front of the other, racing like sculls on a vast river. He drove a little farther until he came to a parking area and a sign with an arrow pointing to Trail No. 3. He parked and studied a marker showing the trail following a circular route through woods, by a lake, past something called "the horse barn," and then into the woods again and back to this spot. He walked into the woods, the only significant stand of trees he'd seen since leaving Houston. Not a dense forest like you might find in New England or even East Texas, but trees, nonetheless, bunched together with a modicum of underbrush.

What was it about this place—Rockport, Indianola, the Gulf Coast—that made him so uneasy? Nothing to latch onto really. And that made him uneasy. Trailer parks and sandy loam. An economy based on transients, tourists, and shrimpers. No bedrock. Impermanence. Dense, muggy air. All those things. But something else. This was not quite the city, but certainly not wilderness either. It was more a purgatory, what city and country had thrown up at their edges, the wasteland at the periphery of existence. Strip joints and dead possums on the highways. Buzzards sitting on fence posts waiting for their next repast from the detritus of civilization, the people or animals who strayed into its margins. And where was Peter Proust? What margin had he strayed into?

The sun was beginning to set. Giacomo Berg left the woods and came to a small lake. Dead black trees stood in the water like sentries. Oily black ibises inhabited the stumps. Several nearby took flight as he approached. They looked more like pterodactyls than birds, and their feathers were dark and wet-looking, as if they'd emerged from an oil slick, flying by virtue of the bones of wings rather than full-feathered wings themselves. It could be an ancient evening were he not here. Pre-human. Under the darkening sky, the lake itself began to look like the primordial ooze, a reflection of the sunset at one end to give it that hint of the original fire.

So this was the Matagorda Bay of the journals of Cabeza de Vaca. He was glad to be reminded of that. What little he could remember of those journals was the constant deprivation of body and spirit and the hardscrabble cruelty of the Indians. As it turned out, those Indians were right. Being dangerous would be their best defense. Constantly moving, gathering grubs and berries. Not able to live off all these birds and fish. He wondered why not. All he remembered was Cabeza de Vaca slowly making his way from one group to the next toward the Spanish colony in Mexico. Bartering himself into slavery—a tall, red-headed man—for two or three years at a time in exchange for his life. It was right around here that he met Estevanico, the Moor, and two others and realized all their other traveling companions were lost at the hands of the Indians, the elements, or crossing the bay. At some point, some of these people moved inland to gather pecans and cactus fruit, taking the Spaniards with them. It was a meager, grubbing existence, eyes always on the ground.

He passed a rotting stable. The path led back into the woods. It had become fairly dark, and Giacomo Berg figured he'd better speed it up in order to complete the circuit while he could still see it.

After walking about fifty yards into the woods, he heard a commotion ahead. He walked more tentatively, trying to peer into the darkening woods ahead. The leaves and brush to his right sounded as if they were being trampled by a miniature stampede. Berg decided to speed up. Suddenly he was stopped by a grunt and a snort just to the right of the path. He was confronted by the two yellow eyes of a javelina, the hair on its back clearly standing on end. He could see that much. Behind this javelina, about beagle size, were two little javelina and the churning underbrush. Giacomo Berg slowly walked along the other side of the path, his eyes always on the yellow eyes of the pig, until he was ten yards beyond it. Then he broke into a run. Behind him he heard what he thought were stampeding javelina giving chase. He didn't turn around until he reached his car, and then, looking back into the dark woods, he saw and heard nothing.

Enough nature. He drove back to the entrance of the park, where a park ranger was standing beside a barricade. "We were just about to go looking for you," he told Giacomo Berg. "The park closed thirty minutes ago. Thought maybe a gator ate you. Ate a golden retriever just this morning. Thought it might want a little dessert." The ranger laughed loudly.

Giacomo forced a laugh, waved, and headed back to the highway. He drove around Rockport and neighboring Fulton. Some wealth out by the condos, but not great wealth. The summer homes of the upper middle class of some inland city, he would guess. The local state representative might have a house here with a boat parked out back. Bank presidents from nearby towns. Judging by the Buicks and unlighted tennis courts, the real wealth went somewhere else. After making several passes through the center of town, he decided to get a motel room to wait for the shrimpers. No sooner done—it was called the "Sunrise"—and checked into, than Giacomo Berg decided he couldn't sit around in the room all evening.

Besides, the windows shaped like portholes bugged him, as did the poor reception on the television bolted to a metal stand bolted to the wall. The parking lot was filled with pickup trucks and station wagons, several with bumper stickers declaring "I'd Rather Be Fishing—Rockport." Although it was just after nine o'clock, there were lights on in most of the rooms. Fishermen playing cards and drinking before going to bed.

He walked the several blocks to the Port o'Call and decided to ride out the rest of the evening in a booth along the wall. A new shift of waitresses. He ordered fried flounder and got change for the pay phone by the door. B.C. was not in her room at the Gulf Hotel. He left the message that he would call again. He called three more times, spacing his calls at twenty-minute intervals. Between calls, he read the local weekly paper and watched the evening run its course.

In one corner a booth of three skinny men in their twenties, longish blond hair, two wearing striped welders' caps. They nursed their beers through the evening, not seeming to say much except to the waitress, blond and mid-twenties herself, but *zoftig*, a word he figured was seldom heard in Rockport. A couple, mid-fifties, was sitting in a booth directly across the room from his. Well fed. They didn't say much to each other, but when they did, they laughed. They knew the waitress fairly well, it seemed. Several times they called "Millie" to where she stood by the pie display behind the counter, asking her for rolls or coffee. Other than a skinny old man, who was sitting next to the cash register, smoking and coughing just as he had been when Giacomo was there in the early afternoon, that was about it. It threatened to be a long evening in the Port o'Call.

After the third call to the Gulf Hotel, Giacomo decided to sit at the counter in order to find out a little more about the place and to ply his photo of Peter with the evening shift. This time the waitress there was a woman with jet black hair, ruby red lipstick, and "Cora" on her nametag. She shook her head when he showed her the photo but took it to show the two other waitresses and the cooks out back. She returned to hand Giacomo Berg the photo and tell him that no one could recall that face. "But wait for the shrimpers," she said. "They've got people who come and go, make a little money and disappear and come back when they need more. They'll be here at three to four o'clock. You say he was a friend of yours?"

Giacomo nodded.

"Well, I was married to two of 'em. That's the biggest joke there ever was. You can't live with a shrimper. The first thing of it is they go to bed at nine o'clock. That's no kind of marriage lengthener if you know what I mean. And when they get home to go to bed they're half-baked and half-drunk to begin with, spending all day long out in the Gulf, peeing in the water and pulling up nets. You can't get near 'em sideways, the way they smell like shrimp all the time. No wonder they have so much trouble with women and just hang around with each other. It's no wonder. After that second marriage of mine, I asked them to put me on the evening shift here so I can leave at 2 a.m. and not be around no shrimpers. You think this place permanently smells like shrimp as it is? Just sit down here at three in the morning when the shrimpers start wandering in. You can get full just breathing.

"Especially with that second one. I don't know what possessed me. I was working here in the early mornings and in he come every morning. And he started sitting right up here at the counter. And he'd put some old Hank Williams song on the juke box at 3:30 in the morning, and that got me lookin'. And then he'd start starin' right into my eyes. He owned part of a boat with his two cousins and a brother, and so that wasn't like the first one, just some kid I married when I was just a kid myself, who dropped a couple of babies into my lap and took off, Lord knows where, to smell up someone else's shoreline with his shrimpy mess. I told him, even back then when I was young and stupid, I told him that I wouldn't have been surprised if instead of babies I was gonna come out with some half-human, half-shrimp specials. Then, after that one, it was seven years before the other one waltzed in here to get his shrimp-smelling clothes mixed up in my wash down at the laundromat. But he stayed up at nights, at least for a while, and we'd go dancing. He could do it real slow, holding on to the belt loop of my jeans the way they used to do when I was growin' up with cowboys out in Helotes, who would hold you real tight so your four feet moved like two, turning and turning around the floor. And that was nice, even though I began to notice back then that the shrimp smell could bleed right through his strong cologne. He did make an effort, right at first there, to cover up that smell. I got to give him that. But sooner or later, you know, he started getting comfortable. And when you get comfortable, you get lazy. And he'd start fallin' to sleep right after his chicken fried steak. And I didn't want to make it hard on him. He was bringing home a pretty sizable check in those days and getting up early in the morning. So I'd wait for weekends. We'd drop the kids at his mother's place and drive over to Refugio. They had a nice dance hall there. Or on nights when we was feelin' more or less like thoroughbreds, we'd head out to Victoria where they'd have some group or another traveling through, playing at the American Legion. And we could dance all night to that. But, like I said, that didn't last forever because he started getting comfortable on me. And a big pickup truck isn't enough and a nice pay check isn't enough when a man starts smelling shrimpy in my bed again. And that was just it. When his comfortableness came on, I also started to notice that shrimp smell again. And I knew it was as good as over. It may be my own failing, but I just can't go through life having my house and my clothes and my bed and my kids smelling all the time like shrimp. It's depressin'. It's like a lower form of life. Want a warmer?"

He nodded. She went back to get a coffee pot and returned with the pot and a slice of lemon meringue pie. "This one's on the house," she said. "It was just sitting there in that pie pan and I thought you earned it for listening to my life story. We would've had to kill it anyway."

Giacomo started to say something when she began again. "Just one more thing, hon," she said. "If this fella's a friend of yours, just hope he ain't no shrimper." She walked back to the kitchen.

It was just past eleven. Giacomo Berg returned to the telephone. This time B.C. Boyd answered. "I'm in Rockport," he told her. "So far I haven't turned up anything. Have you ever been down here?"

"When I was a kid," she said, "we went to Port Aransas a couple of times. Don't think I ever went to Rockport, though."

He told her about the shrimpers and about waiting for their arrival in a few hours. If nothing turned up, he'd head for Flour Bluff and call her from there. He didn't really expect anything to turn up, he said.

Then she said, "Can I talk to you about something? I think you should come back here and talk to these people. They need help."

"Which people?" he asked.

"Stephen, Cara, the whole neighborhood. I had lunch again with Stephen today. He practically forced me to. I told him about the chiropractor. He's done some more checking. There could be something here. Something like fear and trembling and sickness unto death, if you know what I mean. There are people sick all over town. Real, hard-working, well-fed people with good family histories. That's what Stephen says. But you know what he means. I'm sure they could use your help. They're so naive. I told Stephen, for all your faults, that's one thing you're not."

"You've changed your tune."

"I was just in a bad mood, I guess. You know I'm as paranoid as the next person. Won't you just talk to them?"

"I don't know that I can worry about that right now," Giacomo said. "I've got to keep pushing to find Peter."

"C'mon. You know you're not getting anywhere with that. I'm not asking you to do the work. Just tell them what to do next." As soon as she'd said it, she was sorry. She'd been thinking about his calling all evening. Now that he did, she jumped him.

"Hey. Back off a little. You never know when you're getting somewhere until you're almost there." He could let his irritation build, he thought, or he could let it go. "Let me get to Flour Bluff," he said. "Then I'll call you from there."

"Okay, okay. That's fine," she said. "That's good. I know you have to keep looking. I just thought you could fit this in. They seem so helpless."

She'd been on his mind all day. B.C. by the water. B.C. chased by javelinas. It would have been better if she'd come along. He should have made her come, asked her, begged her, offered her a deal. What kind of deal? Where were they?

He wanted to know something about her. "Did you do anything interesting, besides your lunch?" he asked. "You know—museums, movies, homes of depressed oil barons, garage sales of the petro-kings?"

"I just walked around," she said.

"That's it?"

"That and the museums. All in all, it was a pleasant day. But I am thinking about going to Lockhart pretty soon. So, maybe after Flour Bluff. What do you think?"

"Maybe so," he said. "I'll call you tomorrow."

"I'll tell Stephen you might be able to help. Just an hour or two. It won't be bad. It's funny how you feel a certain loyalty to an old love affair even if you can't for the life of you see what precipitated that affair. Good night." She couldn't figure out why she hadn't gone with him. A moment's hesitation when he asked, and then she was stuck with it. She couldn't change direction fast enough. Would this be all there is?

"Good night," he said. He decided he couldn't sit out the next three or four hours in the Port o'Call, so he returned to the motel to watch the nothing that called itself late-night television, read a little, nap, and wait. B.C. She was almost non-committal. Not quite. A little better than that. Midnight.

Three hours later he roused, realizing he had been half-watching and half-sleeping through *Village of the Damned*. A bunch of bug-eyed blond kids. He thought they were in his dreams as well as on television.

He returned to the Port o'Call. Cora was gone, replaced by Sylvia. He had no idea why he was seeing this through. Why would he think Peter was working on a shrimp boat? It was better than doing nothing, a direction to take before abandoning it for some other direction.

A few minutes later, borne on an olfactory wave, the shrimpers rolled in. In a booth by the corner, three older men sat together, smoking cigarettes and drinking coffee. Mid-fifties, turned a permanent burnt sienna by the sun. Glum, the way anyone would be starting the day at three in the morning. In a booth against the wall, four young studs were engaged in livelier conversation. One was intent on popping a glob of ketchup out of a bottle onto his breakfast steak. "Gotdamn," he shouted when one pop from the heel of his hand sent a mortar of ketchup past his plate and onto the table. "Etheline, honey," he yelled to a waitress with dyed jet-black hair standing by the coffee urn. "Will you bring a towel over here and clean up this mess?" Without a word, Etheline picked up his plate and wiped the table, then wiped the edge of his plate. "Done shot his wad again," said the man across from the steak eater, causing the other two to laugh so hard they had to get up and walk around the room.

Gradually, a few other tables and booths were taken over by shrimp-smelling men.

Giacomo Berg had a refill of coffee, pulled out his photo, and started making the rounds. The older men just shook their heads. One said he'd had the same crew for three years now, but there were always new fellas around looking for work and getting it and taking off again. The steak-eater said, "He don't look familiar to me." His buddies concurred. "Course they all don't look familiar," he added, "unless I've worked beside 'em for a month or two. No use even lookin' at a fella 'til he's been around that long. Otherwise you learn a name and a face, and soon as you look up again he's gone and it wasn't worth the bother no how." Giacomo got much the same response from the other booths and tables, though some allowed as how he might look familiar but he was not someone they may have seen lately.

Giacomo's final attempt was a booth in which three Hispanic shrimpers were eating. They looked at the photo and shook their heads. One of the three, coffee dripping from his thick moustache, told Giacomo Berg that he might have come through there but he probably got washed away like all the rest. "If he was just passing through that's what happens," he said. "*El camarón que se duerme se lo lleva la corriente.* The shrimp that falls asleep gets washed out with the tide."

Commerce

"THE MORNING COMES, the night decays, the watchmen leave their stations: For Empire is no more, and now the Lion & Wolf shall cease."

He began the morning with William Blake. Extra spiritual sustenance was required for the journey into Mountain Home. He needed matches. Losing patience with the old ways. That was the stuff of Japanese poetry. He opened his spiral journal and wrote:

Losing patience with the old ways. Flints. Sticks.
The fire in the coyote's yellow eyes. Twice now they have been
the only fire to see by.

Too many words for Li Po. More like Native American poetry. That was it. Had he the matches, he might just as well have danced around a fire singing, "Nam Myoho Renge Kyo." No, that was something else. It all ran together. As it should.

He decided to add a recipe:

HOW TO HAVE A GIRL TURN A CARTWHEEL
Find a place where girls talk together. Plant a sage bush there and water it thoroughly until it is in continual bloom. When girls congregate around the bush, ask the birds to shoot by them in rapid succession. Set free tumbleweeds to roll past them. Set the whole world in motion, so that anyone standing still will feel displaced and not in tune with nature. Grind the sage bush leaves into a powder and sprinkle this powder in the air. Set all the wheels around you spinning. The girls will not be able to stand still anymore. One by one, they will enter into cartwheels and proceed to roll off to the horizon.

He went to the bucket. Using a shirt as wash cloth, he carefully rinsed his entire body, squeezing water from the cloth. He was, after all, going into town. He wanted to write Sara. But what to write? The poem, of course, or was it a song? Again, distinctions that should not be made. He tore a frontispiece from his book. It showed Albion sitting on a rock, head bowed.

The back of the page was blank. He addressed the page to Sara, copied the poem on the rest of it, folded it, and put it in a boot. He arranged the clothes he would wear on the front porch of his cabin. It faced east. He wanted them to bake in the sun, to be warm and inviting when he entered them. That would make the journey that much more pleasurable and ensure that it began on the right foot.

What had him worried was that he would need money. He had money, but he was worried. It was a corruption he tried to avoid at all costs. But now it could not be avoided. He needed matches, pencils, paper. And he needed a postage stamp. He went to the jar he kept at the back of his shelf. He pulled a leather glove from the jar and then the folded dollar bills and coins from the glove. He pulled two dollar bills from the roll and several coins, replaced the glove, then put the jar back on the shelf. He had taken too much money. Matches and a stamp could not cost more than a dollar. But he was afraid of being found out, of someone asking too many questions. If you are to pay for something with one dollar, it is best to pull it from a pocket containing at least two. That way no one would think it was your last dollar and that you might be thrown upon their mercy. That way no one would be inclined to ask you questions. He wanted no mercy and expected none. It was not something he believed actually existed. It was a phantasm, something made up by doctors of divinity and preachers to give some sense of goodness and order to the world. He did not want to be caught in that trap.

And no questions. No one knew he was here. He walked into town taking a different route each time, so no one knew which direction he had come from. There were three stores in Mountain Home. He had tried two of them on his previous two trips. This time he would patronize the third.

They would think, if he were lucky, that he was just passing through. No questions. He wouldn't want to risk losing the cabin for a few matches or a stamp. It wouldn't be worth the risk.

Having collected the money, he then needed a place to put it. He went to the porch to get dressed. He pulled the poem from his boot and put it in his shirt pocket with the money. He poured the remaining water from the bucket on his head and attempted to smooth down his hair. He tied a string through the hole in the door where a knob used to be and tied the other end to a nail on the doorframe. He laughed. What could that keep out? Only something bigger than a rat and littler than a man. He walked down to the road and along the road, crossing the creek. Too difficult to say how far it was or how long it would take. He just walked. Judging by the sun, it was mid-morning. Barbed-wire fences lined most of the length of the road. Gravel and caliche. Not a car or a truck to be seen. This was a lucky journey. He came to a flock of Angora goats standing near a fence. A few started as he walked by, but most just stood there calmly chewing. He felt blessed.

Farther along he came across some kind of carcass that had been picked clean. Once a deer. The brown fur in places. It had been there so long it had ceased to smell. He came to a road leading to a ranch house. Two black sheep dogs ran halfway toward him from the house, barking. He walked on.

Where the dirt road met a larger paved road, he found a portable aluminum building and a space cleared for a parking lot. A long red car was parked in front of the building. On top of the building was a sign announcing "Mountain Estates" with a painting of a deer beside a cedar. This had not been here the last time. This journey had suddenly taken a somber turn. Perhaps he should have turned back and tried it another day. He pressed ahead, knowing in all likelihood that the building would remain.

Not far ahead was the first church steeple of Mountain Home. He stopped to devise a plan of action. He would take the first road crossing this road and circle around the first two blocks of houses, coming onto the main street again in the middle of town. That would put him not far from the market. His stomach began to cramp. He went behind a scrub oak, put his fingers down his throat, and retched. Feeling purged, he set off again into Mountain Home. It was not yet noon. The sun was shining. The walk had been invigorating. But he was experiencing misgivings he hadn't had when he'd started out.

He came to the edge of town and walked down the first road on the right. It led past large brushy expanses and seemed to go forever before finally being intersected by another road, which Peter took. It was a caliche road running between stone houses, each with a cedar tree or two beside it. A couple of roads intersected this one, and he took the second into the middle of town, arriving at Main Street, across from the corner occupied by Koenig's Ice & Grocery. He had been there once. To his left was Rudeloff's

Market; he had been there, too. He thought he'd remembered seeing a third grocery in town. Turning right, he walked two blocks and found it, J & A Ice House and Food Store, Mexican music playing inside. From the street he tried to peer through the screen door bearing a sign for Big Red soda. Should he enter? At this moment? He took a deep breath and pushed the swinging screen door.

He wandered among the shelves of the store, intent upon his quest for kitchen matches. Down one aisle and up the next. He found the matches. A box of 250 would last him over two months, even with wet weather. The package with four boxes of 250 each could take him beyond half a year. Who could think that far ahead? 99¢ That would leave him just over a dollar. He looked for pencils. Finding them among school supplies, he picked up two. With a stamp, that would leave him a good 65 cents still. He'd forego the paper this time. He took the package of matches, turning it over and over in his hands, listening to the shifting of matchsticks. Now he wandered the aisles, looking for something; he was not sure what. He might be thirsty later. He examined the soda containers. All the large ones were made of plastic. The small ones were in six-packs of cans. He could use a large bottle, but not plastic. Deep on a shelf, he found a glass bottle, marked "Grapette" and "Large Size." He figured it had to be less than 65 cents.

He went to the counter, where the man said, "So, this is all you want?"

What did he mean by that? The stamp. He should ask about the stamp. "One dollar and sixty-three," the man said.

"Stamp," Peter said. "I'd like a stamp for this card." He pulled the folded paper from his pocket along with the two dollar bills.

"Hold it," the man said, and turned down the radio beside the cash register. "What did you tell me?"

"Do you sell stamps?" Peter asked again. It was an effort to make himself understood by others.

"No. The only place is down the street at Rudeloff's. They have the post office in there." The man gave Peter his change and put the matches, pencils, and soda in a paper bag, pushing the bag into Peter's arms.

Peter barely noticed. He was preoccupied now with the prospect of going to another store, one in which he'd been before. He walked out the door and looked down the entire length of Main Street toward the Rudeloff Market. He could just forget the letter. He could walk back the way he came. He'd known there was something wrong when he saw that aluminum building. Things had started out well, but then they had turned wrong, and he should have listened to that. He should have turned back when he saw the aluminum building.

He walked down Main Street, clutching the paper bag, holding the letter between his fingers. There were few cars parked on the street. No one seemed to be looking at him. It could be a trap of some kind. Wait for the man to come down off the hill for supplies and then surround him. It was his own laziness that had trapped him, needing matches to light a fire.

He'd thought he was above it all, that he didn't need civilization. But that was vanity. That was false pride. He needed matches. He was still a slave.

He was now in front of Rudeloff's Market. If he carried the sack into the market, would they look inside the sack? Would they think he was hiding something? He went around the corner of the market building and leaned the sack against the building. Still carrying the card between his fingers, he took a deep breath and walked inside. The post office window was to the right. He remembered having seen it that other time. Did they remember seeing him? The man at the counter—he couldn't remember if that was the same person who was there the last time.

The woman at the post office window. He didn't remember her. He stepped to the window and said, "A stamp, please." "Postcard or letter?" she asked.

He didn't know. He held up the letter folded in his fingers.

"That might pass for a card," she said, examining the paper, "but it might be too limp. Just to be safe, let's call it a letter and put it into this envelope. It will only cost you an extra nickel."

He nodded. She took the paper and put it in the envelope with the stamp printed on it.

He handed the woman the change from his pocket. She counted out her portion and returned the rest, staring intently at Peter's confusion.

"You'll have to address the envelope now," she said, offering him a pen. He wrote the address on the envelope, sealed it, and handed it to the woman.

"We'll take care of it for you," she said, smiling. He nodded and walked out the door.

The woman looked to the man behind the counter, who shook his head.

He was out. Peter collected his sack from the side of the market and walked quickly out of town. Out to the aluminum building and then quickly onto the country road. Climbing up into the hills, he began to breathe more easily. When he reached the creek, he removed his boots and walked around on the small stones of the creek bottom. He cupped water in his hands and threw it on his face. Then he climbed the hill to his cabin. There he found his knife with the bottle opener and opened the bottle of Grapette, trying to bend the cap only slightly. He took a sip and spit it out, the sweetness shooting right to his brain. He took another sip, put the cap back on the bottle, tore open the package of matches, pulled out a match and struck it, holding it up to his face. He let out a howl like a coyote. "Owooo."

He had survived another meeting with civilization.

Of Memory and Forgetting

"WITH THE DINOSAURS. Learning to walk backwards. Waiting to be born."

Determining the card had come from Flour Bluff had not been difficult. The trajectory from Rockport seemed to confirm it. But how to find him in Flour Bluff? How to come up with a better run of luck than in Rockport?

To get to Flour Bluff he had two choices: stick to the mainland and cross through Corpus Christi or take the ferry crossing to Mustang Island and drive from there down through Padre Island and back to the mainland at Flour Bluff. The latter sounded more enticing. To reach the ferry he crossed a spit of sand dominated by giants of multinational industry. On one side was a high fence surrounding a sandy expanse that was home to a subsidiary of Bechtel. On the other side, there was a fence running for some distance, broken by gates and guardhouses for Brown & Root and Halliburton. Huge partially assembled oil rigs and offshore drilling platforms lay on their sides inside the Brown & Root compound. One rig, without too much effort, could be seen as a giant preying mantis wading through the shallows of the Laguna Madre in some Japanese post-atomic disaster movie.

He waited in line to board the ferry. It bore the name "Nellie C." A large brown pelican commandeered a post on the corner of the ferry and rode the waves of the bay in that position. Giacomo Berg took this to be a good sign. Not a flashy bird. Large, steady, homely and awkward, except in flight. A utilitarian bird, not lacking in grace. He got out of the car as the ferry crossed the waters of the lagoon. Alongside, three porpoises broke the surface and completed their arcs, hitting the water again in unison, embroidering the surface of the water alongside the moving ferry with a series of loops engaged in, it seemed, for their own enjoyment. "The mind leaping like dolphins," he remembered from Pound. If only his mind were. Great poetry seemed far removed from this place. But auguries were everywhere. He took them to be for the good.

At the other end of the crossing, the ferry met the landing, the gates went up, the cars' engines revved, and they drove out onto the island.

Giacomo Berg followed the signs leading through the tourist enclave of Port Aransas to a long, thin, straight road cutting the narrow island down the middle. Soon the condos and hotels at the southern end of Port Aransas played out, and there was just sand on either side, dunes to the left against the Gulf and flatlands and marsh merging into the lagoon on the mainland side. Grasses and succulents, and every once in a while there was a small body of water inhabited by reeds and water birds. He thought he recognized a roseate spoonbill, though he couldn't be sure of that. B.C. would probably have known.

He crossed the small causeway from Mustang to Padre Island. A couple of boys were standing on the causeway, inspecting large chunks of meat tied to ropes. He slowed down in order to watch them pulling crabs off the meat and tossing them into a bucket. Farther on, he ran into a row of high rises, a strip of surf and shell shops. Then a sign pointing to Corpus Christi and Flour Bluff.

It was difficult to determine where Flour Bluff began. An old sign on a building proclaimed it the shopping center of Flour Bluff. But there was also a Corpus Christi city limit sign and a Naval Air Station sign.

He pulled into the parking lot of the Flour Bluff shopping center, housing a shell shop, a fish market, and the Seaside Grocery Store. Inside the grocery, he found all three shops were merely three separate entrances to the same store. And behind the central counter of this store he found a red-faced man in his sixties, whose stomach was testing the limits of his Mexican guayabera shirt.

"Hello there, stranger," the man called out to Giacomo Berg. "What can I lead you to."

"Information, I hope," Giacomo answered.

"I'll provide it if I can sell it."

"I'm looking for a fella," Giacomo said, laying the photo on the counter. "Ever see him?"

"Can't say as I have. Is he a surf bum?"

"No, a carpenter. Are there any dinosaur tracks around here? Or a museum?"

"No sir. Not many footprints get preserved in these sands. Closest I can get you is that we used to sell Sinclair gasoline out front here years ago. Had a big old green dinosaur balloon flying on top of the building.

Kids liked it. But then we changed to Getty. Thought it was the wave of the future. Well what it was, was a wave goodbye. Ain't nobody down here got a Getty card. So we went out of the gasoline business just when everybody started lining up for blocks at the pump because of the Arabs' embargo. Good riddance to it all I said then and I'll say it now. Whatchou want a dinosaur for?"

"Just a question. Where's the police department here?"

"Well, we ain't got our own since we was annexed, but we still got the sheriff up the way. But don't ask him about a missing person. That's like asking a priest for sex therapy? He's got a lot of theories and opinions and he's even run off and bought himself a computer, but he couldn't find his own asshole with a ream of toilet paper, if you know what I'm saying."

Giacomo said he did and got back in the car. At the sheriff's office a couple of blocks away he found the deputy in charge, a man in his late twenties by the name of Williams. He showed Williams the photo and asked if he'd run into anyone named Proust or Oman.

"He looks kinda familiar," Williams said, screwing up his face to focus more exactly on the problem placed before him. "Let me run it on a computer check. We've got a new computer right over here," he said, sitting down behind a screen on his desk. "Finest goddamned baby in the history of crime control. Now I'll just punch up the name of your friend right here, along with the aliases, and see what we come up with." He punched a few keys and whispered, "Damn. Had to go to a special crime control school in Austin to learn how to run these things. It keeps you occupied." He punched a few more keys. "I see here you've already got him listed with DPS. That's a good thing. That's smart."

Giacomo nodded.

Williams got up from the screen and walked back over to Giacomo. "Well, nothing new. If there was something, it would've come across on the screen. He did look a little familiar, though. Mind if I put that picture up here on our missing persons board? You never know when someone will wander in and know a fella."

Giacomo turned and started to leave. "How much is there to this Flour Bluff?" he stopped to ask.

"Officially or historically?"

"Either way."

"Well, officially it don't exist no more. They annexed it into smithereens. But as a fact of history it's been around for as long as most folks can remember. Used to be the town closest to the Gulf that wasn't blown away by hurricanes. Used to be a tourist spot before they got those permits to build hotels right out on the Gulf. Now Corpus runs from here clean over to there, and we ain't nothing much to nobody no more. It's kinda gloomy."

Giacomo asked, "But, when there was a town, how far did it stretch? What would you call Flour Bluff?"

"Oh, I'd say from the entrance to the Naval Air Station to that big bait and tackle store you see with the painting of a shark about a mile down the road. That used to be the first thing you'd see when you came to Flour Bluff. We still got our own high school, but the team's not worth shit anymore. Not like it once was."

"Thanks for your help," Giacomo Berg said, backing out of the room, leaving the deputy still pointing in the direction of the high school.

He sat in the car, trying to decide his next move. As he turned on the ignition, he noticed that next door to the deputy's office was a nursing home, the Ocean Breeze convalescent home. Peter had worked in nursing homes once in Florida. He decided to try it. He walked through the glassed entrance, where three old women in wheelchairs greeted him with a wave. He asked the woman at the front desk if she recognized the photograph.

"You'll have to ask the director about that," she said, pointing to a door marked "director" behind the desk.

"I'd like to do that," Giacomo Berg said.

"Oh, but he's not in at the present," the woman said. "He won't be for a little while. It is his lunchtime, you know."

"I didn't know. Can I wait here?"

"Certainly you may," the woman said, "but just up here in the lobby please. We don't want to cause any more confusion than there already is around here."

Berg took a seat on a couch near the main entrance. One of the three old women waved to Berg to come over. He did, bending over the woman's wheelchair in order to hear her.

"What's the weather like outside?" she asked.

"Not bad," he said. "A little on the warm side. And muggy."

"Isn't that always the way," she said, turning to the woman on her left, who made no sign of acknowledgment, staring straight ahead. "And who are you here to see?" she asked Berg.

"I'm waiting for the director."

"Good luck. He's a very busy man. I tell him, Mr. Simmons, we're all going to outlive you at the rate you race around. But you know there are a million things to attend to here in a home. There's food and linens and nurses and the other help. And all these old folks. They don't leave you a minute to yourself. What do you want to see him about, if you don't mind my asking? Do you want a job?"

"No. You see here," Giacomo said, pulling out another copy of the photo, "I have a friend I'm looking for. And his family seems to think he may have come through Flour Bluff. You don't know him, do you?"

She took the photo, holding it up close, then as far away as her arms could reach. "Now he does look familiar. How about you girls?" She turned to the woman on her left, but found that she had fallen asleep. "No help from these two, but he does strike a resemblance to someone I've seen around. You know, when you get old, a lot of names and faces run together. You'll find it very frustrating when your time comes.

"My best advice to you right now is to check with one of the men. Mr. Fenola would be a good start. He's still got most of it up here," she said, pointing to her head. "Most of the young men who work here are either cleaning up or they have them tending to the men. The men are heavier, see, bigger bones, and so they need the young men to lift them up. The nurses, they can handle most of us old ladies. Besides, they don't want us getting any ideas. I know I wouldn't mind having a young man lift me up every once in a while."

"Where do I find this Mr. Fenola?"

"Oh, he's usually in the parlor playing cards or taking a little nap. But don't run off. I have more questions."

"I'll be around," Berg said, straightening up. "You've been a big help. Thanks."

"Not at all. Tell him Dorothy sent you."

Could he pick Mr. Fenola from a room of seven old men, four sitting around a card table, three dozing in easy chairs? He approached the card table, betting with himself that it was the man with the diamond pinky ring. He asked the card players if one of them was Mr. Fenola.

"You've got him," said the man to the left of the pinky ring. He was wearing a green fedora. "What can I do for you?"

"I'm looking for this man. Do you know him?" He handed the card to Fenola.

"Yeah. Sure I know him. He used to work around here. Not long ago either. Had a funny name. Sure."

He couldn't believe it. He'd finally stumbled onto something. If he could just nurse this along, from one old man to another, maybe their collective memory would turn up something.

The man with the pinky ring grabbed the photo and said, "I know this guy. A real character with his hair longer than a girl's. But a nice guy, though. Never treated you like dirt like some of them do. He did have a funny name." This man showed the photo to the other two, who nodded.

"How long ago was he here?" Berg asked. "Do you know where he went?"

"Who can keep track of time?" said the pinky ring. "He could have been here a month ago. Or it could have been a year ago. You just lose track."

"Cecil died two months ago," Fenola said. "I remember that. It was a Thursday. I don't think he was still here then. Although I could be mistaken."

"Hey, Cecil died six months ago. You know that. How can you remember when an orderly was here?"

"I still think it was two months ago. Listen, fella, I'm not gonna argue with Benavides here all day long. Let me tell you who to talk to. Go see Jeremiah Smith. He's down the long hall to the right. I think he took a special liking to your friend. It seems that I remember that. He doesn't have any legs, so you'll find him there. He can't wander off. Tell him Fenola sent you."

Giacomo found the door marked "Mr. J. Smith" and knocked.

"Come on in," a voice replied. Giacomo Berg pushed the door open and found an old black man in bed, his head raised slightly, watching television. The man looked at him. "Are you looking for me?" he asked.

"I hope so," Giacomo replied. "Actually I'm looking for a friend, and Mr. Fenola said you might know him." He showed Smith the photo.

"Oh, my, my, yes. He's such a sweet boy. Do you know him well?"

"I used to."

"Well, he's a peach. Where's he gone to? Can you tell me that?"

"I was hoping you could tell me."

"Oh, no, even if I could remember, I wouldn't know. One day he was here, and the next day he was gone. That's how it is in life. I'm resigned to that fact. Look at my legs. Diabetes got 'em. But I can still feel 'em. Just like they were still there under the blankets nice and warm. A lot of the people here, they don't remember things because they can't. I don't remember because I just don't want to. I don't remember my legs are gone. I don't remember my wife is dead. I don't remember my boy Freddie didn't come back home from Vietnam. I just don't remember those kinds of things unless you ask me to, unless you make me stir up my mind. I tell old Mr. Blumenthal he's lucky not knowing who he is or how he got here. I tell him, 'You're sitting here. You're talking. You look like a man of 33'—I tell him that. 'So if you can't remember otherwise, who's to say you're not.'

"Where were we? Come in. Sit down. Oh, yes. You're looking for Oman, that sweet boy. He used to give the nicest baths. Just run water all over your body, get the water all nice and warm. Not one of these quick jobs like you usually get—pour on a little soap, spray you off, wipe you down, and throw you back in bed. No, it was a real pleasure. It was something to look forward to. It was a way to remove your thoughts from all this here."

"But you don't know where he went from here?" asked Giacomo, interrupting the reverie. "He used to come in here and sit when he had free time, and I'd tell him all about my fishing days. I'd tell him about fishing for the old big-mouth bass I used to catch up on Caddo Lake. How you would sit there for hours, from right when the sun came up until well past noon, waiting for the big-mouth, knowing one day, maybe this day maybe the next, that big old fish would bite. But the particular day didn't really matter because they all run together out there fishing, and time is like it just stops dead, throws in a line, and waits for something else to happen. That's what it is. It could be sunup or it could be sundown or it could be noon. But it doesn't matter because time is not the ticking off of seconds on the clock. It's not the measuring of days or months or years. Out there on the water it stops dead still, from the minute you throw the line into the water until the striking of that old big mouth on the line. In between there is no time.

"So he'd be sittin' here where you are, rubbin' that old beard of his, and I'd say, 'Honey'—I liked to call him that just like I called my own boys and girl—'Honey,' I'd say, 'Why don't you get on up here in this boat and we'll do a little fishing here and take advantage of the weather.' So he'd climb on up here on the bed and we'd talk and it'd be outside of time. I'd tell him, 'Honey, this way you don't have to go back to work and I don't have to grow old.' I could tell he liked that."

"What would you talk about?" Giacomo asked.

"Most anything. About fishing. His life. My life. His life, mostly. He did tell me about the troubles that he'd had before coming here, trying to live with the people when they wouldn't have his way of life. I told him, 'Honey, not everybody can always get along.' But he wouldn't let me say that. He'd always come back with 'But they should, Jeremiah. They should.' I just had to laugh and tell him he should have learned his lesson by now."

"Did he give you any idea where he might go after this? Did he tell you anything about his plans?"

"That was one boy who did not have any plans. But where he might go after this—that's something I have an idea about, but I don't want to have to try to remember my idea."

"What do you mean?"

"Let me tell you something else. Do you see that plaque up on the wall? He had that made and gave it to me for my room. It says a lot about him, don't it?"

Berg read the plaque mounted on the wall above the television set: "It seemed as if I might next cast my line upward into the air, as well as downward into this element which was scarcely more dense. Thus I caught two fishes as it were with one hook."

"Two fishes. See there. It makes some sense. That boy, he did make some sense. How well did you say you knew him?"

"We're old friends. Went to college together. Shared a house for a while. Do you know where he lived around here?"

"We never talked about it."

"Did he have any other friends?"

"I wouldn't know if he did. He never talked about no friends. Now the reason I'm asking about you being friends..."

"Why'd he leave?"

"He didn't leave. They kicked him out. Mr. Simmons said he wasn't making any sense. I told Mr. Simmons that boy had more sense than all the Johnny Carsons and Phil Donahues put together. But they don't listen to the old folks around here. Getting a recommendation from one of us is like being put on one of them fighter jets over at the navy base—you gone. But what I really want to say is, seeing as how you're the close friend you say you are and not some kind of spy from that place he used to live that he said might be coming after him or some kind of FBI agent or something, what you should know is sometimes that boy sat up here and talked about taking his own life. He talked about it. Said he had a gun. Said he kept it loaded in case the right time came around. Said he thought he was dying anyway. Said he felt his stomach grinding away into nothing. That boy worried me. I told him to see the doctor when he comes around.

"He said he doesn't trust doctors. Said they fill you full of foreign substances that won't make you live any longer but that you end up dying with a lot of things in you that are not your own true spiritual self. That boy did need help. I know that. And I tried to get him to see a doctor or maybe just put the gun away, throw it in the water and walk away. I tried to talk to him about it, but there wasn't all that much that I could tell him. I couldn't get down off this bed and go down to where he lives and take that gun and throw it in the ocean. Hell, I can't even get down off this bed to go wiggle my hooter over the toilet. It's such a shame. He made so much sense in much of what he said. Who was I, I thought, to tell him to go on living, when I can barely open my eyes some mornings myself? But I thought you should know this. Somebody who knows him should."

Giacomo Berg sat silently taking it in. There were currents running past this man's bed.

To someone of his fatalist dent, this news was not a complete surprise. But suddenly it gave shape to this disappearance. The absence became a presence charged with electricity. As if Peter literally, and not just figuratively, had stepped off the face of the earth.

"Is there anything else? Anything I should know?"

"Once he didn't show up here for three days, and I started to worry, knowing what he might have been thinking. All I could do was sit here and try to put my mind on it, try to believe that that boy was working things out for himself, that he would get himself under control. And sure enough, he showed up here the next day. And he told me that he had taken the gun and he'd gone way out Padre Island down past where the road stops, where there aren't any people to get in the way. And he'd walked until he found a big old sand dune out facing the water. And he sat on top of that sand dune and he put the gun right in front of him, pointed at him, I think he said.

"And he said he was going to just sit there to see if the time was right. And he sat there when the sun went down and all night long, and when the sun came up again, he was still sitting there. And he figured that was not the time. So he came on back here and put the gun away for a while.

"I asked him, 'Honey, how did you know if that was the right time or it wasn't?' And he said, 'Jeremiah, I didn't know it wasn't the right time, but I also didn't know that it was, so it must not have been.' He made some sense, that boy. I hope you find him. And I hope you find him alive. And if you do, tell him hello from Jeremiah Smith."

Giacomo Berg patted the old man on the shoulder and returned to the director's office. "Mr. Simmons has been looking for you," the woman at the front desk told him, pointing Giacomo to the office door. "I'd asked you not to leave this front area."

Giacomo walked into the office to find a bald man of about fifty sitting behind a desk. "You were looking for me?" Giacomo asked.

"I think you were looking for me."

"What I'm looking for is information on someone who used to work here. He used the name Oman. Or Peter Proust."

"What about him?"

"How long ago was he here? Do you know where he might have gone?"

"You a cop?"

"Private investigator hired by his family. He seems to have disappeared."

"Small wonder. The fellow was a basket case. I wonder how we hired him in the first place. He'd come marching in here every day with some complaint. Either we were poisoning everybody with the food or we ought to take out the air conditioning and put in screened windows and porches. Or we ought to let these people have conjugal bedrooms. People who aren't even married, who never met each other until they ate jello together here. I could just see their families' reactions. So I let it run on for a couple of months, and then I fired him. It was just one complaint too many. He was going around the lunchrooms scooping the chop suey off everybody's plate, telling them it was prison food and that it was filled with poisons. That was it. We meet all our inspections. I pulled him in here and fired him. That's all I know."

"How about an address? Do you know where he lived?"

Simmons looked through a file cabinet and stopped, saying, "Here it is. 324 Conch #143. That was three months ago. He came by for his last paycheck and that, as far as I'm concerned, is the end of him."

Giacomo Berg found 324 Conch, a few blocks off the main road. Nondescript, two-story apartment building, maybe 15 years old. The manager was a young woman with two screaming kids—a baby in her arms and a little boy at her knee. She knew nothing. He paid his rent. Was there for three or four months. She could look it up. One day he moved out. Left no forwarding address. That's all she knew. Never saw anybody with him. He didn't own a car that she knew of. He could try other residents, but most of them hadn't been there three months. They move in and out, she said, taking advantage of the first month's free rent at apartment complexes all over town. In and out and on to the next free month. That's all she knew. He paid in cash. Nothing sticks out about his being there. Just a face in the crowd, she told Giacomo Berg. He was here one day and then he was gone.

He knocked on doors. No one home on either side of #143. New people in both, she'd told him. The few people he found around said they didn't know who he was talking about. He hung around the parking lot for a few hours, stopping people as they got out of their cars. No luck. Dead end. It had been a small break, an opening. And then it was gone.

He called B.C. He told her what had happened. She was sympathetic. She asked what his next move was.

"I'll talk to the family," he said. "See if they know anything about this suicide business." She didn't respond.

"So what are you going to do?" he asked.

"I thought you might want to meet me somewhere," she said, "and then we could drive to Lockhart. I have to talk to you about Stephen, too. It's a bigger problem than you might think. It's like quicksand. Every time he takes another step, he sinks in deeper. I thought maybe you could help." This time he didn't respond.

"Of course, that's if you have time. I mean, if you're stuck with this other thing."

"I don't know," he said. "Where do you want to meet?"

She hadn't expected this. But she was ready all the same. "There's a bus tomorrow that stops in Seguin at noon. You could meet me there. It should be right on your way."

"To where?" As if he didn't know.

"To Lockhart, of course. We can go there and talk this out. You'll like it. You'll see." "I've just got to think this thing through. Everything's become more urgent."

"Of course."

They agreed to meet at the Seguin bus station at noon, wherever that was. He called the Prousts. He told them what he'd found—the nursing home, the apartment. He tried to measure the level of anxiety in their voices. He asked about suicide.

There was a pause. Mrs. Proust said, "Well, he did once tell his sister that he was considering it. It was a phone call from somewhere that first time he left the commune. He said he had pretty much decided that sooner or later he would take his own life. I think about it every day that we don't hear. I'm sorry we didn't tell you before. It's something you don't want to believe about your own child—that life could be so hard."

Giacomo waited, thinking she might be composing herself to say more. She didn't say anything else.

"I'm not sure what to do next," he said.

"I've got to think about this a while. I'll call you in a couple of days. Maybe something will come to you or me by then. Of course, if you hear from him again, call me right away."

He put down the phone. He was sinking fast. Rather than spend the night in Flour Bluff, he decided to drive toward this Seguin. He went to the car, pulled out the map, studied the route, and took off. By the time he hit a town called Beeville, he was exhausted. He drove around the main square with its county courthouse and a jet fighter mounted so that it appeared to be taking off from the courthouse grounds. He found a motel, checked into a room, turned on the light to see how it looked, turned off the light, fell on the bed, and was out for the night.

The Brisket Eaters

IT WAS A TALK SHOW coming out of Austin on radio station KLBJ, founded by and for the continued prosperity of the Late Great President and his heirs. The subject was the current President's news conference of the evening before in which the President had apparently defended selling arms to an enemy. The talk show host was keeping a running tally of calls from his listening audience.

Thus far, ten supported the President's position, eleven were opposed. Giacomo Berg had only been half listening as he made the drive north to Seguin. He seemed to have stumbled into Eastern Europe: grocery stores advertising Czech foods, a Czech bakery. A huge Catholic church just off the highway dominated the town of Panna Maria, which was followed closely by Pawelekville. Giacomo Berg had difficulty associating Texas with anything European, anything civilized for that matter.

"Hello. You're on the air," the talk show host was saying. "What do you think about the President's remarks?"

"Well," a man's voice said. "Now it's hard for me to judge because I didn't hear the speech and I'm not familiar with the issue, but just on the basis of knowing nothing that was said, I have to support the President."

"Thank you sir," the host said. "That ties the voting."

Giacomo Berg felt like he had lost a lot of ground. He had picked up the trail, followed it a short distance, and then it had petered out. He picked it up again, advanced a few steps, then lost it again. Would he be able to find it again? And now the bigger question: would he be able to find it in time?

He found himself suddenly engaged in a race not only against space but against time.

Three dimensions were difficult enough, locating Peter as a focus on a grid. But four dimensions. Will he have ceased to exist in time by the time Giacomo found him in space, if he found him, if his ashes have not already been scattered across the wide world or his bones left to bleach in some far field?

What next? Should he wait for divine revelation? For further revelations from the Proust family? What else were they holding back? And money? How would he survive this pursuit beyond a few more days? But mostly, where was Peter? What was Peter? How to get across that great divide?

He waited inside the Dairy Queen for her bus to arrive. The buses stopped down the street. The woman behind the counter of the Dairy Queen—her nametag identified her as Cristina and a Dairy Queen server for four years—said the buses from Houston passed the Dairy Queen before reaching the bus station. They were marked "San Antonio." The buses from San Antonio passed the Dairy Queen after stopping in Seguin. They were marked "Houston," she said. "It's pretty simple. You go one way or t'other. You can't miss 'em, except for those days when they have a football game up at the college. Then they have extra traffic coming through, buses and cars, and you can miss it sometimes in all the confusion. Not today, though."

Maybe one car per minute passed by. He was looking forward to seeing B.C. Not having anything else to go on in the search for Peter, she might start him thinking again in other ways about other things. It might loosen up the cognitive processes. He could use some loosening up. Even a movie would help. A good drunk. A few bottles of wine at an Italian restaurant. Those long legs. Those eyes. He was feeling easy.

"That's it," Cristina shouted across the Dairy Queen. "Bus from Houston. Right on time."

Giacomo waved his thanks, put down his cup of coffee, and walked down the street. By the time he got there, B.C. was standing by the open bus door, helping an older woman and a child down the bus steps.

Always the Good Samaritan, he thought, walking up. She can't help herself. She smiled, still holding the woman's hand. Giacomo picked up B.C.'s bag, and they began walking back to his car parked at the Dairy Queen. "Want a Belt Buster or a Hunger Buster?" he asked.

"Let's wait," she said. "I want to eat in Lockhart. It's not far. You won't be sorry."

They drove to Lockhart. He told her about his travails along the Texas coast. She asked the right questions, provided the right support. She was wearing, he realized at some point, blue jeans, cowboy boots, and a western shirt with pearly snaps. As they reached the Lockhart city limits, he asked, "Is this the way you dressed in Lockhart? Will they let me in if I'm not dressed that way?"

"Oh," she said, a little sheepishly, "it seemed like a good idea early this morning. A little ridiculous, isn't it? We used to dress like this on weekends, for walking around the square or going dancin'. Thought I'd get into the spirit. I mean this morning I didn't want to look like I was coming from New York. Or at least that I was bringing New York with me. Now I'm not so sure. Turn left here."

He turned. She pointed to a parking lot. "Let's go in the back way," she said. "You know, all of a sudden I'm really nervous about this. I'm not sure I want anyone to recognize me. At the same time, I'm afraid I won't see anyone I know or who will know me, like I never lived here, I mean."

They entered the back of a building, walking into what felt like a small room in hell. Fires burned in huge brick pits, tended by two hairy men in undershirts, continually stoking the fires and pulling slabs of brisket and entrail-like strings of sausage from the pits. A man at a big wooden counter was hacking away at beef and sausages, then slid the meat onto pieces of butcher paper for a man and woman standing in front of Giacomo.

"This is what we call the genuine article," B.C. said. She walked him through the process. They got their sausage and brisket on butcher paper, crackers, onions, chile peppers and beer, then sat at a long table, using knives chained to the table for cutting up the meat. "Nothing like it," she said, biting into a piece of sausage, a thin arrow of grease shooting out from the gap between her front teeth.

Every once in a while she darted her eyes around the room to see if there was anyone who looked familiar, who might have recognized her. "You know," she said, "Stephen could really use your help. This thing is drivin' him nuts. He took your advice about the chiropractic clinic. Sure enough, they say they are treating a lot of people for joint pain. But they say it's only normal. You have a number of factors, they told him, that increase or decrease the numbers of cases of joint pain over a period of time, including the weather and biological rhythms and even possibly the movement of the planets. Also, what's in the food and what's in the air. They do give you that. And they admit that recently joint pain has been on the rise."

Giacomo Berg nodded. He chewed. All around them people were tearing at brisket with their teeth, pulling it apart with their fingers, attacking sausage with knives chained to the tables. Primal eating. Not as much talking as he was used to in such a big hall of a restaurant. The eating required concentration. Meanwhile, B.C. continued looking somewhat surreptitiously around the room.

"I've got it figured out," he said.

"What figured out?" she asked, stopping mid-sausage. "Peter or Stephen's problem?"

"Why we're here. Why you're dressed the way you are."

"Oh, yeah."

"It's all tied up with your work. Your ceaseless humanitarianism. Your devotion to some ideal community. This idea of disappearances. You've got to see why it's important. Here we are in a rural village, where you grew up, where people still eat with their hands or with knives chained to tables, grunting and slobbering all the way, not too far removed from Beowulf, or at least Henry II. We certainly haven't reached the age of the Medici here. And you've left all this behind. Disappeared. No trace of you here. And, from what I've been able to observe up until now, not many traces of this place in the known you. So here you are, back among the brisket eaters, and you've dressed what you remember to be the part, and you're wondering where you fit in, if you've been missed, what it means to these people for you to have been removed entirely from their experience."

"Sometimes you are so full of shit. It's not like I was dragged out in the middle of the night and killed."

"Ten years later, twenty years later, you might as well have been. You're gone. A face in the yearbook. A name on the plaque for the permanent honor roll in the main hall of Lockhart High. You wanted to see what community means and loss of community means. With all these refugees pouring through your living room, you wanted to remind yourself what your roots and your rootlessness mean."

"That's enough. Why don't you go investigate yourself. I just want to see the old house. You'll be impressed. Four or five blocks of beautiful Victorian houses. Ours has a roof that slopes so long and gradually that the ceiling of my bedroom on the second floor started out twelve feet high and ended up meeting the floor twenty feet across the room. I used to open the window and sit out on the roof there all evening long. That's all. And if you keep this up, I'll show you my junior high and high school and the houses of my best friends and the park where Bucky Fromlath and I used to go make out or maybe the dance hall where we used to kicker dance at Rumbaugh's, if it still exists. We ought to do that anyway. Did you ever two-step? The way we used to do it, the guys would hitch you up against them with their thumbs in the belt loops at the back of your jeans so you're pressed up so hard against them that you are aware of every nuance and weight shift as they glide you around the dance floor."

"And every nuance of what was going on under those jeans, I bet."

"That, too. It was all part of the plan to get you all hot and bothered rubbing one pair of jeans across another so that it was no trick at all to start a fire on the seat of the pickup in the parking lot."

"But not B.C. Boyd."

"You never know, Giacomo Berg. I'm just glad you've been paying so much attention." And he was paying attention. He was paying intimate attention to every turn of her head, the way her fingers wrapped around her bottle of Pearl beer, her legs crossing under the table, nipping his shin with the toe of her boot every time she crossed them. He was paying absolute attention.

"Let's find the dance hall and then a motel," he said.

"Can't yet," she said, realizing she was sounding more like a local with each sentence. "First we need to see the house."

It was the grand tour: first to her childhood home with sloping roof, time to point out the window to her bedroom, several trips around the block, notes on who lived where and what part they played in the life of young B.C. Boyd. On the third turn around the block, she asked him to stop in front of her house.

"Should I go up to the door? Is that too strange? We sold it to an Austin architect and his pregnant wife. They're probably no longer here. Their name was Houston."

She bit her nails. He examined her anxiety. It was all in the mouth and nails. The rest of her body was in repose, secure and relaxed. It was just from the elbows to the fingernails, crossing to the lips, teeth and jaw that bespoke her tension. Even her eyes seemed calm.

She opened the door and got out. "Can't hurt to try," she called to him. "You coming?"

He followed her to the front door. She was already ringing the bell. No answer. She tried the screen door. It was locked. "Esterbrook," she said, pointing to the name stenciled above the doorbell. "Don't know 'em. Oh well."

"Let's walk," she said and took off toward the courthouse on the square. He dutifully followed, catching up to her as she mounted the courthouse steps. "This was where we celebrated the snowfall," she said, looking out across the lawn. She squinted slightly, trying to make out the faces of people walking in the shade of the awnings of the block of buildings across the street.

She led him on a walk in front of the four blocks of buildings surrounding the square. She motioned to one store after another, told the part it played in her life, but didn't stop. They completed the loop and headed back to the car.

"Don't you want to try to see someone you might know? Drop in on someone maybe?"

"It's not important," she said.

"If it was meant to be, it would have happened."

The Esterbrook house was still locked up when they got back to the car. She had Giacomo drive past her elementary school and junior high and high school.

They went by Bucky Fromlath's house on the way out of town. A blue Ford pickup from the '50s sat in the driveway. "That's the one," she said. "Can you believe it?"

He watched the instant of her excitement and its retreat.

"Hard to figure out how so much could go on inside that little pickup cab."

"Teens are remarkably limber when they need to be," he said.

They passed the Jewish cemetery by the highway. Over a hill, they came to the Catholic cemetery, hidden by some trees. She had him stop by the side of the road. She considered getting out. "This is where I used to come to think in my late adolescence. There were always flowers here, and no one thought to bother me." She didn't get out. Instead, she just motioned for him to drive on. He wasn't sure where.

They passed the Rumbaugh dance hall. She pointed to it and then pointed to the road. He kept driving. He knew the road led to Austin. Did she have a plan? She didn't say a word for fifteen or twenty minutes. It was still early, long before sunset, and he was content to drive.

A golden jetliner seemed to be heading for them. It was descending rapidly. Was it aimed at this highway? They came over a rise and he spotted runways and a control tower ahead and to their right. As they drove along-side the airport, the golden jet was already on the runway and beginning to turn around.

Across the highway from the airport, the flotsam and jetsom of bars and trailer parks, pawn shops and used car lots. A few hotels being built.

"Let's honky-tonk tonight," B.C. blurted out. "I know a place in Austin, if it still exists, that's the quintessential Texas honky tonk, if such a thing still exists. Let's do that. Is that all right? Let's do that."

He nodded. He was happy for any sort of direction. It may be just what he needed: to get plastered and fall into her arms. At least to forget about Peter for a few hours and about his own lack of direction and about the world.

His Oblivion

BEFORE THEY WENT HONKY-TONKING, B.C. Boyd went for a swim. Giacomo Berg called Sara Proust. He'd been worrying about that all day. If it were true that Peter wanted to take his own life, then every move became suddenly urgent.

The investigation into the whereabouts of a lost person, even a person lost to Giacomo Berg, consisted of the continuous tightening of a series of spheres surrounding that person from the known and unknown universes to spheres within a single universe to points on a map to even narrower realms of possibility to a region to a city to a neighborhood to a block to a house to a room to a bed, then boom—the fixed locus in the orbiting spheres of possibility materializes as that person, not so much lost and then found but more a person wrapped in layers of the possible and slowly unwrapped, excluding ever-increasing amounts of extraneous information in order to extrude the possible to find the probable, until the investigation confronted the thing itself, uncovered, bared, waiting to be announced. Time was, of course, always an element in this uncovering, in this narrowing the realm of the possible to reveal the actual. If you found the hotel, the room, the chair, success still depended upon your finding the actual sitting in the chair of the possible at the moment you walk in, not one hour before or two hours hence. It depended upon the intersection of the investigative subject and the investigative object, not only in the same place but at the same time. When he thought about it, it seemed too much to expect. It was as if time and possibility were warped by the continuous movement of bodies in space. How did anything in the world become known? But it happened, almost as often as not, he realized. His job, in fact, was as much a marshalling of elements of the known universe so that the intersection of all possibilities in space and time occurred in the most fortuitous configuration that could be mustered. That was the object. Sometimes it happened.

There was the time he had been asked by criminal defense lawyer Stanley Gaines to do a little research on foot fetishes. It seemed Gaines was defending a drug dealer who had been accused of murdering two women. The women lived in the same city block and had been murdered within six weeks of each other. The thing that had interested Gaines—who said all along that his client was low-life scum who should be put away but not for something he didn't do—was the fact that both women had not only been raped, but that police reports in both cases indicated that the outer garments remained on both bodies except for their shoes and that, in the first case, the big toes of the victim seemed to be covered with some sort of cream while the big toes of the second victim apparently had been spread with grape jam. The police chemist had confirmed that the cream taken from beneath the toenails of the first victim was, in his estimation, much like the ricotta cream used to stuff cannolis, while the second victim's toe hairs were encrusted with supermarket-variety grape jam. They'd grabbed the drug dealer, Gaines said, because he was always in the corner bar making smart-ass remarks to all the women, and these women sometimes went to the corner bar. They did not go together, nor did they appear to have known each other, but a friend of the first victim had told police that this drug dealer had been hitting on the victim one night a few weeks before the murder, flashing his Rolex and talking about his trips to Phoenix and to South America. No one saw the drug dealer with the second victim, but the police figured he was as good a candidate as any, and, as he was a prime suspect in the first murder, they picked him up soon after the second murder—noting the undeniable connection between the toes of the two victims.

Stanley Gaines had been practicing criminal defense long enough to know sexual perversion when he saw it. In fact, more than the thought of the rape and murder of the first victim—crimes he was inured to—the thought of some pervert slapping cannoli cream onto the woman's toes, either before or after she was a corpse, and then licking it off, made Stanley's stomach turn. He said he'd never eat a cannoli again, just thinking about those toe hairs and that dead woman's callouses and toenails. The first thing he did was send the drug dealer, one Tony Spaethe, to a criminal psychologist. They ran a battery of tests on Spaethe and, according to Gaines, didn't turn up any highly deviant sexual proclivities other than those that normally attached themselves to young white males who hang around on street corners and in neighborhood bars preening and harassing women. "He may have acted like a goddamn golden stud rooster just before a cockfight," Gaines had told Giacomo Berg, "but, Jack, there's nothing to indicate he liked sucking girls' toes."

So Berg went to work. He talked to criminal psychologists, some who said there was a direct correlation between foot fetishism and rape and some who said there was none. He checked police records for convicted rapists and deviants who might be living in the area. He worked the corner bar, talking to everyone there who would talk. He tried all the building superintendents in the area, figuring they would have the best sense of the deviant behavior in the neighborhood, as long as it did not involve themselves.

That's when he struck gold. It was fairly obvious really. He asked the superintendent of a building that was fairly upscale for that block if he had ever noticed someone who acted a little unusual.

"I'm glad you asked me that," the super said. "I've been thinking about those murders, you know, ever since they killed that woman in the building next door. I'd see her every now and again. But I've been thinking about the fact that someone wanted her toes. You hear about those things, but you figure they can't be for real. Anyway, when it happened here, right next door, I began to put my mind on what kind of a person would lick a woman's toes. That is what he did, didn't he? Everybody's talking about it. Well, I began to put my mind to it, and it seemed to me that, if someone loved feet that much, that he'd either work at a shoe hospital or at a shoe store or he'd live some place, if he could, where he could watch feet all day long. Maybe next to the subway entrance, I'd say, or maybe some place where people stopped for a while and talked. Outside a restaurant or a bar. See what I'm saying? Look for a basement apartment. Start from there. It came to me because here I am spending all my days looking out from the basement windows of this building. And what do I see? Feet. Ankles. Nothing above the knee. Just feet all day long. It gets to you after a while, but it wouldn't, I guess, if feet were what you wanted more than anything in the world. That's just a guess. But it's my theory. I guess that makes it as good as anyone else's until they catch him."

It was better than a guess. It was better than anything he could get from a roomful of criminal psychologists. Giacomo began ringing buzzers on all the basement apartments. He began by the subway entrance and worked his way down the block. In most cases, there was no answer. At one building an old woman answered. At another, a man well past eighty answered the door after the eighth ring. Other tries produced no one suspicious. He found either people of meager means living in poorly lit basement apartments or, in a couple of instances, he came across young professional types working at home, who had probably paid a good deal of money in order to live in what they called a "garden apartment," as opposed to the basement apartments next door. He wondered how he would be able to determine perversion on a grand scale in such brief interviews, usually conducted with only the interviewee's nose appearing through a crack in a door that remained secured by a chain.

He found he hadn't needed to wonder. Grand perversion announced itself. Two buildings from the corner bar, he rang a buzzer marked "Carabella." The door swung open, and there, facing Giacomo Berg, was a small man of maybe fifty, slight, looking something like an older Lee Harvey Oswald, wearing a chef's apron, holding in his right hand a cannoli shell and in his left a tube of cannoli cream.

"What can I do for you?" the man asked. Giacomo could not answer. Behind the man, plaster casts of dozens of feet lined glass shelves; some were marked in various ways, some unmarked.

"Nothing thanks," Giacomo had answered, for there was nothing more the man needed to offer. That evening Carabella was arrested. Gaines told Berg that this Carabella character had high-speed cameras set up in his basement window and contact sheets covered with feet. He had wine glasses that looked like women's high-heeled shoes. Though they'd tried for weeks, the police couldn't make anything of the dozens of plaster casts, whether they were modeled after other victims or were just some of the detritus of Carabella's fetish. As for Carabella, he'd been working for several years as a pornographic pastry chef, selling his wares to bakeries in Soho, the Upper East Side, and the Village, with mail orders from the West Coast. He was never known to create pastry shaped as feet—at least, not for public consumption.

Sometimes it happened that way. Had Carabella not been home, had he not answered holding cannoli cream, the world might still be safe from Tony Spaethe, but not from Mr. Carabella. It had been a fortuitous conjunction. Time had been the key element there, space playing an important but secondary role.

But, with Peter Proust, time itself was now the overpowering dimension. Time became the dimension not so much to measure against, to chart motion by, not a set of fixed points or a graph, but a constellation spinning rapidly away from the familiar one-foot-then-the-other-foot universe.

Was Peter Proust's time still their own? Had he ceased to exist in his own time as they continued to search for him in theirs? Would he continue to exist only until that moment when they discover that they have arrived in a future he would never know? Was Giacomo in a race against a shrinking future for Peter Proust that may already have been extinguished in a tiny puff of smoke? He no longer had much use for past, present, and future. Instead, he found himself bobbing in an unmarked sea of time, unmarked and at this point unreadable for Giacomo Berg. Time had become a function of moving bodies, one body in particular, toward whose specific gravity Giacomo wanted to be drawn. Thus far, however, it seemed that wherever Peter Proust was, he carried his own time with him.

Giacomo Berg looked at the telephone and dialed. Sara Proust answered.

"I wanted to talk to you about this possibility of suicide," Giacomo said. "Why hadn't you told me? Where does it come from?"

A pause. "You know it's not easy," she said. "We should have told you, but it is not easy. It's something I've been living with for a few years. I only told my folks when we lost track of him. But Peter had talked to me about it when he left the Refuge the first time. He came home a few times then, you know, and he wasn't happy with the way things were there. He really believed in that stuff, Jack. When he found out that they weren't what he expected, that all was not sweetness and light, that they told him what to do and when to do it, it hurt him pretty badly. I think he gave up hope. That's what it was. I think he just gave up."

Giacomo had once known Sara fairly well. Peter's kid sister, she used to come stay at the house he'd shared with Peter in college. She'd idolized Peter. He would not eat meat; she would not eat meat. He would not wear leather; she gave away her belts, purses, and moccasins. But it was his refusal to compromise on any subject that stood out: on beans for dinner, on walking to class even through three miles of foot-deep snow, on what should be read and what should not be read in class; on how to make sprouts. He would wake up the house playing the Rolling Stones' "Queenie" in the middle of the night because that was what he thought the world needed. Sara used to make fun of her brother's obstinance. Sometimes she egged him on. But in the depths of her soul, she idolized him. Giacomo Berg, on the other hand, provided her with some relief. He was the skeptic of the house, the non-believer. It didn't seem like light-years ago that Sara had given him a massage on graduation night as her present. But it must have been.

"We're all getting old, Sara. We're all getting a little depressed. Things aren't working out the way we planned."

"But do you think about it every minute? Are you at every minute working toward nirvana? You know Peter is. You know it, Jack."

"Is there anything else I should know?"

"He thinks he's dying anyway," she said. "The last time he was here he told me he was sure he had some kind of stomach cancer. He says he gets bent over double in pain. I told him to see a doctor, but he won't. I told him it was probably an ulcer. All he eats is dried fruit, beans, and raw vegetables. But he's convinced it's from pesticides. He said it was from building houses for the Refuge in the middle of the rice fields by Houston. He said he was breathing pesticides all day long. That's not to mention, he said, all the pesticides we've been eating since we were children. He really believes he's dying, and there's no talking him out of it."

Giacomo listened. He listened for Sara's voice to crack. It didn't. He wondered how she looked in her forties. She'd been such an open kid. This had probably knocked the innocence out of her.

"There's one more thing," she said. "I have a seven-year-old boy whose father was never in the picture. I don't know if you knew that. He and Peter used to live for each other. Peter wrote books for him; he was the only one Peter ever called. When Peter first talked to me about this suicide business, I asked him to think about what it would do to Davey. I really meant it, but I also thought that might be the one thing that might stop him."

There was silence. Giacomo didn't know whether to speak or not to speak. Not knowing what to say, he chose not to speak.

"The last time he came to visit," Sara began again, this time her voice an octave lower, "I had to kick him out. I don't know why. It was like we weren't even there, like Davey wasn't even there. He knew we were, of course. Why else would he have come? But he was so morose. When he talked, which wasn't much, it was only about his stomach cramps. I couldn't bear to have him around. I didn't want him around Davey especially. I didn't know what Davey would think. It was the wrong thing to do. I may be the cause of all this. He probably wanted my help. I just didn't expect it. We never could really open up."

This conversation moved Giacomo Berg into the lower depths, not just about finding Peter Proust, but if they found him, who would they find? Giacomo Berg had not been his brother's keeper.

"I have to ask you," Sara began again, her voice stronger this time. "Do you remember the time you and Peter drank LSD some girl gave you in a bottle of wine? Does that ring a bell? Do you ever think about that? Did it have any effect on you?"

Giacomo thought about the night and day he and Peter had spent wandering around the town in the snow tripping on acid. It had seemed interminable. They'd watched the sunrise.

They'd visited everyone they knew. Giacomo had watched *Jules and Jim* twice at the campus movie theater waiting for the drug to wear off. They'd visited a friend who told them about having just bought John Lennon's old *Imagine* album and how depressed it had made him. "It made me want to throw myself out the window," the friend had said. "But then I realized I could just throw the album out the window instead. I did and I feel much better." He thinks that's what happened. Giacomo remembered finally going to sleep some time early the second morning. He woke up that afternoon to find Peter Proust still awake. He remembered seeing a look in Peter's eyes that day like the look of a scared animal. That hadn't registered the day before when both were waiting out the solution. Perhaps it hadn't been there. But it was there the third day of Peter's trip. They finally got him tranquilizers, and he went to sleep.

"There was a point," Giacomo said, "when we thought Peter might never go to sleep. I think about it, but I was so far gone myself I couldn't be too sure what was happening to Peter. Why do you ask?"

"He talks about it all the time. He says that's when it started, when he started to lose control of his own life. He says he's never been the same since then. I just wondered," Sara said.

"I'll think about it," Giacomo said. He wanted off the telephone. He wanted not to think about anything. But he asked, "Is there anything else? Anyone else I should talk to?"

"There is Claire Beauchamp," Sara said. "She lives in Houston last I heard. Went down there to work in a factory. I don't know if she kept the job or if she's still there. But he used to keep in touch with her."

Peter and Claire Beauchamp had lived together in the hills of Western Massachusetts during his hiatus from the Refuge. They lived in a house

without electricity in something that resembled a camp more than a commune—five or six ramshackle cabins on a couple of hills with a common
house on the road leading into the camp that the residents of the cabins
shared for cooking, baths, electricity, and a telephone. It had been a hunting lease years before, Peter had told him. Berg had visited once. He'd
spent the night in the cabin with Peter and Claire. It had rained and it was
hell clawing his way up the muddy hill in the dark. Peter and Claire slept
in a loft surrounded by Mason jars filled with preserves. Claire was raised
on a farm nearby. She tended a little garden in back of the cabin and preserved fruits from the market in which she worked in town. Peter worked
with a few other campers on auto and truck repairs.

Giacomo had found life in the camp anything but bucolic. The central building was surrounded by pools of grease, cars and trucks on blocks,
parts of junked cars strewn around the periphery. Claire, though, did have
a bucolic face, as round as a full moon and giving off an aura of robust good
health. She may have been all of 17 or 18 for all he knew, but she was the only
woman he could remember Peter living with for any length of time. She'd
taken them skinny dipping in an old quarry near her family's farm. She was
a hippie's dream. At some point, she'd left Peter, and he went back to the
Refuge. Giacomo would look for her in Houston.

"If there is nothing else, I really should be going," he said. "I'll call
you again soon."

"I'm sending you some money, Jack," she said. "Please find him."

Conversation ended, he lay back on the couch and stared at the ceiling. He yearned for its blankness. He wanted his mind to be wiped clean.
Stomach cramps. Suicide. Acid trips. If he thought of his experiences with
hallucinogens, it was with some nostalgia. But, for the most part, he didn't
think about them at all. When he was in college, he remembered, he'd
thought of LSD as a kind of psychic spring cleaning. When he felt he was
carrying too much mental baggage, he would organize a hallucinogenic
experience, rounding up fellow travelers and those who would remain
moored to the everyday world to help him keep his bearings. A day or two
later he would wake up from his post-trip sleep feeling spiritually cleansed
and mentally reinvigorated.

But Peter questioned his own existence after two beers. More than
once he wandered off into the night from a beer party only to be found in

full lotus in the middle of a field or crouched in a corner, shaking his head, saying "No. Oh no." Clearly, there had been problems there all along that no one had wanted to recognize.

It was at that moment that B.C. Boyd returned from the pool, carrying a magazine. "I've found the honky-tonk; I've found the band. Let's go," she announced and disappeared into the bathroom.

And they went.

He was ready for this. He was ready for anything. She drove them to an old barn-looking building. She sat him down, ordered them each a chicken-fried steak and a pitcher of beer and another pitcher and another. When the band began to play, she dragged him to the dance floor. He was conscious of her jeans rubbing against his, of her arms around his neck, of the tugs every so often she gave him, pulling on his belt loops. In fact, he spent the evening slipping in and out of consciousness, letting the music carry him and the beer and, in point of fact, letting B.C. carry him around and around the dance floor and through the night. He was perfectly content not to think and not to feel, just to be.

He was conscious of her leading him to the car and driving him home. He was conscious of sitting on the bed while she took her boots off while sitting next to him. He was conscious of her legs against his in the bed. But there were such vast areas of blankness surrounding each conscious moment. And it was the blankness he sought. He was conscious of the feel of the flesh of her back and of her legs. But it was the blankness of the rest of it that seduced him, that drew him into its depths. Feeling her hair on his pillow, he fought against his oblivion. But it was a losing battle. He'd known that from the beginning. Finally he just let go, surrendering himself entirely to the ever-inviting, all-encompassing void.

A Trail of Smoke

HE HAD JUST GOTTEN carried away. Was that a crime? Was that a sin? He was usually so careful. He'd built a fire for the pot of mesquite beans. He'd lit the fire. He was feeling so good, so successful after his trip into town, that he decided to fashion a torch out of an old shirt and a tree branch about four inches thick. He wrapped the shirt tightly around the end of the branch and tied it with wire. He'd carried the torch back to an old barrel containing some kind of oily concoction he'd found standing some fifty yards behind the house, and he'd rubbed the shirt end of the stick back and forth in the black liquid. He took his kitchen matches and tried to light the shirt. It required several tries, but finally the fire caught hold. He took off, running up and down the hill around his house waving the branch and its ball of flames, shouting and howling at the moon, repeating a Native American chant over and over: "Hiyohoweyyehhey hiyohoweyyehhey."

At several points during his circumnavigation of that hill, sparks from the torch and pieces of burning cloth ignited portions of the dry brush. Small bushes and clumps of grass began to burn. It had been a dry summer. When Peter Proust returned finally to the pot of mesquite beans, he looked up to see the hillside above his cabin burning. It had not registered before because he had thought the flames at his feet had been simply a manifestation inside his head of the essence of fire he carried on the torch and dispersed through the fire chant. When the smoke began to get into his lungs, however, he realized the burning was not inside his head but was around his cabin.

For a good while, he sat there and watched the hillside burn. The land had been parched, and the grasses and bushes made easy kindling. At the same time, the dry weather had supported only patches of vegetation and not a continuous field of growth, so the fire, he thought, would be naturally contained by the stretches of barren ground surrounding the small bodies of plant life. He was only partially correct. The wind blew the fire up the hillside. The fire died in some places, not being able to cross the baked ground. But, at other points, it seemed able to leap vast expanses, sparks alighting at the end of extended jetés on blades of dry Johnson grass arching out to meet them.

It was in the midst of his reverie on the movement of fire that Peter Proust realized his cabin was burning. Where he saw the flames attach themselves to his porch, Peter poured the pot of mesquite beans. He then began transporting buckets of water from his water trough to throw on the flames around his door. But there was not enough water to battle on all fronts. When he saw the fire smoldering on the cabin's roof, he ran inside to retrieve what he could—his pencils and paper, the journal, a few letters, notes and pictures, his pack of books, his sleeping bag, a jacket, his gun. He took these things down the hill to a stand of cedar trees out of the path of the fire.

The roof was now ablaze and beginning to cave in. The smoke was thick, and he found it depressing, the clean air of this hill made suddenly so oppressive. He walked up the hillside over the charred grasses. It was hot and difficult to breathe. He had just gotten carried away. He had not been careful. Then he heard the fire truck. He ran to the stand of cedar trees and crouched in the darkness.

The truck did not make its way easily up the washed-out gravel road at the bottom of his hill or up the dirt road to his cabin. But it finally did arrive. He watched three men pull a hose from the truck and run it up to the burning cabin. Two other men carrying shovels climbed the hill and began clearing the ground above the fire. Once they began running water through the hose, the cabin fire was extinguished quickly. But from where Peter hid, it seemed there had not been much left to save, a couple of walls at most. Then all five men took their shovels and hoes to the hillside, smothering some flames with dirt, stamping out others, running water on the rest. It was over in a matter of minutes. But the men then spent an interminable period walking up and down the hillside, kicking dirt on smoldering branches, digging at clumps of grass. They spent the most time, though, looking through the cabin, picking up dishes and what was left of his furniture, turning it over, letting it drop. "Is anybody there?" one of the men kept calling out into the darkness.

Was he genuinely concerned? Peter wondered. Or was it a trap? He had no reason to answer. No one who wanted to be known was there.

Finally, the men left the cabin and the hillside. Before leaving the cedar break, Peter followed the sound of the truck down the dirt road and the gravel road and on toward town. He emerged from among the trees and walked around the hillside. The smell was starting to get to him. The smoke was still in his throat and lungs. He decided to put off looking at the cabin until morning. It would be easier to sleep that way. He returned to the stand of cedar trees, rolled out the sleeping bag, and fell asleep. The mosquitoes and horse flies were not a problem that night.

The next morning there was no opportunity to investigate the cabin. He was awakened not by blue jays, as he was used to, or by the sun breaking its eastern light into his sleep. No. He was awakened by the sound of cars speeding up his gravel road. He looked up from his bed among the cedars just in time to see two brown cars arrive on his hill. On the door of each was the insignia of the sheriff's department. Men in khaki uniforms wearing boots and straw cowboy hats got out of the cars and marched straight up the hill to where a thin feather of smoke was still rising from the cabin. They kicked around whatever was at their feet on the floor of the cabin. One picked up a pot and a spoon and banged them together, yelling, "Is anybody home? Is anybody out there?" They broke open his jars of beans and herbs, handling the contents, smelling them intently.

"If you're out there, come on over here," the same man shouted. "We ain't gonna arrest you for smelling bad." The rest laughed and continued sifting through the rubble. There ensued a long conversation among the men standing in what remained of his cabin. They walked out through where the front door had been, and all four of them walked up and over the hill.

Peter Proust figured this was his opening. He grabbed his sleeping bag, stuffed what he could into his pack and hurried down the hill. He stayed off the road, ducked through some barbed wire fences, and made it to the trees along the little creek bed. He decided to wait there a good long while. The first order of business was to calm the pounding of his heart. He sat in full lotus by the creek's edge and began his breathing exercises. He cleared his sinuses in order to rid himself of the stench of the burning hillside. After he felt he had regained some degree of control over his heartbeat and breathing, Peter Proust took off his clothes and lay in the creek, his palms open to the sky. The running water would quench the fire inside him. His face was turned to the branches above him, while what he saw was another place inside his head. He was seeing mountains much larger than the hills he was currently inhabiting, vast plains, large birds floating as high as the mountains over the plains.

Some time later, when the sun was definitely in its descent, he got up, got dressed, put his things in order and set out for the highway that ran past the town. He walked with high purpose. While he was determined to avoid legal authorities, he did not fear them. In fact, he was convinced that they could not touch him now that he was moving again in a direction that he had been able to discern by stopping and listening to the world around him. He reached the highway as the sun was about ten degrees above the western horizon. He found an entrance ramp. He carefully placed his pack and sleeping bag by the highway, turned his back to the setting sun and faced the oncoming traffic. Peter Proust was going west.

Fire in the Belly

BY THE TIME he could bring himself to open his eyes, she was gone. No sign of her. No sound of her in the bathroom. The curtains were open. The light outside seemed overly bright. He closed his eyes again. But he couldn't sleep. Nor could he remember much from the night before. That didn't bother him so much. It might be better that way. But it gave him very little to go on if she returned. She would return, of course. This was not a French movie. Or a particularly serious matter. They had fallen into bed together, at least one of them dead drunk. And they were old enough for that to happen without meaning much one way or the other. No matter what had happened that night. Not much, he figured, though he would like to know. For the record.

He figured if he lay there long enough she would return. She did, carrying a legal file.

Not exactly what he'd expected. How long had he lain there?

"It's almost noon," she said, putting the file next to her suitcase, sitting down in a chair across the room, looking straight at him.

He tried to measure her tone of voice—to measure it against what he knew of her. It was useless. He couldn't detect a thing. Patience. He had to wait her out.

"I went to see some friends," she said. "Not friends, really, but people I talk to quite a bit on the phone. They provide testimony for refugee asylum claims. Central American refugees, that is. I just took a chance and went by their office. They were there. We had coffee. They told me about the detention centers in South Texas—the 'internment camps' they called them. That's what they are really. They said I should see them. They would set me up with their lawyer down there to see them. I don't think I want to. I can imagine what they're like." She looked out the window.

Business as usual? Was it just another day in the life of B.C. Boyd? He didn't think he could trust such a determination. He had to give it more time. He would continue to wait it out.

"Let's go," she said. She was standing by the window now. "Let's shoot some of that Mexican hot sauce into your veins. Let's get some menudo that will take the hair off the dog. That's what we both need."

He gathered himself up and lunged toward the bathroom. Once inside he stood staring at himself in the mirror. He looked old enough to be dead.

B.C. Boyd couldn't help smiling. She thumbed through a telephone book, looking up restaurants. She had him on the ropes. He couldn't possibly remember much, if anything, about the previous evening. She'd pretty much led him around the dance floor and then into bed. He was out. He had spoken every once in a while. But there was no indication in anything he said that he was conscious of what he was doing. She had that on him. It wasn't what she was after. She would rather have been swept away herself. But at least she had this. She knew what Giacomo Berg had done and had not done on a particular evening. And he did not. It was enough to carry her a little ways. Not lift her off the ground necessarily but transport her on small wheels for a few hundred yards. It would make the next few hours interesting. She'd always wanted to toy with Giacomo Berg. This was her chance.

She heard him make noises like he was about to emerge from the bathroom. She studied the phone book intently. The less she said the better. Give him the Berg treatment. She could not resist. She figured he'd eventually become conversational.

And he did. "Find a place?" he asked. She nodded.

"Well, let's go. You spent some time here, didn't you? Graduate school or something?"

She nodded again.

"It used to be one of those big stars on the map," Giacomo said. "Ann Arbor, Berkeley, Austin. For hippies looking for the good life."

"You can see it's changed," she said. That was all she said.

They checked out of the hotel. She directed him to a loud little café with a bakery in the front and formica-topped tables around back. She ordered them each a bowl of menudo. He got up and walked over to the juke box. He found an array of songs in English and Spanish with titles like "You Got What You Wanted, Now Don't Give It Back," "El Corrido de Bernhard Goetz," "Don't Mess with a Mexican, Sr. Ayatollah," and "Leave Me Alone, But Don't Leave Me Lonely." Must have been last loaded years ago. He returned to the table to find a large bowl containing a soupy gray-brown liquid topped with a pool of grease through which several formless masses of meat protruded.

"Mouth watering," he said.

"It's the cure," B.C. countered.

"Tripe," he muttered.

"Innards," she replied.

"Patsas," he said, a little louder.

"Menudo," she yelled. They were standing, their faces inches from each other. She was shaking a corn tortilla underneath his nose. She let loose a laugh like he'd never heard her laugh. From her deepest recesses it came rolling out. He could hear it coming and sat down in order to take it all in.

She began eating her menudo, smiling between bites. For the first time he could see the wild college student in her, unadulterated beauty without all the trappings purchased by experience and caution. Strange how he associated beauty and vulnerability with youth, the ideal still being women in their early twenties he knew when he was that age, though they didn't seem particularly young then or vulnerable. They were lithe, however, taut as bowstrings. Not strange at all, really, given the proximity of the roots for "adult" and "adulterate." "Adulterer" for that matter. To be an adult means to be impure, defiled, falsifying. The process of socialization had worked well on Giacomo Berg. But it was not until this moment that he realized how well it had worked. He realized he wanted B.C. Boyd all that much more because he had finally seen the twenty-year-old inside her. And he realized that didn't make sense. It may even be sick, but there she was before him. Forty-four, he thought he remembered. And the entrance to those 44 years he thought he finally saw in her eyes. They were practically incandescent.

He thought of *King Lear*. He always thought of *King Lear*. This was the big payoff for having been an English major. "Off lendings." Lear stripping off wealth, power, history even, to the essence of Lear. Ur Lear. But when he'd thought about himself, he'd thought most about stripping away the accretions of age, the years since he was twenty-one. His belly gone soft, the hair he'd lost. But most of all it was the fire. He felt he'd lost the fire that once burned inside him, sent him walking through the streets all night long, after furiously listening to Coltrane records or Ornette Coleman, questioning everything, taking nothing at face value, beating his head and fists and feet against the pavement and stone walls of the city just to feel his blood roar. Wildness was what he missed. Off lendings. Could he remember this? That it was not age that held him in perpetual retreat. It was what he'd grown to believe age was. A buffering process.

Holding tightly what mattered while taking on layers of protection. Fuck it. The fire was still in there somewhere. If he could grab it, he could burn his way out. If he could catch that light in B.C. Boyd's eyes, they could fly out of here.

He was staring into his menudo. She was watching him. "Go ahead," she said, still smiling.

He ate a greasy spoonful. The chiles in the menudo burned all the way down. Fire in the belly. This may be the cure. He ate another spoonful and another. It slithered into his gut.

"Did you have a good time last night?" she asked, barely containing herself.

He ate another bite. "You'd probably know that better than I would," he answered. "Did I have a good time?"

"Well, I can't say much for your dancing. For a few moments you floated, but most of the time I had to drag you around the floor. But you were game. I will say that," she said. "I had a good time."

"That's what counts," he said. "This menudo grows on you."

"And inside you," she said. She was afraid he was slipping out of her grasp. She wanted to have more fun with him, but he seemed unusually defenseless. It was difficult to keep her edge.

"What did it mean when you asked me to put my hands in your back pockets on the dance floor, the way the other women were doing? Does that mean you were having fun?" she asked, hiding her smile behind her napkin.

"Sounds like it to me," he said. She was enjoying this. He didn't remember a thing. She was probably making it up. But he could play the game. More than ever, he wanted to see that killer gap between her teeth. But she was hiding it.

"And when you told me I had to pull your clothes off when you hit the bed, was that a good time?"

It didn't sound likely, he thought. But he certainly hadn't had his clothes on when he woke up this morning. He waited for her next move.

She picked up a tortilla, poured hot red sauce across its diameter, rolled it up, then slowly ate it, savoring each bite. Should she let him up?

It didn't seem that he'd suffered much, but she didn't have the patience to string this out all day. Unless he asked for it.

"Back to Houston?" she asked.

"To Houston," he said.

Passing through a town called LaGrange, she placed her left hand on his right leg. It stayed there until they reached the town of Columbus. Then she removed it. He didn't know what that meant, either the placement or the removal. She didn't either. Neither said a word. They simply drove.

A Dead End

THE FIRST ORDER OF BUSINESS was to find Claire Beauchamp. The first place to look was the phone book. In a strip shopping center, he found a telephone booth with a telephone book in it. That would never happen in New York. And there she was. He hadn't expected it to be this easy.

It wasn't. When he called, there was no answer. When he tried again ten minutes later, a woman answered and said Claire should be home any minute. She was the night manager at a 24-hour convenience store, the woman explained, and that meant she came home some time in the morning or at least by early afternoon.

Giacomo decided to drive to Claire's house. He thought it might take some doing to get Claire to remember him, or to talk to him if she knew anything about Peter Proust. He was curious, besides, to see her. B.C. asked to go along.

Claire lived in a red, two-story house in what looked to be a neighborhood of down-at-the-heel houses from the '20s and '30s. A couple of houses on the block were freshly painted, had bright gardens and ferns hanging in pots on the front porch. A flashy foreign car sat in the driveway of one. This block was not without its gentrifiers, Giacomo thought, or perhaps its drug dealers, or perhaps they were one and the same. An African American man with gray hair sat on the steps leading up to Claire's door. His right hand was in a cast, his middle finger on that hand pointing to the sky.

"Good afternoon," Giacomo said. "Do you know if Claire Beauchamp is home?"

"Not yet that I know of," said the man. "I haven't seen her go by. And I usually do. But go ring the bell and ask Mercy. She'll know what's what."

They walked up to the door and rang the bell. A very large, practically billowing white woman came to the door.

"I'm looking for Claire Beauchamp," Giacomo said. "Is she in?"

"You must be the fella who called on the phone. She's not here yet. See, she's the night manager, and if the day shift don't show up, then she has to stay until they do. That's probably what happened. I've told her just to walk away from it when that happens. It's not her fault. The poor child ends up working twenty hours straight sometimes. She comes home looking like a kicked dog. She goes to sleep for three or four hours, gets up to eat, then goes back down to the store. If she'd just eat what they sell there, that would save her a little time, but all she eats is nuts and berries and fruit and vegetables that haven't been sprayed with all those chemicals. She said she couldn't begin to get that stuff where she works. So she don't get to eat on the job like the other employees. That poor child, she's had a rough few years."

"Where does she work?" Berg asked. "I'll drive by there."

"Oh, you can't go there. The company don't let them conduct any personal business while they're working. She'd be fired just like that. I won't tell you where it is. I don't want that on my conscience. You look like you'd just drive right over there even if I told you don't. Is she in some kind of trouble? I wouldn't believe it if you told me she was. You look like a bill collector to me. Does she owe somebody money? I won't tell you where to find her. That poor girl works as hard as she can. Since she lost that factory job making machine parts, she's worked like a durn billy goat just to pay her bills and pay off that piece of shit car she bought. Please excuse my French, but I'm getting mad just standing here talking to you. You look more and more like a bill collector to me. And that girl's like my daughter, so I think you'd better get off my steps, and, no sir, I won't tell you where she works. You're making me lose my self-control."

"I'm looking for a lost friend," Giacomo said. "Someone she knows. I thought she might have heard from him and could tell me where to find him."

"I no more believe that than I'd believe that you'd come to tell me I'm a millionaire. I didn't believe those stories neither, where all those people got a million-dollar check and didn't know what to do with it and how it was supposed to have spoiled their lives. I'd know what to do with it in a New York minute, and I'd be happy about it, too. You wouldn't see any tears rolling down these cheeks, no sir. But why am I standing here talking to you? Go on, get away from my front porch and stop harassing me and my tenants. Claire Beauchamp is not here and I don't know when she will be here, but when she does get here, I'll warn her about you and make sure that I answer the door so you can't get near her."

Giacomo Berg waited for this to end. B.C. was standing at the other end of the porch looking over the neighborhood. He pulled his business card out of his wallet and tried to hand it to the woman.

"Would you mind giving her one of these, then?" he asked. "It's got my cell phone number on it, but only seems to have service less than half the time. I'm not sure where I'll be staying tonight, so I'll have to call her."

The woman took the card, put it in a pocket of her dress, abruptly closed the front door and walked back into the house.

Giacomo and B.C. walked back down the steps.

"I know where Claire works," the man with the cast said. "You're not a bill collector, are you? You're on the up and up?"

"I am," said Berg, pulling out another business card.

"I figured you probably were. Bill collectors don't usually telephone ahead to say they'll be coming round. Mercy gets too excitable, particularly when it comes to somebody she has a fondness for, which ain't a whole lot of people in this world. But she has a fondness for Claire. Otherwise, she'd be right there with you, ready to collect her bills same as she thinks you're trying to do, even if they weren't due yet. But that young girl, she works at the U-Tote-Em at the edge of downtown, you know. Right where the Katy Freeway hits those downtown buildings. Right practically underneath that freeway. That girl works there all night long. I hope she doesn't get killed. I told her to take a gun with her, but she said she don't believe in guns. I told her, Claire, it's not a question of believe or not believe. It's a question of is or isn't. If a gun is pointed in your face, then it's really there. You don't have to believe in it to see it. It's too late for that. I told her I'd go with her to buy one, but she wouldn't have it. She said if someone was already sticking a gun in her face, it would be too late to take one out anyway. This ain't the Wild West, she told me. But you know it is. These streets are wild as they can be what with people carrying Ouzis and gobi balls and attack dogs on short chains and shit. You gotta be able to defend yourself. I told her to just take a gun and wave it around a few times to let people know you have it. That might help a little. They'd know they were taking a chance if they messed with your store. This way they know there's no chance taken at all. But that child won't listen. And a farm girl at that. I was raised in the country myself, and the first thing we knew after learning how to pluck a dead chicken for Mama was how to shoot Daddy's gun. Didn't you ever shoot your Daddy's gun, I asked her. 'No,' she said. Just 'No,' like I wasn't supposed to ask that anymore. But I did get her to carry some iron. I don't know how much good it will do her, but I told her she had to at least carry iron for going to get in her car at night, if nothing else. I got her a good piece of scrap iron, about three feet long, and I wrapped some tape around the end so she could hold it better. She's a strong girl. You don't have to worry about that. So now that child at least has some iron she carries with her in the car. I feel a little better knowing that."

"Thanks very much," Giacomo said and turned to walk down the steps to the car.

B.C. didn't follow. "What happened to your hand?" she asked the man.

"Oh, well," he said. "I got shot in the middle finger. My ex-girlfriend tried to shoot my new girlfriend and I got in the middle. I wasn't trying to be no hero. I just didn't think she'd really shoot that thing. It could have been a lot worse. The police said it could have been between my eyes. Now, my new girlfriend probably feels worse about it than I do, since the old one shot me in my loving finger." The man laughed.

Giacomo watched B.C. turn bright red. She waved to the man and joined Giacomo at the car. He was smiling. She was laughing, but she wouldn't look at him.

They found the U-Tote-Em. They parked next to a beat-up Volkswagen beetle covered with bumper stickers calling for the end of war, the dismantling of nuclear power plants, the rebuilding of the Fifth Ward, and a woman's right to choose. In the middle of the car's small back window, a bumper sticker read, "If God is not a woman, why did She make the sunset pink?" He figured this was Claire Beauchamp's car, but when they entered the store, he found no one he recognized as Claire Beauchamp. The clerk at the counter pointed to the storeroom at the back. There he found her, sitting on boxes, staring at a blank white cinder-block wall. B.C. followed him into the room.

"Claire," he said.

She turned to face them. The same wide face without the ruddiness of the country, where he'd met her. In fact, her skin seemed devoid of color, except for a certain gray-tinged whiteness he'd seen in hospital patients and workers in windowless offices and now in U-Tote-Em managers. She didn't seem to recognize him.

"I'm Giacomo Berg. Remember me? A friend of Peter Proust?"

"Oh, yes," she smiled. And that was all.

"I'm trying to find Peter. I thought you may have heard from him. He's supposed to be in Texas somewhere."

"That was so many lives ago," she said and turned back to the wall.

He waited. She turned back to face him. "I think of him once in a while, particularly the way he scratched his beard, shook his head from side to side, and looked up at the sky. That's the picture I have of him. He used to do that when he said all the gods were speaking to him at once. Sometimes I'm sorry I left him, but I had to go out and do something. He'd been to college. He'd been all over the country. I'd never seen anything but Western Massachusetts. That was good enough for him in the place he was at the time. But I wasn't ready for that yet. I might do it now. But not then. I wasn't ready for it then. Besides, you can't go back. I can't just walk away from here and go back there. Too much happened in between. There are several lives I've lived since then. They're all part of me now. What can I tell you? No, I haven't heard from Peter in several years. I don't think he'd know where to find me. I've moved several times. I used to get letters from him from the Refuge once in a while. But not often and not for a long, long time. Is he that hard to find?"

"His family hasn't heard from him. He left the Refuge months ago and no one knows what's become of him. They did get a card from him from somewhere on the coast south of here, but that's about it. I just thought you might have heard something. It was just a chance."

"I almost wish I had. It might have been real nice. He was always real nice, just sometimes a little confused. If I do hear from him, I could let his family know. Are they still in the same place? And if you find him, tell him Claire says, 'Hi.'"

"I will," Giacomo said, and he and B.C. backed out of the room, leaving Claire to stare at the blank wall once again.

"Let's get to the motel," he said. He felt pretty low.

She Struck a Major Chord

"IS THE WORLD getting more dangerous or are we just getting older?" Stephen Seltzer seemed to be talking as much to himself as to B.C., seated in the front seat next to him, or to Giacomo, riding in back. He was giving them the grand tour of Glasgow Country Estates and environs. Stephen had asked B.C. for help. He'd called some of his contacts from the Optimist Club—the elementary school principal, the pastor of the First Baptist Church, the rabbi at Temple Beth Israel, and the First Methodist minister—to see if they'd noticed any increase in illness among students or parishioners.

They arrived at the principal's office. He was tall, prematurely bald, with a ring of blond hair above his ears. He moved like the small forward he had probably been for some Christian college basketball team, crouching slightly, as if ready to spring.

The principal said that, aside from the rash that had hit a number of students, there had been two cases of leukemia, which the families had wanted kept confidential, and an unusual number of absences for children suffering from some sort of lethargy. It was not mononucleosis or some known disease, but a number of children kept falling asleep at their desks or telling their mothers they couldn't get up in the morning to go to school.

"I'm not talking about your ordinary everyday bellyaching and gold-bricking. At least I think I'm not," the principal said. "Although these kids do get more sophisticated every day. But it's just so pervasive I have to think there's something going on. The school nurse thinks it's some kind of mass hysteria that runs through a school every once in a while. But, if you look at the students it's hitting, they're not the ones I would have picked for hysteria. It runs the gamut—little first grade goof-offs to fifth-grade spelling-bee champs. It's not just girls and it's not just boys. It's not just the kids from Old Glasgow or just the kids from New Glasgow. It's across the board. I'm supposed to report when there's an outbreak of one kind or another. But I'll be danged if I've figured out how to report this one. They might just decide to retire me six years early for not being able to keep my kids in school."

The rabbi, the Baptist preacher, and the Methodist minister said pretty much the same thing: each felt like he had been making a few more sick calls than usual. The rabbi attributed it to the hot, muggy weather holding the bad air from the ship channel over the metropolitan area. The preacher had said that these things always increase at the end of summer when school starts up.

"I wonder if it has to do with the Millennium and Y2K," the preacher said. "After all, it is almost 2000 years on the nose since His death. Not that I think His will will be made manifest by computers exploding and taking what we know of civilization down with it. But I know a number of people are extremely worried."

"It's not so much the funerals," the minister said. "They're holding fairly steady. It's hard to disrupt His plan. But I have been seeing a number of sicknesses—people whose nerves are all just shot to pieces or people who can't get up in the morning at all, can't pull their feet out from under the covers to slide into their slippers. I visited with one of them just the other morning—an insurance executive, a big barrel of a man, somebody who was a go-getter before anybody had even left the starting line. But lately he just hasn't been able to get out of bed. And he won't go have tests. He says there's nothing wrong with him, just that he's tired of it all. Well, his wife called me up, and she said, 'Reverend Channing, John B. is just not himself anymore.' She asked me to come over right away. Said she couldn't fight it anymore. So I went to see him, and I said, 'John B., get up, the world is calling for your energy and your strength.' And he looked at me and said, 'It's gone, Reverend. It's all I can do to change the television station with the remote control.' I know about mental illness. I see it every day in my line of work. This man was not a candidate for that. He has a big house, an adoring family, an important job, and he talks to the Lord on a daily basis. This does not seem like a mental case to me. He is not so much depressed as he is just plain tired. I tried to tell him, 'John B., people are dying every minute. They've been sick since man first took a breath. Everyone gets depressed, particularly for those few despairing moments when you lose sight of God's will. But no one,' I told him, 'just decides to sleep his life away. No one decides he's not sick or depressed or dying, but just too tired to get up in the morning.' I tried to get him to go see the doctor or take a vacation with his good wife. He says he will as soon as he feels up to it. It's a puzzle, a man like that."

Back in the car, Stephen asked again, "I'm serious. Are we seeing hints of an epidemic, is the world fraying at the edges, or are we just getting older?"

They sat in the car in the parking lot while Stephen waited for a response. He got none.

He went on. "Why do I know so many people who are dying or are dead? If it was this way with my parents, I wasn't aware of it. They had friends in college who were killed in the war. If they survived that, they seemed to live one long, uninterrupted moving sidewalk right into their late '60s, at least. You heard about a kid or two whose parents died while they were still in school. Once in a while somebody's old man would keel over from a heart attack. It was just a little reminder, a monkey wrench thrown aboard sky-rocketing adolescence to tell you that sooner or later you would be return-ing to earth. My mother's seven bridge partners—they've played bridge for more than forty years together. No one's died. No one's even been brushed by death. Their husbands are all alive, though some are now husbands of others. Their children have all grown up, most gone to college, most started families, bought houses, opened retirement accounts. Why this sudden change? Is it my paranoia? I don't think so. But sometimes late at night I wonder about that. Why do I know so many people my age, no more than ten years older, who have died or are dying or are in remission or have children whose blood count they monitor every other day? It's not just AIDS and other diseases that pop up now and again. I'm beginning to think—I am embarrassed to say this to you, B.C.—I'm beginning to think that we are only at the thin-nest edge of a worldwide epidemic brought on by our own technology. I stay up every night thinking about this. It's the chemicals and the radiation and the microwaves and the high-voltage wires. I think we're killing ourselves. I think the meek may inherit the earth because they will be the only people not completely surrounded by the instruments of their own demise. And nuclear deterrence? We'll each end up killing ourselves with the radioactive mess we create without ever setting off a bomb."

"I'd like to introduce you once again to Giacomo Berg," B.C. said, gesturing toward the back seat, trying to sound upbeat, then coughing. "He is your partner in paranoia."

Then she realized that she was covered with sweat. It ran from her scalp in rivulets. They were sitting in a hot car in a hot parking lot in humid Houston. She asked Stephen to get them moving again.

"No," Stephen said. "This is not paranoia. It may be middle age, but it is not paranoia. It may be that our parents' friends were dying all around us and that it was at the very time in our lives when we didn't have time to admit that data into our consciousness. I might be willing to concede that. But paranoia—no.

"I also don't remember my own parents making trips to the doctor to see if they were dying. They might have. They easily might have and kept it hidden from me. But everyone I know is going to have moles checked and lungs and colons and breasts and pancrei."

"Pancrei?" Giacomo said.

"Whatever. One minute you're feeling alive and planning a trip to Denver to take the kids hiking in the mountains and see your sister. You're calculating the number of years until retirement when you can collect your pension or when you can cash in that IRA, and the next moment some doctor—he may even be younger than you are—is telling you that you could be dying. And to your ears that means you're as good as dead. So they send you to have a sonogram to check your most interior organs after a routine blood test revealed a body chemistry bordering on formaldehyde. They send you to a nameless clinic, where they give you one of those backless hospital gowns. Then they hand you over to some young man, not even a doctor—a technician who rubs jelly all over your chest and stomach in order to watch your organs on a screen. And he knows more about your insides than you do. And the way he looks at the screen, then looks at you, it makes you wonder, does this kid know I'm as good as gone? Is the monotone he uses to tell me when to breathe an indication of my doom? He plows his instrument so impassively through the jelly on my stomach, my chest and then on my back. The examining table becomes a primordial ooze. What can I read in this kid's face, now reading my future on a screen of sound waves I can't decipher? It gets to you. I felt like I'd aged twenty-five years in the two hours I spent covered with jelly. My horizons were now closing in on me. This happened two years ago. I haven't been able to talk to Cara about it. Nothing was wrong, thank God. That's what the doctor told me at any rate. He fiddled with my diet a little. But, still, I'm not the same. I guess that's just what happens."

Giacomo Berg did not say a word. He, too, was covered in sweat.

"Can you take us back to the motel?" B.C. asked. "I'm not feeling well."

Stephen started the car. "I have one more place to show you." He drove through the middle of the suburb's shopping areas, then turned on a farm-to-market road that ran beside a city park with a number of baseball diamonds and a large swimming pool. Giacomo noticed that a long line of kids was standing behind a diving board while a girl wearing a bathing cap struggled to achieve balance on her toes on the end of the board, facing away from the water with her arms out in front of her. They passed a large uninhabited expanse, then a couple of older homes on large pieces of land that must have predated the creation of Glasgow Estates. Beyond these houses they followed a bayou that ran parallel to the road and about forty feet from it. Then Stephen pulled the car off the road and onto a caliche drive leading to the locked gate of a ten-foot fence enclosing a large piece of property in the middle of which stood a blue corrugated building. On the building there was a sign proclaiming, "Pleistex—A Division of Fischer Industries."

Beyond the building were small hills of red, gray, and brown. Grass grew on some of the hills. On others it did not.

"This is my first guess," Stephen said. "I'm not sure what they make here or what's in those mounds, but I was driving around a couple of days ago, the way I've been driving around looking for answers since all this started happening, and I came across the Pleistex plant. It's been closed a little over a year. But I was driving by and I couldn't help but notice that the wind was picking up dust from those mounds and blowing it toward the park. Now that's a good two miles down the road, of course, but it's something I noticed. And then the bayou runs right across the back of the property. The kids are always talking about 'getting slimed' there. This stuff could find its way into our water supply, couldn't it?"

"It's possible," Giacomo said.

"I don't know what's in those mounds, and it may not be anything to worry about at all, but I just have a feeling I'm right. Or that I may be right enough at least to pursue it further. I've thought about this for the last couple of nights. I need someone to tell me what's in those mounds. I need someone to check the water. Is that about right?" he turned around abruptly to face Giacomo.

"That sounds about right," Giacomo said. "I think I could help you a little on this. I may know someone who can help at least. It might interest him."

"Do you think I may be on to something?"

"Let me say this. You may be dead right. You may be onto something that's right on target. But you may also be as close to being right sitting in this car right now as you'll ever get. Being right about this may be of very little importance when you try to prove it in a lab or in court. But you should know what's there. That's what this is all about. That's why it grabs me. We already know what's right. Or, at least, what's within the realm to be considered. What we have to prove from your observation is not that it's possible or even probable. What we have to prove is, of the different possible outcomes based on your observation, the outcome you predict is overwhelmingly the most likely. We can't describe exactly how the world actually functions. We can only describe how we see the world functioning. Our problem lies in convincing others that our way of seeing the world in this instance has the most merit."

"I can no longer see a thing," B.C. said. "I'm feeling very puny. Can we go back to the motel now, please?"

As they drove back into town, Giacomo said, "I have some ideas." He was thinking of Randall Occam.

"Anything you can do," Stephen said. "I would appreciate it immensely."

B.C. sniffled and snuffled and did not turn from the window.

By the time they went to bed, she was overcome by a cold, full throttle. Her head felt as big as the bed. And there was no room in it for Giacomo Berg.

"This is not the way it happens in romantic novels," she said, by way of apology, though she felt there was no reason to apologize. It was an illness, after all, which she had made no effort to contract. She began to ponder this, somewhat dully. Then she fell asleep.

After reading the sports page, after considering her long legs curled now under the sheets, after pulling out Bernal Diaz's *Conquest of New Spain* and reading about Montezuma's hopeless negotiations with Cortés, after considering her legs again and wondering what had happened the night before, after letting his self-doubt, kept under wraps most of the day, have a go of it, a run around the park on a long leash, but a leash just the same, he turned out the lights and slipped into bed. She was a formidable presence, lying there beside him, turned to the wall, sounds just this side of a death-rattle emanating from her nose and mouth, ears and every pore. It was more like sleeping with some strange gargoyle than with a long-limbed woman.

He sat up in bed waiting for his eyes to adjust to the dark. There was nothing to look at. A sliver of light outlining the curtain, suitcases strewn across a dresser, table and chair, a dark television screen.

Nevertheless he stared.

Then she turned, facing him, still asleep. And the shift in her body's attitude was accompanied by a profound shift in its sound. The sloshing and deep roiling of her influenzaic waters was replaced by a high-pitched rush of air through her finely honed nostrils. At that moment he considered the Roman lineage of that nose, something coming perhaps from her half-Italian mother landed somehow in Lockhart. Centuries of Mediterranean generations had gone into the creation of this precision instrument, through which air coursed as if engaged in some sort of act of liberation. It was not mere intake followed by mechanical expulsion. It was a rush and flow as if the wings of revolution were flying past. He stared into semi-darkness, overwhelmed by the life-force sleeping beside him, this culmination of the complex forces of physics, chemistry, and biology and the less complex forces of chance and her parents' need to rut on occasion.

Then he heard it. At first he was not sure he'd heard it. It was high-pitched and elusive. He thought it came from a television set in a room above or below or beside their own. But it did not. Its thin lines cut through the air in regular intervals, matched, it seemed, to the breathing beside him.

It was an open fifth, the first note and fifth note, the chord high-pitched but exact, the same each time—announced, sustained, then disappearing only to be announced again. And he realized it was emanating from the nose beside him—one nostril perhaps providing the first note and the other, the fifth. Together they produced a high, thin chord. It never wavered. It never changed. He could have listened to it all night. In fact, he was afraid he would. But he fell asleep.

A Quantum Shiver

B.C. WOULD BE SLEEPING IN. Giacomo Berg got dressed, went to breakfast, read the paper. But the paper only took him through his orange juice. He had two eggs, hash browns, and toast to kill. There were definite cultural advantages to living in New York. He went for a walk, but the exhaust, humidity, and blocks upon blocks of strip shopping centers and little else drove him back. He called his friend, Dr. Randall Occam, a health specialist in the Houston Medical Center and star witness for plaintiff's lawyers everywhere who were engaged in suits involving chemical hazards.

"Meet me at Corrine's," Occam said, "for lunch. This is Thursday."

Giacomo had two hours to kill. He tried Bernal Díaz but couldn't stay with it. He found the address for Corrine's on the map. He decided to just get into the car and drive until it was time to meet Occam. Something might come to him while driving. Or it might not. But it seemed that the proper thing to do in order to understand Houston was drive.

He spent the next two hours on a quarter mile stretch of expressway, locked in a traffic jam caused by a chemical truck overturned several miles ahead, precipitating the complete shutdown of traffic in both directions. That was the word passed from one driver to another as they stood there for the better part of two hours on the hot elevated pavement, peering ahead at potential disaster and behind at a sea of vehicles. It was actually a nice change of pace. It was the closest thing to cafe society Houston had to offer. He kind of liked it. Everyone was freed from the moving cages they were locked in on the expressway. One by one, they were pried from their cars by circumstance. They stood together in the middle lanes and at the guard rails gazing at length at what before they had only known fleetingly—stores, houses, trees, office buildings, people in those buildings exchanging papers, moving around. They talked.

"Ain't this a bitch," a tall man said to Giacomo. The man had been in the delivery van behind his car. "I just had two more stops to make and then I was home free. A washer and a window unit. It was gonna be a breeze. And tonight's the night we were going to celebrate our anniversary. It's Sunday actually. But my mother-in-law can only take the kids tonight. I hope this don't fuck that up or I'll catch holy hell."

"But if you can't write into your program that driving on the loop will absolutely include several hours a month just like this at complete stand-still, then your program isn't worth a damn," said a man in a gray suit who had been standing behind Giacomo all along. "Your wife should be able to understand that."

"She won't understand nothin' except I screwed up the anniversary. That's what she'll understand. I ain't got no other program."

Giacomo addressed both men. "This happens a lot?" he asked.

"All the time," the gray-suited man said. "This is the quintessential Houston experience. Everything else is just a pale imitation. Now you can say you've done Houston. I've sometimes thought I should print t-shirts to sell that say something like 'When it's time to be somewhere, how can you be two places at once? Drive the loop.' It would sell. My wife says I should just print them up, keep them in my trunk, and sell them to the rest of you while we're waiting for the traffic to move."

"I'd buy one if the price was right," the delivery man said. "Where are you from?" he asked Giacomo.

"We know he can't say he's just passing through," the gray-suited man laughed.

"I'm from New York," Giacomo said. "The thing that impresses me—I've got to say this—is when this happens in New York, you wouldn't have a lot of people out here talking. They'd be sitting in their cars with the windows up and the doors locked. And half of them would honk every once in a while, like it does some good. If they had a gun in the glove com-partment, they'd be thinking about it, ready for marauding gangs. Half of them would think the traffic jam was an ambush set up by gangs to secure compliant victims. Like bandits on the highways. Two-thirds would won-der why a chemical spill merited extra attention halting traffic, given the certain chemical dangers of land, water, and air within the metropolitan area. And ten percent would be trying to figure out ways to get around the other ninety."

"You're not one of them Yankees that came down here looking for a job, are you?" the delivery man asked. "Because if you are, you missed it by a few years."

"I'm just down here on a little business," Giacomo replied.

"What do you do?" the gray-suited man asked.

He always wanted to evade this question. But this accidental cama-raderie on the road demanded truth. "I'm a private investigator," he said.

"No shit, Sherlock," the delivery man said. "Okay, tell me what I did before I was working this delivery job. Go ahead, tell me. Look at me and what do you see? C'mon, do your stuff. Let me see what you got."

Giacomo would have walked away at this point. He would not even have felt he needed a pretext to walk away in this case. It was so demoralizing to realize the hocus-pocus people think he employed. He could have walked away, but just then horns started sounding ahead. He could see people get-ting in their cars and hear engines starting. As the delivery man walked away, Giacomo said, "Minor league ball, Class B. Worked your way up to AA. You were a pitcher with a decent fast ball but no curve or slider to keep 'em guess-ing. The better batters ate you alive."

"Goddamn," the delivery man said. "That ain't even close." And he slammed his door. The traffic began to move. Giacomo began to move. He felt he had gotten to know Houston a little better. They inched toward the scene of the accident and over the sandy spot where the spill must have occurred. And then the traffic geared up and they were off. Soon he found the exit and not long thereafter he found Corrine's. Inside he found Occam, waving to him from a booth not far from the door.

"Well, isn't this it?" yelled Occam above the disco music, motioning to Giacomo Berg to sit down.

"It's what I would tell my students is a purplish perplex, a concatenation of contradictory vectors all arrived at a single point—me, in this booth here—at the precise moment of measurement when each possibility aches to assume the form of its equal and opposing possibility, that little quantum shiver—is it particle or wave?—when all matter longs to dissolve toward entropy in order to re-form as that which it is not, thereby proving that the only real truth is that which we find in its exact opposite, not in a Platonic sense, mind you—never accuse me of that—but in the sense that we know something by what it is not, thereby allowing us to see that it is as much our own consciousness that we are exploring in the way that it divides up cognition into the real and the unreal, the known and the unknown, the coasting along the edge of the unknown providing that frisson of euphoria that brings us here in the first place."

Occam was on a roll. Here he was, in a red velvet booth in a high-class strip joint in a Houston shopping center, expounding on his presence beside a small platform, labeled "Stage B," upon which a topless woman wearing a g-string was gyrating almost endlessly, stopping only now and then to let a customer insert folding money in the waistband of her g-string—hunkering down like a cowpoke around a campfire or a Vietnamese farmer waiting for a bus—thereby bringing her breasts to eye-level while the customer fiddled with the g-string.

"Meaning?" Giacomo Berg eventually asked.

"Meaning I can't get enough of it. Thursday lunch, Tuesday and Friday nights. When I'm here I exist in that gray area of perception. You know what I mean? They come over to you here—you'll see, someone will do it in a minute—they'll come over and ask if you want a table dance. And you'll say, no, you don't want a table dance, and they might move on, but most will sit down and start to tell you a life story, possibly theirs, and you start to listen. Well, well, you say, this is someone you don't know. And, for me at least, it's someone from another universe—a planet that's just come spinning into my own somewhat slow and tendentious orbit. So, no common experience. No attempt at recognition of similarities. Opposite poles. My anti-Occam. And then she starts to rub my arm and then my leg. And you know how they always say men come here looking for the whore with a heart of gold, the nice girl who got into a jam and had to do this to feed her starving kids or care for elderly grandparents? That's not me. I'm not looking for any kind of salvation here. But that's the thing: You don't go looking for it, but you find it. You talk to a stripper and inside you find her opposite, a nice kid thrown here by one piece of bad luck or another. So how do you measure this light, Jack? As a particle or a wave? The answer's simple: you get thrown into the quantum soup. You come here to a strip joint, where they don't just take off their clothes, they're also stripping off all the bullshit of everyday life, the complicating factors, the complexities, the…"

The stripper on the stage had pulled off Occam's glasses and was now dancing with them nestled on her breasts. Then she put one arm of the glasses in her g-string, smiling at Occam all the while. He was smiling back. "Can't see a thing," he called across the table. Then she put the glasses on one buttock, held in place by an arm reaching into the crack between her cheeks. He reached into his pocket and pulled out a twenty. She knelt down beside him, put the glasses back on his face, let him put the bill in her g-string, and began dancing again.

"Where was I?"

"The complexities."

"Yeah. You come here to get rid of all those complexities. Just naked, performing, nameless flesh. And you've got these lights that make it seem slightly distanced, slightly unreal. You can't see any blemishes, that sort of thing. And you've got this constant loud music that stifles reflection, keeping everything superficial with a single, steady, monotonous controlling cadence. And, so, you think you come in here eager for this unworldly, denuded simplicity, and what is the first thing you find yourself wanting?"

"A woman?"

"Complexity. I find myself wanting to talk to these people. Asking them how they ended up here. Finding out if they're products of a recession. Did they sell real estate? Did they speculate on commercial property? Were they administrative assistants for Shell Oil? Did they sell software? Or did they just run away from home after their father smacked them one too many times? I want to know. I want to pile on layers of meaning. I want to talk to them for hours, find out what makes them tick. Are they happy? Do they have hearts of gold? I buy them one drink after another. No, I say, I don't want a table dance right away. Sit down and talk for a while. And that's the other thing." Occam was so excited by his own disquisition that he was spitting fine spit across the table and wiping drops from his chin.

Giacomo was watching a woman dressed in leather hides circling their table. "What other thing?"

"When I first came here I found it hard to stare at their breasts. We've been so conditioned not to look at them, to be so politically correct, you know. At least I have. One of them would look at me and smile, and I'd turn away. Then I got to where I would stare to show them I admired them. I started talking to these women, getting to know them or the version of themselves that they were presenting. They'd talk through one drink or two or three. And then it would be time for them to do a table dance. That was, after all, the reason they sat down. Not for my good looks. So they say it's time to dance, and it's like I almost can't look because I know them now. It's become complex again. I get embarrassed. At the same time, I have to admit that it's only the ones I know who really turn me on. The others could just be

Venus de Milo for all I care. So there's that old ambivalence and we're back in the real world again. So now I don't know why I came here."

"Because you're a horny bastard."

"No, seriously, Jack. You come in here wanting to be fairly anonymous yourself. That's why the lighting is so crucial. It's hard to make out distinguishing features, the shadows are so strange. But, as soon as one of these women starts to talk to you and rub your leg, you want her to know that you're different than all the rest of leering mankind. And you start to hope they can spot that, that they can find you attractive, too, in a different sort of interesting way, in this cavern of colliding desires.

"And there's something else. Some of them tell me that it's the same way with them. They work here for one reason or another because it's relatively safe and the men disappear into one big smoke-filled blur, and even if they saw them on the street, they wouldn't know it. They like that. But they also say they're always looking. They're always looking for someone to get them out of some jam. They're always in here because of some jam. An accountant or lawyer or even a college professor. Somebody in this high-class place to bail them out. So they don't want to know you, but they want to know you, too. They're out there shivering in that quantum purgatory, too. This place is a writhing mass of ambiguity. I can't get enough, Jack."

"A table dance, Randy?" A woman with long dark hair wearing a sleeveless sweatshirt was standing over Occam with her hand on his shoulder.

"Not now, my dear, but do sit down," he said, arching his eyebrows in Giacomo's direction. "I was telling my friend here why this place is more than it seems to be at first gander."

"Buy me a drink, okay?" He nodded. She signaled for the waitress. "This here is Jack," he said, trying to sound colloquial.

"Another professor?" she asked, batting her eyelashes.

"Well, only in the sense that he professes not to profess a belief in anything," Occam chuckled. "Tell him your story."

"Which one?" she asked, sipping on a Wild Turkey straight up.

"It doesn't matter."

"Well, as it so happens," she said, grabbing Giacomo's forearm, "I was just talking to another customer who reminded me of a $6 million real estate deal I lost. I had it. It couldn't miss. It was a hundred acres of land right beside a ski resort they were going to build in upstate New York. I had my money on the property to hold it for me, but I let it slip away. It just got away from me while I was in court down here. Now I've got to stay down here for two more months while I'm on probation because they say I was guilty of aggravated solicitation of prostitution. Do you believe that? Me? Do you know Harry's Bodego? I was working there and this guy who turns out to be a cop—well, he doesn't turn out to be because I knew it all along. I spotted it right off. He comes up to me and asks me to introduce him to one of the other girls. And so I do and right there he throws the cuffs on both of us. Her for prostitution and me for being a pimp. Me, a pimp? Can you believe it? And aggravated. What did I do? Stare some laser beams into his balls? So I pleaded 'nolo' because I thought that would be the least hassle and I could pay a fine and go to New York to make this real estate money, but instead they lock me up for two months and give me ten-months probation. And what could I do? It meant I lose my kids. I told them that. You mean you'll throw me away for two months and make me lose my kids on a made-up charge? I told them. I can't believe it. But that's what they did. I was in the middle of a divorce, see. And so my husband just took the kids and left. And now I'm stuck here in this town for two more months, or is it four? So now I'm doing this and trying to sell real estate by day. Of course, I don't have a license right now, so I work with this other girl who does. But how can you sell anything in Houston in this day and age? Upstate New York is the place to be. I've never been there myself, you understand. But that's what I hear. What time is it?"

Occam told her it was 1:45.

"Shit. I've got to do four dances before 2. How about it, Randy? One short dance?"

"Not now," Occam said. "Jack and I have business to discuss."

"Look, Professor. I'm just trying to earn a living. I need you to pay me for the time I just spent educating your friend. You think I like stripping for pathetic old men who come here to see if they can get a hard on? Don't be a fat prick like everybody else. Put up or shut up, Professor."

She held out her right hand. He pulled out his wallet and handed her three $100 bills. "That's more like it. Professors discussing business," she said, squeezing Giacomo's forearm. "Never heard of it. Watch my bag, lover. It's got nothing in it but face paint, and they're not your color." She walked off into the pulsating lights.

"What did I tell you?" said Occam. "Isn't she great? I love it when she talks to me like that. You get hooked. These women come right at you with lives laid out on the table. Bare, naked. They're at the same time completely vulnerable and coated with a plate of armor. The beauty of it is they can treat you like shit, and you still don't care. They rub their breasts in your face, and you can't come close to really touching them. It's limbo, weightlessness. There are no spatial axes to latch onto, no permanent foci of understanding. Everything is in motion. It's beyond phenomenology. It's the great quantum leap!"

"Did anybody ever tell you what an idiot you are?" Berg asked. "Let's try to talk a little business before you dissolve into a pool of goo."

Occam was by this time close to falling on his face. He was leaning way out of the booth attempting to follow the gyrations of a dancer on the main stage, equipped with mirrors and poles of various sizes, jutting from the stage at various angles. The dancer, dressed like Raggedy Ann, climbed some stairs to the top of a vertical pole, took off her red wig and Raggedy Ann dress to reveal a harness made of leather straps and slithered and slid down the ten-foot pole. When she hit the floor, Occam hit the floor. It was too much for him.

Picking himself up, and motioning to the waitress for another drink, he straightened his glasses and turned to Giacomo Berg. "What sort of business did you want to discuss, anyway?"

"I want to find out what's in a certain landfill, who's putting it there, and what it can do to people," Giacomo said. "I thought maybe you could break it down for me, tell me how to get a handle on it. Is there a database I can use?"

"What you're talking about is more politics than science," Occam said. "You know that, don't you?"

A blond woman in a firefighter's hat and a red t-shirt sat on Occam's lap. "A table dance, professor?"

"Not now, Lorette. Come see me in a few minutes. I was the fat kid in high school, the bookworm in college," he said, turning to Berg. "You know that. I'm still the fat kid. Not in my wildest dreams did I think I would be living this life. Where were we? Yes. I can get you data. I can get it from the EPA and the Air Quality people and the Water Commission of Texas. I can get you lists out the kazoo. I can tell you that PCBs cause liver damage and pesticides can cause what looks like a stroke. I can stand up and tell any jury in the world that lead can cause headaches and mercury can change your personality. And I'll be right. But that's not the problem. The problem is politics, not science. And the lists the government will give me are incomplete. They'll fight us at every juncture. They won't tell us what a specific plant produces or how much until you've taken them through court, made yourself a pauper, and aged twenty years over a ten-year span. You'll say you've got a toxic landfill next door and you have headaches, and they'll say, how do you know it's not from the petrochemical plant three miles upwind or the city dump leaching into the underground water supply? Or the pesticide drift from the rice fields half a mile away? Or the chemicals in the Diet Coke you drink every day? Or it's just your imagination. Or it's hereditary: your great aunt died of colon cancer. Or you've got HIV. Data is easy to come by. The data you really need is more difficult but not impossible. But the ability to take fact and make it truth for an unimpeachable legal argument, that's the mountain that never gets climbed." He motioned to a woman in an Indian headdress and discreetly situated fringed leather to bring three beers.

"Look," Giacomo said. "I know the odds. I just want to help some friends get off the ground. It may not make that much difference to me. I live across the river from Jersey, you remember. But I thought we might be able to give them some solid footing to start from. They think they've got a problem. They probably do. Kids are getting blood diseases. Old ladies are going screwy three and four at a time. Young men are feeling old. And people like you and me—we're finally feeling our age. And that ain't good."

"I said I'd help. I'll check the database. I'll give you a write-up on what I find. What chemicals might be there and what kinds of symptoms are associated with them. I'll go that far. Any further, and they'll have to start paying into the account. My vices are not cheap."

The woman in the headdress was by then sitting on his lap, having served herself and the two of them their beer. Giacomo looked at his watch. It was almost three o'clock. He felt hemmed in. He suddenly couldn't stand the disco beat, the pulsating lights, the smoke and the haze, the icy air conditioning, knowing it was the middle of the afternoon. He got up and pointed to the exit. "I'll get back to you," he told Occam.

"Wait," Occam said. "I feel a table dance coming on," and he rubbed the back of the dancer on his lap and said something into her ear.

But Giacomo Berg was out of there. Out into the searing heat and the sunlight that overwhelmed everything before it with a white sheen. He stood there, letting the sun burn away what he'd carried out with him from inside. He stood there until he felt his skin radiating heat.

Love's Old Sweet Song

THEY SAT AROUND three empty bottles of retsina—Giacomo, Stephen and Cara Fenster-Seltzer, and sniffling B.C. Boyd. B.C. was alternating hot tea and brandy.

A map of Glasgow and surrounding suburbs covered the coffee table in front of them.

They'd drawn a circle indicating a three-mile radius around the Pleistex landfill. They'd counted the number of inhabited blocks within the circle and calculated the number of volunteers it would require to walk the blocks and circulate questionnaires. Stephen wasn't quite sure where he would recruit the volunteers. Certainly among the few neighbors who had shared their concerns with him about health problems. He'd approach the men's club at the temple. It seemed inappropriate to make Boy Scouts or Camp Fire Girls little statisticians of death. No. He didn't want Tess or Josh in that role. Nevertheless, he would somehow get the volunteers. Or he would walk the entire community himself.

"It's not just the numbers," Cara had said. "The doing itself is cathartic. And it's organizing. It gets people talking about the problem. It could be a kind of centering for you, Stephen. You haven't been centered in a long time."

At that point, Stephen got up to check on the sleeping children, particularly Josh. They did this several times a night now, checking to make sure his nose wasn't bleeding. It was no longer an act done in panic. It was already part of the routine. As he returned, Cara checked his expression, apparently found no indication of trouble, and sipped from her glass of retsina.

They began devising a simple questionnaire. "There's no mystery to these things," Giacomo said. "If you sound like you know what you're doing, then you know as much as anyone. The idea is to make sure the universe you are testing is the universe in which the answers you are seeking will fall. That's all. What we need to do here is not just sample reality but create a new reality. Until we do this, no one will know that the apparent Glasgow of affluent suburbs of two-and-three-acre lawns, sprawling ranch-style houses and nouvelle-cuisine cooking schools is different from the experienced

Glasgow, where parents stay up all night with anemic children, where middle-aged wives of bank executives are one day thrown to the ground on the way to the laundry room by tumors blossoming in their heads, where the high school football coach can't run a scrimmage without at least two strapping kids begging off early from exhaustion. You have to create a new understanding of what's going on here, of what life in Glasgow has become.

"Of course, you already know what's going on—or you have a pretty good hunch. But you want to confirm that hunch. You want to make it look convincing. You want other people to be able to buy into it. So, you create a vehicle, pretty much like a political poll. It asks for family history. It asks for occupations. You already know income levels around here, unless you poll someone's housekeeper. You ask about deaths or illnesses. You ask about pregnancy and births. You ask about physical abnormalities. You ask about mental health, particularly about any changes in the mental health of children. Then you ask if they've ever spent much time in the city park. You ask if they smoke. You ask if they handle hazardous materials either at work or in a hobby. You ask if they've noticed anything unusual about their immediate environment—the water, the land, the air. The ones who seem to have some sort of health problem you go back to with a follow-up questionnaire. Make it look official and scientific. Make it seem dignified. Talk to people for as long as you need to get their answers. It's a lot of work."

"I can't believe you know this stuff?" B.C. sniffled.

"What do you think I do all day long? All I do is ask questions. Either I ask people or public records or a database. I put series of questions together. I rehearse them. I figure out the best order to put them in to get maximum benefit. That's what I do. You know that. I don't carry a gun or ambush mobsters making off with the beautiful daughter of a wealthy drug runner. I talk on the phone, sit at my computer, knock on doors. Old school and mostly tedious," Giacomo said.

He was feeling unusually articulate and focused on the task at hand. It was probably the retsina or what he thought was Cara Fenster-Seltzer's occasional flirtatious foray in his direction. A grounded, earth-centered potter's flirtation, having to do with the way she moved her hands along the coffee table as she sat on the floor, then touched his forearm once or twice to accentuate something she was saying. But a flirtation, nonetheless, although he could not be completely certain of this, nor did it really matter.

But he couldn't help but notice that she'd been paying rapt attention to his explication. Or so it seemed. You can't tell with potters. She may have been listening to an inner world as he'd babbled on.

Stephen Seltzer had been taking notes. He looked over the notes, then went to the liquor cabinet to grab another bottle of retsina. "We do this once a year," he said. "Whenever we decide it's Melina Mercouri's birthday. It occurred to me, shortly before you arrived, that perhaps it was today." He filled the empty glasses and left the room to check on Josh.

When he returned, he emptied his glass, then filled it again. Then he said, "You know it just doesn't get any easier—raising kids, I mean. I'd thought once we'd made the decision to do it, that was the hard part. Once we'd put the thought of nuclear war out of our minds, once we unilaterally decided—Cara and I—that somehow for the next hundred years the world would not run out of food and water, once we'd made that impossible choice to forget all that, or transcend it as we told ourselves, then I thought the rest would be easy. But every time some major disaster threatens, I wonder what we've done to these kids. What act of hubris have we committed, thinking we should reproduce ourselves and that, somehow, everything would work out all right? But this chemical business is getting to me. Just like I can feel a global warming funk sneaking up on me. And a few years ago it was Qaddafi and Khomeini, and now there's no place safe to travel. These things move through us like waves. And my great fear, of course, is that one of these waves is going to break on us. Look at these places where there's no more water and little food or the water they have is so polluted it will kill you deader than starvation will. Millions of children are dying there, and I know B.C. or someone like her will remind me that part of the responsibility for that lies with us and the way resources are allocated and used.

"And I know that, but at a gut level I don't care. No, it's not that I don't care, but I don't care about that as much as I care about the fact that my kids, my family, are living in a country that still has those resources and, if necessary, controls those resources for its own sake, even to the detriment of the rest of the world.

"I used to think, if we brought these kids into the world, that we owed them thirty years free of this kind of worry. I mean the entire universe may collapse in ten thousand million years, so we should be able to spot them thirty free and clear. Thirty years free of nuclear war. We didn't have that luxury when we were kids. We spent six formative years cowering under school desks every time the radar sirens went off. We owe them thirty years without food shortages or water shortages. Thirty years without their lives being thrown into chaos, the way the lives of the children of Lebanon or Northern Ireland or parts of Mexico or . . ."

"Guatemala," B.C. said.

"Guatemala," Stephen said.

"The Bronx," Giacomo said.

"Or the Bronx," Stephen said, "the way those lives are lived in a whirlwind with no sense of security or place or value. I thought we owed them that. I thought, when we had these kids, that we could see ahead a good thirty years. That we could promise them that. Cara, of course, thought we owed them a hundred years, their whole lifetimes free of major disruption. I wish to God we could do that, but I can't see far enough ahead to make that deal. I would never have had kids if one hundred years was the requirement. But I thought I could see thirty. I thought I knew that much. But now, this." He emptied his glass again.

"We're just bombarded by all these contradictory impulses. You want kids. She wants kids. It's selfish to do it. Your mother tells you it's selfish not to do it. There's that primal urge. Everything has its own momentum, you tell yourself, including the reproduction of the species. Don't contradict biology, a voice says. That's all we've really got, it says. That's all we are—a string of biological events that you are too insignificant to consider breaking. You owe it to your ancestors and to your species. Did 3,000 years of Jews suffer so that Stephen and Cara Fenster-Seltzer could decide not to reproduce, not to continue the race? It's your only possible real contribution to the world. It's both an act of pride and an act of humility, an act of arrogance and an act of faith. You are approaching middle age and then old age. Is the time to continue the string now? Or is it already too late? Finally, you just put your head down and bull your way through.

"If we get through this calamity," he continued, motioning toward Josh's room, "it will have been the right thing to do. Until the next crisis. Every day it's more right and more wrong." He looked into his empty glass.

Cara moved next to him and put her hand in his lap.

"What we are and what we think we are are two different things," she said. "This has become one of those times that puts us face-to-face with what we are."

It was time for them to go.

"I went to the doctor today," B.C. said as they drove the lanes of Glasgow and then onto the freeway into town. "Cara had recommended him. He was just across the street in the medical center. I've decided I should go see those internment camps in South Texas. No, let me rephrase that. I've decided I want to go see the internment camps, so I want to get over this cold or whatever it is quickly, so I can get down there."

Giacomo didn't answer. He simply drove.

"Anyway, it was like the invisible epidemic Stephen and Cara are facing in seemingly serene All-American Glasgow. There are so many worlds orbiting out there that we never even suspect, revolving in ways completely alien to our own. I was waiting in this doctor's office, and this family of three women and one skinny little man comes in. The three women were all immensely fat and wearing house dresses. I figured they were among the poorest of the poor. When they sat down, their dresses rode up well above the knee. Their leg fat was dimpled like pepperoni. One of the women seemed to have a little palsy. She pulled out a Louis L'Amour novel and started reading it. The other two women—they could have been 35 years old or 65—and the skinny little man just stared straight ahead into space. A receptionist brought them a clipboard with a form to fill out. She handed it to the man, who handed it to one of the women, who passed it to the woman with the palsy. The woman who had passed the clipboard wanted to know what the form said.

"'They just want your information, Mama,' the palsied woman told her. 'Like where we live, who we are, do we have Medicaid, are you on Medicare?'

"The palsied daughter filled out the form, and then she said they needed to know the answer to a question about when the mother had her 'surgeries.' There was quite a bit of discussion among them. Then the mother answered that the last one she had was last year. Her daughter asked her what it was for. 'Oh, one of my cancers,' she'd said. 'I forget which one.'

"Can you believe that?" B.C. asked. "'One of my cancers. I forget which one.' The kinds of lives people lead. It just blows me away."

They reached the motel.

Giacomo Berg was wrung out. From Randall Occam among the nightingales to self-knowledge dawning in suburbia, it had been a taxing day. He couldn't tell what the night would bring, but he figured the play would not be his. He couldn't figure out where they stood, and he was almost too tired to care. Almost.

She came out of the bathroom and sat on the side of the bed beside him. "I want to do this right," she said. "I think we deserve this being done right. Give me one more day. I've got mega-doses of Vitamin C and antibiotics galore. By tomorrow I'll be in playing shape. You don't want me sniffling in your ear."

"We must be getting old," he said.

She put her hand on his arm. "For some reason I just want this to go well. Tomorrow night," she said, "and we can begin the evening some place other than Glasgow." Then she got up and went to the other side of the bed and lay down facing the wall.

It was just as well. It was a resolution of some kind. He felt so brain-dead that he welcomed this resolution, putting off more serious resolution for another night. Tension allayed, he got up and walked to the couch. His purpose had been to read for a while, to think about other things. But once he got there, first he leaned, then he lay back, and in an instant he was asleep.

B.C. was not. She lay there thinking about what Stephen had said. If the universe collapses in ten thousand million years, what did that mean to B.C. Boyd in terms of having children? That it mattered or didn't matter? That their birth or death was inconsequential except to her and the few others who would know them? That seemed to hold the answer. Why not try to shape matter into a body of understanding? Why not give dust meaning, even if only to her dust? That dust would mean more to her dust than the largest stars of the densest galaxy mean to one another. They would have a pull greater than their gravity. Her time may have already run its course. There was always adoption. There was that. Less than a blip in the ten thousand million year scheme of things, but important to her, nonetheless. That had to be resolved. Not with Giacomo Berg necessarily. She wasn't ready to consider that possibility. But she was paying attention to the milli-seconds of her own life. She was also, she knew, deep down an incurable romantic. She was always listening for love's old sweet song. She'd resolved years earlier that, despite hunger and nuclear war and Guatemala and the ten thousand million year end of everything, it was love's song that would provide her with her ultimate direction. And she realized just tonight, or perhaps remembered that she'd realized it before, one epiphany obliterating the memory of all others. The theme of that song, at least for her, at least now, was, Why not? If we all come from and return to dust and even anti-dust, then why not?

The Ascent of Peter Proust

IT HAD SEEMED like a good idea at the time. But a day-and-a-half of hitching rides across the Texas desert had burned him to a crisp. His lips were split. The bald spot on the top of his head was hot to the touch. At times the sweat ran down his face in torrents and prevented him from opening his eyes to the salt's sting. It coated his beard. He stood in the heat, his thumb out, his eyes closed, waiting for a ride. He did, however, let the sweat dribble into his mouth, trying to decide if he was recycling his own body salts, whether he could become a self-contained sustainable system or whether he was simply partaking of the wastes his body was trying to discard. At night he'd crawled under the barbed wire fence separating a small roadside park with three picnic tables from the rest of the world in order not to be discovered in his sleep by whatever authorities roamed the highways by night. The desert had cooled off quickly after sunset, but the idea of snakes had him spooked. He had a difficult time turning loose of consciousness, lying on the hard desert floor, hidden from view by a stand of dried-out, leafless, thorny brush, watching the stars, trying to discern a slightly altered angle of view from the one he'd enjoyed at the cabin he'd just left.

His first ride the next morning had been to a rest area, where he'd hoped to wash up. Instead, he found the water wasn't running. But a couple seemed to be living in the breezeway. They were sleeping on the concrete of the breezeway when he'd arrived, a mutt tied to the man's leg by a rope. They'd arranged boxes and trash bags filled with belongings in such a way as to cordon off a section of the breezeway for themselves. They'd put a sign up on the topmost box, "Private. Please do not bother." A sterno, a few styrofoam cups, and a bunch of newspapers were strewn behind the partition. A beanbag chair rested against a wall that held a large, framed highway map of Texas. There were signs on both the men's and women's restrooms, saying, "We're broke down and on our way back home. Please give us money to fix our car." The car, he figured, was the one standing in the parking lot, its front axle up on blocks, another mutt tied by a rope to a door handle.

Finding no water, Peter Proust walked into the grass behind the rest stop and sat full lotus facing the sun, hoping to gain energy for the journey ahead. When he arose, he found the couple sitting in the breezeway, watching him.

The man approached Peter Proust, holding the dog as it strained against the rope. They came forward; Peter backed away. He wasn't sure what this meant.

"Which way you headed?" the man asked. "West," Peter said.

"Can I get a lift to the next town?" the man asked. "We're almost out of food." Peter shook his head from side to side and stared at the ground. "I'm hitching," he said and laughed. "I'd give you food, but it just burned up in my cabin. They came and chased me off." It felt a little odd talking to another human being like this.

"It's okay, man," the man said. "C'mon and have some coffee. There's a trucker gave us half his thermos in the middle of the night. It's a little cold, but it will do. C'mon."

Peter Proust didn't want coffee. But he thought he could sit for a while, if this were not some cosmic trick to stop him in his journey. He'd take that chance. Their setup seemed too elaborate to be staged just to catch people like him. He'd never thought of this. Are there others out there like him? There must be. Wandering around. Looking for something. Maybe these two are like him. He'd take the chance. He'd said too much already. He wouldn't say much more. And he wouldn't drink coffee.

The man motioned to Peter to step inside their boxed partition. He motioned to the beanbag chair. Peter sat next to it on the floor. When they poured him coffee, he just put up his hand to show he wouldn't be having any. They understood and poured the coffee back into a large Styrofoam container. He was pleased to have communicated so well without words.

"We was coming from Biloxi, Dedonna and me, going to California because there's no work in Biloxi. It's not that we didn't give it a try. I worked at one thing and another and she worked in a fucking dry cleaners all night long, pressing the clothes of the rich and mighty. But we thought there might be something better out there. We ain't sure. But there couldn't be much worse. That was the plan," he said and sipped his coffee.

"But then we got this far. The car just give out," she said. "It jumped and bolted along for the last thirty or forty miles. They ain't nothing out here to help you. But when we pulled into this rest stop, it just died. It sort of coughed and sputtered and died. We don't know what to do exactly. Our folks don't have no money."

"And we sure as hell don't," he said.

"We smoked it up is what he means. But that's water under the bridge. We been here over a week now, about ten days. I lose count. And nobody much seems to believe us. They give us a few quarters. But quarters won't fix this car. They feed the dogs. And Darrell here gets a ride into the gas station and food store down the road and buys us some beer and dog food, a few gallons of water and Slim Jims and whatnot and then he hitches back. But that's about it. The highway patrol tells us to move on out of here. And we say we're trying. They say they're going to arrest us, and all we can say is 'good. I wish to hell you would.' But so far they won't. And we wouldn't want to give up the dogs."

"I say we just ditch the damn car and take off on the road like this dude," Darrell said. "I've been arguing that for a week. We'd be in California in no time."

"Darrell, we've got more shit in that car than ten years of working in California could ever get us. There ain't no way I'm going to leave my whole life sitting here in some car. You know we decided that we're going back. Then later we can try it again. Want some corned beef hash? We can heat it up real quick."

Peter held up his hand again. He needed to get on the road. He stood up. "Where west are you headed anyway?" Darrell asked.

"I'm not sure," Peter said.

"I hear there's some nice mountains not too far from here, if you like mountains, that is. A number of people coming through here are headed for them mountains. 'Davis Mountains,' one fella said."

That was something, Peter thought. Maybe that was why these people had been put here—to name the Davis Mountains for him. Was that the sign he was waiting for? He didn't know, but he would think about it.

He once knew how to fix cars. He could repair their car, and they could all drive into the sunset together. Too late for that. He needed to go his own way.

He stepped around the boxes and waved to the couple. She was busily lighting the sterno while he was working at the corned beef hash can with his pocket knife. Peter stopped to read the bumper stickers plastered all over the rear of their car. "Evangelists do more than lay people," one read. "Keep America Beautiful. Run Over an Environmentalist," read another. "Life is Hell. And then you die." "I brake for hallucinations."

Peter walked toward the highway. He stuck out his thumb. Sometime later he was off again. Riding in the back of a cigarette salesman's Buick, Peter was surrounded by boxes of Marlboros. The back seat was taken out so he had to kneel there behind the front seat, buttressed by cartons of cigarettes. The salesman didn't say a word. Peter watched the endless landscape of flat, dry land in all directions, broken by the occasional mesa or a ravine etched by a creek that ran either at flood stage or not at all.

When they reached Ft. Stockton, the salesman turned around to Peter. "Going any farther?" he asked. "I've got eight stops to make and then I'm headed on. You can either make the stops and stay in the car all the way to El Paso or you can get out here. It makes me no never mind."

"I'll stay," Peter said. He didn't have a clue as to where he was.

They pulled up to a grocery. The salesman grabbed a box full of cigarette cartons and went into the store. When he got back in the car, he asked, "Don't you ever bathe?"

At the next stop, the office of a motel, the salesman grabbed more boxes and went inside the office. Peter grabbed his things, got out of the car, and began walking away as quickly as possible.

He found another ride, this time in the back of a pickup with a border collie sniffing at his ear. He almost fell asleep in the bed of the truck, but never quite did. After about an hour, the highway began a gradual descent into what by relative standards was a greenish valley. And to the south, a few miles beyond the valley, large-scale, true-to-life mountains suddenly broke the desert's endless plains.

As they neared the exit for the town in this valley, Peter banged on top of the truck cab. The truck pulled over and Peter hopped down. He walked into what the sign said was the town of Balmorhea (pop. 256) and then up the highway toward the mountains. They pulled at him with a kind of specific gravity. By a series of short rides, he was transported into those mountains, the road climbing, winding along a creek bed, dirt roads leaving the main road, disappearing as they approached the base of the mountains. The mountains flat on top like mesas or rounded off by the elements. As the road ascended, the tops of the mountains were nearer and less imposing. Broken rock and sandstone. Small yellow flowers popping from the fissures in the rock. Everything seemed to be getting softer. More welcoming, he thought. It had to work that way, he told himself. The closer you got, the less majestic it seemed. The air was clear and dry here. His head seemed unusually clear.

They dipped into a valley. His last ride stopped at a grocery. Across the street was a reconstructed cavalry outpost. Peter grabbed his belongings and walked onto the grounds of the fort. A number of stucco buildings faced each other across a dusty field. Some were restored. Others were little more than piles of adobe bricks. A flagpole flew the flags of Texas and the United States. He sat in the shade provided by the porch of one of the buildings. Then a loudspeaker clicked on, crackling and buzzing loud enough to be heard across the dusty expanse of buildings. Peter waited for some sort of announcement. Instead, he heard a bugle sound a call to action. Then the loud speaker clicked off. At regular intervals, the loudspeaker clicked on, the bugle sounded, and the loudspeaker clicked off. After a particularly long bugle call, the loudspeaker did not click off. Instead, it carried the sounds of horses' hoofs and horse-like noises of other sorts. Not a person or horse in sight from where Peter sat, but a panorama of sound, nonetheless.

Behind the buildings a trail wandered into red sandstone boulders. Peter followed it a ways. It rose gradually from one set of rocks to the next until Peter, looking back at the buildings, realized he had climbed a considerable distance. The sun was beginning to set. Peter had already decided that he was going to spend the night on a porch swing in front of the house where he'd been sitting. He'd left his sleeping bag and other belongings under the porch of that house. He hunkered down among the rocks and waited for darkness to come. If there were people in the old fort, soon they wouldn't be able to see him.

A horned toad ran out from behind a rock and stopped dead still in front of Peter Proust. Peter decided not to breathe, to see which of them blinked first. But soon he lost track. Had the horned toad blinked? It must have because it was no longer in front of him. It had moved on.

It was dark, and he was now very thirsty. There was water in his canteen. He picked his way back down the trail, walked down the row of buildings until he arrived at the house with the porch swing. A brisk wind was blowing across the compound. His tongue was absolutely dry. He dug out his canteen and drank the water that was by this time tepid. He spat out his first gulp, then slowly let the water dribble into his mouth. He was hungry but would wait until morning to satisfy that need.

He climbed onto the porch swing and lay back. He pushed off against the floor with his right hand and began to swing. Every fifth swing his right hand would push off again. In this way he watched the roof of the porch and the sky from the vantage of a pendulum, seeing all roof at one apex, all sky at the other and arc of roof and sky in between. And in this cradle, gently rocking, he quickly fell asleep.

Only to be awakened at daybreak by reveille. When the loudspeaker clicked on, he started. When the bugle began reveille he sat bolt upright, figured out where he was, and quickly gathered his belongings. His stomach was in full rebellion. It was suddenly tearing him in two.

He had to get food. He made for the Gomez Sac-n-Pac across the highway. He would need food for at least several days. He was going up into the mountains. He would need food for that. He swung open the grocery's screen door and peered in. A woman behind the cash register said, "Yes, we are open. We get up earlier than bugs."

Peter hesitated. Peering into the grocery, it looked to him as if the store were collapsing into its center aisle. But he decided to take a chance. What were his other options? His stomach was grinding one gear against the other. He planned to go quickly about his business. He stepped inside. As he passed the counter, the woman there reached for his bags. He hadn't planned on this. He didn't want to let go of them. But she acted more quickly than he reacted.

She had the sleeping bag and one bag off his shoulder before he had fully realized what was happening. She put them on the counter and motioned for his backpack. He relinquished it without a fight, but with great foreboding. He determined to make his purchases as quickly as possible. He grabbed a carton of orange juice from the cooler. He thought he felt the wooden floor begin to buckle. Then four packs of chocolate cupcakes. Then a loaf of Hollywood bread. It all seemed wrong, out of sync, but he wouldn't stop to contemplate his actions. Catastrophe was at hand. He just wanted to be out of there. Fruit. He grabbed two apples. Then a box of prunes. He looked for yogurt, quickly, quickly, but could find none. Waves seemed to be moving through the floor under his feet. He saw a box of granola bars and picked that up. He had no idea how much money he had or how much he was about to spend. He just wanted out.

The woman rang up the groceries: $6.68. He looked in his pockets. He had three dollar bills, which he carefully straightened, and 83 cents in loose change. He stared at the money, not knowing what to do. He couldn't figure out what food to take back, what would make a dent in the matter of his bill. He was paralyzed. He wanted out. The woman watched him, waiting for him to say something. But he said nothing. He looked around nervously. He just wanted out.

"That's okay," she said. "You can pay me next time." She put the groceries in a bag and the bag in Peter's backpack. He stood there, still not knowing what to do. She handed him the bags and sleeping bag and gave his elbow a little nudge toward the door. Peter walked out, feeling like the store was collapsing all around him, the shelves giving way, the cans on the shelves rolling toward him. He had to hurry out of the store before it got him. He had to hurry through a row of canned goods, but his feet were like lead. The woman behind the register was done for. She would disappear into a sinkhole. The entire store would be swallowed up. He had to get out. He felt sorry for the woman, wanted to warn her, but he had to get out. He slogged through the hills of cereal boxes to the screen door. Boxes of detergent were set to explode all around him. He was close now to the swinging door. He could see daylight and blue sky outside. The store's ceiling fan whirred like an airplane's propeller. He hit the screen door with all his will and then he was through it. He was outside. He hurried across the highway. He didn't look back.

Why was he still so dependent on the world? On these transactions? Why did the grinding in his stomach still control him?

He looked for the trail. He found it among the sandstone boulders and began his ascent. When he reached the first set of tall boulders, where he'd waited the evening before, he sat down. He dug into the bag and pulled out a pack of cupcakes. He tore the plastic off with his teeth and pushed a whole cake into his mouth. He wouldn't look back. Only ahead. Up and ahead.

Up the mountain. Reaching the top of this mountain took longer than he'd figured. The path was rocky in places; it required him to use his hands only a couple of times. But the distance of the trail was what fooled him. At numerous points he seemed to have the top of the mountain within view only to have it disappear and then reappear after several switchbacks.

Then there was the matter of where the top of the mountain actually lay. From the fort below, it had been obvious. But working his way up the mountain, he would decide a small escarpment or a stand of trees or a particular outcropping was the top. He would focus on a point and hold it in his mind while winding up the trail only to find that each point was simply a way-station to a higher point, that the mountain climbed away from the point he'd latched onto from below, that the angle of sight from below was not consistent with the facts of altitude above. Time and again, he would reach a point a few yards beneath his destination only to discover that the trail kept rising, the mountain kept climbing into elevations hidden from those who didn't come this far.

In a way he was glad the mountain kept rising. He wanted to see it all. He wanted a place from which he could look down in all directions, see the world as the eagle does, have no line of sight blocked by something higher, be above everything in the world for as far as he could see. Though it made the going more difficult, the fact that the trail kept rising meant he had not reached the end of climbing, meant he had greater heights ahead, meant the possibilities for elevation were not yet used up, were not yet finite and known.

But, finally, after a switchback and a little scuffling over an outcropping of granite, he was on top. He looked to the east. A plain stretched for miles below him. There were smaller mountains to the south and east. There was a brown haze to the distant south. Mexico was out there somewhere. The plain itself was flat and white with roads crossing it and running off in three directions. To Peter it looked ancient and flat and dry, as the Sinai desert must have looked to Moses from his mountaintop. He looked to the north. There were mountains, but he could see past them. Then he turned to the west. A ridge of mountains rose in front of him. He couldn't see over it. It blocked his view to the west. He was not high enough yet. And another mountain beyond that ridge appeared taller yet. It may not be, if seen from the ridge in between, but from here it appeared to be still taller. This would take more work. It made him claustrophobic looking west.

Peter turned back to the east and sat down. He reached in his bag and pulled out the box of prunes. He ate handfuls of prunes. He pulled out the carton of orange juice and set it beside his bag. He reached in the pack to look for his gun. It should be there. He knew it might not be there, having possibly fallen out along the way or maybe pilfered from his pack while he was sleeping or by the woman in the grocery. He knew he could panic. But he refused to panic. He preferred letting his fingers search slowly and meticulously among his things in a kind of Zen exercise, gliding through his belongings until they felt the cold metal of the gun among his clothes and books and dried beans. And they did. He set the gun beside him. He reached inside the zippered bag inside his pack and pulled out two peyote buttons. He found two rocks, appropriately flat and smooth and about the size of his hands. He put the buttons between the rocks and rubbed one rock in a circular motion above the other, crushing the peyote. He took the crushed peyote and put it in his mouth, washing down its bitter taste with the orange juice. He sat in full lotus facing east. The sun was directly overhead. He sat staring at the plain, his eyes wide open. He was waiting.

It came: a volcano inside him. He ran to a bush and retched and vomited as if his insides were coming out. He was bent over double in pain. The spasms jerked him around in the dust of the mountaintop. Like a knife cutting a jagged pattern across his belly. He lay in the dust clutching his stomach. Then he slowly relaxed. He went back to where he'd been sitting, assumed the lotus position. He felt for the gun beside him, then put both hands on his knees, palms upward, his thumbs and forefingers making two circles.

A Mexican eagle was circling at about eye level out over the plain. He watched it circle and dive and return to circle again. He watched it ride the waves of the wind out over the vast plain, sailing away from him, then sailing back. Sometimes it seemed to just stop in mid-air, making no effort, not going forward and not going back, not going up and not going down, not tilting from side to side or dipping a wing or fighting the wind. It just seemed to stay there, cast as a planet in empty space, its own gravity holding it there. And all around it the void.

Peter watched the eagle sailing. And he watched the eagle holding still. And he watched it and watched it and then he took off.

Out the Window

THAT NIGHT GIACOMO had a dream. He was riding in a car. He was in the front seat on the passenger side. Peter was in the backseat on the other side, staring out the window. Someone else was driving, someone who seemed unimportant to them, or to the dream, or to their being there together. They were riding through New England. He could tell it was New England: the leaves were turning, the roads were narrow. They wound around hills and along rushing creeks. The orange, yellow, and red of the leaves mixed in his rushing vision with the gray stones of New England.

Where were they going? They were going to a farmhouse to spend the night. His old girlfriend Alexi would be there. He hadn't seen her in twenty years. Or was this twenty years ago? Was she waiting there for him? He hoped so, but he wasn't sure if it was his right to hope.

Peter stared out the window. When he was not stroking his chin, his hands were folded in his lap. He had very small hands. When he put them on his lap, they disappeared entirely. The driver drove. New England rushed by in a blur. There was a white farm house in the distance. They were approaching the farm house. Then it disappeared. A little later, there was another white farm house. It also disappeared.

He stared at Peter. Peter was looking for his hands. Then he looked straight into Giacomo's eyes. Peter's eyes were a winter sky blue.

"There was a squirrel back there," Peter said. "I think we got him. I saw him start to run across the road in front of us. We must have gotten him. Oh, man, I was feeling for the thump, but I didn't feel it. But we must have gotten him. I didn't see him run back." He shook his head back and forth and began rocking, saying, "Oh, no; Oh, no."

Then the entire car began rocking. Then it inflated. Then it took off.

Peter's face was directly in Giacomo's face. "You're not even close," he said.

"To what?" Giacomo cried.

"Not even close," Peter said, as he climbed out a window.

"Watch out," Giacomo shouted. "We're flying over Pennsylvania."

Peter turned back to face Giacomo and now Peter was B.C.

"B.C., get back in," Giacomo shouted.

She smiled from outside the window and waved.

The craft let out a high-pitched whistling sound and began to gyrate.

He woke up. He was lying on the couch. B.C. was across the room on the bed, her nose whistling. He remembered the dream. He wanted to think about it for a few minutes. But, instead, he was falling back to sleep. He would make it a point to think about it in the morning. He would concentrate on the dream to imprint it in his memory. But already it was fading. He would try to conjure it up in the morning.

But the phone was ringing. How long had it been ringing? He reached for it, but it wasn't on the end table by the couch. It was by the bed. He turned to lunge for the phone. The bed was empty. Where was B.C.? The phone kept ringing. He picked it up and coughed a greeting.

"Giacomo, I'm sorry to call you this early, but I have news." It was Sara Proust. "I got a card today from some place called Mountain Home, Texas. Do you know it? It was postmarked just four days ago."

"What does it say?"

"It says, well, it doesn't say much. He talks about flints and sticks and coyotes. But it's the closest we've gotten. Can you go there? Is it very far away? I'm sorry to do this to you, Giacomo. I'd come down there to look for him myself. In fact, I'll do that right now if you want me to. I'm just afraid I'll scare him off."

"No. No," Giacomo said. He was only now fully conscious. "I can go. I'll go today. I don't know where the hell it is, but I'll find it.

"That would be great. I don't know how we can ever thank you."

"Sara, you know I've got to do this. I want to do this and I've got to do this. So let's leave it at that."

"Whatever you say, Jack. I just wanted you to know."

"I know. Is there anything else? Can you think of anything?"

"Well, there have been calls late at night to my father's answering machine at his office, when he wouldn't be there. It could be anyone, but my father thinks it's Peter."

"Why does he think that? Does he leave a message?"

"No. There's no reason. He's just convinced it's Peter, that's all. There's a call. The caller just sits there through the length of time they give you to leave a message. It just happens every once in a while. But it's always late at night. My father's convinced, that's all. They haven't spoken in almost ten years. Not to amount to anything anyway. That's all."

"I'll let you know what I find," he said. "Are you holding up okay?"

"No, of course not. This has torn us apart. I can't sleep. Maybe two hours a night at the most. Then I wake up thinking about Peter. I see him wandering around in the dark somewhere. I can't believe I didn't do more for him when he was here. He just seems so helpless to me now. But when he was here, he was still my big brother. I couldn't step out of my role. He just made me angry, and I yelled at him the way I've always done. It makes me so mad. Just like I get mad at you sometimes. I get this feeling over the phone that you're still treating me like a kid sister. I'm 43 fucking years old, Jack. I've got a kid. I'm getting middle-aged. That's all. I just want to make that point. I appreciate what you're doing. Really I do. But I want you to know you're doing this for a grown woman, not to patronize your friend's kid sister. That's all. I'm sorry, Jack. I really am. I don't mean to lay a trip on you, but I've said it and I feel better."

He just listened. It was his turn to speak now. He waited an extra beat in case she wanted to say something else. And then another beat, to give them both a chance to go on to something else. Then he said, "I'll leave in a couple of hours. Wherever it is, I should be there before dark."

"I'm sorry I said all that, Jack. Really I am. You asked a question, and it just poured out."

"Don't worry about it. I'll talk to you tomorrow."

"Could you call tonight if you find anything?"

"Of course."

"I don't mean to be a pain, but this is the best clue we've had yet."

"You're right," he said. "I'll let you know as soon as I find anything."

"And tomorrow, whether you find anything or not?"

"Tomorrow, whether I find anything or not. I'll call you, first thing."

Then they hung up. He got up to look for signs of B.C. He found her suitcase, so she hadn't left entirely. But where was she? She wasn't in the bathroom. That was as far as his search could go for the time being. Then the phone rang.

"I'm just so sorry, Jack, that I blew up like that." It was Sara. "I feel terrible about it."

"Please don't worry," Giacomo said. "I've heard much worse. It's forgotten. Believe me."

259

"I hope not entirely forgotten," she said, "because I did want you to know how I felt. But I had no right to light into you like that. I should have saved it for some time when we were having a nice conversation about something else, sometime far in the future. But I just can't control myself these days. Things are just so heavy."

"All is forgiven. Now I have to get ready to leave. I'll call you in the morning."

"I'll be home tonight, too. You have my cell phone number. I can't go anywhere with this happening."

"Don't stay home. I'll call you if I find anything, but it will probably be in the morning. We don't even know if they have electric lights in Mountain Home."

He knew the strain on her would only get worse. But he couldn't tell her that. The searching is often so much better than the finding. You still had that element of hope to play with. There's very little hope involved when most cases are concluded. More than once he's had to string out a case forever so that the element of hope would still be there. Even the tiniest fraction of hope. The closer you get to your goal, the narrowing of options, the elimination of possibilities, also eliminates most of your hope. It's a sobering process. What do you know about your husband and what do you want to know? Sara probably sensed all this. It was the intimation of hopelessness that made her so desperate now. But only four days ago. That was better than he'd ever hoped.

He got dressed. He was looking for paper to write B.C. a note when the phone rang again. It was B.C. She was with Stephen Seltzer at a coffee shop nearby. She asked Giacomo to join them. She wanted to see Stephen before she left town. "I'm going to the internment camps," she said, "the ones in the Rio Grande Valley. I thought you might want to come. For the ride, at least. Something in the middle of the night just started pulling me there. I can't get this close and not see them. You don't read about it. You don't hear about it. I imagine it was much the same with the Japanese internment camps. But we're holding thousands of people in concentration camps, denying them their rights and then shipping them back to their countries, where some of them will probably be killed. How I couldn't go to the camps is beyond me. I don't know what had gotten into me. But I'm over that now. I have to go, and I'm going.

"For how long?" Giacomo asked.

"Just for a few days. I just want to see it and talk to a few of the people if I can. But I thought we should talk to Stephen before we go. We just can't leave him hanging. I thought you could talk to him a little bit more about what he should be doing."

Giacomo thought probably the simplest thing to do would be to tell her his new plans at the restaurant. It wasn't the most direct route, but it could be the simplest. It wasn't so much that he hadn't wanted to tell her that he now had another direction to take. It was more his disdain for the telephone. Whatever truths were somehow transmitted via telephone somehow didn't count. For Giacomo Berg they had no weight or substance. They were merely electrons riding on fibers and bouncing off satellites, neither right nor wrong, neither truth nor fiction. The telephone did, at least, carry inflection. He had to admit that. But he wanted to be able to see her. He wanted the look in her eyes, the movement of her fingers, whether she began biting her lip. If there were a plant nearby, would she start tearing it up? He would tell her directly, face-to-face, that he was going to Mountain Home and not to the Rio Grande Valley with her. That exchange would carry meaning. For at least a brief moment it would take form on his lips, achieve physical being on his tongue, and then hang or flutter in the air. And she would respond wholly, her body shifting, her eyes looking somewhere not at him. For Giacomo Berg, it was a matter of integrity. It was a matter of affirming his presence in the world. It was a chance to see the way this relationship was developing—or not.

He spotted them at a back table as soon as he stepped out of the bright light of the morning sunshine into the muted tones of the coffee shop. B.C. Boyd was at that moment holding the right hand of Stephen Seltzer between her hands across a black-and-white checkered tablecloth in a coffee shop that was not a hash-browns-and-danish sort of establishment but rather was an extension of an upscale vegetarian grocery next door. Giacomo found his way among tables of people he thought should have been at work but were instead sipping herbal tea while the stress-free sounds of rushing water and sloshing waves massaged their nerve endings, sounds broken only by the whoosh of muscled bag boys wearing tank tops skating by on plastic rollers, bags of groceries in either arm, oddly reminiscent of Union Square. By the time Giacomo reached their table, B.C.'s hands were in her lap. He hadn't seen her register his entrance. When he appeared before them, B.C. seemed surprised. A little flustered.

"It took me a while," Giacomo said. "I got a little lost."

B.C. looked up, knowing he never got lost. She smiled and slid over to make room for Giacomo Berg. But he sat across from her, next to Stephen Seltzer, who shook his hand.

"I just wanted to get a handle on things before we left," B.C. said. "Stephen says they're ready to begin the surveys. I thought we could plan to be back in a few days when they get the results."

"We have another meeting scheduled for Thursday," Stephen said. "I hope we get a pretty good picture by then. Here's what I have planned." He pulled a map out of his pocket and quickly unfolded it on the checkered tablecloth. Each street was highlighted with a different color marker. A large red circle with a cross through the middle marked the dumpsite. Stephen began to recite the questions they'd gone over the night before.

But Giacomo was concentrating on other mysteries. After a few tentative forays, he'd found B.C.'s feet under the table. He placed his feet against hers. He watched her carefully. She didn't look up. Neither did she give anything away by the slightest change in expression. But she also had not moved her feet. And, once or twice, he even thought he felt pressure coming back his way. He knew he couldn't be sure, but just as with a Ouija board, this was no time for doubt. A possible sensation was sensation enough for Giacomo Berg, and he decided to proceed. He moved the pepper shaker across the tablecloth toward her glass, jumping the salt shaker on the tablecloth checkerboard. B.C. was watching Stephen pointing to the colored lines on the map. Giacomo watched her closely. Then, as if absent-mindedly, she wrapped her long fingers around the salt shaker and slowly moved it from one square to another, watching it from the corner of her eye, until it bumped up against Giacomo Berg's pepper. Then, only briefly, like the phosphorous blaze inside the lighting of a match, she smiled. He knew he was onto something and moved his right leg gently up her calf. But she would acknowledge nothing after that.

He looked from her to Stephen Seltzer, who, to his surprise, was looking right at him. "Is there anything I've left out?" Stephen asked.

"It's a good start," Giacomo said, figuring any start was a good start, whatever it was.

Was that pressure he was now feeling against his left calf from a woman's foot? "That is, if all your neighbors are home and they'll talk to you and when they talk to you, they tell the truth. Even when you build in room for complications, there will be complications you don't expect. Leave some room for fuckups. Maybe you won't find anything, or you'll find too much and get overloaded. Maybe it's not cancer and chemicals that's out of the ordinary. Maybe it's high humidity and depression. Maybe the only correlation you can turn up is one between the number of times the Glasgow High football team lost and the incidence of student lethargy. You may be surprised, but the important thing is to persist. It's your survey. Do with it what you want. If you know what you're looking for, then you'll find it. There aren't any survey police running around, checking your data and carving out the permissible range of conclusions. At least, I don't think there are. Besides, even with the cleanest survey in the universe, the other side will bring your numbers into question. That's the one verité in this kind of operation."

B.C. was pleased by this performance. Giacomo was almost animated. He was giving what amounted to a pep talk. She rubbed her right foot against his calf. The trip to the Valley could be something to look forward to with Giacomo in this frame of mind.

"I want to thank both of you for your help," Seltzer said. "I just hope we can put it all together. This whole thing has wrung me out, and we've only barely begun."

"You'll see," B.C. said, "Once you start getting results, you'll feel differently." She knew she didn't know what the fuck she was talking about. Sometimes it would be nice if she were just able to keep her mouth shut. But she wanted to say something, so Stephen wouldn't hesitate.

"Unless you start getting the wrong results," Giacomo said, as Stephen nodded his head.

So much for the boyish enthusiasm of Giacomo Berg, B.C. thought. It was too much to expect.

"We should get going," she said to Berg. "It must be five or six hours to the Valley." They said goodbye to Stephen. Then Giacomo walked B.C. outside.

"I wish I could go with you," said Giacomo. "But I can't."

B.C. was instantly convinced he didn't mean it.

"I got a call a little while ago."

She looked up. "Did they find him?" she asked.

"No. But they have a postcard just a few days old from some place called Mountain Home. I looked it up. It's north and west of San Antonio. It's the closest thing to real contact yet. I've got to go."

She wanted to say, "This can wait another day or two. If he's there, he'll stay there. If he's gone, he's gone." But she knew she couldn't say those things. Instead, she said, "I know you do."

The idea of driving to the Valley alone to see jailed refugees suddenly hung around her neck like an anchor. She'd actually envisioned a dalliance by the Gulf or along the Mexican border over incendiary margaritas. All at once, she was just a soft-hearted social worker doing her job once again.

"Why don't you take me to the airport?" she said. "I think I'll fly instead."

"You could come with me," he said, knowing she wouldn't, knowing she'd see that as a retreat.

"If I do that, I'll probably never get to the Valley," she said.

He dropped her at the terminal of the old Houston airport in the middle of town. "I'll meet you back here on Thursday," he said.

"Unless you find him."

"I won't find him."

Horses

HE'D BEEN DRIVING almost three hours before it struck him that he very well might be coming face-to-face with Peter Proust. This was the first time that even seemed like a possibility, however remote. He just hadn't figured on it, and now he realized he should prepare himself for that contingency. The moment might come. They might find themselves at either end of a sidewalk or creek bed or a bar, and he would have to act.

Since dropping B.C. at the airport, he'd been driving mindlessly, conscious of little more than the straight flat road ahead of him. He and B.C. seemed to be always separating just as they reached the points in their orbits that came nearest one another, those two points ever nearer at each juncture. Like an off-balance mitosil dance, imperfect conjugation followed by incomplete separation, then pulled back into the center to try again. It didn't bode well for the survival of whatever species of relationship they were formulating. He felt like each time they were each being sent out by some centrifugal power only to be reeled back in again to a center, a locus that, somehow, controlled them both.

He'd thought about that for a while. Then he locked into the road in front of him and didn't think another thought until just past San Antonio. It was then, when the land started to rise and the trees to lose height and the vegetation to become more sparse and hardly green, that Berg realized he might be reaching a critical juncture in his quest and maybe its end.

Actually, he thought the end unlikely. These things don't end. Even if the subject ends, the search doesn't end until it catches up with its subject's end, occurring at a time outside his present understanding. So it wasn't likely he would arrive in Mountain Home to find the denouement to this adventure sitting on a bench in front of the IGA, waiting for him to sidle up and take a seat on the bench beside it. For the first time, however, he did feel like there was an outside chance that Peter's time and his own would coincide or, at least, bump into each other.

It was time to think again about Peter Proust. How had he become so lost? The way they used to find him sitting on a snow bank after two beers and maybe a little dope, staring at the stars, shaking his head from side to side, saying, "No. It can't be, guys. It can't be. There's got to be more than this."

It had made some kind of sense to Giacomo then, the way anything back then had made sense. But it didn't make sense that this was still going on, somehow, two decades later. For one thing, Berg just didn't feel anything as passionately as he had back then. It wasn't so much that things didn't matter as much as he didn't have the energy or the time or the attention to devote to them. One thing led to another, and he just followed the ball as it rolled on, one year to the next.

But was Peter still out there in full lotus in the snow? How was it possible? But how was it possible to think of Peter in any other way? He had to get ready for this and for what Sara had told him. He just now realized that he was being sent out once again to bring Peter in from the snow.

That other time, decades ago, they hadn't been able to find Peter for a while. Giacomo went outside to search. It was the early hours of a snowstorm. It was difficult to see. The snow formed a translucent curtain between Giacomo and everything else. And the only sound was his own footsteps tromping in the foot of new snow. He tried to follow what he thought was the path they used to cut through a stand of pine trees between their home and the college. Just before reaching the trees, he saw a gray mass on a snowbank. It was Peter in full lotus, the snow coating his long, dark hair. Berg sat down facing Peter.

"What are you doing?" he'd asked. "It's cold. Let's go inside."

"Not yet," Peter had said. "I'm not ready yet."

So they sat there together in the snow long enough for Giacomo's legs to begin to freeze. "I don't get it," Peter had then said. "Why are we here? What are we doing here?"

"We're going to school," Giacomo had said, hoping to remain concrete, to avoid metaphysics in the freezing snow.

"Then why that?" Peter said. "Taste this snow. Come on. Stick out your tongue and taste it." He opened his mouth, tilted his head, and let the snowflakes pour into his mouth. Giacomo did the same.

"They don't teach you about this in there. They don't teach you what that taste means, what it means to be walled in by snow, all alone, everything silent, on an evening when it feels like you're the only thing living in the world. All they want you to do is think. They don't teach you how to sit here and melt into the world and stop thinking altogether, have no thoughts in your head, and just be." They sat there as the snow covered them both.

"They think the world's a rational place, Jack. They think that. And that's what they want in those classes—how one leads to two, which leads to three. It's just not like that. I thought something was wrong for a long time. I thought something was wrong with me. But over the past two years, I've had this growing feeling that they're all wrong, that we can't always expect two to follow one, that we can't all think in those ways. There's so much more out there, Jack. I don't know how to reach it yet. But it's out there. It's there. Somehow we have to get there, too."

Giacomo Berg sat there with him, not knowing what to say. He was very cold. His teeth began to chatter.

"I'm ready now," Peter said. "We can go in now." He got up slowly. He leaned on Giacomo Berg to straighten out his frozen knees. They walked slowly in together.

Would it be like that again? This time he wasn't being sent out to bring in a kid. It was a man in middle age. They were worlds away from that other time. He would have to understand what drove Peter before he could find him.

Something just off the highway to his right grabbed Giacomo's attention. He slowed a bit. Five horses were standing over a prostrate white horse under a brace of cedar trees. The white horse was most certainly dead. Its legs were stuck out stiffly before it as if it were standing stock still. This should be symbolic, Giacomo thought, but of what? It was a symbol looking for a meaning. The grief of quarter horses. It was the kind of thing an American film director, who'd studied Italian cinema, would use to start a cowboy movie as a tribute to high art. Or something a Japanese director would begin with merely as a visual imprint. Here he was, looking at horses in rural Texas but thinking about semiotics. It put him in a lousy mood.

Compared to the stasis of the horses, Giacomo Berg felt like he was hurtling toward a resolution he was not sure he wanted or even a resolution that he would be able to recognize as such. The more he thought about Peter Proust, the more he realized that his difficulty in finding Peter lay in the fact that he was battling not only a position on a map but also Peter's inner velocity, a system of time and motion that had little to do with the physical world. He had to find that point where the hitherto unknown and lost universe of Peter Proust intersected the known universe of Giacomo Berg in the figure of an aging hippie walking toward him, perhaps, on Main Street in Mountain Home, Texas. Until that happened, he and Peter could be half a block apart in tiny Mountain Home and still be lost to each other. But if that happened, if Peter Proust came walking into Giacomo Berg's field of understanding, then he would have to be ready to throw a net over him and hold him there. As soon as that thought entered his mind, Giacomo was angry with himself for allowing it in—the idea of a net over Peter Proust. Had he sunk to that? Two decades after dragging Peter in from the snowbank, he's ready to throw him in the loony bin. What a corrupting experience life is.

The more he thought about Peter Proust, the more he realized he missed him. He missed that constellation of molecules, thought, and spirit that was Peter Proust and that was so different from anyone else he knew. He missed that otherness in his world.

He was now at the exit for Mountain Home. He wasn't quite sure where to start. Thinking Peter may have mailed his postcard from the post office, or at least bought a stamp there, Berg asked around and was directed to a grocery store. The clerk behind the post office window was a woman in her mid-fifties with a distinctly purple tint to her gray hair. He showed her the photo the family had sent.

"I'm not exactly sure who you mean," she said. "I think I know, but I'm not exactly sure. He looks almost familiar. There was a raggedy fellow in here about a week ago, I think, and he had a scraggly beard and hair that looked like he hadn't washed it in years. He wanted a stamp for a postcard, but I was afraid the card was too flimsy so I sold him a stamped envelope to put it in. He seemed pretty confused. That may be the fellow. I remember that because ever since they convicted that family over in Utopia of running that slave camp for hippies, you get to thinking about that when you see one of these long-haired fellows wandering through. But what are you going to ask me after that? I ain't seen him again and I know nothing about the man."

Giacomo thanked her and moved on. He asked the grocery checker if she remembered anyone looking like Peter, but she did not. She did point him, however, to the other two groceries in town. Berg tried those, but no one in either store remembered anything. One store seemed to be entirely run by teenagers, with the cashier smacking away at her bubble gum, shaking her head to Berg's questions. At the other store, the only help he got was in the form of advice from the completely bald store manager. "That's something I'd talk to the sheriff about if I was you, Bud," the manager said. "Where are you from? Everybody knows everybody around here. I'd suggest you talk to the sheriff and don't bother the rest of us."

As Giacomo left the grocery, a tall, thin, young man dressed in khakis and cowboy boots, a white cowboy hat and sporting a small star was coming toward him on the sidewalk. He looked like a sheriff. He decided to stop the man to ask him questions, but he didn't get the chance. The man got the drop on Giacomo instead.

"I hear you're looking for somebody," the man said. "Can I help you with something?"

"For starters, you can tell me who you are."

"I'm Deputy Sheriff Marvin Jay Steinmetz. Who might you be?"

Giacomo decided the best strategy would be to go the professional route. He pulled out a card and handed it to the deputy. "Giacomo Berg, private investigator," he said, as he handed the deputy the card.

The deputy studied it for a while. "New York City," he finally said, stretching the words out so long that they sounded like a complete sentence. "What brings you from New York City? International drug wars?"

"I've been hired by a family to track down a missing person. They seem to think he may be around here."

"Came here for the night life, I'll bet. Now you ain't lying to me, are you? If you are, I'll call the Department of Public Safety in a New York minute, speaking of New York, that is."

Giacomo pulled out the photo he was carrying and said, "This is the most recent photo the family has."

"The long-haired hippie weirdo. Why didn't you say so in the first place? Someone's looking for him? A few years ago, folks around here would have used him for target practice, until that slave ranch thing. Those people got indicted for pullin' hippie hitchhikers off the road and working them at their ranch and then torturing them to death. Those indictments made people around here think twice."

Giacomo stood there, trying to wait out the kid's obligatory down-home law-and-order posturing.

"So, where is he?" he finally asked.

"If he's smart, he's lit out of here. He burned down a shack on the Ludwig place a few days back. It set the whole hillside burning. With this dry spell he could have burned up the whole countryside, but, fortunately, there wasn't any grass around to burn. Just a bunch of rocks. And we won't have enough fire power for them to ignite until Judgment Day. If you want to see the shack, I can take you there, but I can't today. Too much to do. Maybe tomorrow or the next day."

Giacomo decided to go see for himself. With a little prodding, the deputy gave him directions, if they were to be believed. As Giacomo left, the deputy called out behind him. "Should 'a worn your boots. There are plenty of snakes in that grass." Then he bent over double laughing.

Giacomo followed the gravel road to the dirt road. It wasn't easy going. But that wasn't what concerned him. If the deputy had been straight with him, what would he find?

There was also this: Though he hadn't really expected to find Peter, there had been that dying ember of possibility that had gotten fanned enough by the grocery clerk's description to send up a few flames. There had been that. But the deputy had all but snuffed that out. Here he was on the trail again, and this time it was probably the real trail. But it was also probably Peter's past—not his present and not some ray that will intersect his future. He was still wandering around in a zone that Peter had probably put behind him forever. Unless the deputy was wrong.

But he wasn't wrong about the shack reduced to ashes. The dirt road had disappeared altogether on a hillside. From where he sat, Giacomo Berg could see the charred remains of a cabin about 50 yards up the hill. He climbed out of the car and slowly made his way up the hill, kicking at a half-burned blanket, a pile of wet, charred, torn-up paperbacks—*The Tao of Healing* and an Ellery Queen mystery most visible among them.

He entered what was once the door of the cabin. There was little to see inside the perimeter that had once been four walls. Piles of ash, metal cookware, a few broken mason jars amid scattered charred beans. The aluminum frame from what must have been a cot, a mostly melted and burned-up pair of sneakers. Beyond the cabin he found a steel drum with a large iron pot on top. Inside the pot a soup ladle led into a murky liquid. He raised the ladle and found it full of still more beans. A few had sprouted in that rancid mush.

He wasn't entirely convinced that this had been the recent home of Peter Proust. Nothing to contradict such a conclusion, but he wasn't entirely convinced. Or didn't want to be. This was not exactly the fall of civilization he was witnessing. If this was the final material destruction of Peter Proust, he'd hoped for something more monumental, more telling than the frame of an aluminum cot and an Ellery Queen paperback. He was looking for icons. Something that pertained to what he had known of Peter Proust: a Boston Red Sox cap, for instance, or at the very least, a birdhouse designed to look like a lodging in full flight, something singular, particular to Peter, something showing his stubbornness. The brown beans in the pot. He'd once had a weirdly playful sense of humor. Where was that?

Giacomo Berg sat down on a rock. He was completely depressed. Was there anything having to do with Peter Proust about this place? The sun was going down. It lit up the tops of the hills.

Then it came to him. There was nothing here because Peter was undergoing a painfully slow implosion. The only evidence of his self had been sucked into his belly, as in his yogic deep breathing. There were few extrusions from what went on in there. It roiled and boiled and got swallowed up in darkness. The world was inside his body, inside his head. Carrying it all, Peter was finding less and less room in which to maneuver. At the same time, the world seemed less important, maybe even irrelevant.

A shrieking above Giacomo's head. He looked up to see a hawk in the cloudless sky, seemingly motionless in the immense void. Then it dived and what, seconds before, had been sheer weightlessness, suddenly dropped through empty space like a hundredweight stone. A few seconds later, the hawk was up again, flapping its arched wings, carrying away a lizard the hills had offered up as sacrifice.

This had been, in all probability, Peter's home, Peter's life for a time. But it seemed entirely alien to Giacomo Berg, alien to his conception of Peter. If he were going to see this thing through, he figured he'd better change that perception. As it stood, he and Peter Proust were lost to each other. They were operating in different languages, in different measures of time. They may have passed each other on the street many times over without recognizing each other.

If he was going to find Peter Proust, he had to begin to understand him. If he couldn't pinpoint him precisely on a map, he could come to know him. If he couldn't pierce the mystery of Peter Proust, perhaps he could accept it. That was the only way this would work. He dug in the dirt around his feet. He went to the pot of beans and took one out and began to chew it. He spit it out.

He only had to know Peter, not become him. He made a circuitous route around the campsite. He found small mounds of stones. They were in an area not bigger than forty feet across. He looked at the stones from various angles. They seemed to be pointing in a particular direction, but in the rapidly fading light, he couldn't tell what, if anything, they were pointing to.

He examined a pile of books: a Spanish-English dictionary, *America: A Prophecy*, a bread-baking cookbook, *Be Here Now*, *Black Elk Speaks*, *Tales of Old-Time Texas* by J. Frank Dobie, *Selected Poems of Li Po*, and *The Last of the Just*. This could easily be Peter's library.

It was dark now. A sliver of the moon was edging up over the horizon. Berg decided to try to spend the night on the hill. He thought he might gain something if he took it all in.

Besides, what was there to do in Mountain Home? He pulled a blanket from the back of his car, climbed to a fairly flat spot above the cabin, kicked away a few rocks, and sat down. He was certain now that this had been home to Peter Proust. He was beginning to believe he felt something of Peter's presence here.

He took off his shoes, wrapped himself in the blanket and lay his head back on his shoes.

There were plenty of stars. But what out here would eat him? What could come crawling or slithering through the night? Scorpions? Rattlesnakes? Did he need to fear cows stumbling over him in the darkness? Were there mountain lions out here? Javelina? Wolves? He thought he might build a fire, but then he thought better of it, given the recent history of this hill. They might come out shooting this time. He'd rather take his chances with the wildlife. His back was getting a little sore, jabbed by a few well-situated stones. He thought about looking for a motel.

Then he looked deep into the sky. He figured he'd tough it out. It was something he had to do. He couldn't remember ever seeing this many stars. It rivaled the Aurora Borealis he'd seen once up in Vermont, he and Peter actually, sleeping out on the lawn at Bennington College while a third friend was inside one of the houses, playing the piano, desperately trying to get laid. It was cold, but it had been the right thing to do. They lay there in their sleeping bags watching the lights dance across the northern horizon. When they woke up the next morning, they were covered with frost.

When Giacomo woke up he only vaguely remembered decamping to the car. He was afraid to move his neck. It was curved at an odd angle into the backseat. Slowly he drew himself out of the car and stood up. The sky was light, but the sun had not yet risen in front of him.

He walked in a circle around the car, got his bearings and returned to the ruined cabin. From there he looked up the hill. That was when he realized that, looking from the cabin, the mounds of stones formed an arrow, and the arrow pointed toward a rock formation further up the hill that resembled a lean-to more than anything else. He followed the arrow to the lean-to. The rocks were each about six feet across and between five and seven feet high, seven rocks altogether, leaning into each other and some leaning into a small formation that jutted out of the hillside. One of the rocks formed a kind of roof over the space the leaning rocks created.

Giacomo crawled into that space. At that moment, the sun coming up over the hills to the east threw a shaft of light into the lean-to. It cut right across Giacomo Berg's left shoulder. He looked around. Turning to face the wall behind him, he found the shaft of light illuminating two figures painted on the rock. One was a naked man, bearded, his hand held up as if in greeting. The other was a wolf or coyote. Above both figures, written in large letters, was the word "HOWL!"

And Giacomo Berg howled. It echoed in the lean-to. He howled a little louder. Again and again. Peter lives! He had made a connection. They were talking to each other. All was not lost. This was not so much a clue as a lifeline. Thrown to Giacomo Berg? Who was pulling whom in? He howled again.

With that, the barrel of a rifle appeared, thrust into his reverie through a space between two rocks. "You ain't some kind of werewolf, are you?"

It was, of course, Deputy Marvin Jay Steinmetz. Giacomo Berg climbed out of the lean-to.

"Just thought I'd come check on you, make sure a rattler hadn't left you for dead. Then I heard all this howlin', so I came runnin'. Glad I pack a gun." He was smiling at the ground.

"Thanks for your concern," Giacomo said. "We do that every morning in New York—get a little howling in to start the day off right. Don't you people do that kind of thing? You ought to try it some time."

"You fellas ain't part of some new cult, are ya?" Deputy Steinmetz asked. "We've got no room for cults up here."

"No cults," Giacomo said, waving away the thought of cults. "I'm going now."

"But I brought you some news," the Deputy said. "That friend of yours, your fellow cultee, we saw him leaving town about three days ago. He was tryin' to hitch a ride out to the interstate. Given the road he was hitchin' on, most likely he was going west. One of our people saw him. Now, we could have picked him up for that. But our guy figured the faster he was out of here, the better off we'd all be. He woulda given him a ride himself, but he was afraid your friend would shit in his pants."

The deputy was clearly enjoying himself. Giacomo Berg started to walk away, toward the car.

"What's your hurry?" the deputy called out behind him.

"No hurry," Giacomo called without turning around. "I just need some fresh air."

He stopped at the pile of books, picked out the Li Po, the Blake, and *Black Elk* and walked down to his car.

The deputy was following him down the hill. "Anything else we can help you with?" he asked.

"You've done more than enough already," Berg said. He got in the car and slowly backed his way along the rutted dirt road down the hill.

The deputy, apparently feeling slightly dissatisfied by this encounter, turned his car around and met Giacomo's front bumper with his own, nudging Giacomo down the hill, smiling all the time. When Giacomo backed his car onto the gravel road and began to turn around, the deputy took off, roaring past him in a cloud of dust.

Giacomo was glad to finally be rid of him. He noticed a little creek below the road, stopped the car, and climbed down a rocky embankment to the water, where he planned to wash his face and hands. But when he got there, he couldn't help but lie down in the water. He couldn't resist the two or three inches of water trickling coolly over the white rocks of the bottom. Cypress trees on either side of the creek rustled and whispered and removed this little stretch of water from the heat of the morning. Looking up, he felt an upward pull that he'd felt once in Europe looking up at the vaults of Gothic cathedrals.

The cool water was a balm. He felt as if he'd been running for days. Non-stop. B.C. was in South Texas now, whatever that was like. Lying there in the creek, their recent dalliance seemed so inconsequential when compared to who she was, to what he wanted it to be. Not unentertaining, but largely beside the point. He wondered whether she was viewing the internment camps at that moment. Whether they had gotten under her skin or whether she was just going through the motions because they were there. Or whether she was just wandering through the camps because that was still who she was until they figured out how to arrive somewhere else together.

The water rushed through his thinking. How in this near-desert could there be such trees, sustained by bare inches of water? It seemed to wash through him. He couldn't tell if he felt soaked or cleansed. His mind was no longer racing. Everything had come to a stop, where it could be thought through and examined from all sides, appreciated for its weight and mass. Was he losing his critical edge? Or gaining it?

He knew he was onto something with Peter though. He was certain Peter had lain in this creek. He felt if he just lay there long enough, he would find the way to Peter Proust.

No Way Out

AS THE PLANE LANDED in Harlingen, she no longer had any idea why she had come. All she'd wanted was a justification for visiting the Border with Giacomo Berg. She always needed some justification. Why was that? In case things didn't turn out the way she'd anticipated with Giacomo Berg, for instance. She couldn't just say to Giacomo, for instance, Let's go to the Border. She had to say, I'm going to see the camps, making his accompaniment seem secondary. Had she not set things up that way, in her own mind at least, she wouldn't be on this plane now, rocking a little to the left, then the right as it came down through the clouds that were building over the Rio Grande Valley on this hot, drenchingly humid afternoon. If she'd said straight out, Let's go to the Valley, then if he'd said, No, which he would have, which he did, in fact, say, then she could have gone with him wherever the hell he said he was going or she could have stayed in Houston or she could have returned to New York or she could have done any of a dozen things, gone to the Galveston beach, for instance. But somehow she'd locked herself into this internment camp tour in such a way that she had to see it through. Served her right for her latent Calvinism. Pleasure couldn't be the acknowledged motive here. Or adventure. Or abandon. It had to be political refugees, victims of torture and other forms of physical and economic violence. It had to be a situation that she could actually do nothing to change, in which she could only witness action and its consequences. It had to be a situation in which she was hemmed in by her own indignation without a plan.

It was enough to make her scream.

But she didn't scream. Instead, she gulped rather loudly as the plane hit the runway, bumped up into the air and came down again, speeding past what looked like a collection of World War II fighter planes at a hangar marked "Confederate Air Force." Were they amassing air power to fight the Great Campaign again? From what she could see, it looked like they would surely lose again.

She rented a car and drove to the legal service center in Harlingen that worked with the refugees. A tall kid in cut-offs, sporting a pony tail, gave her directions to the prison and the town of Bayview. He told her how to get to the house in Bayview out of which most of the legal work was being done. She hit the road.

She'd been through Harlingen once before, as a kid with her family driving to the coast on the south end of Padre Island. It had made no impression. Now it did. It was hot and humid and smelled like the chemicals for sale in the office of a garden store. She drove past cotton gins, agricultural chemical warehouses, and textile and clothing mills. Past the mills were plowed fields, the dirt pitch-black. Every once in a while, almost invariably beside a trailer park, she spotted a grove of citrus trees. She drove on. She turned off the main highway onto a two-lane state highway heading east to the coast.

Along this road at irregular intervals were settlements of seven or eight buildings—shacks, small frame houses, cinder-block houses, and mobile homes on pilings. Kids wearing t-shirts advertising soccer teams and motor oil stood around with dogs in the gravel common area among the buildings. Large chemical barrels and drums and cars up on blocks were the only other distinguishing features of these settlements, except, of course, for a few outhouses that still stood in back. There were no trees here. Most of the settlements were carved out of the edge of a field of maize or cotton or sugar cane. These were the infamous *colonias* of the Rio Grande Valley, she thought. This was what the refugees thought they were leaving. Ah, America!

She'd been tooling along down the highway when she saw the line of traffic come to a dead halt about one-quarter mile in front of her. There was something odd, large, and white in the roadway. It appeared to be a house. As she pulled to a stop at the end of a line of cars, she saw that up ahead a white frame house was, indeed, in the roadway. Two men were on the roof of the house, holding up utility wires with wooden poles. A third man up there was leaning against the traffic signal, which was resting on the roof of the house. A crowd of people had gathered around the house and around a car in the road next to the house.

B.C. got out of her car and walked up to the crowd. The house was on a flatbed truck and apparently had gotten hung up on the traffic light. That much she could guess. She looked at the car next to the house. It was one of those little Toyota pickups, not brand-new. Inside sat two old men looking straight ahead, not saying a word to anyone. Between them rested a four-by-four. One end lay on the seat between them while the other end stuck out through the smashed front windshield of the pickup truck.

"What happened?" she asked a man in a blue dairy uniform.

"Well," he said, "I've been wondering that myself. As near as I can make out, they were moving this house down the highway with those three guys on the roof lifting all the traffic signals and power lines so they wouldn't catch on the house. Now what I figure happened is the man who was supposed to get the traffic signal at this intersection slipped or got mixed up or something, but he didn't see the traffic signal coming. So when he tried to catch up with it, he got messed up and dropped the pole that he was carrying. It slid down the roof that way and landed right smack-dab in the middle of that windshield as those two old men passing by. Must have been a pretty big surprise to them. I've been here a good twenty minutes and neither one of them has moved a muscle as near as I can tell. You don't expect to run into a house moving down the highway, much less have a piece of lumber drop off that house and come smashing through your windshield, unless, of course, you are living here in the Valley. Then you know to expect anything except what you expect. It must have come as quite a shock, especially at their age. I don't know. That's just a guess I'm making. But you just look at the facts before you, and you put two and two together."

Traffic was stopped dead still in either direction. An ambulance arrived behind B.C. The attendants ran up and tried to get the two old men out of the car, but they wouldn't be moved. Meanwhile, a fire department hook-and-ladder was being deployed to work on the traffic signal. A few minutes later, a sheriff's car pulled up and two old women got out of the back. They walked up to the pickup and opened the doors on either side. They talked to the men in the pickup for a good fifteen minutes. Then the men, each on his own side, got out of the truck at the same time. They joined the women and walked over to the ambulance. The crowd, by that time well past one hundred in number, cheered. The sheriff and a few other men pushed the pickup over to the side of the road, clearing one lane. Almost immediately, the traffic heading west from the beach poured through the opening on the road. Eventually, some kind of officer in a khaki uniform held up that lane of traffic and let the east-bound lane slowly slide past the house. As B.C. drove by the house, she was struck by a glimpse of ancient red and yellow flowered wallpaper inside. It almost brought her to tears.

She stopped a few miles down the road at the Dairy Queen in Los Fresnos to try to collect herself, keeping an eye always on the traffic from the west in case the moving house threatened to overtake her. She was still a few miles from the internment camp. But the nearer she got, the less certain she was why she'd come. All she could do was be a voyeur. It would inform her work back in New York, no doubt. When she talked about the internment camps, she would know what she was talking about. But that work seemed so distant now. And what could she do for the people she was about to be confronted with? What she wouldn't have given to be heading for a margarita in Reynosa with Giacomo Berg rather than this internment camp.

But she wasn't slugging down a margarita. She was sucking on a chocolate malt at the Dairy Queen. She was not in Mexico. She was in the cultural heart of Los Fresnos, a set of traffic signals on the highway. Old men in straw cowboy hats manned a few booths by the windows. A few families with many small children held the tables by the juke box. All business was conducted in Spanish: ice cream ordered in Spanish, "el rompe correas"— the Belt Buster, called back from the counterperson to the cook. She tried to make it all out, testing herself. She wanted to loosen up her tongue and her ear before hitting the internment camps.

She thought about the camps. It was high time she thought about the camps. Why hadn't she given this more thought? Would they let her in? Could she interview detainees? Would there be others on the outside, working with the legal counsel, for instance, that she could talk to? She'd heard that the prison was not an easy nut to crack. Maybe she wouldn't get in at all. Maybe she wouldn't be able to talk to anyone. This could be a big waste of time. She sucked up the last drops of malt and walked out to the car. She felt the straw hats in the booths by the window turn to watch her walk out the door and then follow her progress through the parking lot to the car. Or maybe she was just imagining it.

She hit the road, making the turn down a narrower road to Bayview. Ahead of her she could see clouds of gray smoke. It looked like fields were burning. As she got closer, she saw the smoke was blowing across the highway. Then she saw a man on the road waving a red flare. As she slowly approached, he raised his hand for her to stop. Behind him the gray smoke moved across the highway like a thick fog. The fields to her right were burning. Men wearing bandanas were running around smoldering bonfires. Other men were throwing cane from the backs of trucks onto the smoldering mounds. Here, under the gray pall that the smoke threw up, there was an end-of-the-world, millennial vision in the middle of the hot, otherwise clear and sunny, South Texas day. Gray figures, wearing red bandanas across their mouths, scurried among the smoking mounds. This could be the Middle Ages, she thought. Where was Breughel when you needed him? The man with the flare was waving at her to keep driving, motioning toward the other lane of the highway. Drive where? She pointed the car where she figured the other lane would lead, if it was straight ahead. She drove into the cloud. She pressed down slightly on the accelerator to assure herself that she was moving. In this cloud it was impossible to tell. If someone were driving toward her in this same lane, she would never know it. She tried to tell herself to have faith in the men with the flares. They had to know what they were doing. Faith. Faith. And then she was out. The smoke in front of her thinned out to reveal another man with a flare, unless, of course, she had driven in a circle. He signaled her to return to the right lane while he held up a line of cars behind him. Then the smoking mounds and the men in bandanas and the gray cloud disappeared altogether, and she was back in the hot South Texas sun, blue sky with a few incipient thunderclouds to the east.

She arrived in Bayview and found the small frame house she'd been directed to. Opening a screen door, she entered the sitting room in which old couches lined the walls. Women and small children inhabited the couches, all looking absolutely wrung out, as if they'd just that minute finished the long march from the Central American interior. Something inside her urged B.C. to turn around and walk out again. Was she ready for this? Long-suffering Indian and mestizo women and children without enough to eat for days, kicked around like dogs by Western politics? She wanted to run, but she was already inside. She smiled slightly, nodded to the women and said, "*Buenas tardes.*"

She walked through the living room to an office with four old desks at which two more young men with pony tails were filling out forms for women sitting at the desks, asking questions in labored Spanish. In a corner of the room a woman was explaining something in a language not Spanish to a group of four refugee women. B.C. had no idea what she was saying. She waited for the woman to look up.

Eventually she did.

"I'm B.C. Boyd," she said. "From the Latin American Political Prisoner and Refugee Network. I called about..."

"You called about seeing the internment camps. Is that right?" The woman stood up and offered her hand to B.C. "I am Carmen Arredondo de Luz. I try to run this place. Like I told you on the phone, your only chance of getting in is to go with the lawyers, say you're our law clerk, and see if they let you in. It depends on their mood and who's at the front gate. They'll probably let you in. We'll be going in an hour or two if you want to hang around. You can go with us then." She sat down and turned back to her conversation with the women.

B.C. remained standing in the middle of the floor. The abstract ledgers in her file cabinets had all suddenly come alive in the people seated and lying around the room. It was as if she had just been run over, not by a Mack truck, but by a mid-sized van carrying the people in her files. She looked around the office and the living room and decided to walk around outside. There she found more families sitting in the shade of a couple of mesquite trees. She decided to begin work, approaching a woman who didn't turn from her gaze.

"*¿De dónde vinieron ustedes?*" B.C. asked. Where do you come from?

"*¿Y quién es usted?*" And who are you? the woman answered in Spanish. A good question.

In her rusty, halting Spanish, B.C. explained that she worked for a human rights organization that fought political imprisonment and worked for the rights of political prisoners and refugees in and from Latin America. She said she had come to talk to people in the internment camps.

"They won't let you talk to anyone," the woman said in very clear Spanish. "Their lawyers even have a hard enough time. They've been trying to see my husband and my brother and my cousin for a long time, and they still can't see them. That's why we're waiting here. We have to wait for them to kick us all out of the country together. Unless the lawyers can find a way for us to stay, that is.

The woman spoke slowly and deliberately. B.C. could follow this.

"What they want to do, of course, is send us back to Guatemala so that my husband and the rest of them will just give up and go back to find us. But my husband will be shot if he goes back. He was a member of the agricultural union. He was even an organizer sometimes. They'll kill him if he goes back. And they'll probably kill me, too, because I was a schoolteacher. Just as a lesson. We cannot go back. Somehow these lawyers will help us if they could only see my husband."

"They don't put you in the camps, too?" B.C. asked.

"They don't have room anymore," the woman said. "They don't have room for women and the children, so they just put us on probation and say we cannot leave the Valley until they say so. And when they say so, of course, it is to load us up to send us back to our country of death. That's what they mean. When they pulled us out of the back of the coyote's truck and sent us to the camps, they asked me to tell them what was the country of my birth. And I said, 'The country of my death, you mean! Guatemala is the country of my death.'"

The woman pulled a small child back into the shade from where she had been playing in the sun. "This is no great paradise," she said. "This is not even as good as parts of Guatemala that I have seen sometimes, particularly when I was still living with my parents. But, as far as I can tell, you can still sit out here under the trees and talk about whatever you like without being worried that the gangs will pull up in a black car and take you away forever, leaving your children here playing in the dust. At least, as far as I can tell, you do not have to worry about that, unless, of course that black car is the Border Patrol."

B.C. Boyd thanked her and got up from where she had been sitting with the woman on the ground. She turned to the woman sitting next to the schoolteacher. That woman shrugged and turned away. "Quechua," said the schoolteacher. "She doesn't speak Spanish."

B.C. saw an old trailer on blocks at the back of the yard behind the house. Two women sat in the doorway of the trailer watching children playing in the yard. She approached the women. As she neared the trailer, they both got up and went inside. She sat down under a mesquite tree to wait for the lawyers.

Not long after that, Carmen Arredondo de Luz came out of the house, carrying a briefcase and followed by one of the pony-tailed young men. "Come on," Carmen motioned to B.C.

B.C. climbed in the back seat of an old white station wagon, which the young man was driving. "This is Tomasito Bach," Carmen said. "He's on leave from Harvard Law School trying to find himself. Instead, he found us and a lot of shit that needs taking care of. What was your name again?"

"B.C. B.C. Boyd."

"B.C.," Carmen said, "what we're going to do is say you're one of our law clerks. Like I said before, there's no guarantee that they'll let you in, but if they do, don't open your mouth and say something we might all regret. Let me do all the talking. If you have a question, let me ask it. We figure everything is taped in there so we have to talk in code. I don't know you. You may be okay, but I can't take the chance on this whole pissant operation going down the tubes because the federales decide they can pin us with supplying guns to the rebels in El Salvador because some New York do-gooder asks the wrong question. *¿Entiendes?* Understand?"

B.C. was a little taken aback. She expected this kind of treatment in New York, but in Texas? It made sense, but the manner was confusing her. "I understand," she said, "but have you ever spent time in New York?"

"NYU Law School," Carmen Arredondo de Luz said. "You take a girl from the Valley and send her to NYU and you come up with the toughest bitch in creation." She was smiling at B.C.

They arrived at a large reservation encircled by enormously high chain-link fences topped with barbed wire. In the center of the reservation were buildings that looked like a small high school. About one hundred men, B.C. guessed, were leaning or sitting against one of these buildings under eaves that provided about three feet of shade. A few men were kicking a soccer ball back and forth across the dusty yard while most seemed to be walking in groups of two or three around the perimeter of the yard.

They entered the first of several buildings. The lawyers, who must have done this hundreds of times, pulled out their I.D. cards to have them perused by the guards. Carmen Arredondo explained that B.C. was a new law clerk and needed to get a prison I.D. The guard slowly looked B.C. up and down. She examined her driver's license, back and front, and asked for any other identification material that might be helpful. B.C. produced her Social Security card.

"You can stay with them today," the guard, a woman identified as A. Moreno on her badge, told B.C. "We'll run a security check on you and give you a card, if everything clears, in the morning. But you can go with them today because we're nice and we know Carmen. You can go, that is, if you let me pat you down to make sure we aren't making a mistake."

B.C. nodded and looked at Carmen. Carmen looked right back at her, indicating nothing.

The guard motioned to a room and B.C. stepped inside. As slowly as she had examined B.C.'s driver's license, the guard patted her body. B.C. steeled herself. She tried to think about other things, as the woman's hands moved up and down her body. All she could think about were the hands. She realized this was not so much a search as a means of humiliation. Then it was over. She came out of the room and joined Carmen and Tomasito.

"That was for our benefit," Carmen told her, as they followed a guard through a breezeway into a second building.

"It certainly wasn't for mine," B.C. said.

"They just saw an opportunity to remind us who has the power here. You provided that opportunity."

They walked to an area in which five or six crude cubicles had been built with particle board and glass on one side of a large cinder-block room with small slit windows near the ceiling. The lawyers gave a guard the list of names of the people they wanted to meet with.

"This will take an hour," Carmen said. "Let's go out in the breezeway, so I can do a little smoking."

B.C. followed dutifully.

"It's already gotten to you, hasn't it?" Carmen asked. "I could tell when we pulled up to the gate. It's a depressing business. These people suffer one humiliation after another, saying goodbye to their parents or their kids maybe forever or their husbands or wives and to everything they've known to pay some coyote with any money they have left to smuggle them across the border because this isn't a free country that welcomes the tired, the poor, and the homeless yearning to breathe free; this is a semi-fucking-fascist paranoid nation suffering a great decline in its fortunes, and it doesn't need starving low-paid immigrant workers just now, thank you.

"It gets to you right away. These are the people with values, with initiative, who want to do right by their families. And we treat them like dogs. The dog catchers round them up, throw them in a truck and take them to the shelter, where they feed them, put them in cement cages and wait for the day when they're sent back to their owners, where they will probably be exterminated, unless somebody claims them in time.

"So we try to claim as many as we can. We win a few. We lose a lot more. The whole thing's a fucking shame."

She'd gone through three cigarettes during the course of her brief explication.

Throughout, B.C. had been scanning the fields and buildings on either side of the breezeway, looking at the faces of the men there. She had a feeling she knew someone there. Among a group of four men about fifty yards away, she saw a face that looked absolutely familiar. Was it Arnulfo? She studied the face for several minutes. The more she looked, the more convinced she was. Her revolutionary. He didn't look in her direction. She began desperately to want him to. But he would not. He went on talking with the group, looking at one man and then another.

It was his moustache. He would talk like that. It was the way an organizer talks. She was more and more certain. If he would just look her way.

"Do you know that man?" B.C. asked Carmen.

Carmen shook her head. "Do you?" she asked.

"I think I do," said B.C. She was becoming very frustrated. Why wouldn't he look at her?

The guard came out of the building to call them in.

"Just a minute," B.C. said. "I have something on my shoe." She took off her shoe and banged it on a steel pole in the breezeway. She couldn't believe she'd been that resourceful. The man looked up and directly at B.C. There wasn't the least acknowledgment of recognition. Then he looked back into the circle of men.

B.C. now was not so certain. It had looked like him still, but why hadn't he acknowledged her? Just a nod, a sign, a gesture. But there had definitely been nothing. Arnulfo or not Arnulfo?

"Why did you do that?" Carmen said, pulling her into the building. "You could get us all kicked out of here for weeks."

B.C. didn't answer. She followed the lawyers back into the building. Six men sat on a bench against the wall. Tomasito went down the line, checking each man's name against the names on their list. Then he motioned the first man in line to the booth in which Carmen and B.C. sat and took the second man to another booth with him.

B.C. didn't say a word. She listened and didn't listen to the first interview Carmen was conducting. Because it was in Spanish, it was easier just to ride on the flow of the language without getting caught up in its meaning. These were all short, wiry, well-built men, peasants, indios, family men, hard workers. Not revolutionaries that she could tell. The salt of the earth. They should be out working the earth, playing with their babies, not locked in a cement and cinder-block prison.

"I am Juan Diego Perez Solas," the second man into the booth told Carmen. "I came here with my family, a wife, two boys and three girls, because the federales came in with bull-dozers one day and destroyed our fields, one day, just like that. And they chopped down the trees almost half-way up the mountain where we lived and they made big bonfires all across the countryside. And they told us we could go work on someone else's ranch or we could move to their camps. And neither one was a choice I was willing to make. And so, I am sitting here in this prison in this great country of yours wondering if the whole world has become one big Guatemala. That would be a sad day with no hope for any of us. We did not come here to this country because we thought it was a land of gold. We came here because we thought it was the only way out."

B.C. had been listening intently. It was not a new story to her, but it had brought her back to earth. Then Carmen asked the man specifics about his village, his age, his politics, and B.C. let the conversation slide right by her.

Perhaps the world had turned upside down, B.C. thought. Perhaps we were just the last to know. The poor, the meek, the oppressed feel all the tremors of upheaval first because they are the most vulnerable. They have no buffers. No place safe to hide.

She, on the other hand, was insulated. The first shock waves do not get through. It is only as the waves build and go crashing into each other, sending out bigger waves, knocking larger and larger ideas of order off their pedestals, that she and her kind begin to feel it, begin to realize what is going on.

Why did this refugee business make her feel so old and world-weary? Ancient. Fossilized. Ossified. Unable to move. Carmen, on the other hand, seemed to be practically giving off sparks. As the men talked, Carmen seemed to pick up energy, shaping her questions, honing in on her prey. B.C. wished she could maintain that edge—even attain that edge and then worry about maintaining it.

The last of Carmen's clients entered the booth. He was obviously an organizer of people. He was not beaten down. He laughed at some of

Carmen's questions. He was not mystified by his whereabouts. He answered Carmen's questions with questions of his own. He looked her directly in the eyes. He was clearly a hero. B.C. was always on the lookout for heroes. She knew it was not her most ennobling feature, but she had always found it easier to fight an uphill battle if she were tethered to some hero leading the charge. She didn't want to believe that this was necessarily an anti-feminist way to be. The hero could be a woman. She preferred to think of it as a general weakness of the 20th-century Western psyche, which could, on many occasions, be ascribed to her. The man was asking about his chances. He asked about the chance of his family staying if he were returned. Carmen hushed him up, saying, "There are many things we will talk about once you've been paroled."

Soon thereafter, the man rose and nodded both to Carmen and B.C. and walked back to the bench to wait with the others. The two guards in the room motioned to the men to stand.

They were marched out of the room. Carmen turned to B.C. "Well?" she said, "did you see what you wanted to see?"

B.C. nodded. "I wondered," she said, "if you could ask about someone I may have seen in the yard?"

"We can try," Carmen said. She did not appear to be as energized as B.C. had seen her during the interviews. In fact, she looked drained.

"What's the name?"

"Arnulfo Gonzalez Barreta of Guatemala."

"And you think he will be using his real name? Did he use any other names?"

"That's all I know to ask for."

"Are you sure you knew his real name?"

B.C. had never thought about this. Was that his name? Had she slept with someone else? "Yes," she said. "I'm sure."

"Will he want us asking for him? It's not always the best strategy if you have another."

"I don't know," B.C. said. Every muscle in her body tightened under this unexpected cross-examination. "I wondered that myself. But I could think of no good reason not to."

"He may think of one."

"Just do it, please."

Carmen approached the guard manning the desk in the room and gave him Arnulfo's name. The guard picked up a telephone and called the query to someone else. A few seconds later, he was shaking his head.

"No one by that name," Carmen said. "Either the man you think is your friend is someone else or someone else is your friend." She smiled as she reported this to B.C. B.C. felt that Carmen was enjoying this. They walked to the door to leave the cell block. B.C. was preparing herself to study this possible Arnulfo again. But when they entered the breezeway, she saw the yard was deserted. Not a soul. She thought she saw Carmen smiling again.

She got in the car behind Carmen and Tomasito for the return to their office. On the way, Carmen pointed to a second fenced reservation, this one of small tract houses. "That's where the guards live," she said. "They are just one generation removed from immigration themselves."

At the office, B.C. got in her car and drove to the coast. Driving across the causeway to Padre Island, she saw four pelicans rowing their great wings through the air just ahead of her. That lifted her spirits somewhat.

But the wall of buildings thrown up on the south end of the island left her confused. There had only been a handful of motels when she was here as a girl. No reason to think this would not change, but Miami Beach? She hadn't expected it. She found a small motel that had survived several hurricanes and the onslaught of speculators and checked into a non-descript, pink cinder-block room with a view of the tennis courts at the condos next door and, if she stood right at the edge of the window, a sliver of a view of the Gulf.

She immediately changed into her bathing suit. The grit of sand in the carpet was somehow comforting. She made for the beach and waded into the water until she was floating off one sandbar toward another. She tested the depth and couldn't touch bottom. She just lay back and floated, carried by the gentle rolling of the waves as they made a surge for the sandbar and land.

She thought about Arnulfo. Was it Arnulfo? She thought about the men lined up against the wall in some of the only shade in the yard. That image imprinted: standing, squatting, sitting men. Men waiting. What would Hannah Arendt call this: the waste of imperialism? Lives wasted standing by a wall. "Expansion is everything." Cecil Rhodes quoted by Arendt and now remembered by B.C. Expansion of countries, corporations. Contraction of lives.

She thought of Giacomo Berg. She felt little pull there just now. Houston? She couldn't conjure up an image, just the name. New York? The yellow curtains of her kitchen window. Arnulfo's suitcase in the living room. Giacomo Berg standing under the electric train running overhead in the Lone Star, where she'd first met him, as he somehow seemed to smile at the train above and her seated below at the same time.

The sun overhead. The waves lulling her body and mind. Floating. Then the sound of the waves breaking ahead of her on the sandbar. Shielding her eyes from the sun. Thinking nothing. Or trying to. Then a wave breaking over her and under her, bearing her up and onto the sandbar.

The next morning she got up early and walked the beach. Very few shells. A few small men-of-war washed up among the seaweed. Styrofoam floats. Plastic jugs, six-pack rings, the refuse of an empire. She was finding it hard to return to Bayview. She thought she should try one more time to figure out if the man she'd seen was Arnulfo. This morning she was certain it was not. Almost certain.

She returned to her room and, instead of packing up and leaving, decided first to call their hotel in Houston to see if Giacomo Berg had checked back in, meaning he'd found nothing and returned the same night. Unlikely.

She wasn't sure that she wanted that. If she were not being self-centered and petty, of course, she would have wished against that, would have wished for him to find his friend. But just now she wanted something, something definite. Giacomo Berg back in their hotel room in Houston would be something definite. But the desk clerk said Mr. Berg had not checked in.

She put on her swimsuit and went back to the water. It was already warm. The tide was out and she had to swim a long way before she could no longer touch bottom. She lay on her back and floated, trying to recover her own inner buoyancy on these waves. That face looking directly into hers at the internment camp. It couldn't have been Arnulfo. She tried to remember his face in her apartment many months before. She tried to remember Giacomo Berg's face. She saw Stephen Seltzer quite easily, sitting in his office. This was supposed to have been a vacation of sorts. A break in the action. Maybe even an adventure. Why did she feel like she was flailing around hopelessly? But now she was floating. She made up her mind to continue to float for the rest of her Texas sojourn. Let whatever happens carry her along.

The wave she'd been riding fell out from under her. Another crashed on top and churned her reverie into the foam crossing the sandbar. She was awake now, relieved of her musing. Stinging saltwater rolling around inside her head. She was ready now, ready to return to the world.

She walked out of the surf, changed, checked out of the motel, and hit the road heading back to Bayview. As she pulled up to the house, Carmen and Tomasito were getting in the car.

"I almost missed you," B.C. said.

"You did miss us," Carmen said. "You can't go with us. The feds called to ask about you last night. They thought you were signaling someone in the yard when you banged your shoe. That's why they cleared the yard. You almost queered our deal. I'm sorry, but we've got too much at stake to worry about you. These people have too much at stake. We talked about it last night and decided you shouldn't go."

Why did she feel Carmen was enjoying this? "Okay," B.C. said. "I understand." She did understand. But she was angry with herself for seeming so passive in accepting Carmen's edict. She should argue just for the sake of it. "You know they're full of shit, though." She managed to say that at least.

"Of course they are, but that's beside the point. It's their show. We're just trying to sneak a few people out the exits before the lights go up. We can't call any more attention to ourselves than we already have." They got into the old station wagon and took off. B.C. looked around the yard. The teacher from Guatemala was stationed for another day with her children under the mesquite tree. B.C. waved and got in her car.

She first turned the car toward the internment camp, thinking she would drive by the yard again to try to spot Arnulfo. She'd driven two blocks in that direction when she changed her mind and headed west for Harlingen and the airport. She found a flight back to Houston that left in a couple of hours. Then she saw a flight that left later that night. She suddenly had a great urge to see Reynosa. Once during her college years, she and a friend had driven all day from Lockhart to Reynosa just to sit at the Triunfo Bar on the zócalo and drink its golden margaritas. Why not again?

She drove to McAllen and then to the border at Reynosa, where she walked across the bridge, caught in a gaggle of white-haired tourists in bermuda shorts. Past customs, through the blocks of curio shops, she walked uphill to the main plaza in front of the cathedral. First, she thought, she needed food. She vaguely remembered a restaurant on the plaza that had sold cabrito. There it was. They threw the smoked hindquarter of a baby goat back into the pit, then served it to B.C. with onions, tortillas, and chile peppers.

She was sitting at a table near the front, where she could watch the business of the plaza. A few shoeshine stands, a raspa stand, people waiting on benches for the bus, others just standing and talking or sitting in the shade watching the world go by. This was more like it. The world was rearranging its pieces in an order she found more to her liking. She finished the goat and wandered through the market a few blocks away, among the mangoes, plastic shoes, licuados, leather belts, and skinned rabbits.

She wandered back to the plaza, where, of course, she found El Triunfo Bar on the corner across from the movie theater. She looked inside. Only men. She looked inside again. It didn't seem threatening. What the hell. She went inside, sat at the bar, and ordered a golden margarita. She knew the men at the other end of the bar were watching her. They had nothing else to watch at that moment. But after the first few sips of the margarita, she cared less about that. The bartender smiled her way. She smiled back. She looked around the bar by looking in the mirror in front of her. Posters for boxing matches and bullfights were on the wall behind her. A shoeshine boy came into the bar, talked to the men first, then came her way. "Shoeshine, miss?" he asked.

She looked at her shoes. She'd forgotten she was wearing sandals. If he'd caught her after another drink, she might have said yes. But she shook her head, no. The world was making more sense now. It was not so troublesome.

"*¿Otra?*" the bartender asked. "*Otra,*" she said, and he smiled.

It was worth it for that smile. Someone played a song on the juke box. A man sang, "I am dancing at your wedding, but I am arranging for your funeral. The girl that you married was really meant for me." She smiled at that. She smiled at almost anything. The second drink was sweeter than the first. She noticed the clock on the wall. It was one hour behind her watch. She smiled at that, too. So civilized. Then she realized by her watch that she should go. She left a few bills for the bartender and waved goodbye. He smiled again.

She walked out into searing heat. Jesus. She had to get her bearings. She walked to the cathedral, and in its cool, damp interior she collected herself. A woman was lighting candles to the Virgin. There was the sweet smell of incense. The darkness in the cathedral was itself a solace. And they say Reynosa is dangerous?

She went back out into the white heat. She found something resembling a coffee shop and had black coffee and a pastry. She then picked her way down the hill, crossing the bridge among Mexican women, each carrying a plaid plastic bag. In customs they looked through her purse and waved her on. She was back in the car and back on the road to the airport without having given anything much thought. She arrived at the airport with still a couple of hours to kill.

For some reason, she decided it was time to call her brother. He didn't have a cell phone. He was afraid of electromagnetic waves bombarding his brain. She tried his house in Ohio, but the phone machine gave a Florida number to call. She called the number. He answered.

"Robert," she said.

"B.C., is that you? I've been worried. I tried calling you in New York. I wondered if you'd gotten close to that satellite. I wondered what you're thinking. I wondered what you're going to do."

"What do you mean, Robert? Whatever are you talking about?"

"You don't know? Where are you, B.C.?"

"Texas. I'm in Texas. Around Houston mostly. I visited our Lockhart home, Robert. It still looks good. Wouldn't be a bad place to live."

"Listen to me, B.C. You can't base where you live on whether it feels good. That's out the window. You have to live some place where it will be safe. Lockhart may be safe. I'll have to look that up. It seems fairly safe for now."

"Safe? From what?"

"The satellite. It fell into Long Island Sound. Like shooting stars. Burning embers fizzling out in the water. Early yesterday morning. About three. People saw it from as far away as Syracuse. But that's not what's got me worried now."

"What's got you worried now, Robert?" B.C. said. She couldn't help the twinge of sarcasm in her voice.

"Plutonium. They're not saying, but I think it may have leaked plutonium into the atmosphere, raining down radioactive dust from Lake Erie to the Hamptons."

"Why do you think that? What makes you think the satellite was carrying plutonium or that it leaked?"

"You just don't know. That's the thing. You don't know. They do all kinds of experiments with those capsules. And this was a military satellite. Military, B.C. Does that tell you anything?"

"It probably had cameras, spy equipment."

"Okay, cameras. What else do military satellites carry? Weapons. It might have had weapons up there. Tiny nuclear fucking missiles for all we know. Otherwise, why aren't they saying what's going on? We have a right to know. It's the beginning of the end, B.C. In a few months, the Millennium. That's how the end will come. Self-inflicted. Your geraniums are probably covered with plutonium dust. Your kitchen sink. Your whole apartment probably glows at night. I'm glad you're not there. You should think about not going back. It was lucky you're not there. Imagine your luck. It's the fucking Millennium, B.C. The year 2000 on our doorstep. This is the beginning of the end. The long slide into home. I'm trying to talk Marian into staying in Florida until we figure out our next move. But she's already packing up. She says the kids need to be back for school and football practice. Football practice? Can you imagine? The world's coming apart at the seams and she's worried about football practice."

Her brother was coming apart at the seams. This fallen satellite had apparently been too much for him. She'd wondered when he would crack. How long could someone who'd spent his formative years driving around in a Volkswagen bus living the credo of free love continue living in a suburb selling insurance in middle Ohio, after settling down and marrying a nurse who had treated him for crabs in a university clinic nearby? How long could he hold it all together?

Thirty years of Kiwanis meetings and backyard barbecues with his Republican neighbors had to take their toll. This was it—the big crackup. The one she knew would eventually come. "Is Marian there?" she asked.

"What's the matter? You think I'm nuts? Paranoid? How can you tell? How can you prove it in court? You can't measure this. We've got tons of radioactive garbage circling the earth, and if one person becomes aware of this and the reality of what's going on hits him between the eyes, everybody thinks he's nuts. I've been reading up on this. I reread the *Illiad* you know. I know my archetypes. I didn't go to TCU for five semesters for nothing. I know about this Cassandra business. Only there won't be any more archetypes after this Trojan horse comes rolling through the gates. This is the end of archetypes."

"All right, Cassandra," B.C. said. "Let me talk to Marian."

Then Marian was on. "B.C., B.C. Thank heaven you're okay. We got worried when you didn't answer for three nights in a row."

"You thought the satellite may have hit me?"

"I thought New York may have done you in. You know I don't trust New York."

"Has he lost it this time?" B.C. asked.

"I don't know. It does seem worse than usual. It's just that there's always a grain of truth in what he's saying. I've learned, just as everybody else has, that when the government says there's no cause for alarm, that's when you have to start packing your bags and bringing out the gas masks. Is this one of those times? I can't tell. Is Robert's intensity level on this thing higher than it's ever been? Yes, I think so. We're just holding tight, hoping it will blow over."

"What about Ohio? He says you're not going back."

"Oh, we're going back. Bren and Suse and I will go back. And we'll make sure Robert goes, too, even if we have to tie him to the hood of the car. You don't have to worry about us. You've got enough to worry about living in New York and all. Why did you call?"

"I can't quite remember. I'm waiting for a plane, and then I got to wondering about you and so I called. No real reason. I've got to go now. It's almost time for my plane. Keep an eye on Robert. I worry about him."

"I'm watching him. We're all right. He just needs a little excitement once in a while."

It was time for B.C. to board her plane. From this, back to the anguish of a Houston suburb. She couldn't bring herself to make the transition. She didn't know how much more of this she could take. She might as well be in NewYork. She felt like she'd dropped into a canyon somewhere, and she had not been able to find her way up one side or the other. She was just stuck there, slithering around with the lower forms of life, heading from one creek bed to another, trying to make her way slowly, muddily, finally, to the polluted Rio Grande and from there into the Gulf.

She turned on her heels and walked out the door. Her rental car hadn't been processed yet. She grabbed the keys and jumped in. She drove from the airport down a narrow highway to the coast. She came to a convenience store where the highway doglegged to the south. She stopped there to get something cool to drink. Behind the store, there were acres and acres of cars parked in a field with people standing among them.

As she bought a Coke, she asked the young girl behind the counter, "Why are there so many people in that salvage yard."

"That's no salvage yard," the girl replied. "People live in those cars. If you see a white station wagon parked a few rows back, that's where I live with my family."

B.C. bolted for the door, jumped into her car and drove away. She couldn't stand it. The world was not going rockingly along, as we were made to think. It had completely fallen apart. Lives were strewn across the landscape.

B.C. returned to her car, rolled down the windows, pointed it toward the beach and took off, pushing the little engine as fast as it would go. She turned the radio all the way up and started shouting. "Fuck it! Fuck it! It's all got to change!" She sang "Jumpin' Jack Flash" at the top of her lungs even as the radio pumped out the sounds of La Mafia.

On Padre Island, she got the same room with the sliver of a view. She closed the curtains and went to sleep. Later she lay on the beach, hoping the sun would bake consciousness out of her. It did not. That evening she walked on the beach for miles. At some point on the way back, she noticed the tiny flashing of phosphorescent sea animals in the surf. She sat on the beach and watched the water. Then she took off her clothes, walked out into the water, and floated in the pitch dark above and below.

The water lifted her up. She let her anxiety drain from her fingertips. Aaah. She was ready for anything.

How to Fly Like an Eagle

"TAKE TWO PEYOTE BUTTONS. Crush them between two rocks. Add gray leaves and purple flowers of the sage bush, crushed. Place the mixture on a rock in the direct sunlight for 36 hours to dry out completely. Make a circle on the rocks around the mixture of branches and twigs, preferably from the piñon pine, to keep the dust from blowing too far when it dries. Spend the 36 hours of drying waiting for an eagle to fly overhead. If one does, call to it, saying, 'What looks like nothing holds great birds aloft.' If no eagle appears, lie out on a big rock on top of a mountain with arms and legs extended to form a wheel with your navel as its hub. Say three times, 'How do you know but every Bird that cuts the airy way is an immense world of delight, clos'd by your senses five?' When the powder is dry, find bark from the madrone tree (this is the most difficult part). Using the bark, sniff the powder all the way up into the center of your skull. This is what the eagle does every other morning."

He finished writing and put the recipe into the notebook with the others. A set of instructions for the rest of the world. Some day, perhaps, someone would find them and give them to the world. He had awakened that morning on top of a mountain. From that mountain he could see other, taller mountains. He determined that he would head for those. Peter Proust gathered into his backpack the personal effects he'd arranged in a loose circle around him: books, notebook, chocolate cupcakes, shoes, gun, clothes, odds and ends.

He set out for the tallest mountain he could see. There was a trail leading down the side of the mountain he was on. He picked his way down that trail, running almost nose-to-nose into a mule-eared deer on one cutback on the trail. He laughed; the deer bounded away. He reached the bottom of the mountain and found a road that appeared to lead in the direction of the mountain he was seeking. He followed the road. He came to a formation of red rocks standing on end, about twelve feet tall. A red stone picnic table was off to one side as was a pole with a blue stand, and inside the stand was a telephone. A gray metal marker on the road called this the "Painted Rock Picnic Area" and talked about Indian pictographs on the rocks. Peter walked around the rocks looking for the paintings. Then he looked up the hill and there, above the picnic site, was a white painting of what to Peter were clearly a deer, a sun, and an eagle. He climbed to the painted rocks and sat there on his haunches studying their message. He could not be sure what it meant, but he knew that somehow it was meant for him. Hundreds of years collapsed like a mushroom puffball. Had he not met this deer on the path downhill? Was it a spirit to guide him to this place? He hadn't been thinking that at the time. He hadn't been open to that possibility. How had he been so blind? But he was given a second chance. The paintings, this message, was that chance. He studied the message but couldn't translate its meaning. He sat there for hours: the deer, the sun, the eagle on the rock. The sun moved from directly overhead to behind a mountain. The rocks now provided shade. He edged up to them. He was almost in their embrace. If he stared long enough, the deer began to move. The eagle floated on wind currents. He stared. Then he knew: this was not a story. This was a record of existence. A place at equilibrium in the universe. The rocks, the sun, the animal on the earth, the animal in the air, all in total, unwavering, delicate balance, as if this were the center of the universe, as if this were neither the beginning nor the end of the world but the place containing both, the world in balance where all beginnings and endings are just transitory significations. He understood.

He felt awakened. Whole? Like solid matter. He felt part of the earth under his feet. He sat in the embrace of the rocks until well past dark.

When he could no longer see the images painted on the rocks, he wandered back down to the picnic table. He took out the cupcakes but decided he would not eat again. He opened the wrapper and laid the cupcakes out for the squirrels. He sat in full lotus on the stone table. Then he walked in an ever-widening circle around the picnic site. The sky was clear, cold and blue, a blue so close to black that most would think it was black, like a dark drape hung behind a stage, a curtain at the edge of perception, pierced in incredible patterns by white pinpricks of light. He was not the only one who saw it that way. He saw a blue extending back into endless space, carrying him back, swallowing him up, enfolding him like a blanket, and the stars were shafts of light and the memory of light leading him deeper and deeper toward the beginning of time, carrying him along as on a moving sidewalk to the creation of the universe, to that time before time. He looked at the stars and imagined himself gliding along an endless mobius, passing back through himself and beyond anything he, or anyone else, had ever known. It was as if it made no difference if he ever moved again. If he waved his arm or a car passed by raising dust from the roadbed, it made no difference. All things were equal, were in balance. He had reached an understanding with the universe, in which his existence was no longer his own. Desire became a running creek. Hunger was tires rolling across a gravel road; anger, the stone face of a mountain; love, the rustling of ferns in a forest; and memory, a shaft of light.

There was little left to do but remove the particulars of his existence so that the general could take over. He had to still the grinding pain in his stomach. He had to wash away forever the thirst that sat on his dry lips and in his scratchy throat. These few temporal needs were standing in the way of his entering timelessness. He couldn't keep from smiling.

One other thing: it was already like a memory from another world now, but he still felt the tug of the thinnest thread from his family, his own personal history. He had to pull free of that. There was a telephone in the wilderness, as if set before him for this purpose. He would call. But first he would write Sara and Seth a message so that, when his notebook was found, they would have a communication from him, though he would already have drifted far away in the universe. He took out a sheet of paper and somewhat laboriously wrote "Sara" and "Seth" across the top. Letters, words, and writing had suddenly become foreign to him, too abstract, removed too far from meaning. He drew a bird, an eagle floating in the full-bodied, uplifting air, and wrote "LOVE" across its wingspan. He folded the paper and stuck it in his notebook. A message they could carry through time.

He went to the telephone, dropped in a quarter, listened for the dial tone and walked away. Could he go through with it? This would be his last act in the temporal universe. Was he too far distanced already? He sat on the table and looked at the stars. Now they were merely pinpricks of light. He was losing his new body. Just the thought of calling had been a sudden constriction on his new life without physical boundaries. He had to call to unravel this last thread. He had money, change that he carried in a small paper bag in his backpack for this occasion. He pulled out the paper bag and emptied its contents in the blue metal phone booth. He called his father's office. First the operator's voice was asking for money. Then his father's voice was talking from the answering machine, talking to him, saying "Please leave a message." Then two beeps and the barely audible whirring of the tape machine. He stood there. What would he say? He listened to the tape running. He hadn't thought enough about this. He could not force a sound through his lips or off his tongue. He finally said, "Dad," then the tape clicked off. He would have to try again. What should he say? He thought some more, came up with nothing, and just decided to speak, no matter what he said. He counted his coins and dialed again. His father's voice again. That always threw him. Then his turn.

"Hello," he said. "I'm calling from a phone booth in the Davis Mountains of Texas. They are beautiful. Deer. I saw an eagle. I am feeling better than ever now. I am calling because I just wanted to say."

And he stopped. He realized he was crying. "I just wanted to say." He was sobbing now. He could barely speak. He had to get it out, but he felt like he was drowning. And what did it mean anyway? Words strung together, thrown out like a fishing line from a boat in a lake. "I just want to say," he managed, not knowing why anymore, "I love you all." Then he hung up. Then he walked behind a rock and retched. Dry heaves. There was nothing in him.

It was done. He felt better. He carried his sleeping bag up among the painted rocks, rolled it out there and lay down to look at the stars. Nothing in his way now. He was cut loose. All he had to do was wait for the right wind current to carry him away. The rocks were like a mother bending over him at night. If the stars were waves of light running out simultaneously in all directions, then the cold earth on which he lay, of which he was a part, was a pebble on the ocean floor washed back and forth by the light waves until it was ground into nothing. He looked at the stars and felt the waves wash over him, rubbing him into the earth beneath.

The next morning he climbed halfway up the hill above the painted rocks to find the mountain he had originally set out for. He found it, got his bearings, and figured the road below would lead to that mountain. He returned to the picnic table, pulled the remaining cupcakes and juice from his backpack and left them there. He pulled out the gun, held it in one hand, then the other, then put it back in the pack. As he stood up to leave, the phone started ringing. It was an irritation he decided to ignore. He crossed the road to a creek bed that the road seemed to follow. Once he set out for the mountain, following the creek bed, he could no longer hear the ringing.

Action at a Distance

HE HADN'T BEEN SURE where to drive. After lying in the creek near Mountain Home for what felt like several hours but was probably more like minutes, Giacomo Berg couldn't decide whether to take the highway where the deputy had told him Peter Proust was last seen hitching—and to hope that either luck or some subconconscious connection would lead him to Peter—or to simply return to Houston to see if Sara had any news, to see what he could do for B.C.'s friends, to wait for B.C.

It was a short-lived epiphany in the stream of Mountain Home. Once Giacomo Berg was out, quickly dry in the scorching sun and back in his car, he was not sure the subconscious was the way to go. He should call Sara, as he'd promised. But not yet. He was afraid that would draw him deeper into this same hole. He needed a new push, new thinking, some kind of affirmation. Sara would find him if she needed to, but for now he felt more comfortable talking to people, figuring things out, seeing B.C. He felt a real need to see B.C. It may have been the barrenness of these hills. It may have been because tracking this missing piece in the order of the universe, this part of his life that had disappeared into a suckhole, this very vulnerable friend, had gotten to him. He wasn't sure of the reason, but he wanted to see B.C. Would she still want to see him? Or was she suddenly engulfed again in saving lives? Was she revived by the chance to do good while all around her evil reigned? He might have to go to the prison gates to retrieve her. That might be a nice diversion. If it weren't for the money he didn't have, he could see staying down here for a while, chasing B.C. while avoiding any semblance of responsibility to his former life.

He arrived at the interstate. With a glance toward the west, he turned the car back toward Houston. Thinking about Peter Proust still out there on a limb made his head hurt. Every once in a while, Giacomo would admit that he, too, was lost in his own orbit, circling life as it was lived by most people. Would he circle forever and never land? Was he facing three or four more decades of weightlessness? Floating until a hip needed replacing or he couldn't hear too well? Or until memory went and his sister placed him in a nursing home to rocket alone into the darkening gloom? Or until he suddenly just ended? He had to snap out of it. He was thinking too much. It was dangerous when he had only himself to talk to—and listen to. He just wanted to see B.C. No good reasons were required.

Suddenly he was starving. But he needed to keep moving. He decided to drive at least to San Antonio before stopping. He kept an eye out for the place he thought the dead horse lay.

But he never found it. Had he dreamed it? He had not. But the image was enough to make Freud proud. Or Bunuel. He drove through the hills heading south and east. He tried to think about B.C., but he found it difficult to think about anything beyond the growling of his stomach. The hills gave way, and San Antonio lay before him. He followed the instructions on a billboard that led him to a Mexican food restaurant beside the interstate. The restaurant was one of two buildings standing in a wasteland in the middle of the city. All around and behind the building for blocks was nothing but weeds and squares of asphalt or cement, parking lots and the foundations of a civilization undoubtedly cleared away by the impulse to plan, reshape, and control. Giacomo Berg could imagine the recent history that led to this desert, but to his eyes, never having seen what loss this denuded landscape represented, he could only see that two buildings stood in the middle of an urban wasteland, not the lives and homes and jobs that these buildings grew out of or the new world some group of engineers and venture capitalists had set down in plans, tacked to the wall of an ultra-modern office in an air-conditioned bank building downtown, never to be realized.

Giacomo Berg pulled into the parking lot of the restaurant, but it was the building behind the restaurant that interested him. It was a four-columned, pseudo-Georgian, three-story white house, the second story porch buckling and caving in on the one below. A neon sign hung above the second-story porch, declaring: "R. Ramos: Midwife." He walked around the house. It was obviously long-deserted. A couple of old mattresses lay in the yard. No unbroken panes in the windows; no doors to the outside remained on their hinges. A "CONDEMNED" sign lay just inside the door. He walked back to the restaurant.

Reproductions of photos of the Mexican Revolution lined the walls. Behind the cash register, he thought he recognized a photo of Allard Lowenstein surrounded by a group of people. It was signed, "Allard Lowenstein 1967. Dump LBJ." Days long gone. There was also a photo of the restaurant itself with the white house standing behind it, its neon lit, and buildings all around. It looked like an actual thriving neighborhood. That photograph was dated 1957.

Four musicians playing guitars and a trumpet held patrons at bay in one corner of the restaurant. The people at the tables in that corner were all turned away from the musical onslaught, except for an older woman with a shawl around her head, who was smiling benignly at the musicians, attempting to keep time by softly clapping her hands.

Giacomo Berg ordered the works: enchiladas, tamales, a taco, beans, rice, and a Dos XX beer—"the cabrón special." After downing half the beer, he asked the waiter about the big white house.

"Oh, it's famous," the waiter said. "They're trying to decide whether they should make it a landmark or burn it to the ground, just like they want to do with this restaurant here. The Midwife's house was the most famous whorehouse in all of San Antonio. But I don't have time to tell you about it. Come back in the middle of the afternoon when we don't have business. My customers are waiting," he said and walked away, waving a hand above his head.

Giacomo Berg had just about finished his meal when the troop of musicians appeared beside his table. When the guitars began, it was not too bad. But when the trumpet seemed about to blow the basket of tostadas across the table, he decided it was time to leave.

He walked around the Midwife's one more time and then he got into his car and headed for Houston. There was so much going on behind the diorama of everyday life. He could never get enough of those kinds of stories. And there he'd thought it had been a clinic or a plot of liberated ground where midwives could advertise and women who could not afford doctors or didn't trust them could go to have babies.

He drove. The sun was beginning its descent behind him. He wondered how this was all going to end with Peter. He figured it would end sometime soon. There was no guarantee, however, that he, Giacomo, would ever know of the ending. There was particularly no guarantee that the ending would announce itself to the world when it occurred.

If there was one thing Giacomo Berg did have faith in, it was the belief that things would work themselves out, one way or the other. Not necessarily for the best, but they would work themselves out, following the dictates of some little-understood universe. And whatever he could do to help things along was negligible. Some corroded sense of karma guided him. He'd picked it up as a child, added what he'd gleaned from 1960s Eastern mysticism, and worked on it until it had taken a form he could use, could carry around and apply to the world as necessary. It was not a hippie-dippy, summer of love, circle-your-Volkswagen-buses and let's-get-down-with-Mother-Nature kind of karma. It was not a do-right-by-the-world-and-it-will-do-right-by-you naiveté. It was more a belief in the finitude of energy, matter, and spirit, in what goes around comes around, in inertia, action and reaction. He believed there were pulleys and levers people operated to get through their lives and what we pulled tugged on us, and what we did unto others we were doing in some fashion to ourselves. It was a Jewish form of karma, he had come to realize some years ago, having taken what little he'd gotten out of the half-hearted Jewish inculcation of his childhood and reduced that to the conception that life is its own reward—how you lived determined not some future compensation but was the only compensation you received. His grandfather, who every summer kept a large vegetable garden in his backyard, always lost half his crop to the birds and the squirrels. Once, at a distance from the garden, watching blue jays hammer away at his tomatoes, his grandfather had told him, "This garden is not just for us, you understand. I'm not the only one tending it. You've got your rain. You've got your sun. You've got your earth. I just dropped in the seeds. So if the birds and squirrels get some of the tomatoes, that's all right. What you have to do is learn to enjoy the birds and the squirrels, and then you won't have lost a thing."

Jewish karma. He believed in this stuff at the core of his being. But somehow, sitting there with his grandfather, he had still been unable to enjoy watching the birds take over the tomatoes.

He had come to realize that his belief in karma was not the best vehicle for transforming himself into a leader of people. He could never quite bring himself to tell anyone else what to do. Not even Pilar Moreno when he explained her job to her. He could lay out the ground rules. But the rest was up to her. She had to live her own life. He could only lay out the options and watch and wait. The future would unfold accordingly.

Because of this belief, he had realized, he would probably never get his life together. He felt like he could never take command of any situation in which he found himself. It was not his right, and, ultimately, it didn't matter. He was responsible for his own actions and nothing more. He would never get ahead that way. But perhaps he would never fall behind. He believed things would all even out. He could not presume to shape his part of the universe, but he wanted to understand it.

To understand B.C., for instance. He could not tell B.C. that, if she were waiting for him at the hotel—not just waiting, but waiting for him— that if she were waiting for him that night, he would from that moment on do whatever she asked. Even though, at that moment, driving into Houston, he felt he might. She would have to figure that out on her own.

But she was not waiting. She hadn't registered that night. It was late by the time Giacomo Berg had arrived in Houston. It had only been a drive of three hours, but he felt completely undone by the time he'd dragged himself out of the car. Were B.C. waiting for him, he was not sure he was up to providing the intensity the moment would require. But he was deluding himself. He knew he could be up for anything if confronted by a force strong enough to knock him out of his present self-absorption. Their rendezvous was set for the next evening. Orderly B.C. would hold to that. Unless something else held her in the Texas Valley. He would assume, for now, that she would hold to their schedule.

It was time to read more from the *Conquest of New Spain*. Cortés was intent upon converting his captive Montezuma to Catholicism. Montezuma saw no reason for it, saying his own set of beliefs were generations old and explained the world adequately. As proof, he explained that his religion had included a prophecy of the coming of Cortés as an envoy of a great ruler and as the avatar of a civilization and alternative system of belief. His system of belief even included a premonition of its own demise. What more could anyone ask of the scope and reach of a system of belief?

If the Aztecs had, indeed, seen Cortés as the fulfillment of a prophecy, if it were not some Spanish coloration of conquest mythology, then they were beaten before they began. The weight of their destiny prevented them from defending themselves. La Malinche as the turncoat was merely a manifestation of how the Aztecs betrayed themselves, or were betrayed by their priests. On the other hand, Giacomo thought, unlike our own, their civilization at least prepared them for its end. They had an understanding of what was happening to them, as Einstein's Jewish agnosticism prepared him for understanding a relative universe. Did that prevent them from resisting their destiny? Or did it prepare them for one last-ditch resistance effort? Does knowing preclude acting or make it possible? Or was this just more Western horseshit? The Aztecs waiting for the Great White Father. Not likely. Cannons and horses and small pox and starvation from a drought year were more likely explanations of Aztec defeat. But he did like that word "horseshit." He was adapting to Texas. He turned out the light and went to sleep.

The next morning there was no sign of B.C. He called her cell but figured she wouldn't be getting any reception in the far reaches of Texas. It didn't connect. He decided to drive out to Glasgow. First he drove to the gates of Pleistex. They were locked. There was no apparent activity behind them. There were seven or eight reddish and grayish mounds around and behind the small corrugated building in the middle of the lot. There was no breeze, nothing to stir up the dust. He walked around the perimeter of the fence. On two sides there was nothing but empty lots and weeds a foot high. A junked car here and there, old tires. He walked the fifty yards to the bayou that ran behind the dumpsite. Nothing particularly noteworthy about the half-foot of brown water in the canal. They should at least run a few tests on the water. He walked back to the car and drove to the park and baseball diamonds about a mile to the west. The only activity in the park that morning was a couple of dozen teenage kids horsing around in a swimming pool beyond the baseball fields. A coach-looking person was standing at one end of the pool, blowing a whistle at regular intervals. Seltzer hadn't mentioned the swimming pool. He had his own.

They had to test the water in the pool. He walked around the baseball diamonds. Nothing unusual to be seen there. He walked into the outfield grass. Where there were brown patches, he dug into the dirt. He thought he might see red or gray dust mixed with the sandy loam. No such luck. But soil samples were needed there, too. He tried to figure out what to do next. He was just killing time at this point. He drove into the center of Glasgow and found a coffee shop.

From there he called the hotel. Still no B.C. He called Occam to tell him about the meeting that night.

"That Seltzer fella already called me," Occam said. "Yeah, I'll be there. But it's only because you asked me, and I figure these rich porkers can fork over a little dough. I also, I admit, love to see Republican suburbanites hit by the truth. Nothing like watching a Junior Leaguer squirm through the first stages of denial.

"You know, of course, this is tassel night back at the old club. I'm giving up a lot for this, Berg, but it's in the interests of justice. Now, if this had been fan dance night, you could just as well have said sayonara to Randall Occam. I never miss a fan dance."

Giacomo Berg conjured up an image of Occam's pudgy body and thick glasses poised at a precisely calculated angle to catch the revelations available in the interstices between fans. He hung up and tried the hotel again. No B.C.

He drove back into town. The traffic slowed, stopped briefly, speeded up, slowed down, stopped, and began again. Office buildings formed an irregular wall on either side of the highway all the way into town. None struck Giacomo Berg as particularly distinctive. Those near Glasgow exhibited a pseudo-baroque post-modern flourish somewhere amid the glass and steel. Closer to Houston, bluish glass and a stair-step architecture were the norm. Closer in still, the heat on the highway was intensified by reflective gold buildings. At the edge of the city proper, brick began to appear on all the edifices, and remnants of the international style dominated the first circle of growth outside the downtown. The center itself, the foundation of power, was a monument valley of granite, limestone, and other rock thrown up to provide the illusion of permanence, old wealth and a rock-hard core, when Giacomo Berg knew this was all founded, and not long ago, on a swamp of fluctuating values. There was some relevance to Montezuma's city here, Giacomo thought, built on a swamp, but this is just a wet dream compared to the Aztec empire.

Finding B.C. still not checked in, he made for the pool, thinking he would see her pass. But he fell asleep in a chaise lounge and did not wake up until it was time to begin the trek back to Glasgow. Before leaving, he checked at the desk again. No B.C.

The rush-hour traffic moved so slowly that he found it difficult to determine if he were moving or standing still. It took him an hour to reach his exit from the central city. It took another half hour to travel three miles beyond that point. He couldn't take it. He got off the highway and found a delicatessen in a strip shopping center.

Lox and bagels. But jalapeño bagels? Cream cheese picante? He ate a bagel with cream cheese and stared at the traffic on the highway. It didn't seem to move. He tried calling the hotel again. No B.C.

He hadn't counted on this. Surely she would show up for her old friend Stephen's meeting, if not for him. Unless the revolution had begun in South Texas. He started making plans. If she didn't show, he would call Sara to see if she had any new ideas. If she did, he would follow them to their conclusion. Or he could try to find B.C. at the internment camps.

But that would require real action on his part. He couldn't just be carried along. Besides, it could be a crucial loss of time in the search for Peter. It was bad enough returning to Houston. He couldn't figure out the right move. He felt whatever this was between B.C. and him had to work itself out at its own pace. Any sudden action on his part might tear the entire fabric apart. Or he could hang around here, waiting for B.C., advising Seltzer on his next move. That seemed the least likely option and the least interesting. It seemed deadly, in fact. He figured people probably began to mildew here in Houston if they remained too long. If Sara had any idea whatsoever, he would buy into it. But if she had no idea?

He finished the bagel and headed for the car. The traffic was now moving at about a twenty-mile-per-hour pace. He inserted himself into the stream and let it carry him to Glasgow.

"Here's what we've found so far." Stephen Seltzer was writing on a blackboard at the front of the meeting room of the Optimists Club, Main Street, Glasgow. "We had sixteen volunteers, who each visited about 20 houses. There were 317 houses in all." He wrote "317 houses" on the top of the blackboard. "We covered 24 blocks from Ivanhoe Terrace to Bobby Burns Parkway and from Loch Loman to McTavish. This does not count the people who were not home and the houses that are unoccupied. There are 47 of those. I had no idea." He drew a square on the board, labeling the sides with the street names he had just recited.

He turned to face squarely the people in the room—200 mostly white suburbanites, sitting quietly in folding chairs, some wearing business suits, others in jogging shorts. From where Giacomo stood at the back of the room, they seemed oddly passive and subdued for a bunch of property-owning, status-seeking white people. Clearly, they were waiting for bad news. "Now brace yourselves," Stephen said. "A lot of these are your families, your children, so you know what is going on. It's hit my family, too. You know something is wrong. But how wrong? When I saw these figures, I couldn't believe them. I asked our surveyors to go back over their questionnaires. And they did, and we still get these numbers.

"You may know about your family. And you may know about your neighbors. And you may know about problems a few kids are having in your child's class at school. And when you go to church, you may have noticed what seemed like more prayers for the sick than usual. And if you read the obituaries, you may have noticed more deaths from around Glasgow and Camelot down the road and Brighton on the other side of the bayou. But listen to this. You won't believe this, but listen anyway. And after you hear this, then we've got to do something. We've got to do something about it."

Stephen began his litany: "23 brain tumors. Out of 317 houses. That's almost one brain tumor per block. Twelve cancers of the mouth and lips. 51 lung cancers—that's people who smoke and people who don't smoke. People who live and work with smoke and people who are never near it. One out of fourteen houses has lung cancer. 28 colon cancers. 189 houses reporting respiratory problems other than lung cancer. 17 melanoma. 6 ovarian or testicular cancers. 22 liver cancers. 68 nervous system problems. 14 pancreatic and stomach cancers. 17 leukemias and other blood disorders. 217 with some sort of unexplained skin rash or other, apparently minor, problems." He wrote all this on the board, then turned to face his audience again.

"And there are so many sad stories. One woman with leukemia had a year-old baby and a four-year-old. She refused painkillers because she wanted to be alert for her children as long as she was alive. She died two months ago. Many of you probably knew her. It's that kind of courage that makes you weep. Our surveyors deserve a lot of credit and a few stiff drinks. It's not easy recording this kind of history." He turned back to the chalkboard.

"Now, compared to average statistical findings for similar populations—age, ethnicity, income, occupation, geographical location, that kind of thing—we are up by 10 for brain tumors, by two for mouth and lips, a plus-19 for lungs, a plus-eight on colons, up 103 for respiratory problems, a plus-two for melanoma, up by seven on liver cancers, plus-41 for nervous system problems, plus-two on pancreatic and stomach cancers, and up 9 on blood disorders. We couldn't find any similar statistics on unexplained skin rashes, but Dr. Spector, the dermatologist at the Medical Center, said he'd never seen anything like it. The good news is we fall short of the average on ovarian and testicular cancer. Birth weight has been normal. Infant mortality is normal. We had almost every house complain of eye irritation for at least one person living in that house—303 houses altogether. And 38 houses reported ear-lining irritation. But there is nothing to compare these to. No one keeps statistics on these."

He looked around the room. Then he walked over to the side of the room where Cara was sitting and fumbled through some papers. From Giacomo's vantage point, the room of white faces now looked pasty-white. Stephen once again was at the front of the room. "That's the bad news," he said. "But what are we going to do about it?"

A white-haired man stood up. He was tan and looked like he spent his days on the golf course. "What can we do?" he said. "We're stuck here. Everything we've got is invested in these houses. And nobody's gonna buy 'em from us. Unless we all keep this a secret. We could do that. Nobody knows about this but us here in this room. We could not talk about it for, say, six months and that'll give each one of us who wants to the chance to get out, even if we lose a little money."

"Word will get out," a middle-aged woman said. "People will find out about it one way or the other. And besides, if somebody asks your realtor about conditions in the neighborhood, then the realtor has to tell them. And don't you think people will start asking when they see 300 'For Sale' signs go up all at once? I used to be a realtor. People ask you all kinds of questions. And you've got to answer. Otherwise, you're liable for whatever happens later. I used to sell back when everybody had money and there were no questions asked about price. They thought whatever they paid would be a bargain two years down the line. But even when they didn't ask about price, they asked about neighborhoods and water and about anything else they thought they should know. They'll be asking double now."

Stephen held up his hand. "What I mean is, not how we can save our investments, but how we can figure out what is going on and stop it so we can go on living here if that is a safe thing to do and if it's what we want to do, or at least we can find out whom to sue. The way I see it, we're a captive community. We're an enclave that the greater forces of the economy have decided will be a necessary sacrifice on the altar of progress. There are always winners and losers in our society. You watch the unemployment rates. The Federal Reserve says that a targeted unemployment rate of four percent or six percent or eight percent is necessary to keep down inflation. So that four or six or eight percent—those are people—their well-being is sacrificed for the good of the whole, for the progress of the economic system. That's the way it works. I'm a bankruptcy lawyer. In order for the economy of Houston to recover, there had to be sacrifices. A number of businesses paid the price. Interest rates went up; their businesses went down. I think that's what's going on here in a very perverse way. I think we're being poisoned, possibly by the Pleistex plant, possibly by something else. We are the unwitting and accidental victims of the chemical industry. They don't mean to be killing us off, but they've got to dump their chemicals somewhere. And it's just our bad fortune that they've decided to dump them on us. That's what I'm thinking. I have no proof. I hope Mr. Occam here, whom I'm going to introduce in a minute, does. But that's what I think is going on.

"It doesn't usually happen to neighborhoods like ours. Not that I know of anyway. I mean, we probably have some chemical industry executives living right here among us, maybe right in this room. We think of ourselves as winners, as success stories, as people who know how to play the system. But things, suddenly, just aren't working out.

"At the same time, we can use our position to our advantage. We know how to make the calls, how to talk to bureaucrats and lawyers, how to prepare for judges and how to gather information. We can use what we've got to get what we need. We are after all, by God, professionals."

There it was. Giacomo was enjoying this. He could see in this speech, which Stephen Seltzer must have worried over all night and day, that he still carried some of that old fire B.C. had mentioned, but at the same time he had never gotten it entirely. He didn't detect any sarcasm when Stephen invoked their status as "professionals." He wondered what B.C. had seen in him. Then he looked to his left and saw her standing in the doorway, smiling. She seemed to be enjoying herself. He walked over to stand beside her. Before he could attempt to say anything, she held her finger to her lips and pointed to the front of the room.

Randall Occam was holding court. He had erased the blackboard and was pacing back and forth across the front of the room. One shirttail was out, his glasses were pushed up to his hairline, his jacket clearly couldn't contain his paunch. Randall Occam was deep in thought.

He stopped pacing and turned to his audience. "I have searched all the available databases," he announced. "This is not something that is easy to do, but I have the means to do it at my disposal, and I did it for you people. You are lucky in that regard. Now I'll just write on the board here what I found in the databases, and then I'll use my years of experience with just these kinds of data to paint a picture for you so that you can begin to understand it. Any questions at this point?"

Yeah, Giacomo thought. Why are you such an arrogant asshole? But he kept his question to himself.

"First, on the release of toxic chemicals reported for this county last year, just this county, there were 632,097 releases of chemicals into the air, 21,800 releases into the water, 18,423 releases on land, 12,453 releases underground, 16,879 releases into public sewage, and 348,879 releases in off-site transfers for a grand total of 1,050,531 toxic releases in the county last year.

"What does that mean for your health? There were 81,379 releases of known carcinogens, 89,765 releases of mutagens, 297,379 releases of toxins that affect development and thinking, 349,821 releases of toxins that harm reproduction, 127,654 releases of toxins listed as acute, 421,934 releases of toxins listed as chronic and 160,623 releases of neuro-toxins. That's a lot of poison for one county.

"But I can get more specific. I can talk about your zip code. And, you'll be glad to know that, since this is by-and-large a bedroom community, your zip code is not contributing a large share to the toxic soup surrounding you. That's good. That's what you want. But still you may be surprised to learn that this sleepy little bedroom community does produce its share of poisons. This homey neighborhood of shade trees and backyard swimming pools, where you come home every night to get away from the problems back there in the city, may not be quite as commodious as you believe. Some of your neighbors are taking some of the joy out of life.

There were, for instance, 2,653 toxic releases into the air last year in this very zip code, right in your own backyard. You'll be glad to know that there were no reported, and I emphasize the word 'reported,' releases underground or into the sewage system in your fair community. But there were

2,328 releases into the water and 16,758 releases on land and another 420 releases in off-site transfers for a grand total of 22,159 toxic releases just in your zip code last year. And what kinds of chemicals were they releasing into your community? 6,432 releases contained known carcinogens, 11,278 contained developmental toxins, 1,765 contained reproductive toxins, 10,689 were classified as acute toxins, 6,432 were called chronic toxins, and 2,987 were listed as neuro-toxins. Doesn't make you feel too well, does it?" He flipped his glasses down over his eyes and stared at his audience.

"If you felt okay coming into this room, how do you feel now?" Then he began to walk around the room.

"Where'd you get that information, anyway?" called a voice from among the people sitting at the back of the room.

"Where did I get this information? Did I get it from some political group? Did I get it from a raving band of environmentalists? I got it from the EPA. For the Republicans in the room, that stands for the Environmental Protection Agency. And that's not exactly a radical outfit. They didn't send chemical spies to collect data out along the fence lines and report surreptitiously on anything they found. No. They sent out something called the Toxic Chemical Release Inventory form. And the chemical producers themselves filled these forms out and sent them back. So this may just be the tip of the iceberg, is what I'm saying. We may not know the half of it.

"This is what the companies that do business with Pleistex, for instance, tell us that they are releasing as toxic waste. They may not be reporting all their emissions or all the kinds of emissions they produce. You are living, after all, right in the middle of a toxic hurricane. Texas ranks second in toxic chemicals released and first in toxic chemicals released into the air. Most of these chemicals are released by your neighboring counties: Jefferson, Harris, and Brazoria counties. Texas ranks first among the states in releases of known carcinogens, and Harris County is the county with the largest amount of released carcinogens. Just over that county line, not ten miles from here. It is also the county with the largest number of toxic chemical releases known or suspected to cause birth defects. So, here you sit, far from the madding crowd, driving into town to make your money so you can come back out to sedate Glasgow to enjoy the fruits of your labor while escaping the consequences. Because, even if you sell insurance or run a health food gourmet restaurant, you are living off an economy that was built on oil and petrochemicals. That's what this town is built on. Oh, a seaport, too, but a seaport for what?

"Petrochemicals. In case you don't know it, in case you are one of those Yankees, like I am, who came down here after Houston already was what Houston is, here's what happened: oil came in in the '20s and early '30s, but the petrochemical industry didn't come in full force until World War II, when the strategic decision was made, with the help of Jesse Jones of the *Houston Chronicle* and FDR's cabinet and some of Lyndon Johnson's closest friends, to relocate a good deal of the petrochemical industry from the Atlantic coast to the Texas coast, out of harm's way and closer to the oil supply. They started making rubber here, more rubber than anywhere else in the rubber-starved world at war. And after the war, things just took off."

"That's right. That's money. That's what made it possible for all of us to live out here," the same voice from the back called. It belonged to a man, probably in his 50's, wearing a business suit, who was by this time on his feet, challenging Occam. From where he stood, Giacomo Berg saw that the most obvious thing about the man's appearance was the fact that, as he talked, his neck got redder and redder and appeared to keep swelling and thickening. "Everything you say is exaggerated and taken out of context," the man was saying. "You can't even eat apples today without getting cancer. You can't let the kids watch TV without killing them off with electromagnetic waves. You can't feed them peanut butter because aflatoxins—and they're natural—will kill them off. Come on, man. That's what life's about—taking risks. We take them every day just getting in the car to go to work. I could kill myself shaving tomorrow morning if I accidentally slipped and cut my jugular, but I'll take that risk. It's worth it. There are risks everywhere. But the risks you're talking about are overstated to scare people out of their senses. I didn't come down here to find out what's wrong with my kid just to have a bunch of socialistic theories thrown at me about the economy. I want facts."

During this harangue, Occam had been drawing a map on the board, locating Glasgow amid its neighboring counties, writing the pounds of toxic emissions generated in each county the year before. Completing this, he turned to the man in the business suit and waited for him to finish speaking.

"So, what's wrong with your kid?" Occam asked.

The man turned away and sat down.

"Here's a fact," Occam said. "What did the petrochemical companies do with the waste they produced? For a long time, they just dumped it any way they could. They burned it off. They took it out to sea. They buried it on site. But they began to run out of room, and they probably had a few chemical engineers who told them that some of the stuff they produced as waste was better disposed of far away from people. So they started finding places out in the country to dump the stuff. A rural industry was born: waste disposal. Little companies would buy up some acreage from farmers and put up a sign declaring themselves waste disposal sites, and the trucks from the coast would begin rolling in. That's what you've got at Pleistex. That dump has been here for over thirty years. It's a good ten years older than most of these houses. I did a little research on it and found that it was originally owned by a fellow named Bubba Pleisocky, who operated about half a dozen disposal sites, dumps really. Let's call them what they are—dumps—and they're spread across a three-county area.

"Well, about eight years ago, Bubba sold out to Grand & Dufy Waste Disposal Systems, which is in turn part of a conglomerate out of New Jersey. Now Grand & Dufy owns 24 dumpsites in this five-county area. Some of them are classified as Class II sites, for dumping non-toxic material, and some are Class I sites, for hazardous and toxic waste disposal operations. I've got news for you.

"The Pleistex site in Glasgow is a Class II site. The companies contracted with Grand & Dufy are supposed to bring things here like sand and plastic and wood and cardboard that they use in their processing, not toxic chemicals that they produce as by-products or use in the processing. So maybe what you think is coming from Pleistex is really being blown here from Texas City or from Deer Park or from any number of places in Jefferson or Harris Counties. Or maybe it's traveling down the bayou from some dumpsite we haven't located yet. Or it maybe it's in your drinking water, leaching into the water supply from some old buried waste pit.

"That's what's so hard about this stuff. You can't tell where it comes from. You can't pinpoint it. All you can do is narrow the range of possibilities and hope you can make them into probabilities. So we could monitor the wind patterns from the coast and see what is most likely to be blowing this way. Or we could test your reservoir and compare it to records of toxic producers and dumpsites nearby. We could do any number of things. But since we start with a dumpsite in your backyard that a few of you, at least, suspect might be the culprit, let's get that out of the way first. That's the easiest thing to do.

"So, thinking that, I got a list of the companies using the Pleistex dump. We've got a few chemical companies, an agricultural chemical company, a degreasing and solvent company, a couple of large oil companies, the electric utility, a steel fabricator, a butane company, and a few other waste disposal companies. So I went through the list of what these companies are supposed to be dumping according to their contracts with Grand & Dufy for their Class II sites. It was mostly sands and lumber, biodegradable material and a few plastics. One company, Fontenot Petroleum Products, admitted to dumping non-degradable plastic here with traces of xylene in it. Now xylene is used in paint thinners and is toxic. I don't know if they can get away with traces in a Class II dump, but that needs looking into. We also need to find out exactly what they mean by 'trace.' I'd guess you're looking at a violation right there. In fact, Grand & Dufy has been cited with 189 violations over the past eight years, 21 at your plant alone.

"Now I want to get serious. There are also some indications that toxic waste was buried on this site before Pleistex, Inc., began keeping records as a corporation. I went back through the county records and found that old Bubba Pleisocky himself had bought the site. And when I looked on the plat—well, I didn't actually look, my assistant Ms. Contreras did most of this research. In fact, she's sitting over there." He pointed to a woman sitting at his extreme left against the wall in the front row. "She deserves a hand for digging up all this information." There was a smattering of applause. "Anyway," Occam said, tugging his pants up with his left hand while waving the chalk he held in his right hand, "the bottom line is, when Ms. Contreras looked up the plat for the land sold to Pleisocky, she found an area, just about where the dumpsite is, marked 'disposal sites,' with three circles drawn in, indicating the sites were each 12 feet in diameter. Ms. Contreras also found that Pleisocky is dead. So we don't know exactly what went on, but we need to find out. We put a call into Pleistex to see about locating and testing those pits, but they haven't bothered to respond."

He looked around the room. A woman near the front raised her hand. "I'm worried about the health situation," she said. "In fact, I have this condition where my ears get bright red and hurt to the touch. It's like they're on fire. And one morning I woke up and my arms and legs were all tingling like they'd all fallen asleep on me. So I want to find out what's going on. But what I want to say is that we shouldn't get caught up in all this negativity. There is probably a good explanation for all this. Or maybe it's all just an unfortunate coincidence. But the chemical companies know what they're doing. They don't want to poison people. My own father was an engineer in Texas City after the war, and he certainly cared about what happened to people, both working at the plant and living near it. And it's people like my father who run these companies, not some monsters like you portray. We have to remember that. These are difficult situations, and a lot of times the chemical companies and the government itself don't know what's causing them, but they're working just as hard as anybody to find it out. Thank you." She sat down.

"Let me tell you a story," Occam said. "It's a true story. It happened not long ago. It was reported in the papers. In 1975, people in Beaumont noticed a brown cloud drifting from a chemical plant near the campus of Lamar University onto the campus. Several witnesses clearly stated that they saw the cloud, emitted like a burp, one said, from the plant and it hovered along right above the ground, pushed by off-shore breezes onto the campus. Three students lost consciousness and female students reported that it melted their nylon hose. A few people got noticeably upset. They petitioned the federal government to investigate. The government didn't seem to be very interested. A few of the students and faculty hired attorneys to find out what the plant emitted in that toxic cloud. There were no laws on reporting like our current laws. The plant never said a word. It was never made to report on the cloud. And 4,857 people on the campus of Lamar University that day still do not know what they were exposed to. But at least they know when and where they were on at least one occasion exposed. They saw the cloud. They saw their fellow students drop. They saw the hose melt off their legs. They can identify that toxic event. But the government and the company surely responsible have done everything in their power to prevent the dissemination of information on the event, much less provide restitution for the ruined hosiery or whatever health problems may have emerged years later. I can't agree with you about the benign motives of these companies or our government.

"But that brings us to the point of my talk here. If any of you care to, you can get this talk from me and various permutations on the subject by enrolling at the Health Science Center in my Corporate Toxicology 101. I welcome all auditors, as long as they are not from the IRS, that is." Occam laughed a little at his own joke and went on.

Giacomo Berg was growing tired of the spectacle. It was interesting, but he wanted them to get on with it, plot a strategy, give him a chance to talk with B.C. He knew that had to wait.

There was little indication from B.C. that she wanted to step outside at that moment. And he knew Occam was just now going into his windup for the big pitch.

Occam was walking around and around the room. His glasses were again at his hairline. He had taken off his jacket. His shirt was by now completely untucked in back. Occam looked at the floor as he made the circuit of the room. On his third loop, he stopped near the front of the room and faced his audience. "What are we looking at here?" he asked. And then he threw a forefinger in the air. "We are looking at a plague. A goddamn slow-moving, insidious, underground and in-the-blood-veins-running, family-sundering, class-ignoring, tortuous, hospital-overflowing, bone-rattling, hearse-filling, mortician-enriching, spirit-breaking, end-of-the-world, community-destroying plague. It does not move as fast as the plagues of the Middle Ages. The Black Death of 1348, for instance, moved through entire villages in just a few days. There were never enough carts to carry away the dead. What we're undergoing is more genteel, more orderly. It works itself out over decades. First your neighbor's child, and twenty-five years later, when you are living halfway across the country in Portland, Oregon, it gets you. Throat cancer here one day and eight years later pancreatic cancer across the street. It's slow, it's silent, it's powerfully individual. It's highly personal. It's lonely. Why me? you'll ask. No sense of community. You're not earthquake victims gathering in a shelter. You're not passengers on the *Titanic* huddled together. You're not the people of Bhopal joined in an instant within a single poisonous cloud. You're dying in your bed in your home, and one thousand miles away, your former next-door neighbor and good friend, who will be dying in her bed three years hence, is playing golf in a retirement community, as carefree as she can be.

"That's the nature of mortality, you say. Every death is suffered alone. I could not agree more. But I'm a scientist. And I'm also an amateur social scientist. And the scientist in me wants to know what the common thread is in all this disease and death. What is the cause? How can we isolate the cause and not its victims? And the social scientist in me looks at a map of the people from, say, this town, as it will be in eight years, and I see people needing extraordinary health care or people dying or people who are dead. And eight years hence, many will no longer be statistics from Glasgow. They'll be living in the Woodlands or Dallas or Hawaii or Riyadh.

"And if those places keep a cancer registry, that's what it will show. Myra X died of bone cancer in Wheeling, West Virginia, at the home of her son, who by the way suffers from dizzy spells and is enormously sensitive to the sun. Ms. X formerly made her home in Lexington, Kentucky. Before that she lived in the Houston area. By that time, it will be impossible for either the social scientist or the scientist to sort this out. That's why this is so insidious. It's a plague that has been creeping across Glasgow for years. And it took Mr. Seltzer here to recognize it as such. It had to reach critical mass. It had to affect enough people at a certain point that its outline finally became obvious to a few people at least. And that is what's happened here." He made another circuit of the room, looking only at the floor.

Giacomo watched B.C. watching Occam. Was she amused, interested, annoyed? He could not read her face. But she was not moving either, not indicating a desire to retreat from the action in the room.

"But what has caused this to happen? Why are so many of you sick? Why do you think you're dying? Is it the Pleistex plant? That's the best candidate for now. But there are so many other possibilities. Why are there so many? Because we are ruled by the modern-day equivalents of the Medici. They call the shots. They tell the government what regulations they will and will not abide by. They control the financial centers. They own the money and trade in this country. Industry is one of their machines to generate more money. And where does that leave you? Living in a semi-feudal society. The idea of nation is now secondary to the idea of money. Each of you lives and works for a corporate entity, in a corporate village, run for the good of the profit line of the corporation. Look at Texas City. People in Texas City go to work in the chemical plants, live outside its fences, owe absolute obeisance to their employers and are being poisoned by what they themselves produce. It is not the most efficient use of workers, slowly robbing their mental and physical strength through poisons affecting those inside the plant and in the villages of workers surrounding its gates. But it is the only system thus far that they have devised to maintain profit margins. Ask someone in Texas City what that funny smell is that's brought into their homes by the air-conditioning units. 'That's the smell of money,' they'll tell you. 'Is it bad for you?' you ask. 'It's how I feed my kids and have this house and pay for my boat,' they say. 'You have to pay a little to get a little,' they say. I know. I've talked to hundreds of people in communities like Texas City. They were nearly blown off the face of the earth back in '47 by that infamous chemical explosion, and still they came crawling back for more. It's a feudal mentality. And the lords of industry and finance… Have you ever visited one of these investment houses? Some of you may work for their local offices. Marble lobbies. Quiet, sedate. Everything to bestow a sense of permanence. On one floor, the younger investment bankers are prowling their computer screens, having Type A, highly intense arguments in glass meeting rooms, which the people in the center office pool glance at once in a while but cannot hear. And on the top floor, in elegantly paneled offices, with furniture of genuine leather, the corporate higher-ups are polite, half-smiling, cold, still possessing the predatory eyes of the younger bankers downstairs, and they tell you nothing. They don't need to tell you anything. They control your world. You are a mere supplicant for information. The same is true in the corporate towers of the petrochemical industry. More chrome. The corporate executive offices more modern, bigger windows, better views, fewer books. They'll tell you of their concern for the health and safety of their workers and their neighbors. They'll tell you in a packaged spiel of their efforts to clean up the environment. They'll send all their secretaries and lower level staff to the beach on Saturday to pick up trash and have the local news stations follow them. But they'll tell you nothing. They don't need to either. They own everyone around them. Some of these porkers are hired just to sit around trying to figure out ways to tighten the vice grip on their workers and threaten their livelihoods. This is a feudal society." This time he walked around the room twice at break-neck speed. Giacomo could see Occam was very worked up. His face was beet red. It would take a long night at Corrine's to calm poor Occam down.

"Why do you think it's so goddamn hard to get any information out of these maniacs?" Occam yelled. "Why does it take someone like Randall Occam to fit all the puzzle pieces together, cross reference lists, put them on maps, identify companies and owners, trace routes for waste disposal? There are only a few Randall Occams in this country. You're lucky to have one here. You people can't do this by yourselves. But you've got me now. I'm worked up. You've got me to show you what you have to do. You have to go to court and claw their bloody eyes out. You've got to castrate these porkers. You'll get some hearing from an agency, and they'll say you have to prove beyond reasonable doubt that Infanticide, Inc., is killing your neighborhood. But how can you control what the wind is blowing and from where? How can you say who put toluene in the water supply? So you sue them all—all the porkers that have been doing this to all of us for the past forty years. Get 'em all and then you'll know you won't miss the fascist among them who actually killed your neighbors. And then, maybe down at the Century Club, the giants of industry will turn on the porker in the club chair they think did you in, and they'll beat him to death with the phones they carry to summon their chauffeurs."

Occam climbed on a table at the front of the room. "There is no way out but revolt, insurrection. They are killing you just the same as if they dropped a bomb right here on Glasgow. Save yourselves! Save your children! Revolt! Get the fuckers and stomp 'em into the ground!"

Stephen Seltzer rushed to the table and tried to get Occam to come down. Giacomo slowly walked up to help him. It had been a good show. Occam was sweating like a pig, and the wildness had not left his eyes. He was red all over. While they were busy calming Occam, a number of people slipped out of the room. Stephen stood in front of the room as Giacomo led Occam to a seat. B.C. was standing there with a cup of water. Occam looked at both of them, at first seeming not to recognize Giacomo. Then his face broke into a broad smile. "Did I get their attention?"

Giacomo didn't answer. He knew that any time Randall Occam asked a question about his own abilities, that question was rhetorical.

Stephen Seltzer was counting heads. About half those who originally came to the meeting remained. If Occam served no other purpose, he had served to weed out the faint hearts in the audience.

"So what are we supposed to do?" a man with a gleaming bald spot asked. "I don't just now feel like blowing up a chemical plant."

"Here's what we can do," Stephen Seltzer said. "The Texas Natural Resource Conservation Commission is holding an administrative hearing on the Pleistex dump next week. We've asked them to come check it a number of times. I just got a call this afternoon that they will, indeed, hold a hearing, first, on the dump and its permits next week. I asked them to postpone it, so we could put together more data, but they said it was now or never. I suspect they really don't want to find anything. And they don't want to give us time to get everyone excited. So they'll run it through the briar patch pretty fast and see how little sticks to it. But we've got to do the best we can. From talking with Mr. Occam, it seems our best strategy is to prove they are dumping illegally. They already have a number of citations. If we can catch them with a really egregious violation that might correlate with this health data we're gathering, then we might have something. So what we've got to do is set up collectors all around the dump and see what we collect. We can hire a firm to take a core sample outside the plant and near the bayou and, of course, we can have water in the bayou analyzed. I'll pay for that. There's a good chance that we might turn up something. We asked the state water people to go inside the plant and test the soil just above the water table, but they have so far declined. They say they are afraid they'll puncture the water envelope and give the dumpsite material a door into the water supply. The state commission says it will take air samples if it is convinced at the hearing that there is any need to do so."

Stephen asked for volunteers to be responsible for various collectors. There were a dozen hands. Enough for the job. Most of these, Giacomo observed, were women. Stephen then announced a training session for collectors with Occam the following evening. Meeting adjourned.

After a few lingerers had spoken to Stephen Seltzer and wandered off, Stephen, B.C., Occam, Giacomo, and Cara gathered around a table at the front of the room.

"What did you think?" Stephen asked B.C.

"It scared the shit out them," B.C. said. "That ought to get them moving."

"I don't know," Cara said. "I don't know who we can count on. Maybe that dozen that volunteered. I think most of the rest of them were there just for the show. I don't think they like to think what we are telling them to think. It's going to take a while."

"It's no way to run a revolution," Randall Occam said. "You've got to focus on what you need. And you need evidence by next Thursday. Those collectors might work—if you're extremely lucky. Those samples outside the plant might work, if you can tie them directly to the plant. But you've got to catch them red-handed. You need a smoking chemical sample. You need to get inside that fence and find those pits that are on the plat and test them. You've got to get samples from those so-called piles of sand."

"They won't let us in to do that," Stephen said.

"Who said 'let'?" Occam asked. "We're talking about breaking and entering. Sleuthing. Getting the goods."

"How are we going to do that?" Stephen asked.

"Why do you think you have a goddamn private eye standing here taking all this in? Make him earn his keep. Put him to work. Get his contribution to the cause. Let's get goddamn Berg to the front line at the barricades."

They all looked at Giacomo.

"Look," Giacomo said. "I'm not that kind of guy. Give me a divorce, a jealous lover. Give me business records at the county courthouse. Let me put a simple tail on an unfaithful husband. I never dress in black and I don't break locks." He looked around the group. All eyes were still on him. He looked at B.C. She gave him one of her enigmatic half-smiles.

He thought about Peter Proust. He thought about his life back in the city going through reams of court papers. He glanced at B.C. He thought about the highly romanticized version these people may hold of what his life is.

"Why the hell not," he said. "If they have an attack dog, it's probably dead or too knocked stupid from the chemicals to attack anything." His eyes were on B.C. Her half-smile became almost a full smile. He could see she was excited.

"Now that we've got you hooked," Stephen said, "I don't even know if Pleistex is checked by some kind of security agency at night. I'll make a phone call about that." He left the group.

"I want to thank you, Randall, for making sure my stay in Houston would not be without its moments of extreme tension and anxiety," Giacomo said. "It would have been too much to ask just to pass through here, taking it all in, regarding all serious action at a distance, meeting a few nice people, having a few good meals. I want to thank you for making it impossible for me to simply remain pleasantly disengaged."

"My pleasure," Occam replied, enjoying Giacomo Berg's predicament. Occam then found a piece of paper and drew Giacomo a map of the dumpsite with the location of the pits he'd found on the original plat.

At that point, Stephen returned. He'd called a friend who lived down the street from Pleistex. "As far as he knows," Stephen said, "Pleistex uses the same security system everybody else uses in Glasgow. He says they usually drive by his place at two-hour intervals. He knows he's seen them at just before midnight and just before two. I guess that's when we should shoot for. So when should we do it?" He looked at Giacomo.

"Tonight," Giacomo said, "or else the thing is left to do." He got up and walked to the door. "I'll be back," he said over his shoulder. B.C. followed him out of the room.

And to the car. "Where are you going?" she asked.

"To get my climbing shoes and other gear," he said.

"I'll drive you in," she said, opening the door to the driver's seat in front of him.

They drove toward the lights of Houston. "I want to go in with you," she said. "I got you into this mess, and I don't think it's fair for you to have to go it alone."

Giacomo realized that she thought there was more adventure here than met the eye. All he was worried about was getting picked up for trespassing. And he was sure Seltzer had the lawyers to get him out of that mess. But she apparently thought there was danger involved. He was almost touched.

"It will be easier on everybody," he said, "if I go inside alone. If they catch me trespassing, they could suspend my license for a little while or I'd have to come back here for a court appearance. That's all. If it's suspense you want, maybe we can work on that after the deed is done." He smiled, always unconvinced by his own attempts to sound hard-boiled.

"C'mon, Jack. I know this isn't one-tenth as dangerous as crossing Times Square on New Year's Eve. You can look across that dumpsite and see it's nothing more than a vacant lot strewn with poisons. That's why I want to do it. I need a little adventure. I've been walking through life lately feeling like I'm removed from everything. I need to jump in. It's like that prison I visited in the Valley. Everyone was behind glass or behind bars or behind fences or standing in the shadows of the yard. There was real agony in some of those lives, but I couldn't get near it. And even if I had been able to cross the physical space, I still wouldn't have been able to get near it. That's what my whole life is about—reading about someone else's agony, but not knowing it, not feeling it, and not, therefore, being able to jump right in and fight it. Let me go find those chemical pits with you. I know there's nothing to it, but at least I could get my hands dirty for a change."

"You want agony? Isn't there enough to go around? Join the Peace Corps. Or the Army for that matter. Look, you were put on this earth to be a white, upper middle-class, highly conscious, guilt-ridden gringa. Isn't that agony enough?"

He watched her as she drove, trying to gauge her reaction. He couldn't. He decided he'd better back off a little. "Let me think about it," he said. "It's so much easier to do this alone and get out than..."

"Than to take some woman along," she interrupted. "That's not what you were going to say, but that's what you were thinking. Look, with my legs I'll be over that fence long before you. In fact, I'll give you a boost and beat you over. I was the fastest fence jumper in all of Lockhart. What do you think these legs are for?"

He didn't answer that.

She enjoyed daring him to stare at her legs. Not his furtive glances. Not his long meandering evaluations when he thought she wasn't looking. She was asking for a direct, head-on analysis. She pulled her right pants' leg up to the knee just to egg him on.

"Jesus Christ," he said, "why do two of us have to get poisoned? I do, of course, appreciate your legs. Always have."

"I know."

He was suddenly feeling better about everything. "Here's what I'm thinking," he said. "I'd like Seltzer to stand near the front gate and you to be around back. You'll serve as lookout and I can pass you the samples through the fence as I get them. Is that too mundane?"

"Let me think about it," B.C. said. "I'd hoped for something with a little more action to it."

"You'll be the first line of defense. You'll have to take the heat if the security guards show up at the rear. Or you'll have to help me get out with all the evidence if they show up out front. They'll probably know Seltzer since he's from the neighborhood, so I figure he can keep them occupied for a while, giving me time to get out. What do you think?"

"I'm still thinking. Why don't I go in and you wait out back?"

"Because this is my job. I know what I'm doing. I've done this before." Of course, he didn't know shit. Who was he trying to kid, B.C. or himself? This was not his specialty. And he'd rather not spend an evening sifting through carcinogens, breathing in mutagens, and hunkering down among the teratogens. But now he was in it, and he had to act like he was in charge. She didn't seem convinced.

They reached the hotel. The red message light on the telephone was lit and blinking. He knew what it might be. But at this moment, he didn't want to know. His cell phone was out of batteries. He plugged it in to charge, saw there were a few messages and turned it over on its face. It was after ten o'clock, and they were locked in an alternative trajectory for the next few hours. There was nothing else that could be done. For this evening, he was committed to this distraction. He would deal with the rest of his life in the morning. He changed into his sneakers, a black t-shirt, and jeans. B.C. did much the same. As he was turning out the light, leaving the room, she came up behind him, grabbed him around the chest, and kissed him behind the ear.

"I love a man of action," she whispered and, of course, then laughed.

He had to stop at one of those 24-hour all-you-can-buy, full-service grocery stores to buy work gloves.

"So you won't leave fingerprints?" she asked.

"So I won't absorb every single cancerous dust particle I come in contact with," he said.

She bought a pair for herself and one for Stephen Seltzer.

Then he took her through the store, looking for the aisle with children's toys. He wouldn't stop to tell her why. He preferred to act enigmatic, at least about the small mysteries even if she could see through his larger attempts. When they found the aisle, he scanned the hundreds of toys in plastic bubble wrappers until he found a hook with cricket clickers like they use on Halloween. He grabbed three. "This will have to do," he said. "It's for signaling me when the bad guys come. You can hear these a mile."

"We can't just yell, 'They're here'?"

"Let's try to follow a script, dumb as it may be," he said.

They drove back to Glasgow and then, by pre-arrangement, to the Seltzer's house. There they found only Stephen and Cara. Occam had waited a half hour but then succumbed to what he called "a desperate need for illusion."

They sat around the Seltzers' house drinking white wine, waiting for the neighbor who lived near the plant to call, saying the security guards had made that round. B.C. pulled out a pack of cigarettes she'd bought at the grocery and began to pace and smoke. She was playing this to the hilt.

Giacomo gave out assignments: Seltzer at the front gate, B.C. at the back. Cara had sterilized more than a dozen small mason jars, the kind used for canning homemade jam. Each jar had a blank, white label, ready for filling in. She had these in a child's backpack, each jar itself in a paper bag to prevent noise and breaking. A government-issue, short-handled shovel was affixed to the backpack. Cara had also thrown in a garden trowel, should that prove more practical. She handed all this to Giacomo and squeezed his forearm. Was he under-estimating the danger here? More likely, they were over-estimating it and him.

"We really appreciate this," Cara said, "seeing as how you got dragged into it and all."

Giacomo then handed out the cricket clickers. He wanted to make it part of a solemn ceremony, but the wine overtook him. "One click," he said, "means you see the security car. That's one click, wait five counts and one click again, and so on. Two clicks means I'd better hand over the samples and get over the fence. Three clicks and I might as well say I got drunk and wandered in and then just pour the samples all over me and wait to die."

No one laughed. Cara and Stephen were visibly tense. B.C. was visibly interested in all that was going on.

"I'll need a blanket to get over the barbed wire. There is barbed wire, isn't there? I forgot to notice." Getting no response, he asked for a bandanna to cover his mouth and nose against the dust.

Cara returned with a lavender bandanna. "That's all I have," she said. "Sorry."

"It'll be pretty dark," Giacomo said. "I don't think anyone will notice." He was kidding. Stephen and Cara didn't act like they knew that. He tied it around the back of his head so that it covered his mouth and nose. "How do I look?" he asked.

B.C. smiled.

He lowered it to around his neck.

"There," B.C. said. "That's the fashion statement you want to make."

Meanwhile Stephen Seltzer sat on the couch, quietly watching them, sipping a brandy, dressed rather stylishly for the occasion, thought Giacomo, in black linen pants and a black knit shirt. He seemed to be almost in a trance.

Cara finished off a glass of wine and leaned toward B.C. "I'm pretty uneasy about all this," she said. "It's just that this morning I woke up to hear what sounded like hundreds of birds crying out. I looked out the window and saw our cat had a young mockingbird in its mouth and was beating it against the back porch steps. And the birds, all kinds of birds, were in the trees and on the phone wire screaming at the cat to let go. Cowbirds, mockingbirds, blue jays, grackles. All of them screaming and yelling at that cat. I'd never known birds exhibited cross-species solidarity." She refilled her glass and drained it halfway. "And I could hear the birds going from tree to tree following the cat.

"I put on my robe and ran outside. I had to chase the cat around the yard. When it finally stopped and put the bird down, I could see its little warm heart was still beating, its little chest was still bouncing up and down. But its head was partially destroyed. I should have picked up a rock and put it out of its misery, but I couldn't bear to. So I let the cat have it and walked back in the house. I didn't know what else to do besides hit the cat a few times. I just thought I'd let nature take its course. But I've felt terrible all day about this. I took Greek mythology in college. I know about omens and portents. Dying birds—that must mean something."

"You're reading too much into this," Stephen said, shaking off whatever trance had held him. "This isn't particularly dangerous what we're doing tonight. And even if we get caught, at most we'll be a little embarrassed, and we'll have to pay a fine."

"That's not what I mean," Cara said. "When I saw that little beating heart still in that cat's grasp, and I didn't know if I still had the power to save it or whether I just had to let it go, I couldn't help but think of the kids, of Josh's tiny beating chest. They're still helpless babies. I don't mean to be melodramatic, but that's what I've been thinking about all day. I just don't feel right."

Then the phone rang. Stephen jumped from the couch and ran to answer it. He came back saying the neighbor had seen the security car drive by. It was time to go.

"I'll stay here by the phone," Cara said. "Paul Goldstein said he'll get anybody out of jail who needs getting out. He said he'll wait up until I call."

"We won't need that," Stephen said and kissed her on the cheek.

"Just in case," she said, and they walked out the door.

The Valleys of the Moon

"WHY DON'T YOU drop me off around back and drive a little ways away, park the car, and walk back," Giacomo suggested.

"Whatever you say," Stephen said. He kept looking in his rear-view mirror as if he thought they were being followed.

"Won't you need a boost over the fence," B.C. asked. Though it was too dark to see, Giacomo could tell by listening that her mouth was definitely shaped in a smile as she spoke.

"Watch yourself," Giacomo said. He figured, slight paunch and all, he could still scale a chain-link fence, though he did wish he had studied it more carefully, particularly in the back, when he'd driven by earlier that day. The last time he remembered scaling a fence of any size was about seven years before, and on that occasion he'd been carrying less weight around his middle and had the added incentive of the distinct and unrelenting presence of a German shepherd on his tail while he was himself tailing someone's husband to an afternoon tryst. On that occasion, he'd had no time for doubt or for weighing the possible against the unlikely. He had simply bounded over the eight-foot fence, conscious only of his own vertical thrust and not of any real physical effort on his part. It had all been a matter of desire. But this time it was a matter for calculation. And he'd not had the chance to calculate. Was the fence, for instance, electrified? That would be a problem. Were the chain links too small for the toes of his sneakers or was the cross bar on top out of his reach? That would alter his thinking. But he hadn't noticed, so he decided that he would communicate his slight anxieties to no one and see if he could pull it off, anxieties, paunch, and all without anyone ever suspecting his doubt. Onward and upward.

As they approached the Pleistex site, Stephen Seltzer drove very slowly, still looking all the while in his rear-view mirror and to the left and right. "Maybe I'd better go around the block once," he said.

"Let's just do it now, Stephen," B.C. said. "There's nobody in sight."

Stephen turned the headlights off and steered his new, dark-blue, family-sized Buick down a gravel road that ran to the rear of the dumpsite, where he stopped. Giacomo climbed out, took the blanket and backpack filled with mason jars, and reminded them about the clickers.

"I'll see you in about fifteen minutes," Giacomo said. "By then, I should be able to start passing jars out the fence to B.C."

The car backed down the gravel road while Giacomo Berg sat in the weeds. When he heard it pull onto the main road, he got up and made for the fence.

The fence itself offered both welcome and less-than-welcome prospects. There was a gate at the back of the fence. With a little push he could work an 18-inch gap between the two parts of the gate, chained together around a pole at the center. This would make it easy to pass the jars to B.C. He'd worried that they were too large to pass through the spaces in the chain link and that the fence was too tall to hand them over directly. He was right on both counts. The chain link squares were too narrow to accommodate the toes of his sneakers and let him get a real foothold. That was the less welcome prospect. He would just have to summon up some upper-body strength and tough it out, hoping the pull of the earth's gravity held not too greatly increased an attraction for his own increased mass.

Two strands of barbed wire ran across the top of the fence. He could see no evidence of electrified wire on the fence, and there was no sign at the gate warning of the possibility of electric shock. He thought he'd take his chances. He threw the blanket over the two barbed wire strands. Nothing to that. He put on his backpack and his gloves, grabbed hold of the fence pole about seven feet up and pulled himself up. He threw one leg over the blanket and hooked it on the fence coming back on the other side. Then he gingerly held on to the blanket, pulled the other leg over and slid down the fence on the inside, rappelling down with his sneakers while he gripped the top fence pole. He was in.

He was not as far gone as he'd feared. In fact, he was rather proud of his quick execution of the feat. If only B.C. had been there to see him. He had, of course, sent her away with Seltzer in case his athleticism had been anything less than spectacular. Oh well. Played it too safe. One of many lost chances.

He walked to the building near the center of the lot, watching for chemical pits in order to avoid stepping into them. The moon was half full. It was split horizontally. With light poles at the entrance to the Pleistex lot and at one of the rear corners, there was almost enough light for him to see what he was doing. He pulled Occam's map out of his pocket, but it was too dark to make out much more than the three large circles near the back of the lot and a square for the building. He would have to just poke around. He took off the backpack and decided to sit a minute to get his bearings.

This didn't feel like criminal trespassing. It felt more like a high-school prank. Of course, whatever this dumpsite contained had been trespassing on the lives of Stephen and Cara Seltzer and their family and friends and neighbors for years. Compared to that, his transgression was small.

Besides, he knew that the trespass had taken place before he'd entered the property. It was not so much what he'd invaded but what had trespassed his own defenses, how he'd made the decision to undertake this act. It wasn't their prodding; it was more his desire to do something, to seize the moment and run. He was sure it had to do with his inability to find Peter Proust. But it also had to do with all his other failures of will, most of which he couldn't even remember to catalogue. For Giacomo Berg, the risks were all internal. Anyone can scale a fence.

He heard someone walking along the gravel at the periphery of the fence. He figured it was B.C. He began pulling the jars out of the backpack. He lined them up—fifteen in all. He stood up to see what he could see.

And what he saw suddenly sent a frisson of hopelessness through his entire being. In the silvered moonlight he could make out three good-sized mounds, a few hillocks and what looked like four depressions or pits. It looked like an ash-white moonscape, devoid of life or the memory of life. The barrenness around him opened up a small desolate wasteland inside Giacomo Berg. It was a hole not wide but monstrously deep, a pinprick of darkness running through him. The mountains of the moon was the description that first came to him. But next was a picture of the earth, this earth, after the bomb or after the chemical cloud. He felt he was looking at a small slice of the end of the world. Not Armageddon, but just after. And he suddenly realized that there were these patches of desolation, of end-time, in every neighborhood, every town, every acre of the world. And these patches were growing, joining one another, slowly taking over the earth, cancerous cells joining hands.

Then he heard a click. One click. He counted to fifteen, then another click. He didn't see any headlights around, but he walked quickly to the rear fence to see what was up.

He found B.C. standing there. "What's going on?' he asked. "Did you see something?" "No," she said, "but I couldn't see you or hear you. I thought maybe you needed some help. I thought maybe you'd fallen into an acid pit and were getting eaten up by chemicals."

"If I was getting eaten by chemicals, you would have heard me," he said. "I'm okay. I'll be back in a few minutes with the samples."

He began to walk back to the backpack, when she called out behind him, "Hey, Jack, nice job with the fence."

He kept walking. He took two jars and the trowel to the first hill. After he'd pulled his bandanna up over his mouth and nose, he quickly dug samples from the top, bottom, and middle of the hill. Then he carried them back to B.C., who was standing by the narrow opening at the gate, saying only "First mound."

B.C. took the jars, marked each with a "1" and put them in a shoe box, as planned, writing "Mound 1" on the shoebox. She watched him disappear into the darkness at the center of the dumpsite. This was not a half-bad way to spend the evening. A little adventure, a little moonlight, a little purpose in life, even a little breeze off the bayou, the weeds rustling around her. Then she thought of what the breeze might contain. She shuddered and took a scarf out of her bag and tied it around her mouth and nose. A few minutes later, Giacomo appeared with two more jars, saying, "Mound 2," and he disappeared again.

This was taking longer than she'd thought. She was sure Stephen, near the front gate, was a wreck. The only noise besides the slight rustling of the weeds was Giacomo's periodic tromping through the gravel of the dumpsite. He appeared again with two jars to be marked "Mound 3." She put these in a third shoebox and marked it.

The jars looked innocent enough. She picked up one and shook it. In that light it appeared to contain a grayish-brown sand. She checked the lids to make sure they were tightly sealed. Funny to think of what kinds of engines of murder those jars might contain. They reminded her of a vial of sand from the Painted Desert she had bought as a child on her family's trip through Arizona. She'd kept that vial on her desk at home for years, never shaking it as she'd been instructed, examining it when she was supposed to be doing her homework, wondering what poor soul had to fill vials with layers of vari-colored sand all day long. She held the jar up to the moonlight and shook it again. No revelations that way.

Then Giacomo came tromping toward her again. "This is from the first pit," he said. "They're right where Occam said they'd be. I had to dig down a little ways through the dirt, but I found something. It felt distinctive." He handed her two more jars. She packed them and marked them "Pit 1." These were not so much like sand but rather like a thick soil or clay.

She looked at her watch. Forty minutes had passed. It was a little after one. The security guard could be expected within the hour. She saw headlights moving down the road in front of the dumpsite. She heard a distant click. It must have been Stephen. She counted to five and heard another click. The headlights approached the front of the dumpsite and then drove on. No other clicks emanating from Stephen. If it had been the security car, he would have had them heading for the hills.

Giacomo appeared with two more jars. "False alarm, I guess," he said. He handed her the jars. "I think I may have found something. These are from the second pit. It was kind of muddy, wet. The ground all around it is kind of marshy. On my way back from that pit, the ground was absolutely soaked. I sank into it to my ankles. I think there's more than greasy sand out there. I hope my feet don't fall off." He began to walk away.

"Jack," she called. "We've only got another twenty minutes before we have to get out of here. Twenty minutes to load up and get out, that is, to be safe."

"We'll make it," he called. "Don't worry."

But he was worried about what he'd stepped into. He took three jars and walked back to the place he thought he'd stepped into the muck. Again he sank. He picked up a two-by-four and prodded the ground in front of him. He could feel it sink in a fairly good distance. Leaning against the lumber, he reached as far as he could go with a jar in one hand and scooped up some muck. He did this in slightly different directions with the other two jars. Then he tried to pick his way out of the sinkhole and back to B.C.

"Watch these," he said. "They're dripping. Hold out a box and I'll drop them in."

She did as she was told. She marked the box "Black Lagoon" and held it out in front of her. He carefully passed the jars through the space and dropped them into the box. The jars smelled like rotten swamp grass. "This place smells like New Jersey," she said.

He turned to go back into the dumpsite. "Jack, we've only got ten minutes."

"This will be fast," he said. "I've only got one more pit to go."

He was into it now. It was so rare that he got to feel like a real sleuth. He took the remaining two jars to the final pit. It was like the previous pit near the surface, consisting of a clay or heavy mud. He decided to dig a little deeper. Three shovels full and the earth softened up considerably. Another shovelful, and he pulled the shovel out of the dark ooze. It dripped off the shovel in globs. He dug again, then let the gooey mixture run off into the last two jars. He'd hit something. Was it some sort of primordial ooze or a roiling pit of toxic chemicals? Was this what the LaBrea Tar Pits looked like as they sucked in beasts of pre-history? He screwed the lids on these samples and then decided to make one circuit of the entire dumpsite to make sure he hadn't missed anything. The front of the lot, as far as he could tell in the half-light of the moon, contained only weeds covering an uneven ground, small hillocks and craters. All of this could be saturated with chemicals, Giacomo thought. He dug into one small hill with the shovel. It felt like sand. It would have to be examined another time. Three hills about four feet high near the front of the property and fairly well-lit by the streetlight formed a basin among them. Seven chemical drums lay on their sides in the basin. He tapped a few. They sounded empty. He tried to read what was printed on their sides, but could not, except for the word "flammable" on one. He moved on. The property was littered with lumber. Piles of two-by-fours and one-by-fours seven or eight feet high were deposited willy-nilly around the dumpsite. Around the building and from the building to the rear of the property, the lot flattened out, appearing to be caliche. The lot seemed to contain only the three large mounds, the three pits, and the sinkhole he had happened into.

There was something, however, leaning up against a chemical drum at the side of the building. On close examination, he saw it was the body of a small, dark, curly-haired dog. He jostled it with his foot, but it didn't move. Clearly dead, but it hadn't been dead all that long. Unless it was preserved by the chemicals it had wandered through.

That was enough for Giacomo Berg. He was gathering up the backpack and the last two jars when he heard two clicks from the rear gate. A five count and two more clicks. Then he heard a car moving toward them on the gravel strip alongside the dumpsite. He ran for the rear gate where B.C. was standing, gripping her clicker with both hands, both thumbs on the metal tongue. He handed her the nearly empty backpack with the jars through the opening and went to the spot on the fence where the blanket covered the barbed wire.

"Hurry, Jack, hurry," B.C. said. "They're almost here." She was running down the fence line with him. He got to the blanket and pulled himself up. But the blanket had gotten bunched up from his previous ascent, and one pants leg caught on the barbed wire. He was stuck on top of the blanket, trying to pull his right leg free from where it caught on the wire as he'd tried to fling it over. He yanked a few times with no luck as he heard the car reach the back of the lot.

B.C. took off for the bayou. "Oh what the hell," Giacomo said and threw himself off the blanket and down to the ground. The wire cut a path down his pants leg and caught a piece of his ankle before letting go. He belly-flopped onto the ground and took off in the direction B.C. had run.

Just then the car pulled up. He heard Stephen's voice calling "Jack, B.C.," and he knew, of course, that this had been Stephen driving to pick them up. He gathered himself up from where he'd thrown himself behind a clump of weeds. A few seconds later, B.C. emerged from a few yards away, trying to carry a load of shoe boxes and a few stray jars.

"Let's get out of here," Stephen said.

They piled into the car and drove back down the gravel roadway, headlights off. As they were about to leave the gravel road for the main street, the security car pulled up and shined a light into Stephen's car.

"Just smile and wave and keep on driving," Giacomo said. And Stephen did.

Back at the Seltzer house, Stephen put the samples up high on a steel shelf in his garage. "I don't want these in the house," he said, "and the sooner they're gone out of here the better I'll feel." He was still pretty tense, B.C. thought.

Cara appeared at the garage door with a tray and three glasses of wine. They followed her into the kitchen.

"I might need to borrow some old clothes," Giacomo said. They all turned to look at him in the light.

"What did you do to yourself?" Cara said, putting down the tray and grabbing Giacomo's leg where the pants were torn above his right ankle. His ankle and shoe were covered with blood.

"Sit down and take off that shoe," Cara said. She returned with antiseptic and a bandage.

When Giacomo took off his right sneaker, he saw that the sole had been eaten almost entirely away. The same was true of his left sneaker. He looked at the fingertips of his gloves. Some were gone.

"I think I'd better go outside," he said, "and take off these clothes. I shouldn't be bringing this dust into the house."

But Cara was already at his ankle, dabbing it with a washcloth, spraying a clear spray on the wound, covering it with a bandage. She worked quickly and efficiently, like a woman who had small children. "You don't really need the bandage," she said. "The spray hardens to make a kind of plastic wrap, but I'm just old enough not to trust it." She stood up, walked backward a few steps, and studied Giacomo Berg. He couldn't tell if she were looking at his wound, judging her own handiwork, or considering his paunch and the inches he carried that Stephen did not on his trim, athletic-club belly as well as Stephen's height advantage. He glanced at B.C. She was watching him with her enigmatic, but obviously amused, half-smile.

"We have an outdoor shower by the pool behind the cedar screen," Cara said. "I'd say you could go for a swim if you like, but I'm afraid the dust might get into the pool, and the children still swim after school." Her voice trailed off. "I'm sorry. Stephen and I sometimes skinny dip late at night when the kids are asleep. But we haven't done it lately." She stood looking at Giacomo Berg.

"It's too late for me," he said.

"I'll get you some clothes," Cara said and walked away.

All this time Stephen had been sitting at the kitchen table staring at his glass of scotch.

As Cara left, he said to no one in particular, "It never hit me until now that this stuff is really out there. It's real. It's poison. It's killing our kids. We don't know what it is yet, but it's there. I'd been half hoping I was getting carried away by my own paranoia. But here's the evidence. This isn't the dreck from a Class II landfill. This is chemicals, carcinogens, rubber-shoe and leather-glove eaters at the very least. I almost can't believe it myself."

Cara returned with a warm-up suit and old leather sandals. "I don't know what size shoe you wear," she said, somewhat apologetically, "but your feet look fairly big to me. These were always a little loose on Stephen and he has fairly big feet, so I thought you should be able to get in there somewhere." She handed the clothes and sandals and a plastic garbage bag to Giacomo and opened a sliding glass door that led to the pool and shower.

He found the shower behind the cedar screen and stripped, dropping each article of clothing into the plastic bag. Then he turned on the water, only cold, and let it wash over him. It felt like pounds and truckloads of dirt, sand, and clay were running down his body. He was creating a regular chemical delta on top of the shower drain. Once he felt cleansed of the muck, he let the water run over him to cleanse him of the experience of the muck. He looked around to see if any neighbors could be watching him bare-assed. But there was only what looked to be a wall of trees. And above were stars. Hard to believe out here with the cold running water, pine trees, and stars there was so much that was insidious and unnatural to be feared. It seemed completely out of joint, but he was suddenly bone weary. He found a towel, put on the warmup suit and sandals, all fitting a little snugly, and emerged from the shower. Cara was waiting at the sliding glass door. B.C. and Stephen were sitting at the table.

"It's almost three o'clock," Cara said. "Don't you want to stay here tonight?" He looked over at B.C.

She returned a barely decipherable frown.

"I think we'll drive back and try to sleep late," he said, "if B.C. will drive."

B.C. was standing up and heading for the door.

"We don't know how to thank you," Cara said to Giacomo, her arm now around his waist, walking him to the door. Stephen followed.

"I almost enjoyed it," Giacomo said, half meaning it.

"Why don't you come over tomorrow for dinner?" she asked.

"We'll see," B.C. said. "We'll call you." And she was out the door.

"Many thanks," Stephen said, shaking Giacomo's hand. "I'll take the samples in tomorrow, and then we'll see where we stand." He stood there holding Giacomo's hand.

Giacomo extracted it and waved goodbye. Then he was out the door.

As they got into the car, B.C. said, "I couldn't take another minute of Stephen's morbidity. I don't know why, but it finally got to me. And Cara. Doesn't she ever get tired of being a good trooper? Let's get out of here."

She turned on the ignition, fiddled with the radio until she landed on a station playing the Rolling Stones' "Jumping Jack Flash," and they were off into the night.

B.C. was glad to be out driving on the expressway in the middle of the night with no one around, just rocketing through corridors of glass and steel. Not a sound from Giacomo Berg. He sat staring straight ahead. She didn't want to let their small adventure drop. Where should she start?

"That was pretty interesting," she said, "that skulking in the dark." There was no response, so she went on.

"Especially running for the bayou when I thought security had found us. It's great to feel right on the edge of something. Although now that I think about it, it must have looked pretty ludicrous to see a woman trying to run furtively through the weeds carrying five shoe boxes filled with clattering jars of toxic gunk. I felt as lithe and smooth as a panther at the time, but I probably looked more like a three-legged moose."

Still no reaction. Was he asleep? She'd try something else.

"Of course you looked like a stuck hen floundering up there on top of the fence. I got to turn back once while I was running just in time to see you twisting and waggling your leg and then belly flop to the ground. It was spectacular. I gave it a 9.9. But didn't they tell you to wait until they filled the pool? Did you do that going in, too?"

Still no reaction. He was definitely asleep. She nudged him. He started. "What?" he said. "What were you saying?"

"I was talking about how much I admired that tremendous leap of yours over the barbed wire."

"Oh, that," he said and said no more.

Then she fired her ultimate salvo: "And Cara seemed impressed. The whole thing kind of turned her on, the way she got you naked out in the backyard and talked about skinny dipping. Then to see you in that stunning warmup suit."

"C'mon. Lay off."

"No, really," she said, and she spider-walked her fingers up his leg, just above the knee.

She figured he would drop off to sleep again. And she was right. He hovered at the edge of sleep, slipping into it, only to be called back every few minutes as her fingers took a walk up or down his leg.

As they arrived at the hotel, an ambulance with flashing lights but no siren was leaving the drive in front of the lobby. She led Giacomo Berg up two flights of the stairway to their room. She opened the door and half-pushed him in. Neither turned on the room light. The curtains were open and the purplish light from the hotel's outdoor lamps provided all the light necessary for their conveyance through the rest of the night. There was also the red message light blinking on the telephone.

As much as she didn't want to, B.C. pointed him in the direction of the phone. "It might be important," she said.

"I know," he said, "but it will still be important in the morning. And there is nothing I can do about it now." He fell back on the bed.

His mind was blank. But suddenly his flesh became the text for the evening. B.C. was at his feet, taking off each sandal very slowly. She was going to undress him, but this time she was making sure he was registering every step.

"I am taking off your left sandal," she said, running her hands around his heel and ankle. "I am taking off your right sandal, my big, strong, hero detective," she said running her hands up his calf.

Then she was next to him. "I am taking off your left sleeve. What big arms you have."

Then she was on his other side. "I am taking off your right sleeve. And what strong fingers." She ran her hands over his right hand and up his arm.

Then she was behind him, pushing him up, running her arms around his chest and unzipping the warmup shirt. She pulled it off him, running one hand down his belly then up his chest. "I am taking off your shirt. Are you with me, Jack?"

He didn't answer. He didn't need to answer.

"And what thick hair you have. I once had a cousin named Harry Cello with black curly hair on his chest, and the girls down at the Lockhart pool used to call him 'Harry Chesto' when he came to visit me." She pulled him back against her and ran both hands across his chest. "Harry Chesto," she said.

She was in front of him, one hand on his belly, the other fooling with the drawstring to his warmup pants. "I'm untying your pants," she said. Her hands were moving along the outsides of his thighs. Then they grabbed his pants at the waist and pulled. "So there will be no questions asked later, this time I am letting you know that I am pulling off your pants."

And they were off.

"And what have we here?" she asked.

The Curvature of Space

HE SPENT HIS FIRST MINUTES awake the next morning tracing the stretch marks on her thigh as she slept. He was waiting for the phone to ring. It was light outside. The sun was well up. Children were chattering and splashing in the swimming pool.

She opened her eyes and watched him for a moment. "There was once a wise philosopher who said stretch marks are a sign that nothing comes easy," she said. Then she put her head on his chest.

"Do you remember last night?" she asked.

"You mean the dumpsite?"

"No. After."

Instead of answering, he moved his hand up her thigh across her back and into her thick, dark hair. She wrapped a leg around him, lifting her head to observe the red light still lit on the bedside phone.

"You're waiting for the phone," she said.

"I am," said he.

"Shall we make the most of it?" she asked.

"We are," he said. "I give it another three minutes." It was three minutes before nine.

And then it rang.

She slid off his chest and into the bathroom.

He sat on the edge of the bed and picked up the receiver.

"Jack. Where have you been? I thought you were going to call me? I was trying to reach you all night. We got a message, Jack. On Dad's office answering machine. But I think he made it two nights ago, and yesterday Dad didn't go in until evening. It was his golf day. So Peter could have called yesterday or he could have called two nights ago. We think it was two nights ago just because he's only called at night before so he wouldn't talk to anyone directly."

Giacomo tried to slow her down, tried to instill calm with his voice. "Well," he asked, "where is he? He left Mountain Home some days ago. What did he say?"

"That's just it, Jack. I'm afraid he may do it right now. Or he may have already done it. He just called to say he loved us and he was crying. That sounds bad, Jack. Usually there's some other sort of message."

"Do you know where he was calling from?"

"The Davis Mountains. I looked them up. They're way out there in the middle of nowhere. He said he was calling from a phone booth in the Davis Mountains. Can you go there?"

"I can go anywhere," he said. "Is that all? I have no idea where the Davis Mountains are, but I'll find them. Hang in there. Is there anything else?"

"There is, Jack. We think he has Dad's gun. I didn't want to tell you that. Dad went to look for it in the attic when all this started. He bought it years ago to protect us, he said. Of course, he never used it except at a target range. We don't even know if it works anymore. But we think Peter has that gun. I should have told you before."

"I think I knew that," Giacomo said. "An old man in Flour Bluff told me he thought Peter had a gun."

"Oh, please hurry, Jack. I think this is really it. We're asking too much of you, but you're all we've got." Then her voice lowered an octave, and she sounded calmer. "I'm asking you to do things, Jack that I should be doing myself. I'm sorry about that, but we just need your help. I don't really think this is going to turn out well. I want to warn you of that. You may be putting yourself through something that will make you feel terrible. I'm sorry about that, Jack."

"I know, Sara," Giacomo said. "I've known that all along. But I'm so far in it, I have to find my way through its center. I'm hoping that way leads right to Peter. I have to see this through. Better me than someone who doesn't know him, doesn't care about him. It's something I have to do. I'll call you from the Davis Mountains, wherever they are."

He hung up the phone and stared at the floor. After a few minutes, B.C. came out of the bathroom, drying her hair. She watched Giacomo's face, trying to discern the substance of the call. He wouldn't look up at her.

"How long will it take to drive to the Davis Mountains?" he asked, still staring at the floor.

"How many days do you have?" she said.

They took a plane to the Midland/Odessa airport. She showed it to him on the map, but it had little meaning for Giacomo Berg: merely a point that had to be reached, from which point they would reset their trajectory for a drive to the south and west, across land that he had never thought about when he thought about the world.

B.C. was going with him. There was no question about that. She didn't ask. She simply made the plane reservations for them both, reserved a rental car in Midland, and drove them to the airport. He was content to let her attend to these details. Now was the time to concentrate entirely on Peter Proust. He had to be prepared for whatever was waiting for him out there in the Davis Mountains. How far gone was Peter Proust? Completely? Dead? That far gone? Or could he be rescued, brought back in from the snow? Was it his place to do that? Was Peter living out a history outside his own, a history that once included him, but now light-years later, lives later, worlds later, a history that would no longer include him?

B.C. was sitting by the airplane window, looking out. He knew she was giving him room to think this through. He appreciated that.

He didn't appreciate, however, the skinny little man with the cowboy hat who squeezed into the seat between them, just as the plane was about to take off. Giacomo had chosen the aisle seat, as he always did, feeling it gave him a greater sense of security, feeling himself at the plane's center of gravity, even as they defied gravity, feeling less subject to the inevitable pitch and roll. He also liked to stretch his legs, liked to get up when he wanted to get up, did not want to feel trapped against an airplane's inner wall or behind a seat whose back rose above his line of sight. All those things. But then there was this little cowboy pulled in beside him.

The man put his hat in the luggage rack and turned, first, of course, to B.C. "Going to Midland on business?" he asked.

She shook her head no.

"It's good and well you're not going to Odessa on business," he said, "'cause there ain't no business in Odessa when the rigs aren't pumpin'."

She turned toward the man. "We're not going to Odessa either," she said. "We're driving west."

With that, he looked over at Giacomo, "Pardon me, folks," he said. "I didn't mean to be splitting ya'll up. You weren't facing each other or talking, so I figured you either weren't together or you'd been married so long you would welcome someone sitting between you." He was smiling an ingratiating smile. "You want me to trade places with one of ya'll?"

"That's okay," Giacomo said. "I have work to do."

"I ought to be going over my books myself, but I'm just too head up about selling two containers of beef to be shipped clear over to Saudi Arabia. Besides, there ain't much else to do in Midland but work so I've got time for that. It was quite a sale. You know so many of us used oil to support our cattle ranching that we forgot how hard it was to make a living just raising beef. I mean, everyone you meet in Midland will call himself a rancher, but what they're really ranching is the oil. Until lately, that is. And then we've really had to work it. This is my first sale to the A-rabs. They don't eat pork, you know. And I don't raise pigs, so we got a nice relationship going. We also both speak oil. They speak it a lot better than I do, of course," and he threw his head up and laughed something like a horse's whinny.

Seeing that the little man would not be ignored, Giacomo leaned toward the aisle as he turned to study the man. He had big ears that stuck straight out as if pasted on his head by a five-year-old. His nose and chin each protruded noticeably from his rather flat face. They were separated by a mouth with virtually no lips, like you'd see on the thin-lipped cowboys in Westerns who said next to nothing and backed up the romantic leads, who had full lips and said what was needed to be said.

But the thin lips next to Giacomo did not stop moving. "You folks tourists?" he asked B.C.

"Not exactly," she said and turned back to the window. Clearly, thought Giacomo, she was annoyed.

"You ever been to Midland before?" the man asked him. Giacomo shook his head.

"Well, I'll give you some advice. Stick to Midland. Don't wander over to Odessa if you want good food or to live the way white people are supposed to live. Here's how it's divided, too. He pulled down the tray in front of him, ordered a gin and tonic from the stewardess, and poured out a bag of peanuts on the tray. With the peanuts, he proceeded to make a large circle on the right and a smaller circle on the left of the tray.

"Over here," he said, pointing to the right circle, "is Midland. It's a financial center. You'll see the bank buildings as we're flying in. You've got some nice clubs, good restaurants, big old houses, bank people, cattle people, insurance people, and oil people. I don't know what you believe in, but in Midland it only makes sense to be a God-fearing Republican." He studied Giacomo Berg.

Giacomo did not flinch. Flinching just wasn't in him at that moment.

"Now over here," he said, pointing to the left circle, "is Odessa. You've heard of Odessa over in Russia? This here's the same thing. They've got the oil supply business and the trailer camps and Mexicans and coloreds for roughnecks and a few discount houses and lots of labor agitation. You wouldn't think that out here in God's Country we'd have labor unions, but we do. And they're always wanting our water. And they're wanting our property taxes for their schools, and they just plain want our money. And they're a bunch of Democrats to boot. You can't figure how way out here in among the Christian people of West Texas we'd have all this class struggle. Ain't it a shame?"

He searched Giacomo's face for a response. But he got none. Giacomo had pulled out his copy of Bernal Diaz's chronicles. He didn't feel like reading, but he had no other defense.

He stared at the words and tried to recover what he'd been thinking about Peter. B.C., against the window, was either sleeping or pretending to be asleep.

The little man slid the peanuts off his tray and back into the bag from which they'd come. He put this bag in his pocket, picked up his drink, folded the tray against the seat back, got up and climbed over Giacomo Berg. He found a seat a few rows back next to someone more compatible, Giacomo suspected. A few minutes after that, they were landing.

They picked up the interstate to Pecos. That sounded fairly exotic to Giacomo Berg's eastern ears. B.C. was driving. There was very little to see. The land was flat or slightly rolling. The sun was hot and high. What was fairly green around Midland and Odessa quickly became dry and sparse as they drove west. At one point, they passed a sign with a picture of Roy Orbison, pointing to the town of Wink somewhere north on a two-lane road running off the expressway. A little later they crossed the Pecos River, where it had cut a dramatic little canyon through the landscape. The green vegetation around the river, which would barely qualify as a creek back East, was the only color for miles around. There was nothing to think about but Peter Proust. Where the hell are you?

At Pecos they left the interstate for a highway going south. The flatness began to give way to the hope of the end of flatness. In the distance to the south and west he believed he discerned mountain-like shapes. Proceeding south, small buttes and mesas gave way to larger land formations. The hints of elevation were a relief to his soul, as if he were lying again in the spring waters near Mountain Home. After so much flatness, lifelessness, sameness of spirit, the imagination needed a spur, an outcropping, an irregularity to latch onto.

At the same time, he realized these must be the beginnings of the mountains where he hoped to find Peter Proust. This was the beginning of the climb into what he knew would, one way or another, be an ordeal, an ordeal not traversed superficially but one that would require him to claw his way through inch-by-emotional-inch. He was trying to steel himself for that. It was for that reason he was glad B.C. was along—for the stone, the foundation, the foothold she might provide when he turned loose of all other moorings.

She had said little during the drive. But, as they left Pecos, she said, "This place was notorious back in the day for throwing any longhair in jail who happened to be traveling the interstate. There were stories ranging from forced haircuts to out-and-out torture. Back then, I suppose, haircuts were a kind of psychic torture. No one denied what went on out here. The sheriff appeared in all kinds of magazines proud of his ability to keep civil liberties out of his town." Glancing back in the rear-view mirror, she said, "It doesn't look particularly forbidding to me these days. Just a poor, dusty West Texas town."

And then she said no more. As the land to the south and west rose ever more distinctly on the horizon, so did Giacomo's ill ease. He took out the map and studied it. The Davis Mountains were part of the string of mountains that ran into and through Mexico to the south and joined the Rockies to the north. He imagined following Peter from one mountain to the next, climbing and descending and climbing again into Colorado, to the Grand Tetons, and on into Canada, always following one mountain behind. Would this end here, where the map had such sparse markings for so great an area? "Old Fort Davis Historical Site," "Fort Davis," "MacDonald Observatory" and nothing else marked, except with the brown shading indicating mountain elevations. Nothing for thirty miles to the south. Nothing for thirty-five miles north.

Nothing for 80 miles west. Nothing for 100 miles east. Nothing. No sign of human habitation. Desolation overtook Giacomo Berg. They approached a sign for the town of Saragosa.

B.C. slowed down. She drove along the shoulder of the highway, as they took in the devastation they were driving through. Beyond the sign were foundations for houses, but no houses. Parts of walls of houses, however, could be seen strewn along the highway on either side for several miles. Blue walls, red walls, walls torn in two, walls with windows, pieces of walls with doors, a tin roof here and there. B.C. and Giacomo drove on, saying nothing. They passed a church half built of adobe with the upper half consisting of two-by-fours and plywood, the roof consisting of plywood half-covered with a layer of tar paper. On one side of the church was a small graveyard with new wooden crosses but no vegetation. On the other side tents and a few small house trailers were huddled in a circle. A handful of children were wandering with dogs among the tents. Farther on, men and women were picking through a dumpsite piled ten feet high with lumber, cinder blocks, sheets of aluminum, tar paper, and the detritus of disaster. A large mobile home was parked by the side of the highway not far from the dumpsite. It bore a sign stating: "Saragosa Tornado Relief Center." That was all. B.C. picked up speed and returned to the main roadway.

They entered a valley. At the bottom of the valley, ahead of them, he saw an oasis: bright green fields, full-sized trees, and what looked like a body of water. Or was it a mirage? No, the trees were blowing in the desert wind. Seeing the green fields against the arid yellow-brown of the desert created an opening in the barren landscape he was carrying inside him. But when he saw the wall of mountains that rose just beyond the valley, he pushed against the seat back with such intensity that the latch holding it popped out of place, and he was suddenly lying on his back, staring at the ceiling of the car. B.C. looked over at him and laughed.

They passed a series of vintage 1940s tourist courts, immaculately white stucco, each with a one-car garage, all encircling a rolling green lawn. Children played on the lawn. Their elders sat among them on green and white lawn chairs. Past the tourist courts was a huge swimming pool brimming with blue-green water. A sign outside the entrance to the pool advertised it as the world's largest spring-fed swimming pool. Had Coronado come this way, Giacomo thought, he would have stopped. He couldn't fathom how settlers passing through here a century ago could push on.

He had an overwhelming urge to ask B.C. to stop the car. He wanted to check into the tourist court, lie in the deep, green carpet grass, dive into the cool of the blue-green pool, turn over and over like a seal in its turquoise waters. It seemed to offer absolute relief. They could stop now and not go on. Or stop and go on later. They could forget the desolation behind them and the desolation in front and bathe in the oasis waters. He wanted to tell her to stop the car. She may have wanted him to tell her to stop. Was she looking longingly at the tourist courts? But she kept driving, and he said nothing.

A bend in the road and the pool disappeared. The green disappeared. The oasis disappeared. Had it been a mirage after all? Now they were climbing into the mountains. He had never suspected Texas would have mountains like this. Not great snow-capped peaks, but formidable rocks, nonetheless. The road wound and climbed into their bosom.

They passed caved-in stone buildings, abandoned wooden cabins, corrals of forgotten ranches. Dry creek beds cut through the mountains at intersecting angles. Cattle grazed in mountain pastures. Goats clung to hillsides. B.C. drove as if locked into the roadway. Giacomo kept his eyes on the mountaintops. Where was Peter? Where would they find him? As the road climbed, the mountains became less formidable. They were not forbidding granite crags. They were of a much more human scale—sandstone escarpments, ridges rather than peaks, as hospitable to vegetation as any of the land in those parts. Piñon trees ringed the ridges. Every mountain was accessible. Most were inviting, each with at least one prospect offering a gentle slope to near the summit.

Giacomo now wanted to get into those mountains and on with it. They rounded a bend and found themselves on a flat plain bounded on three sides by mountains. The road split in two, one way leading into the Davis Mountains State Park, the other to the fort and the town of Fort Davis proper. B.C. stopped the car where the road split and looked at Giacomo Berg.

"Well?" she said.

"Let's go into town," he said, "and see what we can find out. No sense in going into the mountains only to have to come out to ask questions."

"I guess that makes as much sense as anything," she said, "but I kind of thought we should get into the mountains and see if we could pick up his vibes. I think that's the only way we'll ever find your friend. He's wandering in the wilderness, Jack."

"Let's just take a minute and eliminate people from the picture," he said. "When I've satisfied the urge to talk to people, then we can get on with the search, but let's do this first."

He was concentrating now. As she drove into town, he looked at the buildings they passed, hoping for an inspiration, someone Peter might have spoken to—a hippie jeweler perhaps.

But no such luck. A grocery, a drug store, an old hotel, a rock and gem store, an insurance salesman, a seed and feed store, the post office, a doctor. Not a likely candidate among them. He found the county sheriff's office, but only a secretary was inside. She said the sheriff and a deputy were out back practicing for an Old West show.

In back of the building, they found a gray-haired man, wearing a star and a rumpled wide-brimmed hat and chaps. He was whipping around a sawed-off shotgun, pointing it in the direction of a younger man on a horse, shouting, "Bang. You're gone." The young man fell out of the saddle, very slowly, carefully, performing a highly organized roll as he hit the ground.

"Excuse me," Giacomo said.

The older man turned around quickly, still holding the shotgun. It was pointed somewhere between Giacomo and B.C. He quickly pointed it at the ground. His face was beet red. He looked Giacomo and B.C. Boyd over and then said, "We were just practicing for the Old West show coming up." The younger man picked himself up from the ground and walked the horse a short distance away.

"What can I do for you folks?" the older man said, recovering his composure.

"We're looking for a missing person," Giacomo said. "We thought maybe you've seen him or know of someone who's seen him."

"And who might you be?" the man asked.

"I'm a friend of the family," Giacomo said, pulling out his card.

The sheriff looked at B.C. "And I'm guessing you're a friend of the family's friend," he said.

She nodded.

"And who are you looking for?"

Giacomo pulled out the photograph of Peter Proust. "He's about 5'9" and in his mid-40s. He has very light blue eyes and probably weighs no more than 125 pounds."

"You know, we've got quite a few people living in those hills that look just like that. He don't stand out in my mind," the sheriff said. "If you leave me that photo, I can ask around. You know for certain he's been around here?"

"That's what he told his family a few nights ago. He called from a pay phone around here somewhere."

"Well, that's a clue. There ain't but seven or eight public phones in this town and a couple more up at the lodge in the park. Tell you what. Why don't you go ask the phone company where all their pay phones are, and maybe somebody who works around the phones will have seen your friend."

Giacomo thanked the sheriff for the suggestion.

"I guess we can help out you big-city private detectives once in a while. You just have to ask our advice."

"Well, then," Giacomo said, "where should we spend the night around here?"

"You mean you and your friend of a friend?" the sheriff smiled. "I always recommend the lodge in the park, if they've got a room you can have. It's a family place, but I guess you won't have any objections to that." He smiled again, touched the brim of his hat and walked back to where the younger man was standing by the horse. "Good luck," he called over his shoulder.

As they got back into the car, they heard him yell, "Bang," from the back of the building. They looked for what might be the telephone building. It was not hard to find: the only building in town without windows. It was square, light-brown brick, and devoid of any human appurtenance.

"These things were really built with neutron bombs in mind," Giacomo grumbled. "We can all go, but Ma Bell will live on."

She smiled. She'd felt his intensity building ever since the flight. She concerned herself with studying the building, trying to find the entrance.

Once inside, they found two operators plugged into electronic switchboards and a young man in a blue synthetic suit sitting behind them at a desk marked "Supervisor." The man gave Giacomo the list of nine public telephones in the area, including one at the lodge. "I don't know why he said we might have seen somebody," he said. "We don't ever leave this place."

He drew a line on a sheet of paper. The line was the highway and main road in Fort Davis. He drew stars along the line for each public phone and wrote the location of that phone beneath the star. There were five businesses, the post office, the old fort, a picnic site, and the lodge. With B.C. holding the sheet of paper, they began.

First, the post office. The old man behind the counter shrugged his shoulders and shook his head. He called out, "Gertie." B.C. looked at Giacomo, wondering what Gertie signified. A moment later, an old woman came shuffling up, letters held between the fingers of each hand.

"Do you recognize this fella?" the old man asked.

"Hold it up where I can see it," she said. "I got today's mail all sorted in my hands."

She looked at the photo, peered into the faces of B.C. and Giacomo, and shuffled back out of sight.

"Gertie don't know him either," the old man said, "but I'll keep my mind on it."

They headed for the drug store across the street. B.C. seated herself at the counter and ordered a chocolate soda all the way and a hamburger deluxe. "I didn't realize until I walked in that I was starving," she said.

Giacomo sat down beside her, ordered a BLT and a milkshake and showed the photo to the soda jerk. The soda jerk shook his head as he poured the milkshake from a metal canister into a small glass.

Giacomo showed the photo to the pharmacist and the woman behind the cosmetics counter. Neither had seen Peter Proust. The pay phone was on a wall not five feet from the cosmetics cash register. "I would have seen him," the cosmetics woman said.

After lunch, they walked to the gem and mineral shop, the country craft shop, and the lobby of the hotel on the little town square. Five public phones covered and no sign of Peter Proust. They could be way off. Back at the car, Giacomo pulled out the map. "You know," he said, "this isn't the only town in the Davis Mountains. I didn't even think of that. I just made a beeline for the state park. By this map, there's Alpine and there's Marfa. And, by this map, they're bigger towns than this. We could be barking up the wrong tree altogether."

He was gripping the steering wheel as he spoke, opening and closing his right hand around the wheel. She noticed this. He was tightening up.

"I think we're right on track," she said. "It seems to me, in a case like this, you have to go with your gut instincts. He's your friend. You know him. Ever since you got that call this morning, there's been a flow and a rhythm to what you're doing. You have to follow that rhythm through. That's the only way you'll find him. I really believe that, Jack. Let's do this first. Let's go into the park. Let's stay at the lodge. One night at least. Maybe there we can get our bearings. Maybe in the middle of the night, sitting outside under the stars, you'll be able to feel exactly where he is."

This didn't make sense entirely to Giacomo Berg. A little flaky around the edges. But he was grateful for a rationale, even an irrational rationale, a ruling, a definition, no matter what metaphysic it was based upon. He could give one day to this. The chances were just as good here as anywhere. He studied the map. "If he stayed on the interstate as far as he could," Giacomo said, "which is likely, since he was hitching, then this would be a more likely point of entry to the Davis Mountains than Marfa or Alpine. You just never know where a ride will take you."

He got out of the car and pointed to the post office. "I'm going to call the sheriffs in Alpine and Marfa," he said, "just in case they've seen or heard anything, to cover all bases."

She waited in the car. A horse came galloping by carrying a young boy riding bareback and a younger girl holding onto his waist, sitting behind him. About twenty feet from B.C., the horse slipped on the pavement, almost fell, caught itself and kept running. But the little girl on the back fell off in the process and landed in a heap on the street.

B.C. jumped out of the car, but by the time she reached the girl, the deserted square was filled with people. Someone had already picked the girl up and was carrying her toward a doctor's office just beyond the post office, followed by a dozen others. The girl was screaming at the top of her lungs, so B.C. figured she would be okay. Meanwhile, a man in a business suit had hold of the horse's harness on the other side of the square and was waving a finger at the boy on the horse, tearing into the kid like a fire-and-brimstone preacher talking about eternal damnation. How to absolve such sins? B.C. wondered.

"No news there," Giacomo said, emerging from the post office. "Let's push on." They found the phone booth in the entry to the visitor's center at the old fort. No one at the visitor's center had seen Peter Proust. "We could use that beard here," said a young blond woman standing at the tour guide station.

They visited the grocery across from the fort. Giacomo approached the woman behind the cash register as B.C. walked to the soft drink cooler near the back of the store.

Giacomo held up the photo and asked if she'd seen him. He was already putting the photo back in his pocket and turning to look for B.C. when the woman said, "Yes, I've seen him."

Giacomo looked into her eyes. They did not waver.

"Where did you see him? When?"

"He came in here several days ago," she said. "I think he was a little confused. He was very nervous. He bought a lot of juice and some cupcakes. His hands were shaking. He knocked over some cans in front, and he went running out of here. I thought at first he had stolen something, but I didn't find anything missing. I think he was just very confused. I felt sorry for that man. He had the frightened look of a wild animal caught in a cow pen."

"When was this?"

"Why? What's going on? Did he commit a crime?"

"No, no, no. He's missing, that's all. His family needs to find him. Like you said—he's a confused man."

"Okay. You're telling me the truth now, right? It was three or four days ago. I'm not sure."

"That's all it is—he's missing. Can you think back? Which way did he go?"

"I can tell you that. I looked out the window after him. And he ran right across the highway there and into the fort. But my husband saw him, too, you know. He saw him a couple of evenings ago by the Painted Rock."

"Where's your husband?"

"He's in the house, next door. See, he works in the early morning and late at night, and I work in the middle of the day. He says that way he's the one more likely to get shot and I'm the one most likely to talk to all the regular customers. Maybe he's sleeping. That's the only thing. He falls asleep watching the television sometimes. But I can't blame him for that. He closes up at 11 and then gets up at four o'clock every morning. Do you want me to go get him?"

"Please," Giacomo said. B.C. was by this time standing right beside him. She was licking an ice cream sandwich. The woman disappeared through a door at the side of the store. Giacomo nervously made two circuits around the checkout counter. Two minutes later she was back.

"He will be with you in a minute," she said. "Just as I suspected, he was sleeping."

A few minutes later, a slightly stooped man with gray hair and moustache emerged through the side door. "This is my husband Manuel," the woman said, holding her hand out toward her husband. "But I don't believe I know your names, and why are you asking about this poor man?"

Giacomo showed the woman his card and said he was an old friend of the missing person. B.C. introduced herself as Giacomo's assistant. The woman seemed placated. She had simply wanted to make sense of what was going on around her. She turned to her husband.

"These are the people I spoke to you about," she said. He nodded.

"Well, see, sir, my wife told me what had happened with the man acting a little crazy in the store and all, and she told me what he looked like. So when I was driving down the road a couple of days ago, I saw a man like the one she had described. He was sitting on the picnic table at the Painted Rock, sitting cross-legged with his shirt off and his eyes closed. He looked a little crazy to me. So when I got home, I came in and described this man to my wife, and she said, 'That must be the man in the store.' Do you have a picture I could look at?"

Giacomo had forgotten. He pulled the photo out of his pocket.

"I think that's the man. It would be easier if he had his shirt off and I saw his whole body because I was not that close to see his face exactly. But I think that's him, and the more I look at it, the more I think it is."

"When was that?" Giacomo asked. "Two days ago?"

"I can tell you exactly. It was at 4:45 two afternoons ago. Because that's when I come back from making my delivery every other day to the Boy Scout ranch. The same time every other day. I am going again in a few hours, and I saw him the last time I went."

"Is there anything else," Giacomo asked.

"What else could there be?" the man asked. "I didn't sit down and have a beer with the man and trade the stories of our lives. That's all I know."

"Well, thank you," Giacomo said. "Thank you. The picnic table is up the road here?"

"Just about three miles, and it's on your left. There's a marker there, so you won't miss it."

Giacomo walked quickly out of the store. He paced in front of it as B.C. paid for her ice cream. Then they were in the car. Would Peter still be there, sitting on the table?

He drove like a madman. The road was a marked incline, following the twists and turns of a creek bed, marked Limpia Creek. Cattle grazed on the grass poking from among the stones of the creek bed. Twice he asked B.C., "Did we miss it? We should have reached it by now."

Twice she shook her head.

Then a turn in the road and the sign for the Painted Rock historical marker. She pointed to the marker and a stone picnic table among large red sandstones a little way ahead on their left.

He pulled onto the gravel for the picnic area and jumped out of the car. Peter Proust wasn't sitting on the table. Nor was there any sign of him immediately around. Giacomo made a quick circumference of the picnic table, taking in the red rocks that stood around it like a miniature Stonehenge. Two-thirds of the way around the circle he came to the blue stand for the telephone.

"This must be it," he shouted to B.C., who was standing by the table a few feet away, watching Giacomo circle like a dog on a scent. He made the orbit once, then twice. Then he took off up the hill, following the path that led from the picnic table to the pictographs. He found them, painted high on the rock: the sun, the eagle, and the deer. Ancient history. And now a part of his immediate history. He looked around the base of the rocks but found no evidence of Peter Proust. There was, of course, evidence of human activity—a crumpled Coke can, a paper bag with three empty beer cans, an empty can of chewing tobacco. But no sign of Peter.

He looked up again at the pictographs and decided they were his only real connection. Within the last 48 hours, maybe within the last 24, Peter Proust had, no doubt, stared at those same figures. He had, no doubt, sat in full lotus on the ground there and stared at those figures and lost himself inside them. Perhaps he had lost himself in the continuum that joined the painters of these pictographs with Peter and now with Giacomo Berg. Giacomo sat down and looked at the rocks more closely. He had never been comfortable in full lotus. So he just stretched his legs out in front of him and breathed deeply a few times, trying to calm his racing mind, trying to think clearly. He was finally here. Having almost conquered the space between them, Giacomo was now entering the same understanding of time. The more he stared, the more the eagle seemed to float, the more the deer, though stiffly and abstractly painted, seemed to take on life. And the sun on the rock beat down on both of them and its light entered his eyes. He couldn't help feeling that the zig-zagging linear path he'd been following trying to find Peter Proust had now opened out into a field and this field of understanding could now somehow be laid across the field of Peter's life, and, where they meshed, he and Peter would find each other.

He felt like he had done this before. But then he remembered it had been inside the rock lean-to at Peter's cabin near Mountain Home, the rocks painted with the word "HOWL!" Here, now, after the howling, the serenity and timelessness of a deer standing in a field under the sun and an eagle endlessly and effortlessly floating overhead.

The rocks cast a shadow over him. Giacomo Berg felt like going to sleep, but he knew he couldn't sleep. He had to keep his eyes wide open. He felt suddenly attuned to the movement of Peter Proust.

He got up. B.C. was standing behind him. "Ready?" she asked.

"I am," he said. He put his arm around her shoulders, and they walked down to the table.

B.C. headed for the car, but he stopped at the phone booth and called Sara Proust.

"I'm calling you from the same phone booth," she heard him say. "We're not too far away."

They checked into the lodge. It was an adobe building constructed by the Conservation Corps as the centerpiece of the park back in the 1930s. It was situated at the end of a valley between two small ridges of mountains, which comprised most of Davis Mountains State Park. Swallows nested in the rafters and the gutters of the building. Fountains gurgled on the lodge's various patios. An ancient-looking madrone tree shaded one of the fountains. The lodge was elevated and cool, set on nearly a dozen different levels, connected by adobe staircases. Their room was on one of the upper levels. They looked out on mountains to the west and to the east.

Right now, Giacomo Berg didn't give a rat's ass about any of this. Maybe some other time.

"Isn't it lovely?" B.C. said as they stood outside their room.

Giacomo scanned the mountains on either side. No sign of life that he could discover.

He'd asked the lodge clerk about Peter Proust and had shown the photo to the park rangers at the entrance to the park and to two men cleaning up around the lodge's grounds. None had seen Peter.

"Let's eat dinner," B.C. said. "I'm starving again. Then maybe we can hike up one of the mountains before the sun goes down."

As they ate, B.C. told him about her most recent conversation with her brother. "He was ranting and raving about something called anti-matter. He thinks it's sneaking up on us and will destroy all of us in a very short while. He's not sure if it will pick us off one at a time or the entire earth will just be vaporized all at once. And eventually the universe.

"It's got him in a huff. He says for every one of us, there's an anti-person, a collection of some sort of anti-particles walking around in our shape, just waiting to bump into us. And when it does, that's it. Instant non-being. It's got him spooked. He says that's why he's worried about UFO's. He thinks they may be the anti-people come to nullify life on earth. He's really nuts about this."

Giacomo, meanwhile, was chewing his lamb chop, thinking about Peter Proust somewhere nearby. He kept watching the mountain ridge, seen through the window of the restaurant at the lodge.

"What if I'm Peter's anti-matter?" he asked. "By finding him, I may be ending him."

"You don't really think that?" She was looking at him with some concern.

"No, but I wanted to test it against the rational universe. I wanted to give it a hearing. Now that's done. We've got to go. The sun's going down."

As he reached for one last swig of his beer, she reached for his hand.

"Maybe you can get a better feeling for where Peter is by standing up there and looking around," she said.

Made sense to him. More sense than sitting calmly in a café. They finished eating and went outside on the main patio to look around, to try to find the path that would be best to climb to the top of the nearest mountain. And the path that would provide them with the least trouble if they descended in the dark.

Just then a man from the maintenance staff with jet-black hair ran up to Giacomo Berg. "Sir," he said. "I think I saw the man you were looking for. I saw him about an hour ago walking up there among the mountain goats. I was looking everywhere for you to tell you."

He stood by Giacomo's shoulder and pointed to an escarpment at the south end of the mountain in front of them. Below that escarpment, Giacomo saw, by squinting, a small herd of goats, black, brown and white.

"I think it was your man. It's hard to see that far, but he had the beard. I think it was him. My grandmother's always told me I've got the eyes of a hawk. It was him."

Giacomo inspected the mountainside. No sign of a man now. "Which way did he go?" he asked.

"That's when I was looking for you. One minute he was with the goats. The next time I looked up, he was gone. My guess is, though, that he's working his way up to the top through the rocks beside that cliff. Or he's there already. It's not a hard climb."

"What's the fastest way up there?" Giacomo asked.

The man pointed to a trail beginning near the lodge's parking lot and angling to the south and west up the mountain. "Take that trail to the top," he said, "and once you get there, then walk back across the top of the ridge. It's the quickest way."

Giacomo Berg set off immediately for the trail.

"Wait," B.C. called after him. "I'm going, too, but I have to change shoes and get a flashlight."

In the two minutes that took, Giacomo had gone to the lodge office, borrowed a pair of binoculars, and scanned the mountaintop and mountainside. He studied the rocks beside the escarpment. He studied each mountain goat. No sign of a human being. Three people emerged from the other side of the mountain at the north end of the ridge. Giacomo Berg studied them carefully, but they were clearly not Peter Proust. He wondered if the man with hawk eyes had been right.

B.C. found Giacomo at the entrance to the trail. He was, at that moment, pacing back and forth across the stone bridge that crossed a creek at the beginning of the trail.

"All right, Sir Edmund Hilary. Let's get on with it," she said. She knew the anxiety building in Giacomo Berg was in danger of exploding at any moment. She tried to be light-hearted, to take the edge off his next few hours. Was it for her own benefit or for his? She wasn't sure. But it was the easiest way for her to react to an impending crisis. It probably pissed him off.

She followed Giacomo up the path. The first third was easy going. It was simply a matter of walking up a steep incline, with a number of graduated switchbacks. He did not say a word or look back once. Then they reached a series of stones, each rising four feet above the one preceding it. They scrambled over these and then over a series of smaller, but irregular, sandstones that required a zig-zag ascent in search of adequate hand-and foot-holds up a thirty-foot stretch. Over this and they were just below the escarpment. She stopped and rested on the last series of rocks. Looking back down at the lodge, she hadn't realized they had come this far. She turned back to the trail. Giacomo had not stopped but, instead, was walking among stunted juniper cedars to the final ascent, a trail that angled along the side of the escarpment and disappeared behind some rocks. She assumed it reappeared on top. That seemed to be Giacomo's assumption, as he began the climb along the side of the escarpment. She followed as closely as possible. Soon, however, she'd lost him as he disappeared behind the large gray rocks at the top of the trail. She could call him, she thought, but she felt it wasn't her right to cut into whatever connection Giacomo was trying to make with Peter. She was afraid of destroying that. This was a test for her. Could she enter this unknown territory holding her fear in abeyance, not calling Jack, making it herself? She followed the trail behind the rocks. It was made up of a series of cut gray stones, one on top of the other. She clambered her way up, each stone at least four feet tall. The last stone was a good eight feet tall, but, by wedging herself against the rocks along the side, she managed to pull herself up.

And then she was out. Giacomo Berg was sitting on a stone, his binoculars aimed at the far end of the mountaintop.

"Do you see him?" she asked.

"I think I see Mexico," he said, continuing to search with the binoculars.

The wind was whipping around. The sun was beginning to set ahead of them. The valley behind them was green, and the sky was the deepest blue, almost purple, she'd ever seen.

The Pull of Gravity

THE GOATS HAD CONFUSED HIM AT FIRST. What did they mean? They wandered around him like so many thoughts. Peter Proust picked his way through them up the hillside. They hadn't seemed to notice, more intent on the tufts of grass they found growing among the rocks. Had he already become fully part of the natural world, like a shadow skating up the hillside as a cloud moved across the sun? Or less than that? Like the slightest breeze, a zephyr? Or like nothing at all?

He came to the bottom of the bare escarpment. Could he hug it and like a lizard scurry up the rock face? He lay against the stone. It retained the heat of the late afternoon sun. But he could feel a coolness behind the heat, deep in the stone. Lying against the stone didn't transport him upward. His stomach was to blame for that. He couldn't float up with the grinding inside that was tearing him in two. It bent him over and threw him to the ground. But this would soon be over. A brown and white goat grazed near his ear.

He searched the rock for a way up. To the right of the bare rock face was a rivulet of tumbled rocks. He pulled himself up the first rock, which was nearly his height. After that, the going was easier. He then picked his way up the cliff. At one point he rested. He turned to look at the valley behind him and at the ridge he'd climbed two days before. It was now below his plane of vision. He could begin to see the vast plain beyond it, a great waterless lake. He looked south to mountains in the distance, some looking like small, worn-out volcanoes. He continued his climb.

He wondered what the summit would reveal. Would it be an endless vision of mountains and plains? Would he be able to look forever in all directions, not have his view stopped, not having any wall thrown up in any direction to limit his seeing? Would his spirit then be able to lift and leave his body in all directions at once?

As he neared the top, he felt a lifting of some sort already taking place inside him. It felt as if small wings were already beating in his chest and in his throat. His arms and legs felt lighter. The clenched fist of a brain he felt beating against the inside of his head suddenly seemed to loosen its grip, relax. With each ascending step, the lightness grew more palpable. By the time he reached the summit and walked out onto the surface of the mountain, he felt like he was floating on air.

He was above everything. In all directions, as far as he could see—sky and endless earth. No mountains thrown up to impair his vision. He spun around several times, flinging his arms in the air. He was at the top of the world.

The top of the mountain sloped away along a ridge running north. And it sloped up slightly to the west, to the top of a cliff that was the mountain's western face.

Peter Proust walked slowly up that last slope to the top of the cliff. Below, another valley falling away. The late afternoon sun was directly in front of him. He stood there watching it as he took off his backpack, then his boots, then the rest of his clothes. He arranged his goods in a semi-circle around him. The notebook by his left hand; William Blake beside that. Next to that his clothes, two last peyote buttons, several rocks, acorns, and other amulets he'd picked up along the way, a drawing he'd done some time ago of himself with Sara's address on the back. He put a rock on top of that. Then by his right hand, the gun. There were bullets in its chamber.

Everything pointed to this being the time. He had already felt some of his physicality leaving him. He was less there than he had ever felt before. Even the cramps in his stomach had left, at least momentarily. And it could be that momentarily would now mean forever.

He sat in full lotus facing west, his palms pointing upward, breathing in slowly and deeply, trying to feel the rhythm of the moment, of the earth beneath him and all around. The air was fresh and cool. It filled his head the way the water in the Hill Country stream had rushed around him.

Were there any last thoughts to be pondered? He concentrated. He tried to call up images of his parents, Sara, Seth, but they would not come. His mind was already being wiped clean, a blank slate, absolute emptiness. He stared into the sun.

He thought he felt a low vibration working toward him through the earth. The same vibration now in the air. A vibration running lower than the ear could discern or the mind could conceive. The vibration ran through him. He felt it. He felt that he was becoming part of the landscape, losing his singularity, his self, becoming part of the general murmur. This was the time. He no longer existed as a separate being. He was already part of the general buzz. He reached for the peyote buttons, then stopped. He was beyond that. Whatever illumination they brought was temporal. He was ready for more than that.

There was one last act to perform, one last solitary cry in the desert, and then he would be solitary no more. He picked up the gun and put it to his head. He'd never shot anything before. Not a squirrel. Not a rabbit. Not a bird. Always a first time. The eternal moment. Not the before. But the just after. He wanted to be in that eternal moment. Not live in it, but be in it.

But his stomach cramped, knocked him off his seat. He put down the gun and rolled around in the dirt, inside the half-circle of his worldly possessions. He rolled until his stomach relaxed. Then he lay on the dirt staring straight up. He closed his eyes and tried to pick up the vibration again. For a long time there was nothing. Then he felt it coming through the mountain, coming closer and entering his body, passing through him and out into the air. He was there again. He picked up the gun and put it to his head. But a picture of Sara was in his head. He put the gun back down until it passed. He assumed full lotus again. The sun was setting. He waited for the vibration to enter him. He banished all thought as he waited. By breathing ever more slowly, he could slow down his mind until all thought was reduced to a point and that point disappeared. This was what he did. He waited and thought nothing.

Then the frequency of the mountain captured him again. He let it work through him and through the air until he was sure he would not lose it. He picked up the gun, and, as he put it to his head, he had a vision of his old friend Giacomo Berg walking toward him. Why this now? He put the gun down and waved farewell to his old friend. Then he felt for the vibration, and it was still there. It could no longer be stopped. It was still moving through him. This was the time. He picked up the gun and...

Fired.

From the other end of the mountaintop, Giacomo Berg had seen Peter sitting on the summit. He began walking quickly in Peter's direction, B.C. following behind. He was not sure how to approach this. Slowly and carefully he had decided. But then, halfway up the ridge, he had seen Peter put something that could be a gun to his head and then put it down. Giacomo Berg began to run. The ridge was much longer than he'd anticipated. Several times he stumbled and caught himself as the ridge was pockmarked with small holes and undulated in unexpected places. Giacomo Berg refused to take his eyes off Peter, having taken this long to find him.

He was only about fifty feet away when he saw Peter put down the gun, turn and hold up his hand. Was it in greeting or to stop his progress? Berg stopped and B.C. stopped behind him.

"Peter," he called. "I've been trying to find you."

But Peter had turned back to face the sunset. He seemed oblivious to their presence now.

Giacomo watched him carefully. He thought he would slowly walk up beside him. He would get between the gun and Peter Proust, and then he would put his arm around Peter's shoulder to keep him from going over the cliff. He began to edge slowly toward Peter. B.C. remained stock still.

But Peter raised the gun again. Giacomo saw the tension of his finger on the trigger. He began to run for the gun hand, to lunge to pull it away. "Peter!" he cried.

As he dived for Peter's hand he saw it all with absolute clarity: the trigger pulled, the shot fired, the head jerked to the side. Giacomo Berg was suspended in air. This was the moment.

Not past or future. This was the threshold they were going across, the absolute moment the knife entered the heart.

He landed with his head in Peter's chest. Peter had fallen on his side and was trembling. Blood was pouring from his head. B.C. held Peter's head in her hands, patting his hair. Giacomo listened for the heart. Had it already stopped? He began mouth-to-mouth resuscitation as B.C. felt Peter's neck for any sign of a pulse. Peter's body continued shaking. Giacomo breathed into Peter's mouth and listened for his heart again and again. The shaking stopped. Giacomo kept it up though B.C. felt no sign of life. She watched Giacomo working over his dead friend's body.

Then she put her arms around Giacomo's back and pulled him up. "It's over, Jack," she said. "He's gone."

Giacomo got up and walked around the mountaintop, keeping his eyes on Peter's body and the semi-circle of Peter's things around it. He looked into Peter's face from a few feet away. His eyes still had the look of a frightened animal. Giacomo leaned over and closed them. He found a blanket from among Peter's things and covered Peter's body, hugging it as he did. Then he sat down a few yards from Peter's body and just stared. B.C. came up beside him. She thought she'd just sit there. That was the best she could do. The sun had now set, and it was growing rapidly darker.

"We finally found him," Giacomo said. She rubbed the back of his neck.

He stared at the horizon disappearing in the darkness. He thought about Peter with Peter's body just a few feet away. But Peter was as far away as ever. Farther than he'd been when this search began? It was impossible to say. Not worth considering actually. Peter was gone. He was gone when they'd first called. He was gone now. He was going when their eyes met for that instant just a few moments before. He couldn't put it all together. Nor did he want to. He just stared past Peter's body to the images of Peter he could conjure up. And then he just stared at the sky and the stars that were beginning to appear.

This was the present of pain. Not the future you prepare yourself for, knowing that tragedy, difficulty, or death is imminent, feeling beforehand what you know you will feel in the wake of suffering. But this was the moment beyond thought. Peter lay in front of him, and Giacomo Berg was there there there, face to face with the corpse. You had to dig the grave before you could cover it over. He sat there with the searing pain.

Moment dissolved into moment, but together they didn't make any discernible body of time. It was dark. There was a half moon and more stars than B.C. had ever seen. She couldn't tell how late it was or how long they'd been there. She wondered if they would be there all night.

Giacomo waited, rocking back and forth slightly. The huge explosion was over, the searing heat. He was waiting for the dust to settle and the clouds to blow away. He lay back on the ground and stared into space, thinking he could comprehend the depth of field, the distance among stars, which point of origin of the pinpoints of light running toward him was farthest away and which was closest, which stars were burning a hole right through him.

Then a low, deep moan began somewhere inside Giacomo Berg. He felt it working its way out from deep inside, winding toward his mouth. Then it seized his vocal chords, threw open his mouth, and became a high-pitched wail rocketing out of his mouth. He screamed and wailed. It would not let go. It spilled from his mouth. It went on and on, and then it was gone.

B.C. wrapped her arms around him.

B.C. began to hear voices. A beam of light switched on from a dozen yards away, and a man's voice was calling. "Who's there? Are you all right? Stand up. This is the park ranger. Who's there?"

B.C. stood up and walked toward the light. Two men and a woman in ranger uniforms awaited her. One of the men carried a rifle.

"Someone reported a gunshot from up here," the ranger with the flashlight said. "What's going on?"

B.C. pointed in the direction of Peter, and the flashlight beam followed, catching on his blanketed body, then finding Giacomo Berg, now standing a few yards away.

The woman ranger pulled out a pistol.

"It's all right," B.C. said. "We were too late. That's all. Our friend just killed himself."

The ranger with the rifle motioned Giacomo to come forward. He did, holding his hands chest-high. He wanted to avoid confusion, to keep things as simple as possible.

The woman ranger, pistol still drawn, ran up to Peter's body, looked at it, felt it, then called, "He's gone."

The rangers radioed for the sheriff and an ambulance to meet them at the foot of the mountain. They unrolled a stretcher one had been carrying, loaded Peter's body onto it, covered him with one of their own blankets, piled Peter's things together, and put them in his backpack.

B.C. tried to help, but the woman ranger indicated with a look that she would take care of it. The ranger held Peter's gun by its barrel and put it in a plastic container hooked to her belt. B.C. stepped back and grabbed Giacomo's arm. It was suddenly becoming awful to her. What had seemed terrible but meaningful was being stripped of importance, the body became a corpse, the death an incident.

Giacomo sensed that the rangers did not know whether to believe B.C.'s story, but up on the mountaintop they apparently had little alternative but to act as if they did. The two male rangers led the way down the north slope of the mountain, carrying Peter between them.

Giacomo and B.C. followed, and the woman ranger after them, her gun now put away, Peter's backpack and bedroll slung over her shoulders. They marched down the mountainside saying nothing, the only sound the crunching of rocks and gravel beneath their feet. At one switchback in the trail, two mule-eared deer were standing just a few feet away on their hind legs reaching for acorns in a small oak tree. They didn't scare.

At the bottom of the mountain, the sheriff was waiting. "I see you found your friend," he said to Giacomo. Then he ushered B.C. and Giacomo into the car, along with Peter's belongings, to be taken to the sheriff's office. "Let's go to my office to see if we can straighten all this out," he said.

Giacomo didn't say a word but followed the sheriff's gestures into the car, followed by B.C. The ambulance, carrying Peter, followed them out of the park.

The sheriff poured them each coffee.

"Now why were you looking for this friend of yours?" he asked.

"We wanted to keep him from killing himself," Giacomo said. "You see how successful we were."

"Now, I don't mean to imply anything," the sheriff said, "but how did you know he was going to kill himself and how do I know you weren't trying to find him to kill him?"

Giacomo Berg knew they had to go through this, but he also figured the sheriff didn't get much opportunity to deal with murder, so he would probably play it for all it was worth.

Giacomo wanted to keep it as short and basic as he could. He wanted to get out of there. He looked at B.C., who was watching him closely, sipping her coffee, mustering a smile for him, to keep him going.

"Would I ask you for directions to the man I was going to kill, if I were going to kill him?" Giacomo asked.

"That's a good point," the sheriff said. "It speaks well for you. But why did we find peyote beside him?"

"I don't know. Did you check the prints on the gun?" Giacomo said.

"Now that's a good idea," the sheriff said, "but it will take a few days. We have to send it down to Marfa where they can do that."

"Well, why don't you just call Peter's family. They can straighten it all out for you."

"I think I'll do just that," the sheriff said. "By the way, have you got their number?"

"Could you let me call?" Giacomo asked. He was suddenly very agitated. "This is going to be hard for them."

"I appreciate your consideration, but no, I cannot. I'll just break the news in my own insensitive say," the sheriff said, and he walked into another room and shut the door behind him.

"No, No, No," Giacomo said and pounded the desk once. He got up and walked around the room, making dozens of circuits. B.C. watched and waited for him to alight somewhere.

But he didn't sit down until the sheriff emerged from the other room.

"I'm sorry to have troubled you, Mr. Berg," he said. "The family wants you to make the arrangements to send the body and his personal things on home. We can take you back to the lodge."

Not another word was said. They got into the car and were driven back to the lodge. As they got out of the car, the sheriff handed Giacomo a half-full fifth of Bourbon. "You might need this," he said. "Ain't nothing around here open at this time of night."

Then he drove off.

B.C. went into the room, but Giacomo didn't follow. Instead, he sank into a chair on the patio outside their door, unscrewed the cap on the bourbon and took a swig.

"Do you want me to stay here with you?" she asked.

"No, I just want to sit here a while."

"Do you want me to wait up for you?"

"Go to sleep," he said. She took the bottle from him, drank a couple of swallows and handed it back. She went inside but decided to wait up for him. She lay on top of the bedclothes. She fell asleep.

The next morning, with the sun already well up, she found Giacomo asleep in the chair on the patio.

Giacomo Berg arranged with the local funeral parlor to have Peter's body sent back East. He'd found a box and packed Peter's belongings to be sent with the body. The self-portrait, naked, eyes strangely askew, he'd packed on the bottom. Then the clothes and anything worth saving, then the notebook. He'd opened it and tried to read, but he couldn't bear to. The first entry was Blake's "Tyger, tyger, burning bright" written in Peter's hand. He closed the notebook and sealed the box.

He also made the difficult call to Sara. She was, of course, prepared for it. "I'm sorry the sheriff made the call," he said.

"We've been expecting that call for so long now that it was almost a relief," she said. "Not a relief really, but at least something certain." She sounded fully composed. "I'm sorry we put you through that, Jack. But if it makes you feel any better, we feel better knowing you were there."

"Sara," Giacomo said, "I should have been there in time. I should have stopped it. I was this close. I keep thinking about how I stopped to eat or how I was thinking too much and not just running after him. I was this close, Sara."

"Jack, it had to run its course. No matter when you got there, you would have been too late. At least you saw him."

She said they'd send him money, but he told her to forget it. He could cover it.

Then she asked, "Jack, do you think he saw you? I would feel better if he knew someone was trying to make contact, if he knew someone cared."

"To be honest," Giacomo said, "I'm not sure who he was seeing. We looked right into each other's eyes, but I'm not sure he knew I was actually there. It's that look I still see. That's what I can't forget. He didn't seem panicked, Sara. He just seemed calm. He seemed already gone."

Giacomo Berg was not sure he believed what he was saying, but he thought it might make her feel better. When he closed his eyes, he did see Peter's face in that last moment. He'd see that for a while.

She thanked him again, and it was over.

Giacomo Berg climbed into the car beside B.C., looked at the map, and began driving to Houston. Neither of them said anything. The winding trip out of the Davis Mountains seemed to take no time at all. They reached the interstate and headed east. The flat plains of West Texas were a relief. As they logged the miles between where they were going and where they'd been, he began to relax. He felt like driving the car into the ground, driving on and on and on, not stopping for gas or food or anything until they just let it fly into the Houston Ship Channel.

But by the time they reached Ozona, two hundred miles to the east, he had a different idea. He pulled into the parking lot of the only motel to be seen in that dusty town along the highway. B.C. waited in the car. She noticed a jump in his step as he entered the office. Then he was back, dangling a key in front of her. She rubbed his leg. They drove to a room. He opened the door. She walked in. When she turned around from closing the curtains, he was all over her. They made love on the floor, then on the bed of the motel room in Ozona, laughing and screaming, at one point trying to bash the headboard through the wall. After a shower, they drove to Houston. It was almost endless. Neither said a word for 400 miles.

Animal. Vegetable. Mineral.

THE NEXT DAY they slept until late afternoon. Giacomo Berg was eager to return to New York.

He called Pilar Moreno at home because he had no one else to call. He knew she'd be angry. He hadn't called for what seemed like months but was a matter of days. He steeled himself to absorb her sarcasm.

"Let's see," she said, acting as if she were reading a list, "a woman called wanting you to find out where her husband goes every evening when he says he's going to get a cup of coffee and disappears for exactly one hour and twenty-five minutes every time. Then another woman called who thinks her neighbor two apartments down stole her Yorkshire terrier. She says whenever she walks by her neighbor's place she can hear it barking with a kind of muffled sound, like it was in a closet with coats thrown over it. And a guy called yesterday who sells plumbing supply, and he thinks his two competitors are meeting in secret so they can drive him out of business. There's a lot of paranoia out there, boss."

She said "boss" when she wanted to get deep under his skin. He knew he was in for this.

"Oh, yeah," she said. "One more thing. We're closed. We no longer run a business. Or did you forget that, Mr. Very Private Investigator?" She added, "Are you coming back?"

"Tomorrow. Probably tomorrow night," he said. "I'll see you the day after."

"Well, you'll have to go to the Home Depot Training Center in Bayonne. I start there next week. I can work the evening shift and take classes in the morning. How about that? And speaking of which, you owe me my last paycheck."

"What are you talking about? You pay the bills. Pay yourself."

"There's nothing in the account, old boss."

"I'll have your money. But I'm not going to Bayonne to pay you," he said. "We've still got at least a month before they chase us out of the building so they can tear it up. Besides, I have a feeling I'm going to get paid. What else do I have to do anyway? I hope I see you on Monday, and I hope you won't be wearing an orange uniform."

Pilar didn't say a word. After a pause, she hung up.

He sat on the edge of the bed, smiling. He enjoyed this back and forth. He missed bantering with New Yorkers. He was ready to get back. It got his blood flowing again, pulling him out of his fog.

Then B.C. Boyd pulled him down from behind. They rolled around on the bed. She got his shoulders pinned down, then looked him in the eyes and said, "We're not leaving tomorrow. The hearing is tomorrow."

He closed his eyes. He was still too spent to fight even the slightest wave that wanted to carry him out to sea. He would just as soon think about the hearing later. Or not at all. But if she wanted it, then he would go along. What else could he do?

"I just want to get stinking bamboozled," he said. And so they did.

The following afternoon they sat at the back of a hearing room filled with folding chairs at the Glasgow Public Library. A hearing by the Texas Natural Resource Commission was in progress. At a table at the front of the room, four men in gray suits sat questioning a fifth man, who was facing them and away from the audience. The four men had name plates identifying them by agency, two from the Air section, one from the state Water Quality section, and a fourth from the federal Environmental Protection Agency. The man they were questioning was the corporate attorney for the parent corporation of Pleistex.

The hearing had been going on an hour without one neighborhood resident being called. Instead, lawyers for the dumpsite, for the haulers, for the corporations dumping at Pleistex, and for the parent company had all presented their cases, all claiming compliance with the regulations for a Class II dumpsite for non-hazardous and biodegradable substances.

"We understand the concern of the people of Glasgow," the lawyer for the parent corporation was saying, "given the atmosphere of panic created by a few extreme environmental groups, but I am before you today to say that the Pleistex site is not a hazard to anyone's health. There are no toxic substances there."

"Thank you," one of the gray-suited men said. "We will adjourn for 15 minutes and then hear from the complainants."

Stephen Seltzer jumped up from the front row and ran back to Giacomo and B.C. "We've got them," he whispered. "Cara's going to get up there and blow them out of the water. We found more toxics in those little jars than you can find in the Houston Ship Channel. They were just crawling with them. Class II landfill, my ass. They're dead in the water."

Giacomo studied Stephen's face. It was flush with excitement. Would he have been as excited if they'd found nothing and might have been able to rule out toxic exposure from the dumpsite?

"I guess they're glad to see how poisoned they really are," he whispered to B.C. She squeezed his hand and smiled.

Cara Fenster-Seltzer was the first Glasgow resident called. She walked up to the table carrying a large cloth bag over her shoulder. An aide positioned a microphone in front of her, and the hearing began again.

"My name," she said, "is Cara Fenster-Seltzer. I live at 23145 Bobby Burns Road with my husband and three children, ages 18, 16. And 11." Her voice trembled slightly when she began but gained strength as she spoke. "I became concerned about the Pleistex dumpsite when children in our neighborhood and at our children's school began to get sick from some unknown cause. The boy who cuts our yard and lives a few blocks away has some mysterious blood disease. Then my daughter came home from school with a serious rash. The doctor doesn't know what caused it. And my son in the last few weeks has been almost incapacitated by nosebleeds. We were at a loss. We didn't know what to do. The doctors couldn't help us. So my husband and I decided to take a survey of the neighborhood to see who else was having problems—health problems, that is. With the help of our neighbors, we went to every house in a thirty-block area. And the results we got are shocking. Ms. Leah Domenico will present those results to you in a minute. But, let me repeat, the results are shocking. I'm talking about cancer and sickness and weakness. I've never seen anything like it." Cara paused and took a sip of water.

"Mrs. Fenster-Seltzer," one of the gray suits said, "let me interrupt here to ask you a few questions. And I want to ask also that each of you limit your remarks to no more than five minutes as we have a number of people to hear from. But Mrs. Fenster-Seltzer, I sympathize with your problems, and they are real problems, but what we have to determine is whether this Pleistex dumpsite has anything to do with these problems. Why Pleistex? And why did you target your survey to a thirty-block area around Pleistex. If anything was found, then you could point to the plant as the culprit, but how do we know the same incidents of health problems are not occurring, if they are indeed occurring as you say, in some other part of Glasgow or some other part of this region that is far away from Pleistex? I don't mean to disparage your efforts, but I'm afraid your survey can't tell us much until we have controls on it and do it for a wide territory. Then, if we see a particular configuration around Pleistex, then we can start to look at that site. I think we're putting the cart before the horse. But that's my question to you, and to everyone else who comes up here—why Pleistex?"

Giacomo thought it wasn't looking good for the home team. He hoped Stephen knew what he was talking about.

Now Cara's face was red and her voice was shaking again. This time it wasn't from being nervous. It was from anger. "Ask anyone," she said. "Our kids come home from the park with that dust from the dump all over them. If you go look at the swimming pool in the morning, it's got a red film on top of it. And, depending on the way the wind is blowing, some of us near the dump have to keep our windows closed. It gets to be like a dust storm out in West Texas for Christ's sake!"

"Now, Mrs. Fenster-Seltzer," the same suit said, "that may be true. But how can you make this connection directly to the site? This is, after all, a Class II landfill. You heard them say there are no toxic substances at the site."

Cara slowly opened her bag. The man asking the questions quickly looked to the guard in the back of the room, as if he suspected she was pulling out a gun. Instead, she pulled four jars out of the striped bag and placed them on the table in front of her. She picked up a jar containing a greenish-brown liquid. "Does mercury chloride qualify as a toxic substance?" she asked. "We pulled this from a slush pit on the property."

One of the corporate lawyers on the front row jumped up. "That's trespassing," he said.

Cara went on. She picked up a jar of metallic gray dirt. "Does cadmium qualify?" she asked. "How about chromium, nickel, or cobalt?" She held up another jar. "We found these in the samples we took from several mounds in the plant."

The lawyer was still standing, joined now by two others. "They should be cited for breaking and entering," he shouted. "This should be stopped."

Cara held up a jar of brownish liquid. "How about toluene? This came from Pleistex, too."

"This calls for criminal prosecution," the lawyer shouted.

"You're damn right it does," Stephen Seltzer shouted, jumping up from his seat.

"We'll see you in court," the lawyer shouted, marching out, followed by the three minions who'd been sitting behind him.

The gray suits were by this time all standing. The man identified with the Environmental Protection Agency said, "This may be a civil matter."

The gray suit conducting the hearing gaveled the meeting to order. "How do we know these substances came from that plant?"

"Do the testing yourself," Cara said. "We welcome it."

"We're going to conduct a thorough investigation," he said. "You can be sure of that. For now the hearing is adjourned."

The residents of Glasgow in the room jumped up, applauding, and crowded around Cara at the front table.

"I think they did it," B.C. said, hugging Stephen and then hugging Giacomo.

"I hope so," Giacomo said. "You just never know."

In the New World

AFTER TWO WEEKS he felt as if he were finally being lifted an inch at a time out of the abyss by a force he could not identify but that seemed to require no real effort on his part. He got up each day, put on his shoes, had a cup of coffee, and felt himself that much closer to rising from the lower depths to the surface of the earth once again. He felt that soon the lip of the earth would be at eye level, that life as he had known it was just a matter of six inches at most above his head.

Two days after his return to New York, he had traveled to Massachusetts to join Peter's family and a few others for a memorial service. They'd scattered Peter's ashes along an Indian trail running through the woods, where Peter had spent hours every summer day as a child.

They'd sung a few Congregationalist hymns. Someone read the Blake quotation Peter had written out about every bird being a world of delight closed to the senses five. Sara had stood beside Giacomo, holding his hand through most of it.

Giacomo Berg had brought a poem to read, one of Blake's "Songs of Experience." It ended:

> So he took his wings and fled; Then the morn blush'd rosy red;
> I dried my tears, & arm'd my fears With ten thousand shields
>   and spears. Soon my Angel came again:
> I was arm'd, he came in vain; For the time of youth was fled,
>   And gray hairs were on my head.

But he kept it folded in his pocket. The devastation on the faces of the family was too great to add to the accumulated sadness. Giacomo saw the poem as one of the many explanations that had to be hammered together for what had happened. He had stood silently, feeling his best service was at Sara's side.

After the gathering, she'd asked him to stay a few days. He'd mumbled a couple of excuses relating to the work he'd missed while in Texas. She tried to give him a check for his work. He wouldn't take it. They grabbed a bottle of wine off a patio table and wandered through the woods, neither saying much of anything. When it was dark, they came out of the woods and he drove back to New York.

By the time he'd returned, the woman who'd called about the Yorkshire terrier had found her dog, alive and barking, but not in her neighbor's apartment. Instead, it had taken a ride down the laundry chute and was trapped in the basement amid mounds of linens, only to be found by the laundry service that came at the end of the week. The plumbing supply owner had been offered a price for a buyout by his two competitors and had happily accepted, saying he couldn't take the *tsouris* anymore. Then a check arrived from Stephen. Not entirely a surprise, and in this case Giacomo thought it was much deserved. $15,000 would keep them running for a month or two.

He'd received a three-month extension before his office building would be cleared out. He didn't know if that was good or not. It did give him the chance to regain his bearings.

He was currently employed trailing an accountant from his Murray Hill apartment every evening to get a cup of coffee two blocks away and then on a walk, each time in a different direction but each time clocking in at exactly one hour and twenty-five minutes. Giacomo could discern no pattern in the walks. The man rarely spoke to anyone. Once in a while, he wrote something down on a notepad he kept in his pocket. Maybe he was a poet, Giacomo decided. It made for pleasant work, a stroll every evening and then on to B.C.'s place.

There was no skimming the surface there. He was becoming more and more entangled, as his legs were now entangled with hers, as they had been for almost every night the past two weeks. B.C. Boyd poured the wine as they lay in bed. He read aloud from the last of the journals of Bernal Díaz del Castillo. Why, Díaz asked, did the leaders of the Spanish Conquest not remain in Mexico after defeating Cuauhtemoc and the Aztec people but, instead, immediately set out for other parts unknown? Because they realized, he said, that the gold of the Aztecs had come in tribute from somewhere else. The only thing the Aztecs could produce was maize and the maguey on which to get drunk. Cortés alone remained in Mexico. When Díaz came to Cortés to ask for leave to set out on one such expedition, Cortés told him he was making a mistake. Sitting upright and gesticulating in bed, Giacomo read aloud: "'I know very well that you will be sorry you left,' Cortés said. And Díaz admitted. 'We were thoroughly deceived.'"

Then Giacomo Berg fell back on the pillow. And B.C. Boyd wrapped her legs around him. B.C. rubbed a hand across his chest. Then their elbows kissed and they were together. They began working each other's body for meaning, fighting their way through alphabets, creating new vocabularies. Her arms came out and swam around his head, behind his neck, and drew him in.

Then they lay there, side by side. She grabbed his face with both hands and pulled it in front of hers, so his eyes could not look anywhere but into hers.

"Jack, I'm not going to follow you around like a puppy dog my whole life. We hold hands and march forward together. Is that understood? And the next time I want to go somewhere, you're coming with me. Okay?"

He looked across the landscape of her bed and at her endless legs beside his on the sheets.

He closed his eyes. He opened them. He looked her right in the eyes. "Yes," he said, "yes, I will, yes."

B.C. started playing her guitar and singing with two other women, one on guitar and the other on bass. Mostly plaintive country songs—from this country and others. First she needed to drain all that sad shit out of her. After that, rock'n'roll.

She'd decided to find something else to do for a living. Even if it were meaningless. Even if just for a little while. She was ready to not spend most of her time on the sadness of the world.

Giacomo sat over a cappuccino at the Café Dante listening to B.C. sing at the other end of the room. On the wall above him Dante watched Beatrice crossing a bridge over the Arno.

Giacomo Berg was trying to figure out what to do next. He thought he wanted to write a book. He thought he wanted to write this book. He decided he wouldn't.